The Melted Star:

The Life of a Rose

A Novel

Logan Skirha

Any references to historical events, real people, or real places are used fictitiously. Names, characters, and places are products of the author's imagination.

The Melted Star: The Life of a Rose

Book design by Floor de Kok

Printed in the United States of America.

The Melted Star:

The Life of a Rose

Chapter One
Rose Water

Everything is in perfect stillness. Warm light bathes her little corner of Eden in oranges and purples. Rolling hills go as far as the eye can see, and crickets chirp among the tall grasses. The myrtle tree she stands under sways in the evening breeze, the scent of cigar smoke tickling her nose. To think she would jeopardize the promise of paradise for love. But the heart is a fickle thing, and Aphrodite knows this better than anyone.

But that doesn't mean she is immune to the sway of her own emotions. She clutches her hands to her chest to still her beating heart, for it is a warning not to go any further. But the thrill of love is the only thing that moves her.

It is all she has left.

A pair of purple eyes float out from the shadows behind her. A dark voice curls around her as smoke puffs from his mouth. "You realize the weight of doing something like this, don't you?"

"Of course," she turns to face him, "why else would I ask this of you, Asmodeus?"

He steps into the dying light and tucks his cigar from the corner of his mouth. His lavender skin washes out to an almost yellow, black pinstriped suit tight on his wiry frame. A pair of ram horns curl out from his head, with soot staining their tips. His black hair is pushed back into a low ponytail. Asmodeus rubs his leather-clad hands rather anxiously over his jacket.

"Well, it's not every day I have a goddess falling in love with me." His sharp teeth glint as he offers a playful grin. "And I thought you just enjoyed visiting the manor. So, you like me after all?"

"Of course," she repeats with a grin. The cute way his purple eyes twinkle makes her heart melt.

He runs a hand through his slicked back hair, and she surveys his profile; a visage worthy of a statue. Even though he comes off strong, it is moments like these that she appreciates his brooding nature. Asmodeus digs his teeth into his cigar, too deep in thought to notice her gazing.

Aphrodite closes the distance between them with her embrace, and he only reaches her shoulder. The mixture of smoke and cologne permeates even their clothes, but she still inhales the comforting scent. She has grown numb to the overbearing sweetness of Eden, and longs for an excitement unable to be found in the Garden.

Asmodeus is the very thrill she has been searching for.

He whispers, "then why am I nothing more than a secret?"

"You have to understand—"

"I don't understand, that's the thing."

"They can't know about you," she wets her lips, "about us."

He shrugs her arms from around him and takes another drag. There is a restless energy about him, constantly puffing at that cigar of his. Asmodeus paces under the tree with hands tucked into his pockets.

"Why the fuck not? Who cares what the snobby pantheon thinks?" He stops short and stares into her face for a good while with an odd expression she has grown used to. There is longing there, but something darker downturns the corners of his mouth. "I love you. That's all that matters."

"It's not that simple." Her voice comes off as monotone, devoid of the vivid emotion she holds tightly strung under the surface like a perfectly tuned lyre. Above all, she has to stay in control of herself. Aphrodite cannot throw it all to the wind like she so desires. Every step she takes must be calculated, down to every inflection.

That is one thing she admires about Asmodeus; his rebellious spirit. Once upon a time, she too grew like a wildflower, doing whatever she pleased, but the heat of eternal summer quieted her feral heart. There is no longer a rosy sheen to warm her skin, her intensity wilts with each passing day.

She would never say it, but she sympathizes with his plight as a demon. To think, he should be standing where she is, but due to circumstances beyond his control, he can't even step foot on Eden soil on his own. She has a privilege that should rightfully be his.

But as a man with less experience than her, he still has yet to realize the ways of the world. Asmodeus is like a puppy, too often biting off more than he can chew. She has almost no choice in protecting him, and as much as she appreciates his want to bring their relationship out of the dark, it is an impossibility. The so-called "stuffy" pantheon would never let such a thing live for long.

He shuts his eyes, massaging the bridge of his nose with a gloved hand. "I know it's not that easy, Aph. Just let me take care of it, would you?"

She gives a firm shake of her head. "I can't do that."

"What? Afraid I'll fuck it up?"

"No," she says. "That isn't it."

"Then what is it!?" His voice echoes out into the gloom, surprising even her. After a moment of smoothing his hair down, he regains his composure. "I'm sorry for yelling. I just– you're not making this easy for me. We've been meeting like this for months. I'm getting antsy here."

She offers a soft hand for him to take. Her expression droops as she frowns at their intertwined hands. "I just have to think of what to tell him."

He shuts his eyes and inhales deeply. "You can tell Ares he can kiss my fucking ass! I'm not sharing you any longer."

"Asmodeus," she presses his hand to her cheek, "I love you."

"But you know how dangerous it is to love a man like me, don't you?" He leans in close to hook an arm around her bare waist, scruff tickling her neck as he kisses her. "They hate creatures like me."

They sit at the base of the tree, Aphrodite resting her head against his shoulder. She gazes at the full moon with a hand outstretched to try and capture it. If only she could do such a thing, if only her life could be a romantic fairy tale or play. She would be the leading lady and everything would go her way.

But this is no such thing.

"You're not a creature," she says, forcing back reflexive tears. His story is one that brings out the waterworks.

"Sorry. I know you don't like it when I talk badly about myself, but how can I not?" He drops his gaze to the floor, but Aphrodite raises it to look at her. She takes a moment to stare into the purple of his eyes. "I'm a disgrace. They call me a demon, and it's not like I can do anything about it. I'm the runt of the family."

"Asmo, please... don't be so hard on yourself." She lets the silence last until she can return to the more pressing matter. "As far as we go, I'm sure I can keep Ares from knowing."

But Asmodeus shakes his head. "You might've been able to act your way through life so far, but this isn't pretend anymore. What will happen when he finds out?"

"He won't!"

He tightens his grip on her, petting her curly hair. "But he will. He has a knack at finding things out." He pauses, and the hand on her head stiffens. "I don't mind taking the fall if it comes to it."

Aphrodite straightens so she can better inspect his solemn face. "You don't have to do that. I'm sure I can make him understand."

He closes his eyes, and his hand falls back to his side. "This isn't one of your daydreams, doing this will have real consequences—for both of us." He asks a question to the night itself, the glowing moon the only one to eavesdrop on their little discussion. "Are you sure you want to fall in love with a demon? You'll be risking your pretty life here in the Garden."

Aphrodite's gaze falls to the ground, a hand gripping at the layers of pink chiffon that hugs her frame. "If it's you, I don't mind."

He tips her head back to face him, pressing a finger under her chin. "Do you promise you'll stay by my side? That you'll always love me?"

"Of course! I'd offer up my soul if I ever hurt you."

"Now, don't go making deals you can't keep." Asmodeus

grins at her and wags a finger. "You know I'll hold you to it."

"Ah, I'm sorry."

He tucks her hair back from her round face, his fingers lingering along her jawline as he takes a second to soak in her presence. When he answers, his tone is firm. "You don't need to apologize. Not to me."

"I know, I just don't know what comes over me when I'm around you." She grins at how she folds in on herself like a budding flower, an unusual shyness about her. "It's so unlike myself, acting like this."

"You're full of surprises, it's what I love about you," he says.

Every time he professes his love, she bites the inside of her cheek. "Are you sure you won't grow tired of me?"

"Stability is overrated. Speaking of, I really should show you the Rosebed one of these days. You'd love it." He exhales a cloud of smoke that dissipates into the night air. Asmodeus takes her hand in his, squeezing it tighter than he ever has before. He takes one last look at the moon before whispering to her, "we should really get going, by the way."

Aphrodite and Asmodeus giggle like children as they make their way back through the greenhouse. The interior is dusty and worn, but they won't be spending much time in here. The secret door is merely a portal. Stepping out onto the manicured lawns, a permanent storm of lavender clouds churn in the fake sky. Giant evergreens line the property that descend into a dense forest. The wind whips Aphrodite's hair to and fro, carrying the ungodly moans of the damned with it.

She gazes upon the back of a small Victorian castle, its two spires ascending into sharp points. The windows are wide and tinted black, looming at her like empty eyes. The rough path twists as wild bushes of red roses and myrtles overtake the landscape. Transparent figures come in and out of view with large watering cans as they tend to the sprawling garden. She finds it comical that he goes to such lengths for her, as Asmodeus normally hates flowers.

They stumble through the rain to stand under fabric awnings that shield the terrace. She would protest as Asmodeus lays his suit jacket over her shoulders, but the gesture makes her heart skip a beat. They sneak into the ballroom. A mural lays across the ceiling of them together, the colors as bright as if it were just painted. A large crystal chandelier dangles in the middle of the room, refracting light onto the golden marble.

"Can't we stay outside for a bit?" she asks, grinning at the rain dripping over the windows. "At least sit on the patio?

You know how much I love storms."

Asmodeus rubs his chin as if he is actually pondering it. She knows his answer before he even speaks. "I *suppose* it wouldn't hurt to stay out? But only for a little bit, I would hate for you to catch a cold."

"Cold? I'm a goddess, remember?" She sneezes as the words leave her mouth.

"See? You're going to get sick out here. I should know by now not to listen to you, all you ever do is get in trouble," Asmodeus says.

He nudges her through to the den where lengthy couches, along with tables of black wood, sit before a brick fireplace. Narrow bookcases file against the walls, stuffed to the brim with dusty hardcovers neither of them have any interest in reading. A singular window brings in a ray of light, leaving the rest of the den in darkness.

"...I'm sorry."

"There's nothing to be sorry for. I'm going to gather some warm blankets." He stabs a finger at her. "And *you're* going to stay in the den."

He snaps his fingers and a purple flame ignites the wood. She frowns but does as she is told. Aphrodite sits as close to the fire as she can, lightly shivering in her thin dress. The manor is cold and dark, seeming near abandoned. She can't imagine living alone in such a spacious house, but he somehow manages. She would go crazy if she had to live in a place like this.

"...and without shoes, too." Asmodeus comes around the corner, descending the stairs with armfuls of comforters, a scowl on his face as he forcibly wraps blanket after blanket around her shoulders. He sits on the couch with a sigh. "What am I going to do with you?"

"I won't be in your hair for long, remember?" she asks. "I have to go back before he notices I'm gone."

"*Don't* remind me."

"We have to talk about it sometime, don't we?" She turns as much as she can within her prison of downy feathers. "You can't ignore this forever."

He digs his claws into the leather seat. "I know that! I get it. You'll have your fun and then go back to him."

"But what about you?"

He snorts. "What about me?"

"Won't you be lonely here by yourself?"

Asmodeus looks in the direction of the foyer, not answering for a good while. He must be staring at the portrait of her that sits at the top of the stairs, a surprise he sprung on her one day. While he is busy, she frees herself, letting the comforters drop to the floor in a heap.

"You get used to things after a while," he says. "I've gotten used to being by myself, I'm sure I'll be fine without you regardless of where the chips fall."

Aphrodite perches on the edge of the couch beside him. "What makes you so sure things won't work out? I thought I told you that Ares wouldn't be a problem?"

"You say that, but I know better. Things never work out, not for me." He refuses to look at her dead on. "Besides, I hardly deserve someone like you."

She frowns at him. "We both know what kind of person I am. I break everything I touch, and I rush into things. I'll only end up smothering you."

"I'm sure I can handle you, even at your worst." He rises, if only to keep an unspoken distance between them. "I'm the same as you, don't you know? I don't exactly have a sparkling record either, so doesn't that make us perfect fits for each other?"

She hasn't the heart to prove him otherwise, but it would be so easy to crush his heart in her hands like porcelain. Aphrodite is sure Hades and Persephone warned him about her, but his desire beat their well-meaning advice. So even if he stays, she'll never change, not for him, not for any man.

She puts on her best smile—the same she has in that portrait of his. "Of course it does. It's like you said, we're one and the same. I love you, and that's all that matters."

He looks at her with so much love that a sprinkle of genuity warms her face. Even she is unable to remain stone-cold at a gesture like that. "You really mean that?"

"I do." His eyes follow her as she makes her way out of the den. "I'm going to take a little beauty nap, by the way."

"Oh, I can join you if you like?" Asmodeus makes it half-way off the couch before she can answer.

"There's no need for that," she chuckles. "But I'll call if I need you."

The castle's foyer is surprisingly bright, the walls and floor a shiny white. Various carpets overlap on the floor and portraits of his parents and brothers cover the walls. She truly wonders how anyone could stand having several sons. At least Asmodeus is the handsome one.

At the first landing, before the stairs split off to either side, a singular painting dominates the entire wall. It is of herself, looking serene and beautiful as always, her red curls flowing around her plump face, a subtle grin on her lips. Her green eyes glow like she knows something the viewer doesn't.

There are scuff marks worn into the wood at the spot she stands, as if someone has spent a great deal of time gazing at it.

She wanders deep into the castle, the pink door signifying the room he designated as hers. A four-poster bed sits in the corner by the window, the walls done in soothing pastels. A hand mirror in the shape of a sea shell sits on the nightstand with a light covering of dust.

Aphrodite runs a hand over its surface, marveling at the care put into the room. Little painted songbirds flit around the walls and bright flowers crawl up the corners. Did he paint all this by himself? Well, better than bare walls. Stripping out of her single layer of clothing, she crawls into bed for the first of her routine naps. Beauty isn't as easy as it looks.

A few hours later, Asmodeus' name flutters down the hall on butterfly wings, beckoning him to her. The scent of honey thickens the air along with it. With how the floorboards yell, she traces his path—up the stairs and to her door. She scrambles to right herself and pretend she isn't up to anything, but the smell gives her innocence away.

He asks to come in, and the door unlocks. He must be at

a loss for words, with how half sentences to a probable coy speech get lost in his throat. Aphrodite feigns frustration, a hand keeping the thin sheet over her. Exertion flushes on her face, sure it has a pleasant glow to it.

"What do you want?" she asks.

He stands idle in front of her. "I couldn't help but overhear..."

She covers her eyes with a hand, still acting as if he is barging in on her. "Was I that loud?"

They exchange coy smiles, Aphrodite holding his gaze the entire time. This is all but a song and dance before the main event. She pulls the sheet off her, but keeps her thighs closed.

His voice pitches low as he takes her beauty in. "I just want to show you how much I love you."

"What are you waiting for, then? An invitation?" She grabs a handful of his dress shirt and reels him in. "You want to prove your love to me, don't you?"

"Yes! It's all I want to do!"

"Then get to work," she says with a smirk. He hastily kicks off his shoes and undresses himself before diving under the sheets with her. After all the hard work he has put in, giving him a taste of Eden is the least she can do for him. He loves her like it is his only purpose in life that night.

Chapter Two

The First Chorus

Two women sit in Asmodeus' den, side by side on the couch. The fireplace casts no light over them, as if they're not even there. They hold masks on thin sticks in their hands, black tragedy on the left, while white comedy is on the right.

Tragedy's blood red cloak swallows her, light blonde hair falling past her shoulders. Her alabaster skin, gaunt features, and red eyes give her the eerie essence of a spirit. Comedy's fitted ball gown is a sunny yellow. Her bronze skin shines with life, her own dark hair tied into various knots. She has a perpetual playful smile on her face as Tragedy speaks.

"In this manor exists a tragedy waiting to unfold. So the question has been posed; are you a Player or the Audience? Will you act or remain passive?"

Tragedy leads the way up the stairs with a candle in hand. Their red and yellow shadows flicker off the walls like phantoms. The pair peer through their masks into Aphrodite's room at the lovers in bed. Comedy stifles her laughter behind a hand.

"Stuck within a game of truth and lies, of life and death; one vigilant man sacrifices that most precious to him, and a jealous man allows his obsession to consume him. But spiteful little prince, what will *you* lose? No matter what you do, the end will remain the same; no one will be left. Even with such a gloomy outcome, there is no reason to yearn for death when your beloved is by your side. Rejoice! For the tides are in your favor."

But the tides always change. So a cloudless night turns a darker shade of red.

Chapter Three

Red Magic

Aphrodite spends her time as if that night never happened. She indulges in ambrosia, and bathes in the sun every afternoon. A young woman with golden brown skin and a heart-shaped face sits beside her on the balcony. Erato is the only one Aphrodite affectionately calls her friend. A silk dress the color of pink lilies hugs her, its thin straps criss-crossing over her shoulders. Rose petals are sewn into the fabric, its hem reaching Erato's ankles.

They don't speak of much outside the usual gossip, which if not always has to do with Aphrodite. She can't seem to stay away from petty drama. But on this bright day, the topic of conversation is less than ideal.

"Where have you been?" Erato asks. "You disappear for

days at a time, and I can only keep Ares so busy."

Aphrodite fans herself. "If I wanted you to know, I'd of told you."

She glances back into her temple, the back of her statue obscuring line of sight onto the balcony. If anyone wanted to eavesdrop, she would know. Fabrics of red and pink hang from the walls and windows, while fresh rose petals blanket the floor. In each corner of each room, a vase of roses sit in a shelf carved out from the wall.

Aphrodite demands that she be surrounded by beautiful things at all times.

They lean close to one another, their elbows brushing together. There will be times when they have little else to say, but neither wanting to part. So they stare at each other. Aphrodite admires Erato's dark eyes that gleam with stars whenever she smiles, and the soft slope of her cheeks.

"I'm not leaving until you fess up," Erato says, clasping Aphrodite's hand in hers. "I'm your *friend*. Whatever it is, I promise this stays between us."

"I'm not sure." But she grins as Erato tucks stray hair behind her ear, her fingers lingering a moment longer than needed.

"Have I ever told you how beautiful you look today?"

"Don't try and butter me up," Aphrodite says. "I won't fall for it." She folds her arms and looks out at the stretch of blue sky above them. But something bubbles up from deep within her — the urge to spill her secret. "...Fine, I'll tell you."

Erato's sly little laugh, and the way she cups her ear, makes her giggle. "Do tell what the powerful Goddess of Love has been up to these days. The people are *dying* to know. Is it a secret family? Surely you haven't been spending all that time by *yourself?*"

"Of course! A woman such as myself needs solitude, just like any other."

"Bullshit," Erato says.

She grins. "Fine. You win." Aphrodite drops the exuberance, wetting her lips. "I've been seeing someone."

"Another man?" She gasps, as if any of this is a shock to her. "I don't believe that *you* of all the gods would be one to sleep around."

Aphrodite gives Erato a playful shove. "Alright, I get it! I might be a little bit.. impulsive."

She snorts. "A little?"

21

Throwing a hand toward the temple's interior, she says, "if you want to know who it is, I would suggest you leave the roasting for later."

Erato moves into the shade near the door, leaning her head against the wall. She taps her chin with a finger. "Let me guess. It must be someone... someone you wouldn't want Ares to know about, am I right?"

Aphrodite pretends to straighten her skirt. "Maybe."

"Someone close to him, but far enough to be a suitable target." Erato's full lips purse in thought. "Someone he must hate."

Aphrodite grips the edge of the balcony's railing much too tightly, angling her face so she can't see her embarrassment. "It's one of his Uncle's sons."

"*Hades?*"

"Don't make fun of me, alright?"

Erato lowers her voice. "Which one?"

"...The youngest." Aphrodite turns to face her friend. "Listen, he's the only good-looking one, alright? Can you blame me?"

"I can, and I will." She offers a grave nod, pacing in the

small space they have. "But, why don't you tell me about him? What does he look like? I personally heard they're all disgusting on account of Hades refusing Hera's blessing." Erato pauses to calculate in her head. "So how good looking can he *really* be?"

"I'd rather show you than go through this interrogation any longer." Aphrodite holds her head high and beckons Erato to follow into the confines of the temple.

"What do you mean by 'show?'"

She says nothing as she plucks a rose from a vase, and pricks her finger with its thorn. Aphrodite paints a line overhead in the blank air. A rainbow passes over her eyes momentarily. The blood drips over a seemingly invisible door, coating it in red.

"I mean exactly that." She pulls the door open, but all that lies within is blackness. Aphrodite stares into the void. Cold mist curls around her ankles as it sucks in the heat of Eden. "Shall we get going?"

"To where? You have yet to answer me."

She tugs Erato through the threshold, and for a few moments there is nothing else but wet brick under her feet. Aphrodite stumbles in the dark, groping for the next door's handle. When she has Asmodeus' flame beside her, she usually doesn't have to worry about this minor detail. But she recalls the layout of the room. At least she thinks she does?

The floor steadily slopes down until they trip into the dusty greenhouse.

Erato rubs at her eyes, squinting at the empty shelves and flower pots. "Where in Heavens are we?"

"This is the only way I know how to get here." She shoves dead plants out of her face, and makes her way to the front. The beat of rain grows louder, a thing that Aphrodite grins at.

She throws the door open to greet her favorite storm.

That perfect purple sky still churns. She has missed that sight so dearly. Ignoring Erato's questions, they sneak into the ballroom, leaving a trail of water behind.

"Aphrodite! Where are we? What plane are we even on?" she asks, gently shutting the door. "This place looks abandoned."

Aphrodite is too excited to answer, Asmodeus the only thing on her mind. She rushes down the stairs into the den.

"Asmo! Asmo!" she calls, almost tripping on her own feet.

"Where are you?"

Asmodeus rounds the corner with a mug of coffee to his lips. But upon noticing Aphrodite, he nearly chokes and has to spit it to the side.

"Aph!? What are you *doing* here?" He throws a glance to the grandfather clock. "Was I supposed to come get you? Did I forget about one of our dates?" Asmodeus' presses a gloved hand to his mouth and glares. "Are you even supposed to be here right now? Where's Ares?"

"Most likely not." Aphrodite shrugs. "And don't know, don't care. What matters is that I came to see you."

He takes her by the hand, unable to hide his dreamy grin. "Always so full of surprises."

The pair gaze at each other until Erato rounds the corner. She takes a good look at Asmodeus, then back to Aphrodite.

"Are you serious?" She points a finger at him. "*This* is the man you're seeing?"

Aphrodite sneers. "Is something wrong with him?"

"Nothing," she says. "I didn't imagine he would be so... *short.*"

"Hey!" Asmodeus puffs up, straightening to his full five-

and-a-half foot height. "I should have you know, that I'm a *prince*. I refuse to be treated this way by a mere Muse!"

Erato elbows Aphrodite and snickers. "Didn't realize princes were allowed to be so tiny. I mean, wow! Would you look at him? I bet he wears padded shoes."

"I do not!" he huffs. "I'm proud of my size, thank you very much."

"Yeah, okay." Erato's eyes wander around the manor's interior, over every piece of decor. She runs a hand along the leather couches. "Why is everything so dusty? Don't you ever clean?"

"I clean! It's clean!" Asmodeus puffs thick clouds of smoke once he relights his cigar. He mumbles to himself. Stress smoking it is, then.

"And you smoke *indoors?*"

Aphrodite raises a hand at both of them, signalling for the war to pause. "I didn't bring you here so you could make fun of him!"

"But look at him!" Erato throws a hand out. "He's doing half the job just by existing!"

"Is that another short joke?" Asmodeus growls. He shoves himself into the couch across from Erato, kicking his feet up on the coffee table. "Did you have to bring her with, Aph?"

While Erato twiddles her thumbs and tries to stay quiet, Aphrodite settles down beside Asmodeus. Their fingers absently slip together. "I kind of told her about you. Besides, I wanted her to meet you."

She grins, hopeful that her intrusion will be overlooked.

"Wait, you did what?" He drags his free hand down his face. "Aph, for fuck's sake, this was supposed to be a secret! What'll happen if my Mother or Father hear about this?" He pauses. "What if *Ares* finds out?"

"He won't!" she says, indignantly.

After all this time, she is proud of herself for keeping her mouth shut. But now that the secret has left her lips, it will float back to the pantheon, and wind its way back to him.

"Thinking about this is giving me a headache," he says. "I don't know about you two, but I need a drink."

Smoke trails over Asmodeus' shoulder as he passes through the foyer to the dining room. The other two follow close behind, easily outwalking him. The table is wide enough to fit at least ten people, each finely crafted chair shoved neatly into place. A white tea-cup sits at one end, half full.

27

The scent of fresh spring air lingers.

Asmodeus disappears into the kitchen while Aphrodite inspects the cup. Only one person could leave such an impression—the Goddess of Spring.

"Was your Mother here?" she asks.

He returns with a few bottles and glasses tucked under his arm. "What does it matter? If it really bothers you, she left to say goodbye to my Father."

Aphrodite watches him tear the cork out with a claw. "And where is she going?"

"Where *we're* going," he corrects. "That Queen of yours had that doll call her. She wants to see my Mother, and I'm tagging along."

Erato slips into one of the many seats, pouring herself a glass. They share a brief look, but say nothing. For Hera to use Hesperia to contact Persephone... she only uses the vessel in emergencies. What possible reason could she have to request a meeting?

"What do you intend to while you're there?" Aphrodite pours herself a generous glass. "You know we can't be seen together."

"That's why I think it's time we come clean." He swishes his drink around, staring into the dark wine. "I'm *tired* of stepping on eggshells and acting like a wanted fugitive."

"I really don't think it's a good idea."

"Are you *sure* he doesn't know already?" he asks, downing half of his glass in a single sip.

"I think I would know if he knew!"

Erato glances between them with a sigh. "He's not like you, Aph. If Ares is anything like his Mother, he isn't one to slip up."

It is Aphrodite's turn to sigh, downing the drink she takes with a glower. She places the empty glass in the middle of the table. "Well, this has been fun, but I think it's time we leave."

"You just got here!" Asmodeus sets his glass down to better stand in her way.

Aphrodite regards him with scorn before she brushes him aside. "And now I'm leaving. Funny how things like that go. I'm sure I'll see you when you visit."

Erato quietly finishes her drink and joins her companion. Without another word, they depart back through the greenhouse, turning down Asmodeus' offer for an umbrella.

Chapter Four

Spark

Days pass in a blur, until they melt together into a frenzy of color. Aphrodite doubts that even a day has passed for Asmodeus. Surely it doesn't take that long to get to Eden? She practically bites a hole into her cheek as the hours go by.

She lounges among the apple trees, watching the Hesperides do their work. A fountain featuring a statue of Hera herself sits to her side. A pristine chiton cascades down her body like water, a glittering diadem on her head. A look of annoyance dampens Hera's expression, wavy brown hair tied back off her face. Hera clutches Zeus' decapitated head in her left hand, a long scepter in her other.

Aphrodite regards such a thing with disdain. But simultaneously, a mild fear tugs at her heart at the thought of what Hera is willing to do. If a woman can so easily kill her own husband, what would she do once she discovers

Aphrodite has been making deals under the table?

If she ever does, that is.

Upon gazing on the woman she hates, a chipper voice slinks into her ear.

"Now, what's with the sour face?" *Hermes.* Why does this winged freak think she wants to tolerate him today? "I come —"

"—To deliver a message, I assume." She tosses a look to her right at him. His mop of curls partially obscures his sharp face and eyes. A pair of white wings curl around his head. The white of his chiton shows his allegiance to Hera.

He ever-so-humbly presents her with a golden envelope, its metallic sheen nearly blinding her. "Not a message, an invitation." Hermes forces a grin at her, which Aphrodite returns.

"Oh, an invitation? How kind of her to include me in one of her stuffy garden parties!" She plucks the envelope from his hand, and makes short work of tearing out the parchment. She gives the dense letter a quick look over. Hera's small cursive is painful to look at. "*Dear Aphrodite... your presence has been requested. I would greatly appreciate if you graced us with your glowing personality.*" She pauses. "Yeah, I'm not going."

"'Scuse me?" he asks, watching her crumple the paper up into a ball. "I just came all this way out of the goodnesss of my heart to deliver you this message, and you throw it back in my face?" Hermes makes an overdramatic gasp. "What will I tell Hera?"

Aphrodite folds her arms and fires a glare his way. "You can tell her I think she's a bitch."

He flutters into the air, floating close enough to be annoying, but far enough to be out of range. "My word, do you kiss Ares with that mouth?"

She quickly rises, and he jolts backwards from her. With a smirk, she tosses her curls over her shoulder. "*Every. Night.*"

"How does he deal with you and your prickly self?" Hermes' nose wrinkles up, looking down on her from his place in the air. The superiority oozes off him like slime. Light glints off the gold bracelets around his wrists. "You know what everyone says about you, right?"

"Of course I do! But that's all they know how to do - *talk!*" Aphrodite's lips curl into a snarl. She forces herself to walk away. Why does the pantheon think they have her figured out? None of them know a single thing about her and Ares.

It is difficult to ignore—the cold stares, the whispering behind her back. She puts on a brave face for Ares' sake, regardless of the fact he must know what they think of their relationship, but even she has a limit. Sure, the pantheon loves to think of themselves as superior, but Hera is the center of it all.

She labels other goddesses who use their power for themselves as witches. Hera has no use for those who refuse to bow to the crown. But thanks to her, she came to meet her dear Asmodeus.

She climbs the stairs of Hera's temple, all pure and white. No matter how much she loves to hide behind that color, Aphrodite knows her heart is rotted and black. Out on the terrace, a glass table sits with four seats. Three of them are taken.

Persephone is always a sight to behold. Her mahogany skin glows with soft pink undertones, a playful grin on her lips. Wildflowers are braided into her thick, curly hair. Her blousey yellow dress is light and airy, suiting the change in season she finds herself in. With bold red florals covering her, it looks as though she took a flower shower. Although she has never been one for excess, Persephone allows herself a singular ruby ring carved into the shape of a rose.

Asmodeus sits beside her, while Hera overtakes the entire other side. When she seats herself, only Persephone and Asmodeus greet her.

Hera, however, has gone all out it seems. She puts forward a regal aura in her long gown of glittering white, a dusty pink shawl daintily placed over her shoulders. Her neck and wrists jingle every time she moves by how much gold she is wearing. She must be showing off due to Aphrodite's presence. The woman's lips are almost always in a tight line of disapproval. As far as Aphrodite knows, she never smiles.

"You were almost late." Hera sips from her golden tea cup with a sigh. "You should know I value puncutality by now, with how long you've been seeing my son, after all."

Persephone warmly admonishes her. "I'm sure she didn't mean to be late. Why, we were almost late ourselves." She snickers to try and diffuse the animosity. "Right, Asmo?"

"Right." The little man has traded his usual attire of black for a silver a few shades lighter. He hardly touches his drink, or even acknowledges Aphrodite like he normally would, keeping his hands in his lap.

"You two had such a long journey from the dreadful Underworld. I'm sure there was no avoiding it." Hera stirs sugar into her tea. "But dear Aphrodite has no such excuse."

She finally shoves into her seat, leaning against what little free table space there is. "Wow, what a warm welcome."

"I'm sure you haven't been acquainted with Persephone's son yet." Hera motions with her cup to Asmodeus.

Aphrodite and him share uncomfortable looks. She keeps her head bowed low. "I haven't had the pleasure, no."

"Neither have I," he says, voice shaking the slightest.

Perspephone leans over the table to the Queen of the Heavens. She intensely whispers, "what do you think you're doing?"

"Oh, nothing. I'm playing nice like you asked." Hera takes a long sip from her cup as she eyes the pair. After a long lull, she waves them along. "Now, why don't you two introduce yourselves?" More silence. "It would be rude of you to snub my dear husband's family. Perhaps you might find something in common? Or someone?"

Asmodeus turns to Aphrodite to speak, but Hera

interrupts them before they can hardly let out a breath. She holds a bangled hand to her chin. "It's quite a funny thing, you know. I remember when you first met Ares, and I seem to recall you two being rather standoffish as well."

"What are you trying to say?" Aphrodite asks, innocently.

She waves her hand to dismiss the thought, but there is a spark in Hera's eye. *She knows.* "Just an old woman reminiscing, nothing else to it." Aphrodite can spot the way she pretends to take a sip of tea, and suddenly "recall" another thought. "Speaking of my son, do you know he's returning soon?"

"Is that so?" she asks, gripping the fabric of her dress as tightly as she can to stop from snapping. "Coming back from his visit in the Rosebed so soon?"

"I assumed you would be overjoyed to hear of his return." Hera chuckles, staring Aphrodite down. She has no further reason to pretend to notice Asmodeus. "Did something come between you two?"

"Nothing," she lies.

"Come now, you can tell me—I'm practically your Mother as well." The grin she gives makes Aphrodite's skin crawl. The superiority in her tone wishes this table weren't between them.

"You're no Mother of mine," she says through gritted teeth. "I have no need for a Mother—especially not you."

"And here I thought we put these petty matters behind us," Hera quips.

"We would if you'd stop bringing them up!" Aphrodite's face twists the more worked up she gets, until she stands out of her chair. Her fingers grab at the fancy tablecloth. "What do you have against me that you can't let go of, Hera!? Why must you talk down to me like I'm a child!"

"Now, now," she tuts, wagging her finger. "Don't go losing your temper. Think of how poor Asmodeus would feel to witness such a sight—"

"I have no problem with it." He fires a glare at Hera.

"We're all adults here, aren't we?" Persephone stirs some sugar into her tea. "Hera, I thought you wanted to enjoy our company, not make a mockery of Aphrodite."

Glancing slowly around the table, seeing that the odds are not in her favor, Hera folds. She places her empty cup on its saucer and laces her hands together. "Consider the party over. I do hope you all took something away from this." She makes sure to pause on Asmodeus and Aphrodite's faces individually. "And might I add, dearest Persephone, that our local harlot has no trouble doing it herself."

"That's enough, Hera!" Persephone rises with the controlled grace of a true queen. The same cannot be said about Hera, however. The Goddess of Spring looks down her nose at the old woman, meeting her eye, but letting her tight expression do the talking for her. "I don't understand the need to drag me away from my husband, and for what? To gang up on your son's beloved?" She makes sure to run a finger along her rose ring. "We may have our own disagreements, but I would never stoop so low as to publicly humiliate her. Are you not the Queen of Eden? Or is that just another mask you hide behind?"

Hera has little to say to that.

The little meeting dissipates as the four break off. Asmodeus manages to catch up to Aphrodite as she slips away to her temple. They stand at the entrance, Asmodeus halfway up the stairs.

"Do you have a death wish?" she asks, keeping a wary eye on their surroundings. "You can't be seen with me."

"I know, but can you blame me for wanting to have a word before we leave?" That restless energy is back. She can sense it in the way he tugs at his jacket and hair. Without his cigar, he has little to channel his anxiety into. "I've missed you, and you haven't exactly been visting as often." Asmodeus lowers a stare onto her. "I'll take anything I can get, frankly."

The distant sky churns with dark clouds. Lightning lights up her eyes as it rolls closer.

"Ares will be back soon." She sighs. "You can't be around, alright? *Go home, Asmo.*"

"I'll be back," he states, with a loose shrug. "I'll make sure to stay out of sight. The big guy won't even know I'm here."

He says this as if it is fact, but she knows better than to believe him. Ares would strike him down on sight. But she can't bring herself to be straight with him.

"Alright..." She rubs the back of her neck. Rain drops patter onto the warm marble below her feet. Time is running out. This is a bad idea. "Don't come out until I say so, okay?"

Chapter Five

A Thousand Cuts

It is at last, that the man of the hour—the spear that pierces fear into the hearts of mortal men, the God of War—appears. Ares' hair is as bright as his Father's lightning bolt, skin as dark as the clouds he rolls in on. His red suit almost glows in the oncoming twilight. Although his very presence normally announces death, today his intentions are softer in nature.

He is finally home. At last, the scent of roses swirls around him, and he longs for the embrace of his true love, Aphrodite. With careful steps into her temple, he takes a bit more time to gaze at the familiar sights; the kneeling statue of Aphrodite in the middle of the room, piles of roses in her arms as tokens of affection.

"My Love, where are you?" he calls, like a husband returning home to his wife after a long day apart. As he rounds the corner to her private chambers, there she lies on a bed of velvet and silk. Lit candles dot the room.

She has her back to him, but she coyly looks over her shoulder. The thinnest of fabrics drapes her in deep pinks and reds. Ares devours every angle as he approaches her. But her eyes are what reel him in. An unspoken bond of red thread runs between them.

On this black night, with the pouring rain accompanying them, he will feel her like he never has before.

"I love you," he whispers, kneeling against the bed.

She rolls over onto her back, and the robe falls away. Aphrodite makes no effort to cover herself, for why would she? She is in the presence of the man she is most comfortable with. Running her hands up along her sides, she beckons him to her.

He zeroes in on her rosy lips as she says, "I love you too."

As he gazes upon Aphrodite, his chest swells with affection. Because for Ares, at the heart of everything, there is love.

He wraps his arms around her and squeezes. With his face against the crook of her neck, her flowery scent is all he needs. Ares nearly cries he becomes so tender-hearted. Only in her arms does he let himself open up like this.

They lie side by side as they always do, and gaze into each other's eyes. Aphrodite's giggle pulls up at the corners of his lips.

"What is it?"

"Nothing," she says. "It's funny. We're usually so hot and heavy by the time you get home, we never have much time to act like this." She pauses. "Is something wrong? You're so quiet."

"I'm just taking you in, my Dear." Ares tears his eyes away from for but a moment to watch the sleeping sun in the sky. Pink and purple color the clouds, the storm subsiding until he is called on again. "I suppose it would be obvious to say you missed me?"

"I did." Aphrodite crinkles her brow at him in mock annoyance. "And yes, it is."

The crash of waves fills his mind, drowning him with blue memories of the time spent swimming along the coast of her island. They would spend all night among the waves, caressing each other in the shallows under the moonlight. Before the world awoke, bathed in the scent of the sea, Ares would watch the sun rise in her eyes.

He is not sure why he is so sentimental tonight, or what must be in the air to bring this side out of him. But something deeper tugs at his heart—the knowledge that things will change forever. Whatever he does, he has to be careful. His touch is delicate, his words hesitant, as if he could break the moment otherwise.

But the crash of ceramic is what does it instead.

"I'll be right back," he says, steeling himself for what is to come.

Ares descends back into the temple's belly, and what he finds is most peculiar. He did expect an intruder, but to spy those dark horns? He isn't quite sure what to say. The God of War freezes in his tracks, letting the voice his soldiers hear every day come back to him.

"What are you doing so far away from home, cousin?" he asks, taking stiff steps around the statue. "What possible reason do you have to be in Aphrodite's temple?"

Asmodeus had knocked over one of the vases. He clutches his ankle, hissing in pain. "It's—I'm... I'm just visiting."

"Still? It's long after dusk. Shouldn't you be returning home to your mansion?"

"...Yes." He tries to peek around Ares, but he blocks his way.

"What do you need, cousin?" Taking a step closer, he too dwarfs the demon.

Asmodeus is clearly seething, with how he grinds his teeth at him. "I need to speak with Aphrodite. It's important." He glances again to the back room. "But it can wait."

"What can wait? Why do you need to see her?"

He tries to pretend to walk along the steps, but Ares follows. Asmodeus turns back to throw a glare. One of many mistakes he will make tonight. "It's not your business. Just let me see Aph, would you?"

"'Aph?'" he repeats. Ares takes walks slowly along the entrance of the temple. "The last time I checked, you two were barely acquaintances. Why do you refer to her so casually, then?" He stops to face Asmodeus. "I'll ask once more—*why are you here?*"

He doesn't expect Aphrodite to come out, back in her red dress. Did he lose his nerve somewhere and forget to control his volume?

"Asmo?" she chokes out.

The demon in question scramble for words, face strained under Ares' constant glare. "Aph, it's, uh, not what it looks like!"

"Get out of here!" She actually shoos him away. What is the meaning of this? Why does she look so frantic to help him escape?

Asmodeus tries to descend the steps, but Ares catches him by the shoulder. He turns him back to face the God of War. Each ringed finger of his digs deeper into his collar. Ares' expression is blank, but his eyes radiate a blood-red corona.

He has no intention of hurting him, only to scare him really. But then Asmodeus has to speak those cursed words. "Do whatever you want, but you can't stop me. I love her too!"

"What are you talking about?" he asks. But he doesn't want an actual answer, he wants to let loose the feelings he has held back for so long. To think his own cousin would try to steal Aphrodite away in his absence. Perhaps the whispers he has been hearing have some truth to them. "How long has this been going on now?"

But it is ridiculous to pretend any longer. Ares has

always known. Magma bubbles up within him, from some dark corner he refuses to acknowledge unless on the battlefield. A thick heat sweeps up through his arm into his fingers. He hardly recognizes the hand that lights his cousin alight as his own.

Chapter Six

Burn

Asmodeus' screams ring through her head, and her pretty world burns down in an instant. He writhes on the floor of her temple, flames licking up his right half. His skin burns and blisters, shrieks growing louder as the seconds pass. Ares' features have none of the expected malice. His dark skin glows among the flames as he stares at the violence.

"Ares!" Aphrodite attempts to step out from behind him, but he holds a hand up to keep her from approaching.

"Don't get any closer! Who knows what tricks this demon has up his sleeve?"

"Fuck you!" Asmodeus' sobs grow louder.

"That was a warning shot." Ares shoos him away like an impudent child. "Why don't you go limp to whatever hole you crawled from?"

Black blood stains the perfect marble floor. Asmodeus

holds a hand to his half-charred face, staring at Aphrodite with his good eye. Tears bubble up from within her, but she can't cry now, not in front of Ares. She clamps a hand over her mouth to muffle the pained noise that tries to escape; a bird caught between her hands.

"You have to let me see him! Please!"

"I can't risk that," Ares says. Aphrodite pushes through to kneel before him. The sweet scent of flowers is overpowered by the stench of burning flesh.

Asmodeus' voice fills the temple again, bouncing off the marble pillars and statues of herself. "Why did you do this to me!?"

He drags his body across the floor, leaving smears of blood along the way. His fingers grasp at her arms. He is a pitiful sight, staring at her with those pleading eyes. It is not like she can do anything to help, she has already played her cards. Still, he tries to stand, but hasn't the strength to last long.

"Asmodeus, stop! Please! You're hurt enough as it is!"

He sways, unable to keep his balance. "Just tell me everything's going to be okay!" Silence. "Tell me you still love me!"

She glances back to Ares with a knot in her throat. He

watches the scene play out with a glare, hands idle at his sides. "To think that a demon would try and persuade my Love to fall for him. First time for everything."

Asmodeus scrambles for the right words, unable to properly speak as blood dribbles from his mouth. "What does he mean? You love me, don't you?"

He grabs at her leg, bloody fingerprints soiling her robes. The longer her silence goes on, the more obvious the betrayal becomes. "I'm sorry," is the only thing she can muster. She doesn't have an answer for him, not now. She failed to keep him safe.

He lets out all his frustration and pain into a single howl. It is the cry of an animal backed into a corner, realizing that he has been had. At last, he is able to stand on shaky feet, malice rolling off of him in a hazy cloud. His death glare cuts her deeper than any knife.

"You don't give a shit about me, do you!?"

"I do—"

"Liar!" He spits blood in her direction. "You used me! What am I to you, a toy?"

She can stay calm no longer, repressed feelings can only be pushed down for so long. Aphrodite trembles as blood blooms in her eyes, spilling out from the corners like tears.

Her face flushes as she yells. "I did everything I could!"

Aphrodite tears at her curls, the flame inside her rising into an inferno. A hurricane unleashes in her humble temple. The wind tears at her rose bushes and whips her hair around her. Fear momentarily crosses Asmodeus' face at the sight.

But after a few moments, her outburst fades to a lazy breeze. She doesn't have it in her to strike fear into her lover's heart. They stare at one another, unable to speak, tears running free.

"Please come with me! I beg you!" Even as badly hurt as he is, Asmodeus' love is stronger than the pain and anger. He extends a trembling hand to her. "We're meant to be together, aren't we?"

"Asmo, I—"

"That's enough of this silly game." Ares makes a beeline for Asmodeus as sparks fly from his fingertips.

Aphrodite, however, turns to face him. They stand toe to toe, rubbing away bloody tears with the back of her hand. As she stares into his face, it is clear that Ares doesn't want this to happen as much as she does. The red and gold of his eyes shimmer with a wetness unlike him, while the hand he means to finish Asmodeus off with trembles.

"I'm not letting you kill him," she says.

"He crossed a line, my Dear. Just let me finish this and we can go home."

"*Only* if you let him go."

Ares looks over her shoulder at him, regret the only thing that paints his face. "I always knew," he confesses, "that you were seeing someone else. I just didn't think it would be him of all people."

"What's *wrong* with him!?" Her hands clench into fists at her sides and like the sun coming out from behind clouds, her anger is back full force. Her shrill voice bombards him. "Why can't you be happy for me?"

Ares' face is stony, cool as the marble that surrounds them. His voice is an attempt at staying collected, but his own feelings seep through the cracks. "All I *do* is for you, my Love. I hope with time, you can forgive me for this." He lets out a deep sigh, barely able to look at the carnage. "Leave here."

She looks back over her shoulder at Asmodeus; his bleeding, blackened skin seared into her memory. Even with his injuries, he gazes at her like she is all that matters.

Asmodeus yells, "I'll come back for you! I swear on it!"

They watch him stumble down her temple steps, crying and panting like a dying animal. She still cannot bring herself to help. When he eventually fades from view, her brave front

51

crumbles to dust.

Ares watches Aphrodite collapse onto the floor and sob into her hands. Only now, with no other eyes to see a display unbecoming of the God of War, does Ares break down. Even though he has a reputation to uphold, comforting his partner is more pertinent.

His voice cracks. "I'm sorry. It'll all be okay."

"When?" she demands. She looks at him with sorrow straining her face, eyes puffy and ringed in red.

"I don't know," he says. "Maybe one of these days, one of these nights. Everything passes eventually, even this."

It seems Aphrodite has no patience for flimsy words tonight. A storm of conflicting emotions consumes him; guilt at his actions, yet a relief that Asmodeus made it out alive. What will she do now that their bridge has been burned? What outlet will she pursue next?

"Let's get going, alright? It's going to be dark soon." He kneels beside her, resting a gentle hand on her shoulder. "We can talk about this later."

"I don't want to talk anymore," she snaps.

"We don't have to do anything, then." He sighs. "Best for things like this to fade away on their own."

They take their time in returning to Aphrodite's quarters, enjoying what little of the night they are able to. With an arm around her shoulders, Ares keeps glancing at her down-turned face. Her curls obscure her expression, but even he can guess how she must feel. He isn't one for flowery words in times like these. He is a simple man with simple desires, and right now his only desire is her comfort. It pains him to see his love at odds with herself.

But is he not at fault as well? After all, he is the one who cast the first stone. He let his pride outweigh his original intentions, to allow this affair to continue under the table. Ares doesn't blame her whatsoever, for the wonders of paradise do grow old and mundane, and the heart longs for anything to spark excitement again. Asmodeus has his charms, sure, but an affair is all it would ever be. To let things go any farther would be crossing a treacherous line.

His patience can only go so far.

Asmodeus should be happy The Fates granted him another day. Hopefully he doesn't squander it. But knowing him, he will show up again and again, until Ares squashes the little pest. He tenses the more he thinks about it, a thing Aphrodite must notice.

"I'm sorry." There is no life to her words. Maybe it was a

mistake to step between them. She wipes at her watering eyes. "I'll make sure I don't make this mistake again."

"I'm not angry with you. I don't even care why you started seeing him, I just want you safe, my Love."

They walk along concrete paths flanked by rows of giant oaks, their branches forming an arch over their heads. The flash of fireflies adds a sense of whimsy to the otherwise somber night. Aphrodite usually smiles at this, but tonight she pays it no mind. She seems to be elsewhere, somewhere darker. His mind races with a typhoon of words, of things he should have said sooner. But it is too late for that now.

She spits out a question. "Why wouldn't I be safe with him?"

A frown sits on Ares' handsome face. He doesn't know how to proceed. Is this question meant to trip him up? "He was—is—a demon, my Love. Who knows what he would have done if not dealt with?"

Despite catching himself, he isn't entirely sure the man stepped foot off Eden's soil alive. He could have succumbed to his injuries outside the temple, and they would never know.

"What does that have to do with anything?" Irritation oozes into her voice. Aphrodite's temper is a dangerous thing to toy with, a thing even Hera fears. To think his Mother of all the gods in the Garden would be afraid of her. She is the Queen of the Heavens for a reason, is she not? What could she possibly be wary of?

To Ares, she has always just been his spontaneous Aphrodite. After the cool nights and hazy days they've spent in each other's arms, it is strange to think it would all but scratch the surface of a being such as herself.

He knows the stories of the lives she has taken, the war that was started in her name. It is difficult to think she could commit such atrocities, but he too has blood on his hands.

"I mean nothing by it," he says.

"Do you think I'm stupid enough to let him take my soul, Ares?"

"I didn't *say* that—"

"It sounded like you did." She tosses a glare at him. Despite her fragile ego, he loves her, for they share a bloodthirsty rage that only the other can sympathize with.

"I only ever express my sincerest concerns for you, you know this."

"Of course I know!"

They circle the giant fountain to one of the two entrances to her room. Thin silks act as a makeshift doorway, candlelight passing through. Erato meets them at the threshold.

"Whatever is the matter?" she asks.

"Nothing. It's nothing." If he wanted to spend the rest of the night gossiping, he would have gone to visit Dionysus instead.

"Do you not realize how late it is?" Erato's worrying over Aphrodite is almost nostalgic after the night he has had. "I thought you were with," she nods to her, "*you know.*"

Aphrodite nods to him. "Erato, it's okay. He already knows."

"Oh, my apologies." She stands in the doorway, rather unsure of what to do. When neither of them can even crack a smile, she asks, "I take it that isn't a good thing?"

"No, it isn't," is all he has to say.

Ares covers her with his cape to keep the pestering at bay for tonight. The room they step into is lit by hundreds of candles along the window sills, soft cushions and couches are the only furniture she has. Carpets cover the otherwise cold stone floor. He leads Aphrodite through the room to her bedchambers, the Muse at his heels. "Ares, what happened?"

"We'll talk about it. But not right now. Please, just give us some space for tonight."

Thankfully, he has an actual door to close and lock tight.

He carries Aphrodite to bed, holding her to his chest like the wounded swan she is. Her room is small but cozy, the perfect place to slip away to when the outside world is too much. Layers of colorful blankets, comforters, and pillows make up the ocean that is her bed. They practically sink into it, lying side by side.

His fingers dance up her side, tucking hair from her face. Once the sheets caress her, Aphrodite is out cold. Only while asleep does Ares get the chance to see her in her purest form. Without the perfume of lust or veil of anger she typically wears, only then is her true self shown. She curls in on herself, looking more like a tired woman than a frightening deity. He wonders if Asmodeus has ever been given this opportunity? Most likely not. Ares blows out the single candle lighting the room.

Maybe tomorrow will be better for them?

Chapter Seven

Camouflage

Aphrodite and Ares share less than a few words every morning and night, to give her what she needs most—space. Their love will mend and she'll surely forget the spontaneous affair in due time. Because that is what it was, right? Spontaneous. This couldn't have been premeditated, he knows her right down to the way she thinks. His Aphrodite is not one to do much planning besides a vague idea. So how could this have transpired right under his nose?

She would have been gushing about it to someone, anyone who would listen. His Rose isn't actually good at keeping secrets, especially her own, but she likes to think she is. Word gets out, and the rest of the pantheon talk until it falls into his lap. Normally, he doesn't even need to acknowledge it—the relationship fizzles out and she comes running back to him. It is just how things should be. No one, especially not a slimy soul-stealing demon, will ever take her away from him.

They sit under the glass-walled pavilion in armchairs set across from each other, a lit chandelier between them. Grass and vines sprout from the cracks in the stone floor, empty flower pots piled high in the corners. Aphrodite curls up on her chair, the red skirts of her dress falling past her feet. Black embroidered roses hug her hips. She rests her cheek in the curve of her palm, staring at the foggy scenery through the glass.

Ares folds his hands together as he watches her, his various rings shining in the light. He is dressed in a burgundy suit, collar open and tieless, a thin gold chain the only thing holding his shirt closed. It is all purely to blend in with the filth of the city.

"So, you're going?" She phrases this as if it were an accusation.

Aphrodite doesn't even direct her scorn at him anymore, only showing it through otherwise passive quips. Which is odd, as she isn't one to be indirect about anything. If he weren't the son of the late Zeus, things would be much different. Would he even be allowed in the Garden? To be torn from his lover; a fate worse than death. Perhaps he can sympathize with Asmodeus—but only the tiniest bit.

"I'm afraid so," he says. "I have to check out something else in the Rosebed. We've been getting more and more reports of a black cat crossing people's paths." Ares takes a moment for his question regarding the blonde-haired witch to sink in. "You don't know anything about that, do you?"

She shifts away from him, letting her feet dangle off the edge of the cushion. "Eris? We're not even on good terms. Why don't you ask her yourself?"

Ares nods along. "The last I heard you two were quite good friends."

She directs another cold observation his way. "Whoever told you that deserves to be executed."

He leans back in his seat and drags a hand down his face. Did burning Asmodeus really put that much of a rift between them? He can see it in her eyes, the anger she holds close to her heart. One wrong move and she'll bite his head off, but he doesn't have time to play her game.

"Does he really mean that much to you?" His stare is as

hot and pervasive as Apollo's sun.

"What kind of stupid question is that?" she asks.

"Are you going to answer me or are we going to sit in silence until I leave?" Ares shoves out of his seat to lean over her. "I love you too much to let this fester. I don't know how many times I can explain myself, I did what had to be done. I don't regret it."

"My answer isn't changing." Aphrodite twirls a lock of hair around her finger.

"So you loved him?" He lowers his thick sunglasses enough so he can get a better view of her.

With a sneer, she balls fistfuls of her skirts into her hands. "If I say yes, will you drop it?"

"Until I come back, yes."

She fidgets further, and he watches the tension in her face gradually melt away. Aphrodite sighs. "Then the answer is yes."

Ares crouches beside her chair so he is at her eye level. "I don't mean to make you more distraught than you are, my Love. I just need to know what you're thinking."

Aphrodite looks over her shoulder and she is as radiant as ever; the way the light caresses her face and the soft curl of her lips makes his heart stop. He has to let out a slow breath to relieve the pressure. No matter what she does, he can't stay mad at her, for their love is like an overgrown rose bush, equally as beautiful as it is dangerous. Ares doesn't even mind the prick of her thorns as long as he gets to be beside her.

She doesn't answer him, but all they have is time. They'll come out of this mess stronger than before, he's sure of it.

"I love you," he says.

"I love you too."

He kisses her forehead and she tries to stifle the smile that inches its way onto her face. He chuckles at it. "Ah, is that a grin I see?"

"Perhaps. What of it?"

At least he's able to bring back her wit momentarily. By tomorrow she'll be laughing again, but he won't be there to see it. Ares holds his arms out for a goodbye hug. She tosses away her petty anger for a moment to   throw herself into his embrace. Ares squeezes her a bit tighter than usual.

"I love you," he repeats, the rose-scent of her perfume soothing his anxieties.

"I'm still mad at you," Aphrodite mumbles into his shoulder.

"I'll take what I can get, my Dear."

They break their final embrace for a good while, but Ares lingers at the pavilion doors. She stands a few feet away, acting rather shy with how she hugs herself, refusing to let him catch her staring.

"When will you return?" she asks.

"I'll be in and out," he kisses her hand, "I promise."

But she doesn't smile, an unknown weight forcing her to frown. "For both our sakes, I hope you're right."

The couple walk into the overbearing heat and Ares takes one final look at her. He puts her face to memory, for it's all he'll have for a good while. A storm brews overhead, the clouds turning dark and gray. The roar of thunder is his cue to exit the stage. A single bolt of lightning envelops him, and within that split second, he's gone without a trace.

The moment Ares departs, Aphrodite flees to the one place where she can be alone, the myrtle tree. She takes her time in hiking up the grassy hill, an unlit candle in her hands. She sets it at the base of the tree, nestled against the flowers she lays down. She lights the wick and offers a quick prayer to wherever Asmodeus is, her regret evident in the apology she mutters to the candle.

Silly a silly thought, as if he can even hear her. If only her words could reach him on the wings of a bird, they would perch on his hand, stare into his eyes, and relay the message. But things are not that simple. Smoke wafts past her nose and it takes her whole being not to cry. Erato would pester her with questions at the sight of her puffy eyes, but this is her secret, as it has always been. It is the one thing she cannot speak to anyone.

No matter how much she yearns for someone to comfort her and tell her everything will be alright, this is her mistake to mend. She must go it alone. She prays day and night, abstains from socializing and sex. She covers herself in heavy fabrics and no longer smiles or laughs. As lonely as she is, this is her act of repentance. As the days pass, she builds an entire shrine under the tree with dozens of candles and dried flowers. She looks forward to it every morning and night as it's the only joy she allows herself to partake in.

A vision comes to her as she sleeps of Ares and Asmodeus. They're in silhouette, dueling each other. The sparks from their blades clashing light their faces. She can't get between them, she can't even scream for help. Aphrodite is but a member of the Audience. She glances to either side at the rest of the pantheon as they watch alongside her. It is just another tragedy to gossip over for them.

Aphrodite wakes all alone to a black room. Surprisingly,

she feels nothing, only blank space within her. She has one thing on her mind, the city she never got to visit, the Rosebed. The want was there, but she couldn't leave Eden without the rise of talk. She's grown used to being the subject of gossip among the planes, but is it her fault she lives the way she wants?

She is without bindings, free to do as she pleases. Other gods are only jealous that she does what they cannot, for she has an immunity that other women below her would kill for. No matter what atrocity she commits, she'll be forgiven. But will Asmodeus give her the closure she yearns for?

Erato's voice drags Aphrodite out of her thoughts.   She stands amidst the tall grasses that sway in the breeze, their pink robes stark against the golden scenery. "You're really worse than I thought, aren't you?"

"Thank you for pointing out the obvious," Aphrodite says.

"You really miss him, don't you? Whatever happened to that demon you were seeing? Why aren't you with him?" When she gets no response, Erato tries to coax an answer out, taking a few steps closer. "Ares told me something happened, but that's it. What did he not want me to know?"

Aphrodite tears at the grass between her fingers. "Asmodeus told him off. He had to give him a piece of his mind, and look at what happened because of it!"

Erato holds a hand to her mouth. "Is he dead?"

"He let him live," she says. "But what am I going to do?"

"We can't let anyone else know about this. My lips, for one, are sealed." The Muse kneels beside her, squeezing her hand for comfort. "What *are* you going to do? I haven't the slightest idea of what you're talking about."

"They'll find out, they always do!" She whirls around with wild eyes, gripping at the air. "I'm sure someone is watching us right now."

"Oh, don't be silly." She tries to soothe her, but Aphrodite glances back and forth as if trying to discern an invisible presence.

"I have to get out of here, Erato."

"What do you mean?" she asks. "We're safe here, this is paradise. What more could you ask for?"

"I'm stifled here! I'm like a caged bird." She gestures around them. "There's nothing left for me here."

Erato blinks at her with a perplexed look. "..But where else is there to go to?"

"Like I said, I'm leaving."

They stand together, Erato clutching at her heart. "Don't

tell me you're going to the Rosebed?"

"I have to, he's waiting for me."

Aphrodite takes a few steps away, but Erato grabs her by the wrist. "How are you so sure?"

"I have no choice but to try," she says, with a shrug.

Erato gives it her all as she goes on, speaking a mile a minute. "And what of Ares? I'm sure he wouldn't allow you to wander the city by yourself and if he finds out who knows what he'll do—"

"No man controls me, dear Muse. My mind has been made." With a flick of her hair, Aphrodite allows herself a grin as she pulls Erato in close. She whispers, "I'll make sure to keep a low profile."

Her eyes try to calculate an elaborate lie, staring into Aphrodite's face. "But what shall I tell Hera? She hates you, doesn't she? This will be the perfect excuse for her to justify punishing you."

She waves a hand in Erato's general direction. "Make up whatever story you like. I doubt she'll buy it, but I only need time to make my getaway."

They walk back along the misshapen path to Aphrodite's room, discussing it with hushed voices. The sun casts them in yellow hues. "When do you intend on leaving?" Erato asks.

"About now, I think." Aphrodite presses a finger to her chin.

It's time for Erato to make another shocked gasp. "They won't just let you through the gates! Ares would kill anyone who'd let you slip out!"

"*Ares would kill anyone,*" she mocks, with a twirl of her skirts. "There'll be no one to kill because no one is going to know! Erato, I've got it all figured out."

Her chambers are empty late in the afternoon, the light seeping through the cloth-covered windows. Aphrodite tip toes along the carpets, eyes darting along mementos and paintings of herself. What does she take with her? Ares always tells her it is best to travel light, and she would hate for any of these precious gifts to be broken on the way down. Gathering her dress in her hands, she regards it with scorn. This is a product of Eden, a thing she would rather leave behind from this day forth. Aphrodite tugs it loose and lets the fabric fall where it may.

"What are you doing!?" How is Erato still shocked?

"What I should've done long ago." She eyes the window, at the open air and endless sky. If only she could fly like a butterfly, she would be truly free from everything and everyone. As dainty as she may seem, she is not easily broken, for the spirit of violence and blood, of war and ruin, beats in her chest. She was born to stir conflict. An oasis on its own plane is not where she belongs. She's chosen to ignore this for so long, but she's meant to live in chaos, thriving on the ocean of life, being thrown to and fro by its endless waves. It is about time she returns to that older self.

Aphrodite climbs onto the open window sill and almost immediately loses her footing, the wind stronger than expected. Erato clings to her waist to keep her steady. "Aphrodite, please! Rethink this. It's not worth looking for him, you can't leave like this!"

Her hair whips around her face like the beat of grand wings. "I'm not turning back now!"

The Muse loosens her grip and stares at the sky with Aphrodite. The endless blue spreads out before their eyes. Her hands slip away from around Aphrodite, instead gripping the window sill, lips a firm line. They share a tender look.

"You're my friend, what will I do without you?" she sighs. "I know this place has been killing you, but I'll see what I can do."

Aphrodite leans her head back and boisterous laughter streams out. "I knew you'd come around!"

"Who else is going to keep that old hag guessing where

you've went?" Erato asks, dropping the proper act. "Hurry up before I go with you myself."

They share a final grin, Aphrodite squeezing her hand. "I'll make this up to you one day, I promise."

Face to face with the cliff's edge, she takes a breath and leaps.

She falls for what seems like ages, laughing all the way. The brief thought that she's acted rashly enters her head, but impulse beats rational thought at this point. Her hair cascades behind , rippling like the curtain in her room. Never before has she been so alive, a flower blooming in her chest.

She looks back as the room she occupied for centuries grows smaller and smaller. The further she falls, the darker the sky turns, layers of clouds blotting out the moon and stars. Distant thunder roars through the sky as rain clouds hang below her. The closer she grows to the boundary between Eden and Earth, the more her golden aura wavers.

Gods can only leave their paradise through means of the gates, lest they hand over their godhood. Aphrodite has little use for it anymore, having to go incognito for her little visit.

Wind whips past her outstretched fingers and she bids a final goodbye to her home. If she will ever see it again is unknown to her, but she can't worry about that now, she has to carve her own path. Piercing through the thick clouds, she enters a world buffeted by a storm.

The soft golden glow around her wavers, and her aura peels away from her, dripping though the sky in a myriad of colors like oil paint. To a far-off viewer, it would look like a melted star falling from the Heavens. She curls in on herself, her own form morphing before her eyes. Her skin glows and true bliss overcomes her for the only time in her life. She doesn't know what change is taking place, but her heart still thrums at what her new self will look like.

Aphrodite plummets into freezing water.

Chapter Eight

The Pearl

A light shines on him, washed out colors that make his chest burn. Rough calloused hands hoist him from the water and into a small boat. The patter of rain assaults his senses. Holding himself gives him little relief as water drenches everything.

"Oh, would you look at the sight of this one!" A deep brogue bounces around in his head. A man in a breton cap and heavy wool sweater sits on the other side of the boat, a gold insignia of a horse shining on his hat. His bearded face is thin and sharp, with salt and pepper streaking his otherwise long dark hair.

"Who are you!?" A lower voice leaves his mouth that shocks even himself. He looks down at his hands, the fingers thinner and more delicate. How are these his? The rest of him is lighter as well, and he momentarily laments the idea of losing so much weight during his metamorphosis. No wonder he is unable to brave the cold ocean breeze.

"I should be askin' you the same thing, shouldn't I? It's not everyday I catch a siren in my net, you should be thankful I found you." The fisherman stares at him, elbows resting on his knees as he leans forward. Even though water drips down his face, his eyes remain locked on him. "What's yer name?"

"I don't *have* a name," he says, returning the man's stare with equal intensity. If he has to rip out his throat to get off this boat, he will.

The fisherman rubs his chin with a gloved hand as a mischievous grin crosses his face. He has a single golden incisor. "Well, I suppose since you fell from the sky and what not... how about Ariel? Fittin' for an angel, don't ya think?"

"It'll do." Ariel flicks wet hair off his face. "I'm not a siren, by the way."

"That's what they all say."

The man eyes him for a few more seconds with a hunger Ariel is very familiar with. It is safe to say he plans on staying on the other side of the boat for now. He still has a part to play, however—the naive and coy siren that this man desires. Ariel is more than comfortable giving a man his fantasy as long as he gets what he wants.

When all the boat does is rock for another few seconds, he seethes. "Shouldn't we be moving?"

His grin turns dreamy as his eyes drag along Ariel's body, going as far as to affectionately sigh. "Don't get all impatient now. I'm just takin' a good look at ya. You're awfully cute for a siren."

"We should be getting to shore, shouldn't we?" he asks again. Ariel has had enough fun and games, but the fisherman is insatiable.

"You know, I have a nice warm bed—if you're interested?" He most likely thinks that grin will make his heart melt, but he remains blank. "...As well as some dry clothes, can't forget about those."

"I just need to know the way to the Rosebed." Ariel tries to hide his disgust and ignore the man's comment. "I'm meeting someone."

His new friend rows assuredly towards shore, the waves rocking the wooden boat. They sit in silence for all of thirty seconds before he opens his big mouth again.

"What's a cute little thing like you lookin' to get in the Rosebed?" He waves a dismissive hand like the thought itself is a pesky fly. "Place is full of criminals. Not worth it, might run into the wrong crowd. Safer out here, if ya ask me."

"I *didn't* ask you." Ariel's anger flares up and he does his best to not bare his teeth, but the way the fisherman has his lecherous eyes glued to his body reminds him of a certain King of the Sea. They certainly are too sharp and intelligent for a mere fisherman. It is not a coincidence he found him on the open sea. Poseidon always was a pervert, unable to keep his hands to himself.

"It's a real shame you can't stay, y'know. You say you're meetin' someone, eh?" Poseidon cocks his head, still smiling. "You just met me, didn't you? Why don't we get to know each other better?"

Ariel sneers. "I'm not interested."

"You're cold now, but I'm sure you'll warm up just fine." His playful nature falls flat to the man who's heard every line in the book. "Besides, I still require payment, don't I? For savin' you and all?"

"Does it look like I have money?"

Poseidon's eyes drag up and down Ariel's bare body for so long, they hit shore and he doesn't even realize it. "I was thinking somethin' of a more... physical nature."

Ariel is done playing pretend, snapping even though he is naked and defenseless. "I'm not sleeping with you,

Poseidon."

His demeanor shifts from flirty to cold as the sea he carried him out of. He slips his cap off. "Do I happen to know you? I don't recall meetin' a beauty like you before." But then he frowns after a moment. "Well, there was a time I knew *someone* like you. But she was... a lot different."

That dreamy stare comes back, his fingers toying with the fabric of his hat all the while. A softness pours in that he can't ignore. Ariel can still recall the fruitless pursuits from Poseidon years prior. All the gifts and trinkets he would give him when they were in Eden together. Sure, he might have given him the time of day, but he never slept with him. Ariel sighs. To think there was a time when all he had to worry over were how many suitors he had.

The anger from before sloughs off, and he is left with a heavy guilt in his chest. If there is one thing he knows about himself, it is that he can't stay mad at old suitors. "And who was she?"

This gets a grin out of Poseidon that twinkles with nostalgia. But there is a sadness in his eyes that Ariel almost regrets causing. "She was beautiful. Out of my league." He pauses to cough into his hand. "We should be getting inside, shouldn't we? I'm sure you don't want to hear an old man ramble about a lost love."

Ariel folds his arms and eases out of the boat, keeping his eyes on Poseidon the entire time. They walk along the wet sand in silence.

There is a wooden cabin set along the edge of the beach. It is small but expertly crafted, made entirely of full logs set on stilts. Light from the lanterns set by the window and door call to him, a siren song he can't resist.

Ariel enters Poseidon's abode, aware of the eyes crawling all over him. The door locks behind him. A bear pelt covers the stone floor. A fire roars, casting dim light over the model ships and naval paintings along the walls. There is the bare essential in terms of furniture, a handmade table and pair of chairs that sit in the makeshift kitchen. Ariel leaves a trail of water wherever he goes.

"Oh, let me dry you a bit." Poseidon has a towel in his hand, which Ariel snatches before he can get any closer.

"I can dry myself, but thanks," he says, dryly.

"No reason to be short with me." Poseidon crowds him close to the fire, standing a bit too close. "I'm just tryin' to make a beautiful man such as yourself feel welcome."

Ariel shoves the towel into his hands, trying to laugh the comment off. "I really don't need to be worried over,

Poseidon."

He frowns at Ariel, and the brogue disappears at the snap of a finger. His eyes glow that typical gold. "Are you sure we don't know each other?"

Ariel bites his tongue. He would rather die than give himself away so soon.

"...I must be mistaking you for another person." Poseidon stiffly swallows and continues on. "You still need your clothes, don't you?" He grows closer, the scent of the sea rolling off him as his fingers barely touch Ariel's sides. "You know, it's been quite a while since I've been this close to anyone."

Ariel only knows how to deal with rowdy men, so he isn't sure what angle to play. The memory of the reckless God of the Sea doesn't match with the older man in front of him. He shifts to an angle that better shows off what little curves he has left, the fire lighting his silhouette in the dark of the cabin.

"And what kind of man are you exactly?" He hopes the question comes off as innocent.

Poseidon's grin is rather strained as he sits down at the kitchen table. "Ah... I'm not very sure anymore. I'm certainly not a good one." When Ariel has yet to move, he taps the seat beside him. "Please, take a seat."

"What makes you say that?" He refuses to move. They stare at each other, the dripping of water the only sound.

"I've done some horrible things," he says, Poseidon's eyes shining in the lamplight. "And because of it, I've lost the people I loved. That's all I'll say."

"Are you sure they won't forgive you?" Another coy question, but Ariel knows well the crimes he committed. The assault of Medusa was a spectacle the pantheon could not stop talking about for years. Ariel refused to be apart of such disgusting gossip. One day Poseidon was at the top of the world, and the next he abandoned them.

He laces his fingers together and gazes at Ariel. "I've long since accepted that I'll never be forgiven. And that's fine, I hardly deserve such a thing."

"So you've been here all this time?" Ariel pretends to look over all the knick-knacks along the walls and shelves, holding the damp towel around himself.

Suspicion enters Poseidon's voice. "How do you know I left somewhere?"

But he too is quick on the draw. "Why else would you live on a beach in the middle of nowhere?"

The God of the Sea leans forward a bit, and sits that much straighter. His sharp eyes pinpoint his every move. "I never said anything about leaving. But sure, let's go with that." He pauses. "So, why don't you tell me a little about yourself? That is, if you can."

"What is that supposed to mean?" Ariel snaps.

"I think we both know what I mean." His grin is so smug, a thing he would love to smear with his hand like wet paint. But he is not the same powerful being he once was.

Ariel slowly inches closer to the bedroom. It is the one place he still reigns in. If he can just wrap Poseidon around his finger without letting his identity be known, the rest will go swimmingly. But he acts as if he knows already.

His voice drops an octave. "Cut the bullshit, Poseidon. Why don't we stop dancing around the issue?"

"I don't know what you're talking about." He heaves out of his seat and steps closer as he speaks, almost corralling Ariel into the bedroom. "The only issue here is that you're not in my bed yet."

He closes the door behind him. Ariel has the pleasure of watching him strip out of his sopping wet sweater, dozens of little scars along his hairy torso. He has a swimmer's build. Ariel bites on the inside of his cheek. Is he really about to do this?

"Why don't we get to business, eh?" Poseidon leans a

knee onto the bed, and it creaks under his weight. He has to wave Ariel over. "Why are you still so shy? I thought you of all people would be used to things like this."

"So you know?" he blurts out.

"Ha! I knew the moment I laid my eyes on that gorgeous face of yours." Poseidon hums contentedly to himself. "Now come over here."

"I don't listen to orders."

He lifts Ariel off his feet rather easily, and can't help but get swept along in the moment. The feel of his thick arms around him brings a thrill to his heart. Poseidon tosses him onto the bed, towering over him. Their shared dampness gleams in the lowlight.

"You do now." Ariel melts.

But he nearly forgot, he has somewhere to be. "Wait!"

Poseidon goes to lean down, but pauses. "What is it?"

"I have to get to the city." Ariel scrambles to sit up, but his suitor barely acknowledges his words.

"You don't *have* to go anywhere," he says. "If you mean the Rosebed, it isn't worth it. Full of criminals. It'd be better if you stayed here—with me."

"I can't—"

"If you think I'm going to let you slip out of my hands again, think again." Poseidon's touch gains the slightest edge to it, pushing him back down onto the bed. "Or did you forget that I love you?"

Ariel can hardly recall most of his flings, but he forced himself to when it came to Poseidon. The man has an unhealthy obsession with him. It didn't matter that he was with Ares, he cared not. Whatever the God of the Sea wants, he takes.

"I wouldn't use those exact words, but sure, let's call it that." Ariel shifts his face away from him. "The only thing I remember is the fixation you held for me."

"Held?" Poseidon tuts. "My Dear, you underestimate me. Even after all these years, I've never forgotten you." He runs a soft hand through Ariel's pearlescent locks. "Don't think I didn't know how badly you wanted me as well. All those little smile you'd give me from afar, you little tease."

"I don't know what you're talking about." Ariel tries to roll out from under him. But he brings him down so their bodies are flush against one another. Poseidon's gentle hands wind along his arms to his wrist. He tries to pull away, but he has him in his net. "Don't try anything!"

"I wouldn't dream of it," he says, romantic words rolling

off his tongue. "You don't need to be scared of me. I'm quite the gentleman–when I get what I want."

Ariel unwinds and lets his guard down, but there is still a tight ball in his chest. Cigar smoke curls around his thoughts like vines. "You sound just like the man I'm trying to find."

"So I take it you have good taste after all?" Poseidon folds his arms under his head as he repositions, spread out like the haughty king he is. Ariel sits on his lap.

They stare at each other, the joke inevitably falling flat. "Just so we're clear, I don't like you."

"You say that now," Poseidon chuckles. "But I'm sure I can win you over some day."

Ariel is more than tentative about placing his hands on Poseidon's chest, sure he has something up his sleeve. But he waits and nothing happens, growing closer until he is lying on top of him. Poseidon's heartbeat, along with the steady motion of his breathing, soothes him. There is nothing to worry about, this is just another night with another man, no different than if he were with Ares or Asmodeus. Poseidon's strong arms wrap around him, cradling him against his chest as he pets his damp hair.

"Forgive me. I've spent quite a while on this edge of the realm, all by my lonesome. One forgets how to act like a god and more like common pond scum."

"What are you apologizing for?" Ariel asks.

"Maybe I'm a better man than you take me credit for."

"Good men haven't assaulted people." Ariel tries to pull back, but Poseidon keeps him in place. He is slow to answer, but Ariel is content listening to the patter of rain on the roof.

"I've done bad things, I don't deny that. I was a stupid young man with the world at my fingertips. I like to think being exiled has humbled me."

He lays back down against Poseidon with a sigh. "You're just like every other selfish man I've known. You're only nice when you want to be."

"But are you not the same as me? We both come from the same place, we're two sides of the same coin." His gaze washes over Ariel and he's sure those eyes pierce through his disguise, yet he doesn't call him out. "You craved freedom like me, right? Why else would you leave the Garden behind?"

"I have to—"

"—find someone, I know. But why did you really leave?" Poseidon asks.

"That doesn't matter." Ariel tries to slip out of his grip, but there's no escape from Poseidon's clutches. His fingers dance along his waist as he coaxes him back down.

"What's wrong with staying the night? We can head for the city tomorrow morning, bright and early." When it doesn't convince him, he tries another approach suffused with roses. His large hands slip around Ariel's, an unexpected gentleness in the way he touches him. "I promise I'll take you where you need to be, you just have to trust me."

"I don't trust anyone," Ariel says.

Poseidon's golden tooth glints as he grins. He pulls him into a warm embrace, and he has the pleasure of hearing his rough voice rumble deep in his chest. "There's a first time for everything."

A curiosity rises within Ariel from that alone. He is a hummingbird whose eye is easily caught by every blooming flower he passes. Poseidon is a color he has yet to experience, sure his royal blue will enrapture him one day. But that is a thought for another time in the distant future, as he has a city to reach in the morning.

Chapter Nine

The Rosebed

The next day, Poseidon's thick arms ensnare Ariel, but the more he tries to wiggle away, the tighter they get. He really wouldn't have pegged him for the clingy type, even before he fell, but appearances are deceiving.

Ariel elbows him in the chest. "Let go of me, you big oaf!"

Poseidon grumbles, yet his eager hands slide away without protest. Sleepy fingers trail through Ariel's hair, voice soft in the silver light of dawn. "What are you hitting me for? I know you're eager to leave, but can't you let a man get his sleep?"

"You were touching me without my permission!"

He rubs at his closed eyes, willfully ignoring Ariel's rain of scorn. "Oh, so now you decide to say something? You were fine and dandy cozying up to me last night."

"It's not like I had a choice." He folds his arms, pouting as Poseidon hooks a scarred arm back around Ariel's waist, reeling him in close. He squashes his face against Ariel's chest, and gazes up at him from his vantage point. This early in the morning, his face is like the placid surface of a lake, the malice from last night nowhere to be found among the gold. His rough fingers massage Ariel's lower back, half-grinning at him.

"What are you smiling at?"

"Nothing, nothing..." he hums. "Just enjoying your company is all."

As much as he pretends to not be flattered, his ego bends, forgetting all about the silver tongues most of the pantheon possess. They know how to get their way with the subtlest of compliments, or perhaps Ariel is just a sucker for praise and flattery. The look Poseidon gives him is full of... something. He would hate to call it infatuation, seeing as he is probably only looking to butter him up, and to give it a name would mean to acknowledge it, but Ariel doesn't have feelings for anyone other than the two rowdy men he calls his.

But, then again, neither of them are here, so if he chooses to sleep with Poseidon, they will never know. It is not like he has anyone of importance to tell, the secret will stay between them in this cabin. He has no intentions of letting things go any further than sex, but the serial dater in him longs, yearns, even aches for a man's tender touch. It doesn't matter who, as long as they can shower him with the affection he deserves.

Ariel runs his fingers over the side of Poseidon's face, relishing the coarse texture of his beard. He even goes as far as absently toying with his lower lip. How will that beard feel pressed against his neck amid the whirlwind of desire? He can picture the mild pain as his teeth sink into his skin, injecting the sugar he craves into his veins. Hopefully he leaves a wonderful mark, or two, or three. However many he wants really.

One could call Ariel a slave to his impulses, but he is a slave to none. He uses his sex as a tool and a bargaining piece, for the only things that can truly sway a man's loyalty are sex and money. The pleasure he gets is but a bonus, so it isn't his fault he knows how to get what he wants.

"I see." Ariel ticks away at just how to wrap this man around his finger, pressing his thigh between Poseidon's legs, and clinging to him that much closer. This gets little reaction out of him. Usually Ares and Asmodeus are like fireworks, hot and explosive with their needs, every touch getting a stream of praise and dirty words directed at him, but

Poseidon only grins into his face.

"You look rather annoyed."

Ariel pouts. "I am most certainly am not."

Poseidon titters, "whatever you say. I'm not one to argue with a lover. I'd hate to ruin the mood before we start."

"I'm not your lover," Ariel says.

"Yet." A hand squeezes Ariel's hip, fingers tiptoeing along the line of his inner thigh. He almost wants to stop playing hard to get, sure Poseidon's tongue would have a number of other uses. "I'll make you mine one of these days."

"You sound so sure of yourself."

"I always get what I want—and right now I want you."

Ariel shrugs the sweet talk off. "You'll get exactly what I give, and nothing more."

"Bold of you to doubt my ability, Pearl."

He lets out an annoyed breath at the pet name. "Pearl?"

"Cute, isn't it?" He strokes Ariel's hair. "I thought on account of your hair being shiny and all, it'd be a fitting nickname."

"...Yeah, okay." He can call him whatever he likes for all he cares. Although he didn't expect something so unusually specific, there is a first time for everything.

"Let's take a bath, shall we? I'm sure you're aching for some relaxation." He further kneads Ariel's muscles. "Besides, you're so... tense."

"Just lead the way." He shrinks away from Poseidon.

There is an open doorway on the other side that leads to a rather large bathroom. With the makeup of the house, it should be impossible for a room of this size to fit, but gods have their way, he supposes. The tiled floor and walls are painted over in shades of blue resembling the flow of the sea, a porcelain tub sitting in the center with gold leaf lining the edges. Candles in sit wax-smeared precipices along the wall.

Poseidon runs the bath while Ariel stands awkwardly off to the side. He only peeks through the door, the air is much too cold for him. Poseidon doesn't seem to mind it, like a polar bear wading through the frozen tundra. All that hair and muscle is good for something after all.

With his back turned to him, Ariel can make out a tattoo of a killer whale across his shoulders, a seal in its jaws. Steam rises from the water that Poseidon runs a hand through, and takes one good look at Ariel before stripping and stepping in.

With a relaxed sigh, Poseidon lays his hands on either side of the tub, head resting against the lip. "Care to join me, Pearl?"

Ariel tiptoes along and covers himself with his hands. Casual intimacy is unusual to him, to be vulnerable is to open oneself up for pain. Poseidon could drown him if he so wishes, but he will just have to take the chance. He slips in and situates himself between his spread legs, his knees poking above the water. The warm water is indeed heavenly after the day he has had. They stare at each other.

"You're so pretty," Poseidon muses, leaning back further in the water. "You don't have to be afraid of me, you know?"

He extends a hand for Ariel to take, pulling him into the place against his chest like a telescope aligning a constellation. He must love having someone to hold after so much time alone. With a snap of Poseidon's fingers, dim light throws soft shadows over their faces as the candles light. After a few minutes, the sweet scent of flowers fills the air.

"So, what's this man you're looking for like?" Poseidon absently runs his fingers through Ariel's hair.

"He's a real piece of work," is all he says. Best to keep it vague for now.

"Do you always tend to go for difficult men?" Poseidon runs water over Ariel to work out the knots in his lower back, kneading at the muscles with surprisingly deft fingers.

"Usually." Ariel lays his head down. He flicks through

faces that blur together in his mind, but lingers on Ares'. Hopefully he won't hold this against him. When this is all said and done, they can return to their quiet life in the Garden. Everything will go his way. "He has quite the temper."

"Doesn't everyone from the Garden have a short fuse?" he chuckles. "Now, what's this hot-head look like?"

"Well... he's kind of short." Ariel frowns at the facts he let slip through. What *does* Asmodeus look like now? He never thought it would be an issue. "Other than that, I'm not sure anymore. But I'll know when I see him."

"So you don't even know who to look for?" Poseidon muses in silence for a few minutes. The question that bubbles up is an odd one. "But what do you intend to do once you find him?"

He falters, words catching in his throat. "...Apologize?"

This gets a good raspy laugh out of him. "You don't even have a plan? That's not going to get you anywhere. You need to tell it to him straight."

Ariel gives a firm shake of his head. "You don't understand, that wouldn't go anywhere."

"What do you mean? Of course it would!" Poseidon says, with a grin. "I haven't lived this long on just good looks. I mean, they've helped, but these days? I'd be lucky to snag a minnow."

Ariel leans back in the tub to appraise him. If things were different, perhaps he too would be down on this empty beach. "You look just fine to me."

Poseidon is actually taken aback. His voice turns silky smooth. "You really think so?"

"Of course!" Why is he humoring this old bastard? What is wrong with him?

He peppers kisses over Ariel's palms. "Oh, sweetheart, I'll do whatever I can to help you with your boy trouble. You just need a man to sort things and take the weight off your shoulders."

Ariel leans back in, wet hair falling over half his face like a thick curtain, and a spark catches between them. Poseidon's hands wander below Ariel's waist as he looks off to the side with a bashful grin. "So... you really think I'm still handsome?"

His delivery is dry. "Would I be in this tub if I didn't?"

"You're right." He laughs at himself. "You make me feel young again, you know that?"

"I do now." Poseidon squeezes wherever he can reach. It is clear that he wants him, but they still have a city to reach first. The duo are quiet for a few moments.

"So..." Poseidon begins.

"So?" Ariel coaxes him to continue with a flirty glance, but it only makes him flounder more.

"What would you say to me staying in the city for a while? For your safety. Not, uh, with you, just nearby—"

"I'd be fine with it."

The old man can't hide his excitement, his eyes crinkling as he continues to grin. "I'd be just a call away. When would you like to leave, by the way?"

"We can take our time. I'm in no rush." Ariel stretches out along the length of the tub, put at ease knowing that Poseidon will be wrapped around his finger soon enough.

There is a spring in his step as they get dressed, Poseidon pulling out a navy blue suit from deep in his closet. It's a bit snug, but in all the right places. He still wears his Breton cap with his hair tucked back. He unfolds a pair of horn-rimmed glasses to wear. All in all, he looks like someone's father.

He lends Ariel a white dress shirt and high-waisted black slacks. Thick lace lines hangs over his hands like flower petals. Poseidon ties his hair up for him, as "it's the least he could do," or so he says. The pair of black loafers he also loans him are a bit worn, but they will do.

They sit at the small table next to each other. Poseidon shifts his seat close to Ariel's, their knees grazing. "Shall we get going?" he asks, crossing the cabin to the door.

Poseidon shoves his arms through a rain coat. "We have quite the journey ahead of us."

"Can't we wait a minute?" He rests a hand along his shoulder as he steps beside him.

"For what?"

"To say goodbye." He takes in the rhythm of the rain, along with the gentle waves that roll in, for a final time. It reminds him fondly of his island of Cyprus, a place he misses dearly. But there is no way he could visit it now. He has a man to find.

With a deep sigh, Ariel slips down to the beach. Poseidon follows, leading back to the docked boat with a black umbrella. Ariel holds it while Poseidon pushes the boat out, and they row along the coastline. The rain is lighter today, a fine mist coats the lazy waves that roll in. Poseidon hums a tune, but otherwise they don't talk much. Ariel focuses on the scenery, dipping a hand in the cool water. He gazes at the distant clouds that graze the horizon.

Poseidon leans back into the rainfall. Ariel steals a glance at the water dripping down his face, but he catches him in the act. "Something the matter?"

Ariel looks away. "No. Nothing." A moment passes between them. "So you really don't mind the rain?"

"I don't mind getting my hands dirty." He instantly regrets everything at the mere implications.

Ariel pretends to not hear him, and he resumes his humming as if nothing happened. The whoosh of the oars cutting through calm water fills the silence.

They eventually reach the only thing sticking out from the fog, a rotted dock. Poseidon steps out, helping Ariel with a hand on his waist. A group of glowing eyes stare at them from above that fill the top of the stairs, the wood creaking under their feet. They have dark suits and fedoras on. Smoke trails from their grinning mouths.

The tall man at the front speaks. "You know there's a fee to dock here, grandpa."

"I've been coming here for years," Poseidon says. "You'd best speak with respect when addressing me, boy! What possible fee could there be? This is a public dock."

"It's under new management, pops. So get with the program." The man rubs his fingers together. "All the cash you've got."

Poseidon stares at the state of the dock and scoffs at the obvious disrepair. He takes a step up the creaky stairs. "You're clearly doing a terrible job at upkeep. I don't have time for this, move aside."

The leader cocks his head while the others leer at Ariel. "Why don't you let us have fun with that arm candy of yours? I promise we'll be gentle."

"I'm not for sale, you loser," Ariel pipes in.

"Ay! That's uncalled for!"

"He's right. You're just a bunch of low level trash that shake down the pigeon tourists that come to dock, isn't that right?" He takes a long look at each of the demons. "Can't even do it alone, either. Step aside."

"Or what?" The gangster sneers.

Poseidon climbs the remainder of the stairs and grabs him by his pressed collar. He pulls him in close, letting him hang in the air. "Do you realize who you're talking to, runt?"

His voice is thin. "Some old man?"

"I'd rip your tongue out for that, but I'd hate to make a mess of my suit. So I'll have to settle for less." As the man opens his mouth for another witty retort, Poseidon delivers a clean left hook to his jaw. The sharp crack resounds through the air, knocking the gangster off the dock. The rest of the group, without their leader, give them a wide berth. Poseidon glares at them as they leave.

"Are you alright?" Ariel asks.

"I'm just dandy." He frowns and dusts himself off. "I'm sorry you had to see that."

He leans against him like a damsel in distress. "No, it was kind of hot, actually."

Poseidon shakes his head at him. "You really have a thing for violent men, don't you?"

"What can I say? They're exciting." He bats his eyes as innocently as he can, clutching the umbrella in both hands. Every look wraps Poseidon further around his finger. At least he hopes they do, as he isn't sure how far his charms can go anymore. He is a perfect pearl, relying on his looks to get him where he wants. But maybe he isn't as perfect as he thinks.

Poseidon keeps a steady hand on Ariel's forearm. "Excitement doesn't necessarily make them a good man."

"Does it really matter in the end?" Ariel walks forward a bit. "I'm only here for a good time."

Poseidon only shakes his head at him. "Thoughts like that won't get you anywhere. It's no wonder you left the Garden, and for what? To pursue a man?"

He tugs the god along by the tie, adopting a solemn tone.

"You misunderstand. What I'm truly interested in isn't sex, what I'm after is love." Ariel glances Poseidon up and down. "This man is special, and I can't just let him go. I'll do everything I can to see him again."

For some reason entirely unknown to Ariel, he huffs at his words. It is not like he cares much, however. No matter how much Poseidon spews his affection at him, he will never be his.

They walk along the dock to the streets, barren and empty. Even in the gray, the neon signs and lights shine like an angler's bait. Casinos, brothels, and clubs boast their wares with gaudy slogans. Life-sized marble statues are set up at random; they sit at storefronts, street corners, wherever they can take center stage. Black lights shine at their bases, making the stone glow. The only people that pass by are in dark formal attire. They keep their heads low, hands in their pockets, eyeing the pair from afar. Does everyone smoke in the Rosebed?

The rest of the apartment buildings are dilapidated or abandoned, or at least they look like it. It could all be a clever front. Poseidon keeps close to Ariel, an ever present hand on his forearm. The rain keeps up the whole walk. After many a turn down streets that all look the same, Poseidon's grows increasingly unraveled, dabbing at his forehead with his sleeve.

"Do you have any idea where you're going?"

"It's been quite a while since I last visited... nothing looks the same anymore." He can't hide the disappointment that furrows his brow. "I'm sorry. I would ask for directions, but I'm not in the mood to deal with these fast-talking city folk. All they want is a deal out of you."

Ariel pretends to examine the bland buildings. "Like me with you?"

He's quick to reply, squeezing his arm a bit too tightly. "That's different. You're not like these soul-sucking leeches —"

"And to think I was just about to ask if you needed help," a man sighs from behind them. "But I'm just a soul-sucking leech."

Ariel looks over his shoulder at what looks like a peacock in human form. He is short and compact, his pinstripe suit fading from a shiny purple to green. Gold rings adorn his fingers, a pair of reflective sunglasses at the tip of his nose. His sculpted face is scruffy with a cupid's bow mustache. The only thing that dampens his visage is a horizontal scar slashing across his right cheek and nose. He oozes slimy vibes as he smiles at Ariel, both his canines dipped in gold.

"What's a cutie like you doing with a geezer like this?" He nods to Poseidon. "I didn't realize the old folks' home let their patients out for walks."

"Do you need something?" Poseidon asks, with a sneer.

"I was just in the area and I couldn't help but overhear you needed assistance." The loser presses a hand to his chest. "And like the good Samaritan I am, I thought—"

"So you were following us?" Ariel is unimpressed to say the least.

He runs his gloved raccoon-like fingers over his mustache. The smile refuses to waver. "I like to call it 'Following Really Close Behind.'"

"So you *were* following us!"

"What about it?" he asks.

"Go steal from someone else!" Ariel moves to stomp the pest, but Poseidon has to hold him back.

They turn back to continue their walk, but the gangster pops up beside Ariel with a hand out. "The name's Judas, nice to meet'cha. The only stealing I do is stealing hearts, Love."

Ariel stares at his hand. "I'm with someone."

Judas leans in close and the overpowering stench of his cologne makes him dizzy. "Do you think I care?"

Poseidon muscles his way between them, puffing his chest out. He easily has half a foot on Judas, Ariel a few inches more. Are all mouthy men short? "Unless you have any business with us, I'd suggest you leave—before things get ugly."

Judas flicks out a shiny gold business card that has his name engraved on it in ugly cursive. He forces out a nervous chuckle. "I offer my business, actually, and it won't cost you a thing. Like I said, I'm a good guy. I'm not like the other low lives mugging people." He lowers his voice to a whisper. "I can show you where the hotel is. That's where you're headed, right? I have pretty killer intuition, if I do say so myself."

Ariel moves further behind Poseidon. "You talk too much."

Judas runs a hand through his coiffed hair. "You have a rather sour mouth on yourself, too. But I love when they talk back."

Poseidon snatches the business card. His neck is taut, breathing heavily through his nose. "You show us the hotel and that's it, understand?"

Judas splays his hands and backs up a bit. "I'm not looking for a fight, pops. I just want to help a pretty doll in need."

"Fine, you can help—but that's all you do. You lay one finger on him and I swear—"

"I'm not gonna touch him." He places his hand on his heart. "Scout's honor."

The trio amble along the streets, and while Judas leads the way, Poseidon stands between them to keep a vigilant eye on their so-called help. After ten minutes, Judas spouting bullshit the entire time, they reach the steps of the Grand Hotel. Unlike the rest of the buildings, it glitters with light. Finely dressed men and women funnel in and out of the revolving doors, some loitering outside to smoke, most having some combination of white and gold on.

The trio step inside the lobby and it stinks of glitz and glamor and rich people. The floor is waxed to a reflective finish. They approach the front desk, wide and made of mahogany.

Ariel rings the bell while Judas leans against the counter with an elbow. "You can leave now—what was your name?" He grins at him. "Judas."

"Right." He gives a nod to the revolving door. "Scram."

Judas puts on that predatory grin again. "I know the people here, I can get you a good discount."

Poseidon groans.   The gold-suited receptionist appears

103

with the smell of a cigar following him. His claws click against the wood. "How may I help you?" he asks in a monotone voice.

His yellow eyes are flat, looking as much of a rat bastard as Judas, but with even more jewelry on his person. Ropes of gold decorate his neck, with a diamond-studded crucifix pinned to his jacket. His face is clean-shaven, save for an ugly goatee. "Getting a room, I assume? How interesting."

"Yes—" Poseidon starts.

"Make it a suite, Mammon." Judas snaps his fingers in the demon's face. "These people are in a hurry."

Mammon slowly slides a dirty look over to Judas, while he reaches for the key. He shoves it into Ariel's hand. "Your suite key, sir. By the way, the front desk is open twenty-four hours a day. I practically live here." After a pause, he continues. "That was meant as a joke. I would introduce myself, but this idiot ruined my speech."

Poseidon lingers while the other two head toward the elevator, leaning over the desk. "I didn't realize this was a demon-owned establishment. Whatever happened to Barachiel?"

"New management," he says, idly sniffling. "I'm sure you'll find everything to your liking. How long are you staying for?"

Concern makes Poseidon's brow furrow. "I'm not quite sure. What does it matter?"

Mammon steeples his fingers. "We implore our guests to stay as long as they like. We like to think of our humble hotel as a family. Family never separates, does it?"

"I truly can't relate," Poseidon says.

"Can we just go up to the room?" Ariel asks, stretching rather dramatically. "My feet are *killing* me."

The two men say in unison, "I can carry you if you like."

Poseidon shifts so the slime ball can't see Ariel, but Judas cranes his head around him anyway. "I can show him up to the room–promise I won't even hold his hand."

He gives in, clearly wishing to do nothing more than squash Judas, but he releases them from his fatherly gaze. They take a glass elevator to the top floor where burgundy carpets and gold-streaked marble greet them. The suite takes up the entire floor, a no smoking sign resting outside on a plaque. Judas ignores it and lights a cigarette.

"Seriously?"

He gestures with the cigarette tucked between his first two fingers. "I'm itching for a smoke, Love. Can you blame me?"

The room they enter is luxurious, with furnishings of dark wood and silk. A chandelier dangles in both halves of the room; the first half is more of a living room area. Bookshelves and a grandfather clock sit against the far wall to their left, while the wall across from them is made entirely of glass that lets in the morning light. Ariel settles on the lengthy black couch in the first half, resting his feet on the coffee table.

Judas smokes by the cracked open balcony door. "So what'd you come to the city for?" He blows smoke out into the cold air. "Planning to fuck that old man and take all his money?"

"I'm looking for someone, actually."

"Oh? Who?"

"I'm not about to tell a criminal my business." Judas slithers to the couch, getting closer as he talks. "It's a real shame, I'm really a nice guy you see. You really shouldn't judge a book by its cover. I can be real nice if you'd let me."

His hand slides over Ariel's, but after he closes his eyes, with a split second and one punch later, Judas clutches his gushing nose. He retreats to the other side of the couch. "Fuck!"

Ariel shakes the soreness from his hand. "Don't touch me."

Even with blood dripping down his face, the ugly bastard grins. "You really know how to hit a guy, huh?"

"Let's say my boyfriend taught me."

"Aw, so you got yourself a man back home?" Judas slides back over for more.

"You could say that."

With his sour tone, Judas takes the chance to press the issue. "Trouble in paradise, Love?"

He grits his teeth. "That's none of your business, is it?"

"So I'm taking old guy isn't your man?" Ariel stares. "Alright then," he swallows. Judas adjusts his tie, and glances out the window. The clock steadily ticks away. "It's funny."

"Hm?"

"I'm looking for someone too. But I haven't seen them yet."

He pretends to space out, but the loser looks to him as if expecting him to have questions of his own. "...What do they look like?"

"They're a real babe, kinda like you. I'll know when I see them, though. So it's a good thing we bumped into each other, eh?"

He nudges Ariel with his elbow, and he goes to raise his

hand. "Don't make me hit you again."

Judas grins into his face. "Maybe I like being slapped around a bit."

He makes the effort to not look at him. "Are you going to leave yet?"

"What say we help each other out? Make a little deal?"

"I'm not stupid, Judas," Ariel snaps. "I don't know what you're talking about."

He puffs away at his cig. "I help you find your man, you help me find the girl I'm trying to find." Ariel slinks away into the bedroom to dig through the mini fridge beside the threshold. He pulls out a bottle of water and stares at Judas as he drinks. "Could you get me some?"

He nudges it closed with his foot. "No."

Judas sucks in air between his teeth. "*Cold*. You treat your boyfriend like that, Love?"

"He knows better than to mess with me." Ariel does everything but look into his eyes as he leans against the wall. "So, I was told this place is rife with demons. Is that true?"

"You could say that," Judas says, voice caught in his throat.

"I was just wondering, since I have a thing for them." He tilts his head and stares him down, taking a long moment to unscrew the bottle and take a sip. After wetting his lips, he goes on. "You wouldn't happen to know where to find any, would you?"

He snubs his cigarette out on the armrest, speaking through gritted teeth. "What's it to you? I thought you divine types hated them. They're worth less than the dirt under your feet, am I right?"

Ariel laughs into his hand and bends over the couch. "What? You talk as if you know what it's like to be one," he says, tone softening. "I mean, are you though? I won't tell. I'm only asking because you look the type with that cheap suit and ugly mug of yours. Only demons wear those, right?"

"Don't fucking toy with me!" Judas grabs him by the sleeve, but Ariel catches him off guard with a hand caressing his jaw. He means to transfix him with a single look, Judas' eyes reflecting in his like a mirror. Gone is the spoiled brat, a snake shedding its skin.

Honey rolls off Ariel's tongue, fully expecting him to give in. "Do you want to hurt me?"

"Why are you touching me? All of a sudden you want to feel me up now?" He leans into his palm.

"..Huh?" Judas' eyes remain a bright gray. He shoots a knowing grin at Ariel. "You tryna' do something here? If so, it ain't working."

His face contorts as his touch turns hard. "Why aren't you charmed?"

"I think you've lost your touch." He nudges his hand away with a finger. "What're you, a siren?"

Ariel almost yells at him, but chooses to sit as far away as he can get and brood. Judas crosses his ankles, the smug tone trickling out of him. "Don't pout because your little tricks don't work on me, Love. If you'd like, we can make up later after the geezer falls asleep."

Ariel spits out a "fuck you."

"That's the whole point, duh."

"You can leave. The door's right there." A heavy knock resounds through the room, but Ariel is too annoyed to answer the door. "*It's open!*"

Poseidon steps in, glancing between them like a concerned chaperone. He hangs his suit jacket on a hook by the door and takes a seat between them, legs spread. "So what have you two been up to?"

"Nothing," he says, sneering. "Can you kick this loser out now?"

"Something happen while I was gone?" He directs his glower at Judas while Ariel takes his turn to gloat.

"I didn't do anything, for fuck's sake!" He tosses a hand out to Ariel. "He's only mad cause he couldn't hook his claws into me."

"You're just overreacting," Poseidon says, as he adjusts his glasses. He tugs the gangster from his place on the couch.

Judas is incredulous, face bright red, tossing a hand to Ariel. "Why the *fuck* are you defending him? He punched me!"

"For all I know, you probably deserved it." He nods to the door. "I think it's about time you leave, or do you prefer being carried out like a stray puppy?"

Judas takes his time in sauntering to the door, muttering under his breath. But he makes a point to hold Ariel's gaze. If he didn't want to hurt him, he's sure he does now. Ariel gives him a curt wave goodbye. No matter what, he always has to have the last word. The bastard slams the door shut behind him, and he listens intently to the sound of his footsteps descending the hall.

"Run me a bath, would you?" Ariel asks, unbuttoning his shirt.

Poseidon nearly trips over himself after jumping from the couch and rushing into the bathroom. "Ah, of course!"

He spreads out along the cushions, tugging his hair from

its tie and letting it lay in a mess. The faucet squeaks on and Poseidon returns. "Is there anything else I can do?"

Ariel considers it with a thumb pressed against his lower lip, glancing to him through half-lidded eyes. "Yes, actually," he whispers. "We can take another bath together."

"Ah, already?"

"Do you have a problem with it?" he asks.

"No, no..." Ariel notices when the flush in his cheeks grow brighter, the more the old man stumbles over his words. Poseidon's eyes follow his hand as he caresses his own chest. "We already took a bath, it seems–" Ariel motions him closer with a finger. "...Yes?"

"Strip out of that suit. *Right now.*" Ariel's slips some desperation into his voice to hurry the scene along. "Don't you want to really feel me tonight? I can give you what you want."

"I.." He lets a hand slide over his stomach, and into his slacks to tease Poseidon, even going as far as forcing out soft little gasps. He leans over the couch to hoist Ariel in his arms, but doesn't speak as he carries him to the bath.

Chapter Ten

The Fool

IT is funny to think that something as simple as a man in his life could clear up his cloudy skies. They have spent the last few days together in the room, Ariel doing little else outside drinking wine from the mini fridge, napping, or lounging in the bath. Poseidon doesn't even mind taking little trips into the city to find what he so politely asks for. Perhaps he is jumping the gun, but with a beautiful man such as Ariel by his side, he has a purpose. He is sure he will be able to make up for past mistakes.

Age has given him many things to regret, and ever since his self-imposed exile, he has had nothing but time to think things over. He has grown blind to the rest of the world in the comfort of his bubble. The rest of the pantheon may call him selfish and rash for leaving the Garden, but he needs nothing more than to be out on open water. Poseidon is a man who craves excitement and the thrill of danger. He has needs as any other person does.

Watching his spoiled Pearl from afar, his old heart swells, as he has never cared about anyone other than himself until now. He gets lost in those eyes of his, as deep as the ocean itself, and with many shadows lurking beneath the surface. But he overlooks them, as no one is perfect, especially not him. This can be his chance at redemption, all to prove he's a better man than others believe.

"What would you like to do today?" he asks.

Ariel lays in the fancy tub built into the wall of their bathroom. A glass of wine rests in his hand, hair falling delicately around his shoulders. He has been distant ever since Judas left a few days ago, but Poseidon is used to the silent treatment. He sits on the edge of their bed, shirt undone, hands in his lap. He tenses at the thought of using that word. Theirs. It is such a foreign concept, sharing something with someone.

"Well, what is there to do in this dull city?" Ariel flicks a look at him, and even annoyed he's gorgeous.

"We can see the sights?"

"What sights are there to be had? This hardly seems like a tourist friendly place." He steps out of the tub and wraps a towel around his waist. "Why don't we visit one of the clubs? I think it's high time you unwind, old man."

Poseidon shakes his head. "Oh, that isn't quite my scene. I'm more than happy here where it's quiet."

"You really are old, aren't you? Maybe I'll call up that loser from earlier." Ariel leans against the sink to brush his hair out.

He bristles at the thought of letting that that scum take Ariel out in his stead. He would rather die than let that happen. Poseidon puts his glasses on and fetches a clean dress shirt. "That's not happening," he mutters. "Aren't you afraid of what'd he try? What if I'm not there to stop him?"

Ariel slams his hands down on the counter, staring into the mirror. "You don't have to worry, I can take care of myself. I'm not a child!"

"What are you going to do? Punch him?"

"I would, but I'm afraid he'd like it too much." Poseidon sits back down to fix the rest of his clothes. Ariel steps into his peripheral, assuming he is impatient at how long it is taking to get ready. "I'll be just a moment—" he glances up,and the towel drops. "Are you alright?"

Ariel places his hands on Poseidon's shoulders and crawls into his lap, skin still damp from his bath. Poseidon is at a loss for words as Ariel slips his glasses off. He leans in closely, much too close for him to keep his usual cool attitude. His hands are limp at his sides, but Ariel places them on his hips.

"We're going out tonight, do you hear me?" Between his silky words and skin, Poseidon gets lost as his hands wander over Ariel's curves. He squirms in his grip if to spur him on further, even going as far as to bite his lip. The little tease. "Pretty please? I'll make it up to you if you do this little thing for me."

Ariel leans him back onto the bed, taking an eternity to undo his shirt button by button. "I thought we were going out?"

"We will. Haven't you ever heard of slowing things down? We can get to know each other a bit better." His lips are so close yet so far away. They have yet to even kiss and here he is, grinding on his lap, heart ready to burst through his chest. Ariel's nimble fingers outline each of his scars. Poseidon grinds back into him, but his clothes too restrictive for what he wishes to feel.

"Please let me," he begs.

"Let you what? Use your words, old man. I thought you had all this experience to show off?" Poseidon isn't sure which hurts more, his uncaring tone, or the nails that scrape against his skin. "What happened to all that big talk before?"

"It's not that simple."

"So you're just a coward?" Ariel asks. "I thought you wanted me."

"I want to do things on my terms, not yours."

"You don't *get* a say." Ariel sneers and gives up on the flirting. "You're going to listen to me or else."

"Or else what?"

His smile is tender and warm, but a cold wind passes over Poseidon. "I have connections. It'd be a shame if someone were to find out where you were."

"You wouldn't dare," he gulps. Before Ariel he is but a frightened old man.

"Try me."

Poseidon shoves him off, if only to keep distance between them. He can't form coherent thoughts when he touches him, all semblance of self-control slipping away once he lays those eyes on him. "I'm not afraid of your empty threats!"

No smile comes to break the choppy current. He's serious this time. "I don't bluff."

"And I'm Zeus himself!"

Ariel changes subject to the gangster from before, slithering back into the bathroom to tie his wet hair up in the mirror. It seems that he has grown bored of arguing, or perhaps he knows Poseidon is right. "You wouldn't happen to have that card still, would you?"

"Don't tell me you're thinking of actually going out with him?" Poseidon asks.

Ariel pulls into fresh clothes; sheer white formal wear that hugs his frame, along with a black collar. He leaves the first few buttons undone, letting most of his bare chest show. He slips into the next room without answering. "So do you have it or not?"

"You don't even know him!" he calls from his place on the bed.

"It's better than staying in this cramped room with a god that's lost his spark." When he enters after him, Ariel shoves a hand into his face. He clutches the phone receiver on the wall to his ear. "Give it."

Poseidon's shirt droops from one shoulder, but he leans into his touch rather than shrink away. Try as he might, the power he had fails to leave him. "You know that trick doesn't work, right? I don't have to listen to you."

"I don't care. Give me the card."

"I refuse," he says. "I can't have you running around the city all by yourself."

He drops the phone and lets it dangle. "Fine, I'll find him myself. I don't need you anyway." Ariel means to move to the door, but Poseidon blocks his path.

"Without my help, you wouldn't of even made it here. There's still the means of my payment. You're staying here."

He looks down at Poseidon like he's a piece of trash he found on the street. "Are you ordering me around?"

His bravado falters. "...Yes?"

"Then why don't you *make* me stay?" Ariel wraps his hands around his own neck. "I want you to make it hurt. Throw me on the bed, tear my clothes off, convince me that I should stay with you."

"I don't want to hurt you," Poseidon says, taking a step back.

There is a heat that runs through Ariel, a dark shade of red Poseidon can't quite put his finger on. The manic look he gives chills him to the bone. Every time, just when he thinks he has the upper hand, he spits in his face and laughs. Ariel comes onto him, unbuttoning his shirt to reveal the shimmery rainbow fabric that lines it.

A kaleidoscope passes over Poseidon's eye and a multi-colored light fogs his vision; shades that tint his world a rosy pinks. It should be romantic, but all he can feel is dread. Every color is much too bright for him to look at, shielding his eyes as if he were squinting into the sun. Ariel's pastel hair glows like he is some deep-sea predator attracting prey.

"If you won't," he says, "I'll find someone else who will. Don't you want to keep me? Make me yours?"

The longer Poseidon stares at him, the more he loses his train of thought. He can only dumbly agree at this point, Ariel's words the one thing he can focus on. "Of course! I want nothing more than that!"

"Then do as I say." He places Poseidon's around his neck and presses close to him. Ariel holds his gaze and he swears his eyes shift in color, from pale green, to   pink, then lavender, and back to green. "Just think of how pretty I'll be with all those marks, marks that you'll put on me. Isn't it romantic to think about?"

He tries to take his hands away, but Ariel holds them in place. "That's not what love is."

"Love is sometimes cruel," he says. "So come treat me

harshly." He tugs the rest of Poseidon's shirt off while he whispers the sweetest siren song into his ear. "Paint me with those pretty colors. Eat me."

How can he possibly say no to that? He sweats and his throat dries up. "I'm not sure that's wise, I haven't indulged in such things in ages. I'd be a bit rusty."

Ariel cups his face in his hands and his sweet smile is so unlike his words. "It doesn't matter. Hurry up before I change my mind."

"Right, right..." Poseidon lifts him, arms wrapping around his lower half as the siren shoves his face into his neck, allowing free reign over him. The rose-scent of his skin makes his head spin as he presses him against the nearby wall. He is like a starving wolf as he marks up Ariel's neck, teeth digging into skin so delicate he's afraid he might actually break it.

However, the little noises he manages to coax out makes it all worth it, purple and pink that bloom below his jawline. He huffs fire at the sight before him, at the bruises he causes. Could that little shit Judas do this? He wouldn't even know where to start.

"Don't stop," Ariel breathes.

He lays his prize on the bed and Ariel stretches out

across it. His damp curls glimmer across the dark sheets, and with just a single lust-glazed look, Poseidon does his best to give him what he wants. Leaning back to survey his work, flower petals trail down Ariel's neck and chest. The object of his obsession gazes at him like a content cat.

He pants, "forgive me... I don't quite have the stamina I used to. I might have to take a break."

"I thought I told you to ruin me?" Ariel asks. "You still have a job to finish, old man," he grinds into him, "unless you really want me to let that ugly man to do it for you?"

Poseidon practically froths at the mouth. "As if I'd let him even touch you!"

"Then devour me." He's so soft with eyes half-lidded, and fingers gripping at the sheets. That hunger remains even as he struggles to breathe.

"Have I not done enough to satisfy?"

"We're not done just yet." Poseidon gingerly rubs at the bruises with a frown. What is it about Ariel that brings this ugly side out of him? Those eyes force his thoughts to darken and fester. All he can ponder are ways to bring more cute noises from behind those supple lips. But, of course, there is a limit to even his lust. "I said I wasn't going to hurt you."

He almost growls, "I didn't say you could stop!"

122

Poseidon pulls away a sweaty mess, goosebumps rising at the daggers that fire his way. He puts on a firm look to hide the fear that creeps in. "I don't care, you little siren. You might be alluring, but I draw the line at real pain."

Ariel bares his teeth. "Coward."

"Sorry I'm not like the reckless minnows you're used to swimming around with."

He curls up on his side, turning away from Poseidon to hug himself. The gentle patter of rain rolls in as the view darkens with Ariel's mood.

"I hate you."

"Go ahead and hate me." He damps at his sweat with a fresh towel. "You'll get over it soon enough and we'll be back where we started."

Poseidon teeters on the tightrope between comforting him and retaining his distance. The bruises aren't the same romantic brushstrokes he pictured, his stomach drops at the sight of such delicate skin full of his teeth marks. A younger version of himself would have happily done such a thing without a second thought, and though he likes to think that he has grown from such disgusting pursuits, the fact of the matter is that he nearly assaulted him just days prior. They are still naught but strangers, but a line runs between them.

"Why are you still here?" Ariel asks. "Other than the obvious."

It is true, he doesn't have to stay. He could have easily shut his mind off and gave him what he asked for, but he didn't. There is a feeling gestating within him that Poseidon can't explain, for it is too soon to give such a thing a voice. "I'm not quite sure myself." Ariel keeps his focus outside the window. He won't warm back up unless he gives him what he wants, as much as he hates to do so. "Shall we go out, then?"

"I thought you said partying wasn't to your tastes?" Ariel asks.

"I know what I said. I'm only going to keep an eye on you. I hate stuffy parties, I prefer–"

"–A more personal atmosphere, right?"

"...You could say that."

They take their time in redressing, Ariel whining incessantly about that idiot gangster the entire time. Judas answers the phone with a smooth line which crumples the instant he notices it is not who he is hoping for. "What do you want, geezer? I have more important things to do than waste my time with you, like that little babe of yours–"

Poseidon cuts him off. "To show us around. I'm sure a miscreant like you knows of some clubs?"

"Know them? I practically live there!" He pauses. "I'll be waiting in the lobby."

They arrive downstairs, Poseidon keeping a protective arm around Ariel's waist. Judas waves them over, the bright red sequins on his suit nearly blinding him. His entire outfit is covered in them, down to the fake devil horns on his head.

He tuts at their outfits. "That's no way to arrive to a club! How are we meant to let you out in public looking like... that?" He jabs a mini pitchfork at Poseidon.

"What in the Heavens do you mean? I look just fine!"

Judas slips the tie from around Poseidon's neck and undoes a few buttons. "You have to look like you belong there, pops. Don't want someone jumping you cause they think you're loaded." He turns to Ariel. "You look perfect though, Love. Wouldn't change a thing."

Judas leads them again through the city, away from the glittering splendor of the Grand Hotel, down dark streets and alleyways, closer to the sound of pulsing music. A red sign glows against the black backdrop of the buildings surrounding it, The Black Mamba.

"We're here," Judas says.

Men and women clad in black suits form a line behind the velvet rope. Smoke drifts above their heads in thick clouds and their eyes glow in the dark. They openly eye Ariel as Judas cuts the entire line.

"Where do you think you're goin'?" the bouncer asks., flipping through his clipboard. "I don't see your name."

Judas taps his pitchfork at the paper. "The proprietress of the club is expecting me."

"And who are your friends?"

"Oh, I'm with the pretty face. The old man was only here for the ride."

"Excuse me!?" Poseidon's thick fingers wrap around Judas' neck from behind. "Don't make me throttle you, boy!"

He taps his hand to signal him to stop. "I wouldn't do that if I were you."

Every single demon in line stares him down and Poseidon eases off the bastard. "I'm accompanying Ariel." He tugs on his sleeve. "C'mon, we don't need this loser to show us around, we can find someplace else."

"I *like* this place," Ariel says. "You don't want to make me unhappy again, right?"

He sighs. His heart folds at his beautiful face, and he can't say no. "Of course not..."

Ariel runs a hand along the shape of Poseidon's wide shoulder and grins. "We can finally have some real fun.

C'mon, what're you, scared?"

"Me, scared?" he says with a chortle. "Nothing scares the King of the Sea!"

Ariel moves in close to whisper against his skin. There is an endless depth to his eyes that Poseidon loses himself in. "Then what's the hold up? I want to let loose."

"Can you two hurry up?" Judas asks as he unclips the rope.

With more complaining, Poseidon enters the so-called establishment. The walls and decor are red velvet, the floor pitch black. Red lighting drenches the crowd. Pulsing, synth heavy music fills the space. Mortals and demons alike mingle together at the bar, in the booths to either side, or the dance floor. A good portion of the club goers openly snort cocaine and pop little black pills.

"This is deplorable," Poseidon says with a sneer.

He jabs at him with the pitchfork again. "As if you're any better than them. What's it to you how people choose to let off a bit of steam?" Judas steals them a booth off to the side and orders a round of drinks. Ariel sits between them. Poseidon can pick out the glittering eyes that throw glances at the trio. It seems this is business as usual for the gangster.

"Should we really be here?" Poseidon asks.

"Don't worry, this is neutral ground. Fights are only allowed outside. The blood would ruin the upholstery." He folds his hands in his lap. "We're just waiting for the Lady of the House to finish getting ready."

"She your friend or something?"

"She wouldn't call me that, but sure. Let's go with that."

They nurse their drinks for a good while until the heavy curtains pull to each side of a small stage. A single spotlight illuminates a woman in a tight cobalt blue dress with layers of fringe that act as a hem that reach just over her knees. The Black rhinestones that cover her bodice and her umber skin gleam in the bright light. Her hair is tucked away under a blue cloche cap. A man offstage lights the cigarette holder in her hand for her.

"She's beautiful," Poseidon says. Almost too beautiful in his opinion.

Judas gives a smirk. "Just wait til' you hear her sing."

A somber piano plays a slow tune accompanied by a low saxophone. Her commanding stare quiets the crowd. They're at her full attention. Her voice stretches out like the branches of a poplar tree, breathy and low. The Lady sings the blues with such feeling that even Poseidon finds himself tearing up. She puffs away at her cigarette, letting the tendrils of smoke curl around her face, and takes a long look around as the saxophone blares behind her. She sends a chill through the audience. As she exits front stage, the crowd gives her a wide berth.

She approaches Poseidon's little trio and her serene smile is but a smokescreen. Upon closer inspection, he knows that face, one he hoped he would never see again.

She speaks with a mouth full of smoke. "What a surprise to see you of all people loitering in my club. Who's your little whore for the night?"

He loses his voice somewhere in his throat. It seems to be a common thread since coming out of hiding. Perhaps he lost his nerve somewhere down the line. He would never let anyone speak to him like that when he was in Eden.

All he can do is choke out her name, "Medusa."

"So you haven't gone senile yet?" Her eyes glow a toxic yellow. "Tell me why you're in my city, pervert. You'd best choose your answer carefully."

A sea of lights stare at him. The music cuts. Ariel scoots out of the booth and barely gives Poseidon a second glance. Medusa and Ariel stare at each other.

"Oh, of all people, it's you," she says. "Why am I surprised? A pervert and a harlot."

"I don't know what you're talking about," Ariel says. "I'm no one."

She blows smoke in Poseidon's face. "I'd suggest you leave if you want to avoid getting blood on those pretty clothes of yours. Unless you're with him?"

He spares a glance to the old man. His eyes are empty as a doll's. "Who?"

Medusa chuckles. "You might be nothing more than a fallen woman, but I always did like you."

"Man for the time being," he corrects. "Unfortunately, I never came to enjoy the scent of violets like you do."

"A true shame. We would've been great together."

Ariel slips into the crowd toward the bar. With a snap of her fingers, the situation dissolves and the throbbing music picks back up. Medusa perches on the table with her back to Poseidon. There's no one left in his corner. Judas must have slipped away during the commotion for who knows what. Slipping off her hat, a dozen snakes uncurl as she shoots a look over her shoulder, mint green blooming over her skin. Within the smoke cloud around her head, thirteen pairs of snake eyes paralyze him in place.

Chapter Eleven

The Soldier

Ariel steals a seat among the rush of suited men sitting alongside him. More smoke clouds his vision, wrapping him in an intense heat that surges in the air and makes his clothes stick to his skin. There is only one thing on his mind —to find a suitable toy for the night. Poseidon has grown old and tired rather quickly, for he lacks the sharp edge Ariel longs to feel on his skin. He wants nothing more than a man to tear him apart. There is little difference between pain and pleasure in his book. Maybe if he wishes with all his heart, he will find the love of his life tonight in this very club.

Among the black and grey, a red blur stands out at the

very edge of the bar. He can't make out the face, but the bartender leans in to hear the man's order. After a few moments, he brings over a second drink to Ariel with a napkin wedged under it.

"I didn't order this."

He nods back to where he came from. "It's from the gentleman down the way."

The red suit is gone when he looks over, so he glances down to the napkin. A rose is messily doodled ink. A heavy hand lays itself on his shoulder and a beard tickles his neck. The rings on his fingers tell him exactly who it is.

"I thought I told you I'd be in and out," Ares says.

"I don't know what you're talking about, sir? You've got the wrong person—"

"Don't give me that." Ariel spares a look at his partner's face and his grip softens. "Why did you follow me? This isn't where you belong."

He avoids his accusatory gaze. "Maybe I wanted to visit? What's it to you? When did you become my keeper?"

Ares takes a quick look around, and tugs him off to the side, down a dark hall and out the back. The music fades to a dull murmur and the rain drips down the sides of the awning. A red exit sign paints their skin pink. "Tell me, why are you

132

here?"

Ares asks, hands tight at his sides. "Do you not realize how dangerous it is?"

"I've been fine so far." Ariel leans back beside the door, a hand on his hip. "If you want me to go back, I doubt I even could."

Ares stares out at the depressing grey, and his words come off as amusement trying to school itself into disappointment. "Typical of you to leave without permission."

"How did you realize it was me anyway?"

He manages to get a grin out of him. "There's no one who knows you as well as I do. Or did you forget that?" He lets the moment pass. "Beside the fact that I miss you, you still haven't answered me."

Ares squeezes his hand and his gaze burns a hole into Ariel's skin. There is only rainfall as the seconds pass. He hopes he drops it, but he knows better than that.

In a mousey voice, he says, "I have to find him."

"Don't even start with that!" Ares takes a few steps back and bites down on his lower lip. The anger he holds on a tight leash oozes through the cracks. "Why are you so obsessed with that demon? He's probably dead for all we know! Why can't you just let it go?"

"I know he's here. I just know it."

Ares' face grows dark, restlessness dancing under his skin. He can do little but fidget as he glances at the doors they came through. "Why are you here with my Uncle?"

"Sorry?"

"Don't play dumb with me. You know what feelings I have for him – that my *Mother* has for him."

Ariel moves into his orbit so they stand on equal footing. "What are you going to do, then?"

He goes for the door handle, shoulders and jaw tense as he grabs it. "I'll just be a moment. In and out. Then we can pretend this never happened."

He moves into Ares' path. "You can't just kill him! He still has to help me find As-"

"Don't fucking say his name," he whispers. When Ares looks into his face, his eyes are wet. "Do you not realize how stressful it is? To be the perfect son, the perfect lover, the perfect soldier? I don't think you even have a fucking idea. Everything I've done, everything I do is for you and yet it's never enough, is it? You just take and take and take–"

The God of War collapses and clings to Ariel like he's the only thing he knows. Ares presses his face into his shoulder as he wipes at his eyes. "Why am I not enough for you? I'm going to go back in there and wrench that disgraceful fucker's head from his shoulders. Maybe then I'll be good enough."

"Don't do something you'll regret." Ariel holds his face in his hands as if he were glass, able to make out the spider web of cracks. "Look at me." Ares' eyes flick between the door and him. "Look at me," he insists,   pressing a soft kiss to his lips. "I'm right here, okay? Everything's okay. I'm sorry for leaving."

Ares presses their foreheads together. "I love you. Tell me, you didn't...?"

"With him?" He shakes his head. "No, of course not. I'm forever yours, remember?"

"Of course, silly me." His touch turns tender as his hands slide down around his waist. They bask in the moment of finally being in each other's arms, Ariel taking his time in rubbing at the leftover trails of tears. "So, what will you do? Leave me in pursuit of that despicable man?"

"I love both of you. But what's it to you? I bet I've barely crossed your mind these days."

"You don't cross my mind, my Dear," he says. "You live in it. But I'd rather lose a hand than reach for you while you're like this."

He can only find it in himself to grimace rather than

make a full-blown scene. "Then why show yourself, if you're just going to leave?"

"I wanted to step in before you get too ahead of yourself. You don't realize who you're getting involved with. But you don't care who you hurt as long as you get what you want, right?" He steps back, caution in the way he views him. "What am I to you anymore?"

The embers spark back up. It seems that no matter what he says, the fire will only grow. With no way to defend himself, he knows he is a selfish creature moved only by desire. Ares is the only one to ever hold him to his actions.

"Are you angry with me?" Ariel asks.

He takes a few steps around the perimeter of the awning, careful not to let his suit get wet. His rings shine as his fingers fidget with one another, and it is clear that his decision is a difficult one. "I can't stay silent forever. I'm not blinded enough by love to let you walk all over me like you do everyone else. I'm not your sword and shield and I'm not going to let you destroy yourself over a demon."

Ariel looks away. "I'm sorry, but I have to do this. You don't understand, he loves me."

"Obsession and love are two different things, a thing you clearly don't understand." Ares takes him by the hand, unable to truly be rough no matter how disappointed he is in him. "Why don't we get you home? You don't belong here."

"I can't leave yet! I have to make sure he's okay!" Ariel struggles, but without his usual strength, it's a futile gesture. "Let go!"

"I'm not letting you stay with my piece of shit Uncle," Ares states.

The back door opens and Judas stumbles out of the dark. There is a warm flush to his face, and his eyes are unfocused. He has a drink in hand and his suit jacket is missing. It takes him a few moments to get anything out once he sees Ariel.

"Ah, there you are. I was wondering where you headed off to." He glances to Ares. "And who the fuck is this? You leaving early or something?"

"We're just talking," Ariel says. "It's a private conversation. Why don't you go back inside and enjoy yourself? This is none of your business."

"Hey! I'm the one who's supposed to be showing this babe around!" He stands half a foot shorter than both divine beings. "So I suggest you step off, buddy."

Ares shoos Judas away with a laugh. "I'm not going to humor you, mortal. He's not yours to have."

He pulls Ariel to his side to better stare the little man

down. He rests his head on Ares' shoulder. Why is it that he attracts the most irritating of men? Small fries that can only talk big.

Judas shoots a look to him. "Wait, what? I thought you liked me?"

"So you think getting punched means I like you?" Ariel fake gags. "As if."

He makes some crude gestures with his hands. "You know, like some friendly flirting? C'mon!"

Ariel turns his head with a sigh. "On second thought, let's get out of here. I'm tired of humoring this loser."

They step out into the rain, Judas staring after them. A bolt of lightning strikes and in an instant they are gone. Warmth pours over Ariel's body as they ping pong back and forth in the cloudy sky. Everything passes by much too fast to process until the scenery blurs together into one blob of paint streaks. Before he knows it, they are in front of the Grand Hotel.

Ares rushes them into the dark lobby. This late at night, it is all but deserted. Loners sit among the couches, smoking under dim lamps. They ascend the stairs hand in hand.

"Aren't you still mad at me?" Ariel asks.

"I am. But it doesn't change the fact I've missed you."

Once they are on the first landing, in the light of the moon, Ares pulls him in for a quick kiss and melts in his arms. Ariel's lover undoes a few of his buttons to feel his bare skin again, but glowers at the purple marks.

"Listen, I know what it looks like…"

"I thought you didn't do anything with him?" His attempts at protest are cut off as Ares tightens his grip on his shirt. He presses a deeper kiss to his open lips. "Tell me the truth."

Ariel leads the way upstairs. "I might've tried to."

"But?"

"He wouldn't listen to me," he pouts.

"Well, unlike him, I'm no coward. He's nothing but a weak-willed man with a fragile ego."

Ariel pauses with a hand on the railing while he tugs his ponytail out. "Do we really have to wait to get to the room then? Why don't we have some fun right here?"

"I can't allow that." He works another grin out of him.

"Oh, so now you're the one who makes up the rules?" Ariel goes ahead of him. "I thought you didn't care what others think?"

"That's you, my Love. I value privacy."

The moment they reach the room and the door closes, they can't restrain themselves any longer. Ares all but tears him out of his clothes, but strips slowly himself. Ariel has no time for waiting, so he pounces on him from his place in bed, dragging him down with a flurry of kisses.

"Why don't you fuck me already?" Ariel squirms underneath him. "I've been waiting so long."

Ares pulls back, a strand of saliva connecting their lips. Ariel curls up on the bed like some elegant prize to be ripped apart and sullied. "Is it so wrong of me to want to take my time?"

He runs a finger over the marks on his neck. Ariel almost regrets allowing Poseidon to even touch him, but in the moment, it seemed so natural to do. He is sure Ares will happily cover them with his own. "I know how impatient you are, my Love, but let me savor this night with you. I'm going to treat you as you deserve."

He takes him into his arms and their limbs entangle. Ares' steady hands leave trails of heat wherever they touch. Their love burns like a distant star, a thing Ariel can faintly see even through closed eyes. His mind runs through rosy thoughts as he presses into Ares, who is acting like he is trying to memorize his body, albeit much too slowly. He goes lower and lower, painting his love over him with his hands and lips. But there is a restraint in his muscles, a certain tension Ariel can sense. Even as Ares finally gives him what he wants, he barely dips his toes into his waters.

"Is something wrong?"

He pulls back from between Ariel's thighs. "I'm sorry... I don't know what's wrong with me tonight. I can't seem to just let go like we usually do. I'm afraid of hurting you."

There are those ever familiar words. Why does every man treat him like he is made of glass? He might not be godlike, but he can still take a beating. Ariel leans over for a kiss. "It's alright. If I get hurt, it's just getting what I asked for, right? You don't have to hold back with me, you should know that."

Ares smiles but keeps his distance, again running a hand over the bruises. "I know, it's just... you're so much softer. I'd hate to ruin you like he has."

"What if I want to be ruined?"

He shakes his head. "That's not the kind of love I hold for you. I've only ever held you in the highest regard. If I were to even think of being cruel to you?" His eyes glaze over with tears. "I wouldn't be able to forgive myself. I'd sooner die than raise my hand to you."

Ares climbs over to rest his head against Ariel's chest and their fingers fit together like puzzle pieces. "Silly me, I should know better. We were destined to be together, it was written in the stars." He holds Ariel's hand to his heart, a steady beating against his skin. "And don't you forget it. As long as this heart beats, no matter what, even now, I'm with you till the end."

That night, a quarter past midnight, their hearts converge into one, their hands fitting together too perfectly. Their heads are full of sweet dreams, golden monuments that attest to the purity of their love. But a thing so bright can only last for so long. Like a dying star singing its swan song, it has yet to realize it has been long dead before the final blow has been dealt. They will go to the guillotine with rosy cheeks, not even feeling the blade strike their necks, or how the hot splash of blood clouds their vision.

For true love can never die.

Chapter Twelve

The Second Chorus

Down in the depths of Medusa's club, in a dark room with metallic gold furniture and walls, Comedy and Tragedy sit together at a mini bar. It sits along the far wall, long leather couches flanking either side of the statues put on display. Bottles of red wine crowd the counter.

"Have you heard the news?" Comedy asks. Their shadows dance on the wall.

Tragedy is deadpan. "What news? Tell me it isn't something stupid again."

Comedy laughs as Tragedy downs her glass of wine. "No, silly! It looks like the vigilant man has finally reunited with his love. Isn't it touching? Have you ever seen something more beautiful than true love?"

Tragedy pours another glass of wine. She swirls it around and watches how the light filters through it. "The only good that can come out of it is a heart-wrenching ending."

Comedy frowns and her voice lilts with rising emotion. "What do you mean? But what about how 'love never dies?' That love transcends death? What happens after the curtains fall and the credits roll? What's left after that?"

Tragedy pours her glass on the floor. The shimmering mess resembles a pool of blood. "Two cold corpses."

Chapter Thirteen

The Rat

Further down a steep flight of stairs, in a lone back room, Poseidon seethes. His hands are bound behind his back by handcuffs that dig into his thick wrists. He stares down the woman he could only describe as his worst nightmare come back from the dead. Medusa perches on the table in front of him, puffing away at her cigarette. Her eyes have grown cold over the years, the naivete hewould grown used to is gone.

"What are you doing here?" she asks. "You still haven't answered my question."

"I don't answer to your kind." She slips off a glove and runs her bare hand over his face. With the slightest twitch, she leaves red scratch marks, but Poseidon refuses to yelp in her presence no matter how it burns. Venom dribbles from the wounds.

"Oh, you will." Medusa takes one of her earrings off and unscrews the top. "Now, open up."

"What? Poison? I'm surprised you'd choose such a non-direct method after what I've done to you. Where's the anger? The lust for revenge?"

Her face remains set in stone. "I'm sure you'd love me to scream out my anguish, but I've let go of all that years ago. I hated how it ate me up until there was nothing left but rage." She swirls the black liquid around. "Poison would be far too easy. What I want is to ruin your life."

Poseidon's smugness slips through with a smirk. She backhands him with her free hand, glowering down on him. His cheek stings and a metallic taste is left in his mouth. "There it is." He shifts in his chair, getting a tad too excited. "C'mon now, show me more! Hit me again! I want to feel your anger!"

"You're disgusting," she says, shaking her hand out.

His glee drops off, though the smirk persists. "Don't make me slip out of these handcuffs. You'll find I'm not as much of a gentleman once I'm pissed off. But you already know that, don't you?"

Medusa's eyes light up and her snakes hiss. She snatches

something off the table he can't quite see. Pressing the edge of a kitchen knife to his face, her yellow eyes are all he can see.

"You aren't the first to threaten me with a knife," he chuckles. "Although my little Pearl is arguably a better looker."

"I'm going to petrify your limbs and smash them one by one. Don't worry, I'll leave enough feeling so I can watch the pain pass over your face." There are tears in her eyes. "You'll beg me to stop like I did to you."

The door unlocks behind her and Judas falls through, needing to press a hand on the wall to keep himself steady. He runs a hand through his messy hair as his eyes float over the room. He speaks in sing-song. "Hey... I got something to tell ya..."

"Are you high again?" she asks. "I thought I told you not to shoot up on the job, Judas." Medusa takes a look back at him. "Why are you alone?"

He waves a heavy hand at her. "It's not my fault! Some guy took him away!"

She brandishes the knife at him. "You mean you let him get away!?"

"You mean he ran away with another man...?" The reality of the situation sets in; he has lost his treasure. "Who stole him?"

Judas groans and holds a hand to his forehead. "Fancy suit, blonde hair, different colored eyes. The babe was all over him, seemed like they knew each other real well."

"My nephew!? He's in the city?" He rocks the chair side to side. "Get me out of these handcuffs! Why is he with Ariel?"

"You think I fuckin' know? What do I look like, a mind reader?"

Medusa stares past Judas at a dark corner of the room and pinches the bridge of her nose. "You were supposed to keep track of him. You had one simple job!"

"It's alright, I'll fix it." He flicks out a switchblade, adjusting his hair with it. "I'll make sure he follows along, even if I have to rough up that pretty face a bit."

"Don't you dare!" Poseidon yells. "I'll kill you myself before you lay a finger on him!"

Judas cocks his head with a malevolent grin. "As if there's anything you or anyone else can do to stop me. You're really in no position to protest."

"You're going to be punished for your impudence, boy." He has had enough of dealing with Medusa's games. With a deep breath and a metallic snap, his hands separate. He lunges for Judas from his seat, but the Snake stops him in his tracks with a glance, freezing him mid-air.

"That pleasure isn't reserved for you," she says.

From behind Judas, a shadow creeps along the wall   in the very corner. It leaps from the wall and wraps around his face. He flails around, choking on muffled screams and tripping over himself. The black tar forces itself down his throat, his nose, his eyes, wherever it can get. He chokes on the goop as well as his own blood. His lower jaw dislocates with a sickly crack and every last inky bit disappears, leaving blood in Judas' eyes.

Bones snap in and out of place until he abruptly sits back up to pop his jaw back in. His cloudy, dead eyes gain a purple glow. He grabs at the corner of the table to stand and adjust his tie. Fresh blood drips from his chin.

"I thought we were saving him for later, Asmo?" Medusa asks. "How're we going to find your lost love now?"

"You should know I don't take lightly to people threatening what's mine." Asmodeus stares down at the blood covering his hands. "Everything's going to be fine, Deuce. We still have one chance left."

She jabs the knife at Poseidon. "You really mean to tell me you're thinking of trusting him to bring that slut—"

"Don't call him that!" Asmodeus pounds a fist into the table. "What other choice do we have? I need to see him again, just once." He grabs at the right side of his face. "At least he won't be put off by this face you picked out."

Medusa circles Poseidon, her heels clicking against the concrete floor. "Listen, patron god of perversion, here's the deal; you're going to bring him back here. Or you can die." She finally lowers her gaze and allows him to move once more. "Will you agree to our terms, or will you tuck your tail between your legs and flee back to that filthy hut like the mutt you are?"

"I suppose I have no choice now, do I?" Best to follow their lead and wait for his chance to defect. He is sure they have their suspicions, that he won't willingly give over Ariel so easily, but he lives to defy expectations. At least until he gets what he wants. He smiles into the ex-priestess' face. "I promise I'll be a good boy."

She smiles back. "You're incapable of being good, swine."

Asmodeus reaches into his jacket pocket and tosses something to Poseidon. He catches the unlit cigar out of the air and rolls it between his fingers. "What's this for?"

"Just something to persuade him with. I'm sure he won't believe I'm here without proof."

He squints at the cigar and looks back to Asmodeus. "You mean the person he's looking for... is you? What business could he possibly have with a demon?"

"The kind of business only kindred hearts can understand," he says, tugging his jacket a bit tighter. "Love."

Poseidon tucks away the cigar into his pocket, mulling over this new information. "I've heard rumors of a certain holy whore spending her time with a demon. Even though I haven't mingled with the pantheon for some years, their gossip reaches even here. I assumed they were just that. But, tell me, is it actually...?"

"It doesn't matter what you've heard from the pantheon." He lays a cold stare onto Poseidon. "What matters is that he's mine, and nobody fucks with him. Do you hear me?"

"You always did love to push the envelope." His smile broadens. "You sound so sure of yourself, yet apparently he's with my other nephew? How peculiar."

"I don't appreciate your lackluster commentary. Until I see him with my own eyes, get out of my sight." Asmodeus props the door open and waves him through. They exchange a parting look before it swings shut, leaving him in the dark.

On the way back to the hotel, Poseidon conjures scheme after scheme in his head. How can he make this work out in his favor? How can he come out on top? His greed knows no bounds. Once he hooks his teeth into someone, he refuses to let go.

He passes by the front desk, a pair of women standing at the front desk in red and yellow, but their conversation stops short once he approaches. The duo look him up and down through the masks they hold, and his skin crawls. It is like they are able to see into his very thoughts.

"Do you need something?" He stops in his tracks, unable to ignore them.

"I hope you realize your actions have consequences," Tragedy says. "You'd best be careful, lest your greed consume you."

He furrows his brow and spits out a reply. "I don't know what you're talking about, but I think you have the wrong man. I've never done anything wrong."

"You tell yourself that every night?" Comedy clicks her fingers against the desk. "You should heed good advice when you hear it. It'd be foolish not to. One day it might come back to haunt you."

His blood boils at their assumptions, as if strangers know anything about him or what he has been through. Before the geyser can erupt, he pulls away and stomps up the stairs. All he has to do is follow these simple instructions and bring Ariel back to the club. At least that is what he was told to do, but he has never been one to follow the rules.

He tries the door but finds it locked. Ariel must've taken the key with when he abandoned him. Outrage at being utterly humiliated burns in his stomach that he can't shrug off as much as he would like to. Some things are unforgivable, and for those that treat him as replaceable, he has no mercy in his heart. Poseidon will make Ariel realize who he's messing with.

"Ariel?" he calls as sweetly as a songbird. "I know you're in there. I must have forgotten the key, I don't have it with me. Could you let me in?"

When he doesn't get an answer, he quickly changes tune. Wrapping his fingers around thin air, he conjures the only thing he has left that is reminiscent of Eden, his golden trident. It is rather worn from misuse, but it'll do the job. Wood splinters as Poseidon plunges it into the door, stabbing a hole big enough to fit his arm through. With his chest already heaving, he slams the door open.

He searches the room, and finds no one but Ariel lying asleep in bed with tousled hair. He lets his guard down and his skin crawls again. Someone's eyes are on him. But from where? It could just be that he is on edge after the night he has had, but after another look, he swears he must be forgetting someone. Was his nephew not with him?

The wind knocks out of him as someone tackles him from behind. Elbowing the attacker off, it is none other than Ares, half-dressed, shirt undone.

"What are *you* doing here?" Ares asks. "Shouldn't you be rotting away in solitude where you belong?"

"I'm here to claim what's mine." Poseidon eyes Ariel with none of the fondness Ares has. He is the last trophy in a collection that he desires, no matter the consequences. Ariel only now stirs from his slumber, bathed in a silk robe as he stretches out, still soft and dreamy. He shouldn't be an issue.

Ares makes the move to wrench the trident from his hands. They fight back and forth, knocking over empty glasses on the coffee table in the other room. But Poseidon has the upper hand, forcing his nephew down to the floor with the pole against his throat. No matter how he struggles, he refuses to let up.

"You made a mistake coming here," he intensely whispers. "Just know that this wasn't only fueled by my envy."

With a crash, Ariel smashes a lamp over his head, and he loses focus. His grip on the trident falters and Ares rams the pole into his face. With a yell, he grabs at his forehead, crawling along the carpet as blood drips. It fogs his vision as he stares at them stand over him. He gropes at Ariel's foot as a final attempt, but his Pearl stomps on his hand. Ariel's eyes blaze with a fire known only from the Goddess of Love herself, confirming what Asmodeus said as true.

He shoves Poseidon onto his back, kneels over him, and curls his fingers around his neck. Any softness that he thought he knew is gone. Ariel leans close enough for Poseidon to see himself reflected in his eyes, and even like this, his beauty is unparalleled.

"Touch him again and I rip your throat out with my teeth," Ariel says. "Do we understand each other?"

"My Love, aren't you going a bit too far?" Nervousness tints Ares' voice. "He's down, you can stop now."

"I accept my death with open arms," Poseidon croaks. "Go ahead and kill me! I'm not afraid of some harlot."

Ariel squeezes, but Ares sweeps him to his feet with his arms wrapped around him. "Stop! He's not worth it!"

He manages to dig the cigar from his pocket and Ariel locks onto it like a bloodhound. "What is that!?" He wrestles out of Ares' arms to steal it, holding it like a piece of gold. "Where did you get this?"

Poseidon props himself up against the wall, slowly getting his breath back. He keeps an eye on where his nephew is, as even without his trident, he is still a force to be reckoned with.

"There's someone who has a vested interest in you." Poseidon sings like a bird once more, dangling the promise of that demon in his face. "We made a little deal, the two of us. Of course, he doesn't intend for me to get anything worthwhile out of it."

"Where is he?" Ariel asks. He is so close to taking the bait, standing a few feet away. Just a little bit closer.

But then Ares tightly grips his shoulder. Can he stop ruining his plans? "I'd advise you not to listen to him. He's nothing but a snake."

Poseidon frowns at his nehpew. "Oh, come now! I have nothing but good intentions. Do you really think I'd hurt him? Don't you trust me? I'm family, after all."

"It's disgraceful to think that you still call yourself my Uncle," Ares says, glowering.

Ariel interrupts them and shrugs off Ares' hand. He takes a few steps closer. "Aren't you going to answer me? Where is he?"

The pistol fires and he seizes his only chance. Poseidon captures Ariel by the arm like a shark clamping down on its prey. He reels him in close and holds him in the perfect position to snap his neck. As he struggles, the snare tightens further. Oh, to feel this beautiful body squirm between his hands, to see the animalistic fear in his eyes. Poseidon would be lying if he said it didn't excite him. The impulse grabs him to lick his neck, if only to aggravate his nephew.

"Let him go!" Ares' eyes burst into flames.

"Ah, ah, ah... one wrong move and he's dead." He caresses Ariel's face, clamping a hand over his mouth. "I'd hate to snuff out such a pretty life before I've had my fun with it."

Sparks fly from Ares' fingers and his face contorts with rage. The trident's metal crumples within his grip. "You think you can do this without consequence? Your name has been on Mother's list for years, Poseidon. I'm sure she'd love to hear of your whereabouts."

"Why don't we go have a little chat with The Bitch of the Heavens herself? I'm sure she'd love to see the great Aphrodite grovel on her knees for mercy." He flashes a smile, one much too confident to be a bluff. Poseidon shifts closer to the door. "You must think very highly of her. But, let me fill you in on something–she's the same as me. She's rotten to the very core."

"Why do you keep lying? My Mother is the beacon of the pantheon, she's our guiding light. She'll have no choice but to see my side." He gives him a once over, and scoffs at his wounds. "It's not like you even have a leg to stand on. You'll finally get what you deserve."

His grin refuses to falter. To think even after all he has seen, his nephew is still so naive. "Care to test that theory?"

"Care to take your filthy hands off him?" Ares retorts.

The moment Poseidon shoves Ariel away, Ares chucks the trident at him. As it flies through the air, it bubbles and evaporates away. To think that he'd try to turn his own weapon against him. But he's not surprised, to say the least. Ares steps towards him and Poseidon, expecting yet another low blow, squares up. His nephew grabs hold of his wrists and a pair of golden shackles, woven from pure light, binds them together.

He stares down at his hands. "Is this really necessary? I haven't even done anything yet."

He's only given a disdainful stare as an answer.

Ares spirits them away to the one place they can contact Hera. The Cathedral is the sole place of light in the dirty city of the Rosebed, the one monument left to show the might of the gods. The perimeter is walled off, the golden gate the only way in. The main tower is made of glittering, multi-colored stained glass that reaches high into the clouds. Crowds of the faithful line the walkways in white and gold, yet Ares pushes through to the front, parting them like the sea. He wedges the door open enough for them to get in.

The inside of the lobby is as one would expect, spacious and grand. The floors glitter like the crystal chandeliers that hang at intervals on the ceiling. Gold-ringed pillars flank the main walkway, leading to two large archways that reveal the rest of the Cathedral. Shining staircases and doorways draw the eye, but there's too many to count. A Muse sits at the front desk just beyond the arches, a golden circlet atop her head. Her perfect hair is pulled back from her sharp face, robes as golden as her crown.

The Muse doesn't bother looking Ares in the face as she slowly flips a page. "Why did the doors open? We're not meant to let visitors in until the trumpets sound." She spares a glance from her book and nearly falls from her chair. "Oh, my stars! Lord Ares, what are you doing here on such short notice!?" She scrambles around the desk, tucking her hair back into place. "Forgive me, but we aren't officially opened yet, not–"

"Until the horns sound, I know." Ares looks down at her like she is only an obstacle. "I'm here on business, Calliope."

"Oh, business? I suppose I can make an exception, then." Calliope swallows, tightening the grip on her guestbook and pen. She grows more frantic at the sight of Poseidon. "But what is he doing here?"

He ignores her question. "I'm here to request an audience with my Mother."

"Well, in that case... I suppose it wouldn't hurt?" She checks them in as fast as her nimble fingers can go and leads them upstairs. She looks back over her shoulder at the first landing. "What's the meaning of your visit today?"

"That's between my Mother and I. I don't discuss sensitive matters with Muses." They climb flight after flight of stairs until they reach the top. Calliope opens a pair of golden double doors to a chamber in similar taste to the lobby. The walls glow as light flows through the stained glass, those present being cast in a hazy fire.

"Hesperia will see you now," she says with a curt bow. Calliope closes the doors behind them.

Gigantic tapestries of the finest silk hang from the walls

in a mimicry of privacy. Hesperia sits at the base of the tree, but doesn't bother turning her veiled head. Pounds of silk robes shroud her, with thin sleeves of white lace peeking out from underneath. A golden glow emanates from around her. The tree's wide branches, full of golden apples, sway from an unknown breeze. She towers over them even while sitting, an aura of serenity about her. She clutches a tall pitcher in her hands, a thick liquid sloshing from within. White swans float in the moat around her hill.

"What is it you need?" she asks, splintered voice coming from everywhere and nowhere at once. Hundreds of different pitches form a beautiful cacophony of echoes.

"I demand an audience with My Mother," Ares says.

Hesperia merely looks over the other two, but pauses on Poseidon. "Ah, the pervert, in chains as he should be. But who else accompanies you?"

Ares blocks Ariel from view. "That's not important. May I see Mother now?"

"You cannot force the sun to set," she says.

But Ariel steps out from behind him. "How long must we wait? That tree doesn't look like it needs that much water, does it?"

Hesperia tilts her head and rises to her full height of

several feet, robes hanging from her frame. She glances down to the man in question with his hands on either hip. "What is it you need, my child? I'm willing to overlook this blatant disrespect. Clearly you two are in desperate need of some kind."

"I demand to speak to Hera this instant!" Ariel smirks up into her face as though he has pulled some fanciful trick. "Aphrodite wishes to speak to her."

"Oh. I thought I recognized that haughty tone from somewhere." Hesperia sways in Ares' direction. "Tell me, why did you try and hide her from me? Why don't you want Hera knowing of her whereabouts?"

"With all due respect, he isn't exactly what he used to be." Ares pulls Ariel back to his place beside him. "I ask you to ignore him. He isn't involved in this."

"So he fell from grace? Is that so?" Hesperia bristles at this. "I think a fellow god defecting would be at the top of the list, don't you?"

She gazes at the orange-purple sky through the glass, and slips the veil from her eyes. Foggy light streams out like a spotlight, spreading through the chambers until it covers everything in its brilliance. The fog morphs and shifts into more discernible shapes; a projection of the Garden of Eden.

Thick, gnarled roots of trees crawl through fertile dirt, grass tall and bright green.

"Hesperia," Hera's commanding voice booms through the air. A throne is the last thing to form, rising from the floor. The Goddess of the High Heavens sits with her sceptre set over her thighs. Around her sit white peacocks, some wandering through Hesperia and the others. "Now, what is it?"

Ares bows before his Mother, while Poseidon and Ariel glower on. An unusual grin crosses Hera's face while she taps her cheek with a finger.

"Your son wishes to speak to you," Hesperia says.

"So, after all these years, you decide to show your face. Everyone always wants to come crawling back." A look of pure disgust crosses her face as Poseidon grins. No old broad scares him. "But you're not the matter I'm interested in. I'll deal with you in time."

"What!?" Ares jumps to his feet. "Mother? What are you saying? He nearly killed us, and you're just going to–"

She raises a hand to silence him. "Rest assured, he will be dealt with. But I didn't expect rosy-cheeked Aphrodite to waltz into my domain." She waves her scepter at Ariel. "Now, you have something to ask for?"

"Yes—" he starts.

"If I were you, I'd be groveling right now." She claps, a deafening sound that fills the chamber. "But that's another matter. Now then, state your case." Ariel kneels but refuses to look Hera in the eye. He spreads his hands out on the marble floor.

"He isn't involved in this, Mother! Please, listen to reason!"

"I ask that you restore my godhood," Ariel says. Ares tries to bring him to his feet, but he shoves him away.

"My Love, get off the floor. You don't have to do this!"

"I'm sick and tired of being useless! I can't do anything anymore!" He returns to his groveling. "Please, restore me to my previous state, Hera. I'll do anything."

Hera scoffs and takes slow steps around the shamed god. Her slow clapping resounds with malevolent intent. "That's what I thought you'd say. Do you truly believe a state like this can be turned on and off like a switch? You were born into a blessing, that might I add, you took for granted. You left to become mortal, to chase after a demon. Why would you want to return here? If you meant to, you surely wouldn't have pitched yourself over the edge of the mountain, would you?

She leans down to tipping Ariel's head to look at her

164

smirking face. "What happened, Aphrodite? You were just like me—powerful, revered, respected. You were certainly an image of perfection. Leaving Eden was a slight against me, and it's much too late to apologize."

"Can you blame me for missing Asmodeus? You expect me to just forget about him?" Fat tears roll down Ariel's cherubic face and his lower lip quivers. He rakes hands through his hair, letting his emotions get the best of him. What a sorry sight, a god reduced to a mortal throwing a tantrum. Oil-like tears roll down Hera's cheeks.

"Your desire twisted your heart and hurt my son! Did you ever wonder for a single second how he felt? Seeing you spend all your time with that creature? He truly thought you would stay true to him, but I know you better. You really meant to walk back into his life like the last year you spent cheating him was just a mistake? Is this what I'm hearing?

"You expect this type of humiliation to be hand waved? To be forgotten? Unlikely. I'm going to make you wish the fall had killed you. You'll know the pain you've caused. This is the least you deserve. This is my mercy laid upon you." Her face hardens with her final decree. "From seafoam whence came Aphrodite and to sea foam she will return."

"Mother...?" Ares trembles at Hera's judgment. His

molten tears hit the floor as he steps close to Ariel. "Please! I beg you to reconsider!"

"Move," she orders.

"I'm not letting you kill him!"

"What do you propose I do, then? I won't allow this slight to go without punishment." Hera spares a glance to Poseidon. This entire time he's been in the back, a bystander to this melodramatic scene. "Poseidon. It must be by the Fates' will that you be here, for suddenly I have the perfect job for you."

"...So you're not going to smite me?" he asks.

"I'm only doing this to humor my son's foolish plea. You will be under my thumb as Aphrodite will be under yours."

"Can you explain that any less vague?" Poseidon raises his shackled hands. "And could you do away with these? They've been cramping my wrists and it hurts like a bitch, which you would know all about, I'm sure."

"I'm going to pretend I didn't hear that," she says. "I want you to tear the rebellion from Aphrodite's very soul. I don't care how you do it, I just want it done." Consider his interest piqued. With a snap of her fingers, his bindings melt off. He massages his wrists. "What of the little brat?"

"My son must be barred from seeing her. I fear for his

sanity, you see. The only thing that'll come out of this continued dalliance is ruin." Ares devolves into a crying mess as he clings to Ariel. The only words that come out are angry sobs that curse his Mother and everything she stands for. Ariel stares Hera down as she leans from her perch. "Do you have something to say, dear Aphrodite? Do you not feel regret at your actions?"

"Regret?" he asks. "I have no need for it."

"Oh?"

Ariel's features contort with something strange, neither the expected rage or sorrow that would ruin his beauty, but a spiteful grin. Even in the face of the Queen of the Heavens, he refuses to back down. "You think you might have won now, but rest assured that I will come back. A man doesn't eat man, but I'm nothing of the sort. I'll hunt you for sport and eat you alive."

Hera cackles at his empty threats and fat tears of joy stream down her face. "I await that day with bated breath, my Dear. But don't worry, you won't be left without companionship." Her smile drops along with her voice. "You'll be needing someone to mend your wounds, after all."

From behind the golden apple tree, Erato steps out from its shade, her hands bound with gold. She keeps her eyes low, most likely out of embarrassment.

"I caught her trying to leave," Hera says. "I can only wonder why she would do such a thing, but I digress. Until we meet again my dear, sweet Aphrodite."

Hera raises her scepter and with a flash of light, the ghostly scene vanishes. A silence falls over the chambers as Hesperia collapses to the ground. Poseidon scoops Ariel into his arms despite how he struggles. The little Pearl gives him a slap across the face. The taste of blood is almost erotic. He twists Ariel's arm sharp enough for him to cry out.

"The woman upstairs gave me free rein over you, so don't think I have any qualms about hurting you anymore." Ares threatens Poseidon again, but he pays him no mind, as a banished prince is nothing to be afraid of. He tosses the cigar to him as a trinket to remember this day by. Heavens know he won't be needing it anymore.

Before Poseidon reaches the exit, Ares yells after him. "I'm going to get you out of here, my Love! I promise!"

Good luck with that one, hero.

Act II

The Cathedral

Chapter Fourteen

The Deal

All alone in the empty suite, Ares stares at the cigar in his hand. The debris from their previous struggle lies on the carpet like some kind of bizarre art piece. He knows he must do the unthinkable; contact that despicable demon. It is the last thing he wants to do, but it's his only shot at getting Ariel back.

Rolling the cigar along his fingers, he lights it with his thumb. He takes a long drag and grimaces at the bitter smoke. As much as he hates it, he has to grin and bear it. Asmodeus is but a phantom hiding in plain sight, the very shadows clinging to his heels. He refuses to speak his name. To do so would admit he is still alive and kicking, but the cigar is definitive proof that the pest survived.

Distant thunder signals another spring storm. He snuffs out the cigar between his fingers and steps out onto the balcony to watch the black clouds roll in. A stream of rain darkens everything it touches. He raises his hand to the sky the moment lightning strikes and becomes electric. Normally he wouldn't waste his time in sightseeing, but today he lingers a moment longer.

He stares down at the city in all its chaotic nature, the seedy back alley deals, the inequality and poverty, and the faithful turning a blind eye to it all. Is this what Hera sees when she looks down from her throne, so high up in the heavens? No wonder she chooses to stay in her Garden. She's unable to face reality, so she chooses to cling to the ruins of her ego and execute those who doubt her. But the world has had enough of her reign.

The patter of rainfall on the pavement, the whistle of the wind—they should be soothing. But Ares can't rest until his other half is beside him. To think of what Poseidon must be doing, the pain he must be inflicting upon him at this very moment, makes his anger glow like the neon red below him. With a heart as heavy as the clouds that carry him, he descends upon Medusa's club once more.

He tucks his hands into his pockets and approaches the front of the line. The bouncer doesn't even manage to utter a single word before Ares cuts him off. "I'm here to see him," he says. "Let me through."

"Him? You'll have to be more specific." The demon

thumbs through the clipboard. "Is his name on the list?"

Ares lowers his sunglasses to stare into his eyes. "You know exactly who I'm talking about. I have business with one of your employers. Now let me through."

"Oh, I don't know about tha–"

A woman stands in smoky silhouette just past the open double doors. Her black, wide-brimmed hat casts a dark shadow over her face, but even in the low light Medusa's eyes gleam like headlights. "Are you bothering one of our guests? Need I remind you that there's a *line?*"

The bouncer gulps and fidgets as she approaches. Her lavender pantsuit's jacket is left open, chest bare. A pink tulle bow hangs from around her neck. Without even looking, she places a manicured finger on the very top of the list, Asmodeus written in overdramatic ink that takes up a quarter of the sheet. Medusa unclips the rope and lets Ares past her. She takes a brief second to grill her employee while he enters.

The atmosphere is sensual and slow with purple lighting and little stars that twinkle on the ceiling. Smoke obscures his view. Medusa steps back in, tapping his shoulder so she can lead him to a private room in the back hall.

She grins at him the whole way. "I'm sure you've been dying to see each other again."

"How'd you know I came here to see... him?"

"Everyone always comes to me when they have problems. It's only natural, my word carries weight in this city." She fishes out a key from her jacket pocket and pushes the door open. "Besides, he's been expecting someone. Not *you* exactly, but he has no room to complain."

The walls and decor of the room they enter match the rest of the club with its shades of violet. Sheets of silk cover any windows that look in on them. A circular table sits in the middle with three chairs set around it. One, however, has already been taken. Purple eyes stare   Ares down; the same eyes that he tried to burn. A flame bursts to life in his chest, trembling at the very sight of him. Medusa takes her seat beside Asmodeus, who lights her cigarette.

"Still sore? I was sure burning me alive would be more than enough to quell that anger of yours." Asmodeus chokes out a laugh. He leans into the light, Judas' clean-shaven face greeting Ares. The demon runs a gloved hand over his jaw. "If it weren't for you, I wouldn't have to be in this meat suit. We would both still have what we want."

Ares shoves his own seat out to make sure he keeps his distance from Asmodeus. He isn't sure he will be able to stomach sitting next to such a despicable being.

"Don't speak of him like he's something to be owned. Now, explain yourself." Ares tosses the cigar onto the table as if it were a dead rat. Asmodeus regards it with care, fingers hovering over it like he is afraid to touch it. "Why would you employ my Uncle to bring Ariel back to you?"

"I had no other choice. I just wanted to see him again."

"I don't understand why he still clings to this idea of you," he says. "Why he would throw away his place in Eden to search for you."

Asmodeus' features soften at the mention of Ariel. "You mean he's been looking for me?"

"He *was*. That fucking bastard took him from me. And do you know the worst part? Hera stood by and let it happen." He clenches the edge of the table, and as fingers melt impressions in the wood, fire bubbles from his eyes. "Why would she forsake me? Her own son?"

"I'm not exactly surprised, she isn't exactly the sociable type." Asmodeus shrugs his statements off as if it were another fact of life. "My Father always warned me to steer clear of her."

"Don't give me that shit!" Ares leans over the table. "*Your* Father left us to hide in the Underworld! What has he been doing all these years?"

He leans back in his chair. Lacing his fingers over his chest, with his elbows on the armrests, Asmodeus glowers from the shadows. "Keeping his nose in his own business. You'd do well to tell that bitch upstairs to do the same!"

With a sigh that can only be described as the end of his patience, Ares flips the table like it were a twig in his path. Medusa calmly takes a puff of her cigarette, holding a hand between them as Asmodeus stands toe to toe with him. "I would really appreciate it if you didn't get blood on the carpet. Can't you two solve this without beating each other to a pulp?"

Asmodeus tosses his jacket off, rolling his sleeves up so he can stretch his arms. "Just let us get this out of the way, would you?"

She heaves out a sigh. "I'm adding this to the rent you still owe me."

"Are you really sure you want to do this?" Ares asks, discarding his own coat.

The demon waves him forward. "C'mon, let's do it. I'm not backing down now."

Asmodeus squares up, but Ares immediately delivers a left hook to his jaw, and he collapses to the floor with a groan. Light burns mark his face.

"I told you," Ares quips.

He sits with a hand cradling his face while Medusa watches from her seat. Asmodeus tries to put on his best sympathetic face. "Care to help?"

She blows smoke at him. "No, sorry."

"Fuck you too, then." Ares is the one to offer a hand and help him to his feet, except he holds him in place when he tries to step back. "What is it now?"

"I think it'd be in your best interest to help me. You want to see him again, don't you?"

"Of course I do!"

"Then act like it." Ares' grip tightens. "Hey, you're hurting my wrist," he only squeezes harder, "hey! Okay, fine! You win!"

The God of War is merciful today. He could break his arm, but Ariel would resent him for it. All he wants is to have him back in his arms, and if he has to work with the very demon he had an affair with, he will.

"Think of how scared and lonely he is right now!" Ares' eyes glimmer at his own words. "He needs us more than ever. Don't you realize that? You have to help me."

Asmodeus stares at the floor, rubbing at his eyes with the back of his arm. Black tears fall onto the carpet. "Don't make me feel guilty. What am I supposed to do? I can't do shit in this state! I may as well be useless!"

Ares places a delicate hand on his shoulder. Asmodeus' neck is taut. "Anything that'll return our lost love will be more than enough."

They silently cry, both keeping steady with their

emotions. But no matter how the boat sways, it doesn't capsize. A moment passes between them. It is the only connection they'll ever have.

"Can you stop that? It's making me uncomfortable," Medusa says from her corner. "Can you do this later,when I'm not here?"

They ignore her. Ares offers his other hand to shake. "So, what do you say? Do we have a deal?"

Asmodeus eyes him with suspicion but submits in the end. Even though he doesn't seem happy about it, he knows their goal is the same. "I have only one term. At the end of this, we'll settle who really deserves to stand next to him, fair and square."

"You want to fight again?" Asmodeus pulls his hand back to hold it against the burn. He glowers, but it's to be expected. "Now did you really have to go for the face again?"

His smile is much too light for his choice of words. "I wanted to remind you that I'm not afraid to set you alight again. I'm going to make sure you don't worm your way out of this little deal. Besides, I thought you enjoyed a challenge?"

The demon primps his hair back into place. "I'll put up a fight, but it's not like I really stand a ghost of a chance. You're her number one."

"Who knows? Maybe you'll surprise us both."

He doesn't return the gesture. "We'll see. Deuce and I will put something together." Asmodeus falls back into his seat once more, dropping his gaze to a dark corner. He bites the leather of his glove. "You're staying at the Hotel, right? Expect me to be in touch within the next few days. Until then, you'll just have to keep yourself occupied."

A silent tension hangs in the air. Medusa exchanges a glance with Ares and shrugs the sudden brooding off. It's oddly comforting that the demons' attitude is still there. At least something has yet to change in his life. He dusts off his jacket and slings it over his shoulder.

Ares stares him down, but Asmodeus avoids it. "Thank you."

"For what?" his rival spits out. "I haven't done anything yet."

"I didn't expect much out of this, certainly not that you'd agree to work with me. All I can do is be thankful for your cooperation. But don't worry, you won't have to get your hands dirty. I know it isn't your style."

"Can you leave now? Like I said, I'll be in touch." Quick and to the point. Asmodeus doesn't spare a glance as he leaves.

Ares takes the back exit and walks to the Hotel in the rain. He needs time to think this situation over, to put aside his distrust. Best for the downpour to wash it all away, to baptize him anew. No longer will he stand in his Mother's shadow. He has but one goal, to burn everything that holds him back and forge his own path. No matter what he has to do to get there, he is sure he will be forgiven. Even if the world ends in fire, he will get Ariel back. For they are meant to be together.

He showers and lies in bed. His hands grope at the empty space around him, yearning for the familiar touch of his love. Ares has no one to soothe the shadows in his mind tonight. He stares at the stars, shining like droplets of paint flicked onto the sky. Ariel's beautiful face keeps him awake, though it isn't long before exhaustion catches up to him. Even in the depths of sleep, his fingers curl around his love's absent body.

Chapter Fifteen

The Star

Lying on a plush mattress, Ariel holds anger close to his heart. He is but a flower withered between the pages. Layers of blankets and pillows surround him. He stares down the man he longs to let all this rage onto, to stab it into his neck like a dagger — Poseidon.

His bed lays in an open clam shell, casting Ariel in shadow. The bastard lounges on a pristine white couch across from the shell. Erato sits beside him on its twin, but she only has eyes for Ariel. Vases full of roses sit throughout the room on little tables. Poseidon tugs the collar of his white suit loose, his wavy hair falling around his shoulders. He's the epitome of smug with that stupid smirk. Ariel's stomach churns at the sight of it.

The falling rain reverberates through the expansive room. Humid heat clings to Ariel's bare skin, as Poseidon only gave him enough thin silk to barely cover himself. A giant projector looms behind him, dim lights glowing behind every lens. The ceiling is pitch black, much like the distant sky. Their room sits atop the highest floor of the Cathedral.

"You look so angry with me right now." Poseidon cups his chin like he is viewing a piece of art. "You'll get over it soon enough."

Erato plucks one of the roses. "I don't see the point in any of this. Why would Hera forsake one of her own?"

"It's not meant for you to see. If you had the foresight we had, you'd be able to understand." He takes a rose as well, marveling at its fragrance. "You're but a Muse. It isn't your job to wonder."

"And you're but a playboy with an oversized ego."

His grin tightens. That golden gaze covers Ariel in slime. "That may be so. But, tell me, why would you risk your place in Eden for a simple whore?"

Erato leaves the flower on the cushion beside her as she stands and brushes off her skirts. "You have no sense of honor or loyalty, do you?"

"I'd suggest you quell that loose tongue of yours while you still have it. I've had enough of your comments."

Poseidon crushes the rose in his hand. "If you don't need to mend my Pearl, you have no place here."

She crosses the room to Ariel as a final act of defiance. Erato leans over to extend a hand to him. They meet for but a brief moment, the Muse squeezing his. She pulls him close so she can whisper. "You're going to get out of here. I'm sure of it." Unspoken fury fills her eyes and Ariel nearly tears up himself. Without another word, she departs.

Once they are alone, Poseidon takes his time in unbuttoning his shirt. He leaves the comfort of the couch to pace around Ariel. Closing in on him, he crawls onto the bed. He can't move once Poseidon touches him, fingers sliding up his arm and around his neck.

Poseidon chuckles to himself. "You're so much prettier like this... when you listen to me for once." Ariel looks anywhere else but him. "What's the matter? Don't you want me to make you honest?" He smears a finger across Ariel's lower lip.

"What does that even mean?"

His other hand runs up Ariel's thigh. "Don't you want me to make you sweet? You're nothing but an evil witch, charming and cursing men. It's the one role you know how to play." Poseidon's voice and touch turn hard. He presses his chest against Ariel's shoulder. "But after I'm done with you, you'll be back to your old self—nay, better than your old self.

You'll finally be something beautiful, and you'll be all mine."

Ariel turns his face away from him. "I'm not yours."

"That's where you're wrong." Poseidon squeezes his leg harder and harder, with eyes that swallow him. "Look at me. What happened to your passion? Where did it go?" He forces his face against Ariel's neck and his hot breath burns like steam. "Why are you so quiet? Try and enjoy yourself."

"I hate you," he says.

"Then why don't you put up a fight?" He frowns. "It's no fun if you give in so easily. I want to hear your heart race, see the pain in your eyes. So why won't you look at me?"

Poseidon forces Ariel's face towards him, but this is the last straw. He bites at the finger closest to his mouth hard enough to draw blood, but he doesn't even flinch. He slaps Ariel across the face. He lies in a heap, staring up into those hollow eyes he longs to gouge out. The walls of the observatory lower, throwing them into darkness. The rain subsides to a hum. The projector whirs to life. Every star in the sky shines on the ceiling. Poseidon's silhouette blots out the light while greedy hands explore Ariel's body.

"I'm going to make you love me. I'll make you into the perfect Pearl."

The universe is the only one to watch this scene unfold. There is no sympathy to be found in the night sky. The

Audience stares on.

Over the next few days, he spends time recuperating in Erato's greenhouse on the Cathedral grounds. Rows upon rows of rose bushes line the crystal clear walls. Gentle air soothes his sore skin. His shirt hangs open, slacks rolled up to his calves, revealing bruises and bites that mark his body. He lays his head down on the table they sit at. Steaming cups and a pot of tea crowd Erato's side.

She blows on her tea but doesn't sip. Worry permeates her features. "I'm sorry."

"For what?" He slumps back in his chair. "You couldn't do anything. Your hands are tied."

"It just isn't fair! To think his crimes would be forgiven for - just to..." Erato's hand shakes and her cup rattles against its platter. "I put this on myself. If I can just reclaim my godhood, this will all be worth it."

"He's going to break you before that!"

"I don't care!" He shoves his chair back, chest heaving with the most minimal of exertion. "Don't you realize how useless I feel? I may as well be a mortal, living in dirt! I need to become a god again! If I have to trade my sanity for a shot at that? I'd gladly spend the next hundred years like this."

"I'll help you as much as I can," she says. "Please, just try and enjoy the time you have away from him."

Ariel leans against the side of the table, barely sipping his tea. He doesn't have time to waste having a party, he has a plan to unfold. How he will do it, he hasn't the slightest idea yet. But he is sure it will all come into place. "Will I ever get to see him again?"

Erato pours herself more tea. "Ares is barred from the grounds. I'm not sure if or how you'll be able to–"

He puts on the voice that gets him everything he wants. It has yet to fail him. "Can't you make it happen? I'm sure Calliope would listen to reason, you're her sister after all."

"She only listens to what she wants." The greenhouse door opens with the squeak of rusty hinges and Poseidon fills the space. He is put together this time, every hair in place, looking the part of the suave gentleman. A warmer hue replaces the malice he saw prior, something almost like love. To think Ariel thought of him as a love-struck fool, when he only wears the jester's hat to distract from the monster underneath, the shark that only shows itself in the dark waves of sheets and blankets. Poseidon has the nerve to smile at him.

"How's my Pearl doing today?" With hands in his pockets, he stares at him without a single tender thought, like a blood-sniffing shark. He leans down beside him, if only to look at himself through Ariel's eyes. "What's wrong?"

Poseidon slides a hand along his forearm, but he flinches away. "Don't touch me."

He plays the huffing off as concern. If he were a dumber man, he'd have fallen for it, but Ariel is no man's toy. "Can I not worry over you? You're like one of these delicate roses. It's my job to take care of you."

"How do you explain these marks then?"

"...I'm sorry? What do I have to explain myself for?" Poseidon looks at him as though he's speaking gibberish. "The way I see it, I only did what was necessary." He stands behind his chair, curling each ringed finger around the arms of it. He twists it around so their faces sit inches apart. "You weren't listening. What's a man to do when his fiancé won't listen to him? I had to get rough with you — to make you listen."

"Fiancé?" Ariel looks away. But no matter how much he tries to ignore, his stare persists. "You must be joking."

"There I go, jumping the gun like always." He laughs at himself. His rough hands probe the purple and red marks on Ariel's arms. "I would never joke about something as serious as love. As your prince, it's my duty to save you from yourself. But I can only do that if you let me. I can picture our honeymoon now..."

He waits for him to finish, but he must be too caught up

in his gross fantasies. Ariel eyes Erato across the table. Death radiates from her. Who knew such murderous intent could possess a being of romantic sighs.

"What exactly are you doing here—in my garden? You don't belong here."

The old man puts all that energy into bawling like a child. He grows red in the face, turning his anger towards Erato. "Are you saying I can't spend time with my fiancé? What did I ever do to deserve such scorn?"

But she isn't one to be intimidated by immature men with fragile egos. She blinks at the delusional questions. "He's not yours to begin with. Now get out."

Before Poseidon has a chance to speak, Erato directs a finger to the glass door. He has no choice but to follow the rules, it is her domain after all. He makes a scene out of being forced into the newly pouring rain, but goes on his way. Ariel watches him trudge back to the Cathedral through the wet grass.

He sips his tea to bring back the calm Poseidon interrupted, and it only irritates him more. Erato continues their conversation, but Ariel has his eyes on the sky. The way the clouds roll over one another brings back visions of the sea. Oh, what a wonderful thing to get lost under. To huddle against Ares after a night spent among the waves and wake to the crushed light of dawn. They have spent an eternity together, hand in hand, and now the Fates have torn them apart.

Where is he now? Lost to the city, most likely. Hera will pay dearly for this. To think she can impose her will upon whoever she wants. If she thinks the God of Love can be so easily locked away and forgotten about, she is sorely mistaken. He will break free from this controlling tyrant and head straight for her. If it is a fight she wants, it is a fight she will get.

A bell rings above the door. It is connected to a line that leads to the nearby tower. They both know what it means; it is time for Ariel's return to the main building. What little peace he has is over for now. Erato reaches the door before him.

"Shall we go together?" She gestures to his lack of a coat or umbrella as she ties a scarf around her own head. "I'd hate for you to walk in the rain alone."

"You just don't want me to be alone with him, is that it?" She pulls the door open and the fresh scent of rain rolls in. "Well, partially. But what about Ares or... him?"

"You can say his name, you know."

"Okay–*Asmodeus*." Erato grins like she broke a rule. "I'm so used to keeping it a secret, I almost forgot things like that don't matter anymore."

"So what about them?" They keep to the dirt path, keeping close to any trees to avoid getting caught in the rain. It doesn't stop Ariel from getting his feet wet.

"I'm just curious. I'm sure Ares is going to burst in here any moment to whisk you away - with the demon perhaps? But, I can't help but wonder... what will you do if he doesn't?"

"He wouldn't let me stay here and rot! He loves me." Ariel wrinkles his nose at her. They stop at the heavy wooden door. "But if he doesn't, I'll find a different way. I don't need to rely on anyone, remember? What's the point of being a god if I can't even save myself?"

They slip back into the lobby, Ariel leaving puddles behind. Hopefully Calliope won't notice the mess. A crowd of faithful surround her booth with gold coins falling out of their pouches. With the most patient of hands, she takes their donations, and signs them in. Calliope bids them an excellent visit with all the grace of royalty. As the Eldest Muse, it is no wonder she has been chosen to deal with the public. Her circlet is a beacon, letting the pair know how far to keep their distance.

On the way back to his room, Poseidon swoops in and cuts them off on the stairs. He comes from behind, tripping over his own feet, spewing half-hearted apologies at Ariel he can't stand to hear. Erato shoves him ahead to buy time. He locks the doors behind him. Even though it'll only be a few seconds before Poseidon borrows the key from Calliope, he will get to spend it alone. As familiar as he is with the concept of playing hard to get, it is a much different story when being pursued by someone you have zero interest in.

Poseidon's yells turn hushed when the knob jiggles. "Let me in, please. Let's not have a repeat of the other day." Ariel covers his mouth to muffle his breathing. Something hits the door, most likely his fist. "Don't make me pry this door open, you ungrateful whore! This time my nephew won't be here to save you!"

Poseidon's muttering grows quiet. Maybe he has given up? Ariel strains to hear every minute sound, kneeling against the door, but can't make anything out. He jumps when his voice comes out of nowhere. "If you don't listen, I'll have no choice but to punish you—and I won't be nice this time."

He speaks as though Ariel is but a rebellious child, that this can be fixed after an uncomfortable talk. But Poseidon has no way to express himself other than through violence. If he has been nice thus far... Ariel isn't sure he wants to find out how mean he can get. Maybe he should let him in after all?

Chapter Sixteen

The Snake

Downstairs, a golden Cadillac pulls up to the curb outside the Cathedral. A woman steps out into the rain, high-heeled foot first. She tugs her fur coat tighter around her frame. A pair of bright yellow sunglasses sit over her eyes and a golden helmet covers her head, topped with an owl statue and a brilliant red plume. Curly black hair sticks to her face, sneaking out from under the helm. Her skin is a beautiful dark brown. A pendant sits around her neck; a screaming face adorned with snakes.

Medusa turns to the car. "Are you coming?"

Asmodeus steps out along with her and the car idles. He quips to the driver, "we won't be long."

His blinding white suit is tight around his shoulders and chest. Black shades obscure his eyes, and his fox fur coat droops off his shoulders as he slouches.

"Shall we get going? We won't have much time." She nods to the Cathedral's doors, fussing with her clothes. "It won't take Poseidon long to figure us out."

He tugs at his jacket and makes a face at the color. He can't focus on the plan when he looks so grotesque. "Did you really have to stuff me into these ugly clothes? I doubt he'll even recognize me."

"That's not my problem, now is it?" Medusa props the door open long enough for Asmodeus to slip through. "I'm only here to keep you from getting yourself killed."

The lobby is full of worshippers scrambling to keep their place in line, each one in their Sunday best. Asmodeus shoves their way through. Calliope sits at the front desk like she always does. "Cutting isn't allowed. If you'd be so kind as to... Oh, Lady Athena! First a visit from your brother and now you? Forgive me, but we have procedures to follow and you can't just–"

Medusa looks down her nose at Calliope. Funny how one as observant as she would fall for this simple disguise. "I have business to take care of, Muse."

"...I suppose you want to see Hera as well?"

"You ask too many questions."

It is Calliope's turn to make an unamused face. "It's my job. I can't be letting in just anyone anymore. After what happened with Ares, so much has changed around here." She plays coy, putting that buttery voice to work. "What happened up there by the way? In Hesperia's chambers? Why is he banished?"

"What my brother did is none of your business. Do you always pester your guests like this?" Medusa does her best to imitate Athena's commanding aura. Her fingers wrap around the front edge of her desk. "My time is very important. It'd be a shame if someone were to put in an unkind word about you to Hera – oh, a sure shame."

"Okay, okay, I get it." Calliope gives in and writes their names down with a flourish. "Do you need someone to escort you upstairs, My Lady?"

She shakes her head, brushing past the Muse towards the stairs. Asmodeus discreetly burns part of the page when she isn't looking. "I can find my own way."

"Are you sure?" Medusa stops in her tracks with hunched shoulders. "Are you really doubting me, Muse? Need I remind you of what happened with that priestess?"

Calliope bows her head. "Of course not, My Lady. A thousand apologies."

She spares a single glance back up. "May I ask one more thing?"

"Speak."

"Who are you here to see?"

Asmodeus hooks an arm around Medusa's, turning her away, forcing her to wait by the stairs. The grin he directs Calliope's way is too bright. "Forgive her, this has been a difficult time all around. You know how dysfunctional families are." He laughs, smooth and good-natured to put her off her balance. "But, if you must know, we're here to see your latest guest."

No quick remark falls from her tight lips. The crowd is restless. She keeps her eyes anywhere but on Asmodeus. "I don't know who you're talking about. We don't have guests here."

He wipes his upper lip with a shrug. In his head, he crosses her face out with a red X. "Have it your way. Don't think we won't remember this."

They move up the stairs and Asmodeus sulks as their walk turns into a trek. He didn't expect it to take this long. The same white walls and marble statues pass by with each landing. Medusa tugs him by the arm to hurry up, and after half an hour—more like an eternity if you would ask him—they reach the top floor. Halfway up the final flight, a shadow eclipses the light from the hall. Poseidon huffs as if he ran to make it here. With his unruly hair and flushed face, one can only imagine what he was up to beforehand.

"A-Athena?" He stands, resolute to bar their way. Asmodeus isn't given a second thought. "What are you doing here? Hera didn't tell me you were coming."

Medusa ascends the steps one by one. Tension runs thick through her arms with how she tightly grips the railing. Poseidon stammers on, but she talks over him. "I thought I'd pay you a little visit, Uncle. I'm looking for answers."

He backs up against the wall as she moves closer. "I don't have any for you. Now if you'll excuse me, I have somewhere to be."

She leads him by the shoulder down the hall. "Why don't we take a little walk? It might jog your feeble memory."

"What of your little friend?" Poseidon asks.

"You have bigger things to worry about." When he tries to get a better look at Asmodeus, she turns him away by the chin. "Like explaining to me why my little brother was banished."

"Oh, well, you see…" His voice fades as they round the corner.

Now with some wiggle room, Asmodeus is free to do as he pleases. As long as he doesn't disturb the peace in any meaningful way, no one will know he was here. His throat dries out as he steps closer to the pearly gates and finds the door locked. "...Ariel?" A whimper answers him. "Darling? Is that you?"

"I'm not opening the door!"

He tries it again. "Babe, it's me... it's Asmodeus. You have to let me in."

There's a long pause. "You're lying. I know that voice! You're that scumbag from the club."

How could his baby not recognize him? His hand slips away from the door. "Take one look at me and I promise you won't be disappointed."

After a few moments, it opens and there he is, the love of his life, the only thing that keeps him going. He could never forget the beautiful face he spends countless evenings thinking of. Even with a different coat of paint and some frilly clothes, Asmodeus knows it is him. He slips his sunglasses off and watches as the skepticism melts into something softer.

"Oh my god," is all Ariel can get out before they fall into each other's arms. Ariel grips the back of his jacket so tightly, he fears he might tear the seams. He doesn't mind how damp his tears are, all he cares about is that he gets to see his baby. Asmodeus would cry himself if he weren't inhabiting a corpse, so all he can do is squeeze his hand to soothe him. If only he could truly feel the rush of his skin again. He will have to save it for another time, another place, when they can have a proper reunion.

"I nearly forgot, I have something for you." He pulls out a small velvet box from his pocket.

Ariel wipes at his leaky eyes and rosy cheeks. "Are you seriously giving me jewelry at a time like this? You have to go before he gets back!"

"Listen, just listen.. We don't have much time right now. She can only distract him for so long. Just take them."

He holds the box to his chest. "...What are they?"

Asmodeus takes him by the shoulders and stares into his face one last time. Time slows down for him as he marvels at every feature like a favorite painting he hasn't seen in years. But he saves those ocean eyes for last, the serenity within them able to still his beating heart if he had one. He would pull Ariel in for a kiss, but he doesn't want the icy lips of a dead man to be his last reminder of him. So a kiss to the hand will have to do.

"You'll see. Open it when you're alone. Now, don't you go worrying, alright? I'll be back for you." With a final embrace, he manages to get an "I love you" in before returning to the staircase. As if, even in the midst of this mess, he could forget that their love is the most important thing. But no matter what, he can never give him enough. He will never be able to measure up to the likes of Ares. It is like trying to fight the current, hopeless.

Now it is not like he wants to surpass Ares, no, he is through playing childish games like that. Love isn't a competition to be won. Asmodeus only wants to be in the same spotlight they bask in, no more hiding behind the curtains offstage and watching with a chest full of resentment.

All he needs is for them to see him as an equal. But just when he gets his hopes up, he remembers, he's a creature of the night. He has no right to impose on their happiness, fine with being pushed to the background. Yet the tear that longs to fall tells him otherwise.

Medusa and Poseidon come back around, faking their laughter all the way. He tries to hug her, but she brushes him off. They hardly bid each other farewell before Medusa hurries down the stairs, leaving Asmodeus on the first landing with his hands in his pockets.

Her voice bounces up to him. "Come on, Romeo. You know I don't have all day." He forces his feet to move. A dumb grin sits on his lips. "You didn't forget how you got in this situation, did you?"

She probably hopes to wipe the smile off his face, but not even her pointed tone can move it. "Must you bring up the past, Deuce?" he asks with the subtlest hint of annoyance. "I think this is the opportunity I've been waiting for to prove myself to him."

She chuckles at him and her snakes laugh along with

breathless voices. "Are you really this stupid? I thought after what you went through, you'd have learned a thing or two. But clearly you don't."

"Well, you'll be the one in the wrong here when I," Asmodeus jabs a thumb into his chest, "win over Ariel like it was nothing."

"You think you'll be able to just do that?" She walks ahead of him. "Awfully confident for the prince who nearly died to Ares."

"Why do you hate me so much?" At last his grin deepens into a frown. "Aren't we friends? Why else do you keep me around?"

"The entertainment," she hisses.

Asmodeus trails behind now, mumbling to himself, and throwing a miniature pity party with a full tea set. He stops at least three times on the way back down, leaning dramatically against one of the ugly statues, throwing a hand over his forehead. He only does it to annoy her. "My life sucks so much right now, Deuce! I keep trying to make things better, but nothing works!"

Medusa's head snaps to the side. "Maybe you should stop being so dumb, have you ever thought of that? Can you go any slower? Do you want me to leave you behind?"

He laments as if he were the main character of a tragedy.

"Oh, whatever will I do without you? Die?"

"One can hope!" She fires the cherry on top at him like a bullet.

"I think I'll stay back after all," Asmodeus grumbles in return, sniping her back. "I'll see you afterwards—the later the better."

Despite their bickering, Medusa waits at the foot of the stairs for him. At the end of the day, she's his only friend, no matter how many times she threatens to kill him. The lobby is nearly empty, a few stragglers resting against the walls. They move past Calliope's empty booth and part ways at the Cathedral's gates. Medusa steps into the car at the curb and rolls down the window to throw an elegant wave goodbye. Asmodeus doesn't bother with more than a nod in her direction.

Outside the gates, neon signs glare at him from every street corner and shop, filling the city with a bright light akin to that of a warning siren. The chaotic glow that makes his home away from home. The rest of the people he passes have dead faces, mere husks with glowing eyes. Thankfully, Asmodeus has a body, no matter how temporary it is. To feel the sun again on his actual face again would be a dream come true. Hopefully Ariel will be by his side to see it. But what will he do once he has him? What will it feel like to finally have the love he deserves?

One day he'll get to find out, but in the meantime, fantasies will have to do. The stairs are in sight, a warm red glow that he's grown so fond of during his stay with Medusa. At intervals along the sidewalk, beautiful statues are set up in a haphazard fashion, black light illuminating the white stone. Their expressions are so life-like one would think they were actual people.

Why does Medusa leave her work littering the streets? As if any of these people have an eye for the arts. With the majority of the populace having been killed off, possessed, or used in some fashion, there is hardly any reason to remain in the shadows. The only ones safe are those blessed by the gods, and that opportunity hasn't reached the Rosebed yet.

He wanders down the hall to his door, fumbling with his keys as he unlocks it. The light is dim within the apartment, a mortal standing in the middle of their living room, wires and rope holding him in a pose worthy of a Renaissance painting. All around the room spotlights are set up that shine directly onto the poor fool.

Medusa sits nearby on a stool. She lowers her sunglasses at the sight of Asmodeus and waves him towards her. "Come, you have to look at my latest piece before anything else, it's of the utmost importance!"

"How did you get home before me?" He slips off his

shoes at the door, shuffling into the living room. "And when did you find the time to kidnap someone?"

"That isn't important! What's important is that you give me your honest thoughts." The two appraise the man–who is clearly paralyzed–like a work of art. Medusa clasps her hands together, quivering with anticipation. "So, what do you think?"

He snorts. "Do you always bring your work home, Deuce?"

"Well, inspiration is inspiration, isn't it? I can't exactly control when it appears. I'd be a much more famous artist if that were the case." Her snakes curl out with a yawn. She snaps her fingers to get their attention. Medusa takes careful steps to her art piece, deciding where the petrification should begin. The snakes lash out one by one, biting along the man's body, their venom slowly turning him to pristine marble. When the transformation is complete, she unhooks her masterpiece, and turns back to Asmodeus. "Well? How much do you think this will go for?"

"Honestly? It's worthless."

"Oh, shut up! You're just trying to get a rise out of me by insulting my art!" She folds her arms with a hiss.

"Listen, I don't have time to argue. I have somewhere to be." He tosses his coat onto the couch and unbuttons his shirt. "You have anything I can borrow for tonight?"

Medusa sits beside him with a grin.

"...What?"

"You really have a death wish, don't you?"

He tosses his shirt at her. "Keep your noses out of my business!"

"I'm sorry, who's the one squatting in my apartment?" she asks.

Asmodeus stalks across the room to keep his distance from her. "Wasn't that Judas' debt?"

"Regardless, I expect to see some cash in my hand."

"I'll be paying my half in due time," he says.

"When?"

He throws his hands up. "I don't know, okay? You'll get it when you get it."

Medusa opens a dog-eared page in a magazine, one she's read multiple times. At this point she only looks at it when she's roasting him. "So, where are you taking the harlot?" She slowly flips a page. "Just a word of advice, try not to get caught. If anyone asks, we don't know each other."

He moves in front of her, keeping his shoulders hunched to try and intimidate her. It's such a shame Judas is also short. "What did you call him?"

She waves a hand in his face. "Can you get out of my light? I'm trying to read here. Who knew a prince could be so rude?"

"Cut the bullshit, Deuce!" He pulls the magazine out of her hands.

With nothing to hide her sour face, she openly seethes. "Word gets around you know. People talk. Those fancy Muses think their Cathedral is air tight, that nothing could possibly get out. Little do they know, we have someone on the inside."

"We do?"

She shakes her head like a teacher scolding a pupil for failing to see an obvious answer. "See? You're as stupid as I thought. You'll most likely meet her tonight. So,where are you taking him? If you can even manage to get him out the door."

He coughs into his fist. "...The Grand Hotel?"

"...Is my club not good enough for you?" she probes.

He grumbles and leans against the gaudy patterned wall. Why is she always like this? If he wanted someone to scold him, he would've stayed in the Underworld with Persephone. "What was that?"

"Fine! I'll take him there. Eventually."

She points toward her side of the apartment. "You can take something pretty for him, and please do something to cover up that stench of death." She fans herself with the crumpled magazine. "You don't want to repel him, do you?"

He stalks through the expansive rooms, past dozens of

portraits of the snake herself and her various art pieces. Vintage furniture and decorations that look as if they came out of the Victorian era litter her half of the apartment. Vases of flowers and fake fruit cover every surface. The sickly smell of lit candles fill his nose, only fueling his irritation. Why did she feel the need to light every candle they own? Did she enjoy messing with his sensitive nose? Or when she would create her "art" and blast what she referred to as classical music. He didn't hear a single scream of the damned or even a lyre. Classical his ass.

He wrenches the door open to her room, gripping the jewel encrusted knob tight enough to crush it. The room is as ornate as the rest of her section; a four poster bed, lace curtains, a bust or three of herself on pedestals throughout the room. Asmodeus digs through her jewelry box, taking a pair of golden spectacles and a pearl choker. He also snatches her best bottle of cologne, a thick pair of sunglasses she won't miss, and returns to the living room.

He wanders down a long hall to his room, secluded from the rest of the apartment, which truly isn't much to write home about. The only furniture are a bed and nightstand in one corner, with a dresser on the opposite wall. The closet only has suits in it. Neon light from downstairs filters through the blinds that washes him out in red. He stares at the blank television set in the corner, not bothering to flick it on, knowing he would only get the pleasure of watching white noise.

He lays the items on the bed and saunters out to the bathroom. He strips his pants and draws a boiling hot bath. He has to look picture perfect for Ariel. He lays in the water, feet propped up over the side.

Asmodeus makes an afternoon of getting ready. He stays in the steamy bathroom with hands on either side of the sink, staring at himself in the mirror. The bags under his eyes, the sickly pallor to his skin; all thanks to the drugs Judas abused before. It's times like this that he wishes Medusa had other ways of keeping underlings around her finger.

The only sign he cares about is the bright glimmer in his eyes. As long as his mind is intact, he doesn't care less what happens to this vessel. He bundles up in a pinstripe suit, a clear vinyl raincoat over it. He takes his time in doing his tie and slipping on his black leather gloves. The daylight wanes as he steps out of his room. Medusa beckons him over, still reading one of her many magazines.

"What is it now?"

"I have something for you." She stands, tucking a white rose through his coat's buttonhole with a pat on the shoulder. "You still look ugly, but I can only do so much."

Asmodeus leaves without as much as a thanks.

Chapter Seventeen

The Fox

The walk to the Cathedral is uneventful, with the newly fallen rain making the usual busy streets empty. He has to be careful not to step in a puddle or scuff his good shoes, they are the only pair he has. Hopefully this vessel will last, he would hate to be forced to live inside something ugly. It has taken him long enough to find a body that suits his needs.

He centers his thought on the focus of his desire for the umpteenth time today, his precious Ariel. He can picture it now; his hands gripping at bare skin, feeling every inch of Ariel's body. But he couldn't possibly make love to him in this sorry state. Everything has to be right for their rendezvous. His fingers twitch, his teeth grind. Sure, he's impatient, but if it's to see his baby again? He would go to any length, tell any lie. He can't pass a chance like this up, he'd be crazy to.

Asmodeus, mustering up all the energy he has inside him to remain a relative state of calm, approaches the Cathedral's giant doors. He squints and raises a hand to knock. No one answers, of course. He must look like an idiot, but it wouldn't be the first time. He pulls on the handle as if it would open, and surprisingly, it does. Asmodeus weasels his way through the empty lobby and up the stairs, doing his best to be silent. The halls are dark, with shutters covering the windows to keep the cool air out.

He's a thief in the night, preparing to steal away a museum's precious gem. However, there isn't a single sign of life through the Cathedral. Asmodeus takes it as time to relax. So he shakes his nerves from his trembling hands, lighting his cigar with a snap of his fingers. The pinkish-purple embers light up the dark. He exhales a cloud of smoke, his anxieties all but leaving him. He's got this, there's nothing to worry about.

Once on Ariel's floor, near the door, a warm light comes around the corner from the other side. It's one of the Muses holding a small lantern at her side, the brightness of the stars shining within her cloak. Her dark hair is tied back into a high bun, stray curls falling over the side of her face. When her eyes fall on him, she doesn't yell or scream, but smiles at him as if she were expecting him at this precise moment.

"You're just where I thought you'd be," she gloats. "I'm who they call Urania, Asmodeus."

"What the fuck? How do you know me?" He eyes the door. Maybe he'll be able to make it before her.

"Your friend told you about me, but that isn't important right now." The moment he makes the slightest move, Urania raises a hand to stop him. "Why are you so nervous?"

"...You haven't called for help yet?" Asmodeus might have a chance at killing her if he's fast enough. She holds a hand to her mouth to stifle her laughter, shoulders shaking with the effort. "What's so fucking funny?"

"You don't get it, do you?" She closes the distance with slow steps, and wags a finger at him like a stern aunt. "I've been waiting for you all night and you're late."

He sneers. "I show up when I want to, lady."

She leans in a bit too close for his liking, holding the lantern up near his face. "I expected someone a bit more... handsome. But you'll do."

Asmodeus bares his teeth, biting down on his cigar. "Do you want me to rip your throat out, Muse?" He decides to simmer down, but pouts at the comment, toying with the placement of his coat. "I look just fine, by the way."

"Hm. Sure." She grins into his face. "Regardless, you would be wise to leave me unharmed. You wish to see the

Pearl, don't you? I was going to escort you myself."

"You serious?" he asks.

"I'm nothing but serious when it comes to Fate." She lets out a little sigh and glances off to the side. "I hope one day you're able to comprehend the fact that everything is predetermined, right down to your awful personality." Just as Asmodeus is about to retort, she hushes him with a finger. "You don't want to wake him yet, do you?"

She unlocks the door with a bronze key, opening it enough to let Asmodeus in. Before he is completely through, she stops him with a hand on his arm, whispering one last thing to him. He could swear her eyes look almost cat-like in the dark. "You have to bring him back before midnight."

He tries to pull away. "Yeah, yeah–"

"Do we have an understanding? You have no choice in this."

"Yeah, I get it." Asmodeus pulls his arm away, surprised at how strong her grip is. Ariel's room is dark, the only light pours out from cracks in the shell. The projector looms overhead as a constant reminder of Poseidon's hold on him. Asmodeus pries the shell open, and there he is, sleeping beauty, lying peacefully among an ocean of blankets and sheets. Asmodeus kneels at his bedside. "Ariel?" His voice betrays him, shaking just the slightest. He slips his gloved fingers through his, whose eyes flutter open.

"Asmo..?" He grins, half asleep and groggy, but panic blooms in his eyes. "What are you doing here? Where's Poseidon? You shouldn't–"

"I had to come see you." He squeezes his hand. A cloud of smoke hovers around his head like a veil. "Don't worry about him, he shouldn't bother us. This is the only way I could make it happen. I told you I'd be back, didn't I?"

"I didn't expect you so soon," Ariel says with a frown.

His black heart swells with love at the way he looks at him. His skin glows against the lights inside the shell.

"Well, I live to exceed expectations." Asmodeus pats his hand as he stands. "Come on, we have to get going while the night's still young."

Ariel rubs at his eyes, but still holds the sheets close, his hair sticking out in all directions. "Where are we going?"

"Out. I want to show you the city."

"But where?"

"It's a secret."

Ariel takes his time in dressing himself, his shirt half-on, pants still sitting where they were thrown after a few minutes. Asmodeus waits with his hands in his coat pockets. It seems like he still has no sense of urgency. It's almost like they're back at the manor, waiting for him to get ready so he can escort him back over to Eden.

The door opens and closes again, Urania entering the room with a small metal cup in her hands. She places it on the nightstand, snatches the brush to roughly run it through Ariel's hair, and ties it into a ponytail with a pink ribbon. When she nudges him to turn, Asmodeus takes his chance to secure the choker around his neck.

"Where'd you get that?" Urania scrutinizes the jewelry with the cup in hand.

"A friend loaned it to me."

"Looks cheap," she says.

He tries not to let this dampen his mood. "Ariel, what about the earrings I gave you?"

It is the cutest thing to see his face light up like that. Always so forgetful. Ariel digs under his pillows for the box, taking out the pair of dangling pearl earrings. As he puts them on, Asmodeus slips the glasses he "borrowed" from Medusa on him. He only has a moment to admire him before Urania has Ariel drink from the murky liquid, a thing as black as the hole within him. He makes a face, but drinks it nonetheless.

"What was that?" As Ariel speaks, his hair loses its luster and shine. It turns a dull pink.

"Something that'll help you remain undetected outside. You might be but a mortal, but you still have traces of your godhood inside you." She shoots a look at Asmodeus. "Just remember, you have to be back before midnight."

"As if I'll forget. What do you take me for?"

"An idiot." Once Ariel is ready, they're lead outside by Urania.

Ariel is in awe at the sight of fallen rain, hopping in puddles like a child with his face to the black sky.

"You've haven't been outside yet?" Asmodeus asks.

"They barely let me leave my room half the time. I nearly forgot what it's like to be outdoors." He wanders along the path to the gate, and runs bare fingers over trees, taking in the scenery.

Asmodeus catches up to loop his arm through Ariel's. "Well, just stick with me," he says.

"I'll make sure nothing goes wrong tonight."

"..I also forgot how short you are."

"Hey!" Ariel snickers to the open night air as they walk down the street, arm in arm. The statues that dot the city almost glow in the dark this late at night, a rainbow of color blending from the street lights. The buildings are dark shadows with blacked out windows. Ariel's all smiles. The weight of their hands together comforts a small tender piece of Asmodeus, a flower that blooms in his empty chest. He

215

allows it to be known to not even Ariel, keeping it all to himself.

They make it to the Hotel in all its splendor, although Ariel doesn't seem to be very impressed. Has he been here before? They reach the front desk and Asmodeus rings the little golden bell. His older brother Mammon makes an appearance, looking gaudier than usual. The haughty asshole. He could smell the superiority complex a mile away.

Mammon leans against the counter and his various chains and watches jingle like little chimes. "Oh, you're back at last?" he asks.

"Excuse me?"

"Your friend has a room here. I was wondering when he was going to show up again."

"We don't plan on staying long," Asmodeus says.

Mammon frowns and folds his hands together. "Will you cut the shit, Asmo? What are you doing up here?"

"Can you let us go up already? I don't have a lot of time to waste arguing with you!"

The trace of a grin barely upturns the corners of his mouth. "It'd be a shame if someone were to tell Mother or Father."

"You wouldn't dare!"

Mammon poises a hand over the phone on his desk. "I

could call them right now. What would they think of precious little baby Asmodeus running around in the city all by himself?" He coughs into his hand. "Oh, I nearly forgot. The room's been taken already."

He has had enough. If he has to commit fratricide tonight, so be it. His parents would thank him to be rid of one of their despicable sons. Asmodeus grabs Mammon by the collar and pulls him halfway over the counter. "What do you *mean* it's been taken!? You just said it was Ariel's!"

"Another man has holed himself in the room. I think you know who it is? Tall and blonde?"

Ariel practically shoves Asmodeus out of the way. "You mean Ares is here!?"

Mammon straightens the folds out of his crisp shirt. "You could say that."

Asmodeus is fuming at this point, so he foregoes Mammon, and stalks up the stairs by himself. Ariel rushes past him into the elevator, and almost doesn't wait before pressing the button fifty times. They hardly speak a word the ride up.

Asmodeus leans back against the wall. "Are you really in that much of a hurry to see him? Aren't *we* supposed to be together?"

"I know, but... it's been so long! And I miss him!" His

217

eyes sparkle with glittery tears. "Don't get me wrong, I love you both, it's just... different with him."

"So I'm not good enough for you?" he asks. "Is that it?"

Frustration wrinkles his pretty face as he holds himself. "It's not like that at all..."

"Then what is it like? Tell me, I'm all ears." The elevator doors slide open and Asmodeus has to drag him out into the hall. "So what am I to you then? Some fun for when you get bored of Prince Charming?"

"No! I love you both!" He takes Asmodeus' hand in both of his. "You have to believe me. Would I really risk my life leaping from Eden to find you if I didn't–truly, truly, truly– love you?"

His mouth gapes like a dying fish. "I... I guess you wouldn't of, huh?" He wraps his other hand around Ariel's. "I didn't mean to blow up like that. You know how I get when he comes up."

Asmodeus pushes the suite door open and leads the way into the picture perfect room. Ariel looks around in awe for some reason. Asmodeus would set the mood, but he can't take the chance of Ares lurking around some corner, ready to behead him at a moment's notice, so he keeps the lights bright. He settles down on the couch and rests his feet on the coffee table.

"You want a drink?" Ariel returns from the other side with a bottle of wine and sets it on the table.

"I don't know if I should."

"You know you can relax, right?" he asks.

"I know that. But where's Ares?"

Ariel shrugs. "The room's empty. He must be out."

Asmodeus smokes like a chimney to keep calm. He eyes the bottle and his dry mouth gets the best of him. He drinks straight from it once he tears the cork out, not even minding the fizz that oozes over his chin. With a hefty sigh, he sinks into the upholstery. It has been forever since he has had alcohol, let alone some pretty okay wine made for rich people, but he still can't relax.

Ariel's hand slides over his thigh. "What's wrong?"

"Nothing."

"You're not enjoying yourself, are you?"

"I am." He makes a point to take a longer sip of his wine this time.

"Don't lie to me." Ariel shifts closer, laying an arm over his shoulders now.

"You trying to sit on top of me or something?"

"I could if it'd make you feel better." Before he can protest, he takes a seat in his lap. Asmodeus allows him to slip off his sunglasses and loosen his tie. "Is something wrong?"

He looks into his eyes for but a moment. They are not his to gaze into. "I don't know, it might sound dumb."

Ariel lays his head on his shoulder. "Try me."

Asmodeus hunches his shoulders. He shuts down, concealing his face in the collar of his coat. "I just love you so much."

Not even his laugh, or the finger that makes little circles against his dress shirt can brighten his spirits. "Well, I knew that. But is that a problem?"

"No."

"Then what's the matter? Cat got your tongue?"

"...I don't know if I should trust you again."

He frowns. "What makes you say that? I'm plenty trustworthy." Ariel looks at him with the sharp eyes of a hawk. It is as if he has been playing a game with him this entire time, playing the role of the coy and naive mouse. They both know perfectly well what it is. He just wants to see him spill his guts all over the floor and bleed out. Asmodeus nudges him back to his side of the couch. "Did I do something wrong?"

Back is the mouse, but Asmodeus knows what he saw; a venus flytrap dangling bait right in his face, waiting for him to fall for the honey-coated trap. He has to say something, but starting is always the most difficult part. Words bubble up in his chest like so many little fish, their scales gleaming under the water's surface. They look so easy to grab, but it is easier said than done. He has to pace the length of the table for a minute to get out the nervous energy. They stare at each other for a second before Asmodeus takes his seat again. He swallows another swig of wine.

"I love you, you know that. But then I remember what happened between us and.. I just don't know." He waves a hand in front of his right eye. Even with new eyes, half his vision is cloudy at best. At least it is better than being half-blind. But what will he think when he sees his scars? If he ever lets him. "I can't help but wonder, do you love me as much as I love you? All this time I thought it was true, but I don't know what to think anymore. Tell me I'm not crazy."

"Of course I love you." Honeydew melts on Ariel's tongue and his words give him a warm hug as they stick in his ears. But there is nothing in those eyes of his. He wishes there were contempt or hatred, anything to replace the indifferent glaze that coats his pretty face. Ariel curls up on the corner and looks down on him. Asmodeus leans over, hands on his thighs, head on the edge of the coffee table. He wants so badly to cry, to hurt, to feel anything in this husk. But there is only numbness.

He may as well be digging his own grave, but he can't stop himself. "Please? Will you be honest with me?"

221

Ariel wets his lips and purses them in such a way that makes him want to wipe that look off with a kiss. "How many times do I have to repeat myself before you believe me? You believe me, don't you?"

"I don't know."

"Why?"

Asmodeus can sense the guillotine blade growing closer by his tone. "It's dangerous to be with someone like you. I thought I was the one you should be wary of, but I was wrong. It's the other way around."

His hand runs over Ariel's, up his arm, and along his neck, to cup his jaw in his hand. His thumb rubs just below his ear. He clutches at his heart, at the false heat radiating like a swallowed sun. It isn't real, he tells himself, none of it is real. Ariel acts as if he didn't hear him, but he only hears what he wants. "Why don't you take your gloves off?"

"I'd rather not stain you."

Ariel ignores him and tugs one off so he can slide their fingers together. The tips of Asmodeus' are black, stark against Ariel's pale skin. With even the slightest movement, soot streaks along the back of his hand. The dull sensation of skin on skin isn't enough for Asmodeus, so he tears the other glove off with his teeth, needing to feel as much as he can. He appraises Ariel like one would art, but with the black coating him, it looks more like a toddler doodled over a masterpiece with charcoal.

There is something else that churns in his heart, a darker thirst that longs to be sated. He knows that his love could suck him dry if he wanted to, and maybe that's what he wants. When the remaining light eventually fades from his eyes, he hopes Ariel is there by his side. Better yet, to die by his hand would be a dream come true. He aches to snap between his hands, to be bathed in his own blood. Only then will he be clean. Only then will he know what sweet innocence feels like. If he confesses his sins, will Ariel plunge his knife deep inside him? Cut out all the black mold that suffocates his young heart? Asmodeus' life will be his to take.

He channels that malevolent energy into something soft, going in for a deep kiss that Ariel presses back into. Asmodeus has a firm purchase on his hips as he lays him down. Ariel's fingers run over the fine silk of his open shirt, pulling him down by his tie.

"I want to know everything," Ariel breathes. "Will you tell me?"

Asmodeus can't stand to look into his eyes again. "I've done terrible things."

"That's okay, I'll stay with you." Asmodeus pulls back after a moment. "What's wrong?"

"I don't want to hurt you."

"Why would you?"

Hewould only be fooling himself to think he is more than his desire. "I'm afraid I won't be able to control myself."

He coaxes him back down with gentle words. "I'm sure you're just overreacting. As if you could ever hurt me."

They ease back into their romance. Asmodeus does his best to put his impulses on the back burner, but they sit there, whispering in his ear. It would be so easy to snap Ariel's neck like a twig, to squeeze his throat closed until he turns purple. But he loves him more than he loves himself. He would sooner tear his own heart out and present it on a silver platter. He wonders how it would taste. Would it be enough to satisfy his love?

Ariel's shirt is half off when he fires a look at the clock on the wall. His voice tickles against his skin. "What time is it?"

"What does that matter?"

"I have to be back, don't you remember?"

Asmodeus still pulls at Ariel's shirt, hands staining his body as he explores. "I'm sure we'll be fine."

"I really think I should go. I can't stay." He tugs his shirt back down despite Asmodeus' begging, rolling out from under him. He is halfway to the door before he can make any further pleas.

"I'm sure I can do something-" The door slams shut.

Asmodeus sits on the bed, alone and angry. He nearly tears the door off the fridge as he opens it, snatching every bottle from inside. He takes a few gulps from each one, decides the wine is too sweet for him, and smashes them on the carpeted floor. He relights his cigar, takes a long drag for the walk home, then tosses it onto the spilled wine. He slams the door behind him just as Ariel did. If a fire breaks out, that isn't his problem. He is sure his brother will be able to deal with it.

On the way out, someone calls his name from the opposite direction. When he turns, it's none other than the big soldier himself standing in the living room. The patio door sits open.

"What the fuck do you want? I'm not in the mood!"

Ares holds the damp cigar in his hand, red eye shining like a siren as he looks over the room. "I thought we had a deal? I never thought you'd be as brazen to go behind my back and sneak into the Cathedral." The cigar evaporates into ash and he dusts his hands off. "I give you props for having the courage to sneak him out, but you're nothing but a cowardly rat after all."

"What's it to you? You only care about keeping him all to yourself! Maybe if you weren't so selfish, we wouldn't be here!"

"The only selfish one here is you. I tried to be civil, and to

225

think you were capable of change. But trying to stake a claim you have no right to make? I should've killed you before. I'm not going to make that mistake twice." A sphere of white hot magma bubbles to life in his palm. As he closes his fingers, it lengthens into his signature gold spear. Ares closes his eyes for a moment of silence. "Ariel, forgive me for what I'm about to do."

Asmodeus scrambles to the stairs. Ares watches as he makes a fool of himself, approaching at a leisurely pace. He escapes to the bar by the lobby. The overhead lights casts a blue sheen over him. He orders whiskey on the rocks and sips at it. Just calm down, Asmodeus, everything is going to be okay. He won't find you in here, it is too dark.

Until someone lays a hand on his shoulder, maybe to ask if he is okay. Whatever it is, it doesn't even register. He smashes the glass into the man's face, bits of it lodging in his fist. He is immediately kicked to the curb, so now he is alone and even more pissed off. Add in the shitty rain, the fact that Ares is out on a manhunt for him, and the dousing of blood on his suit, it all makes his situation even worse. But the worst thing is that Ariel is gone, and it is all his fault.

Asmodeus curses the whole way home, holding his injured hand against his chest. Black blood drips down his arm onto wet pavement. Fuck Ares. Fuck Ariel. Fuck all of them. They think they are better than him. As he rubs at his eyes as he crosses the street, he becomes aware of something different rising within him, but chalks it up to frustrations. Ariel must be getting to him. He trudges home in silence.

He almost kicks the door open as he loudly complains about his hand. Medusa sits on the couch, flicking through yet another magazine. "Did you get stood up again?"

"The fuck you mean by 'again?'"

She flips a page and adjusts her sunglasses. Her snakes curl into a short bob, body bathed in black velvet. "You know, you don't have to yell at me like that. If you need help, you can just ask, you idiot." He shows her his hand, and Medusa makes sure the blood doesn't get on her magazine or clothes. "Now what did you do? Get into a bar fight?"

"Yeah."

She has to close her eyes and rub her temples to process what he just said. "Why are you so fucking stupid?"

"It's part of my charm," he says with a grin.

"You're right, I love my men big and dumb." She snaps her magazine back open, sparing but an idle glance at his wound. "Why else would I put up with you?" Her snakes pick at the broken glass in his hand, but Medusa can't be bothered to actually help herself. "You can wrap that up yourself." She points to small dresser between two of the bookcases.

Asmodeus retrieves the bandages, albeit awkwardly, and uses more than he needs to fuck with her. He flexes his hand and mild pain throbs through his knuckles. "Thanks," he says, oozing sarcasm.

She doesn't reply.

He goes to lie in bed and stares at the ceiling, but his mind runs far too fast to fall asleep, so he has little choice but to stew with his thoughts. Once his eyes grow heavy, he knows it is about time for his body to fade for a few hours. But Asmodeus doesn't dream, for dreaming is a luxury, a waste of time he can't afford.

What is the use of getting caught up in empty visions that lead nowhere? He never understood the obsession. Instead, he views it as a necessary evil, a means to recuperate, to plan his next move. There are no sparks of color or nostalgia-tinted movies that play, only an empty black. It is another thing that reminds him of home, of the endless pitch that makes up their hidden sky downstairs. He hopes his pain fades by the time he wakes.

Chapter Eighteen

Rose Petals

In his rush to leave, Ariel forgets the way back to the Cathedral. He had been so distracted taking in the sights, that he didn't bother to pay attention. The rain picks back up. He shivers through wet clothes as he wanders down street after street. He doesn't know where he is or which way he should be going, at this point he just wants to go home and go back to bed. Maybe he should have stayed with Asmodeus and forgotten about his curfew. At least he would of had a warm bed.

A meow catches his attention. A black cat sits atop a metal fence, staring at him with amber eyes. It jumps down at his feet to rub against his legs. When Ariel reaches down to pet it, the cat wanders away a short distance, running away every time he moves. He follows it for a while, still not knowing where he is going, until he stumbles upon the Cathedral's brick perimeter. Ariel trips over his own feet through the gate. The door slides open and warm light pours over him. He looks up to thank whoever it is, but the feeling is short-lived. Erato stands at the door with a lantern, a shade of blue painting her face.

She shakes her head and pulls him in by the hand. "What are you doing outside?"

It is as if she knew he would be there. He twiddles his thumbs. "I just wanted to see what the city's like. That's all."

She slams the door shut. Ariel avoids her gaze. "It's not safe out there, you of all people should know that. I thought someone had stolen you away. If I let someone take you, well, I don't know what would happen–to me or you. I'm only glad you came back in time." She guides him up the stairs without another word. The light from her lantern casts amorphous shadows on the walls and statues they pass by. He isn't used to having anger turned around on him for once.

"I'm sorry." He really isn't.

"Don't apologize," she says. "You'd better be glad it was me who found you and not one of my sisters. Don't let this happen again." That's all Erato has to say on the matter for tonight.

As he falls asleep, his thoughts turn to Asmodeus. His voice sticks in Ariel's spine like a tune he can't forget. For some reason, he wants to see what he was hiding. Those eyes of his pierce into his heart, and the wanton desire in them makes him shiver. What would happen if time hadn't separated them? Imagine the pleasure Asmodeus could bring him. What would happen? He doesn't know. It invokes a thrill inside him, something ancient awakening again to the light, like a sealed tomb being opened. It has been forever since he has had a curiosity as visceral as this. It seems only natural Asmodeus would be the catalyst.

A singular droplet rolls over the edge, thick and sweet as honey. Images blur into existence of Asmodeus' hands, his mouth, all doing things he knows are right. It carries a soft tint, a romantic air; sweet meetings destined by a higher power. Ariel aches for his man, to be with him once more if the Fates would allow it. His thighs brush together as he tosses and turns. A thin sheen of feverish sweat covers him. All alone in his room, he glows pink in the night.

The silhouette of a cat runs circles around him. It grins with the knowledge of a well-kept secret, a marble-sized pearl stuck between its teeth. Each time he tries to get a better look at it, it's just out of view. It speaks without sound, branding words into his brain.

"Tell me what you want. I may make your dreams come

true." He opens his mouth to speak, but nothing comes. He is a puzzle missing a final piece, a star falling through the sky. "So you're going to ignore me? You can take your time, then. I'll wait for you."

Even with these words, Ariel can't settle down. The black cat's swishing tail taunts him till morning.

Erato doesn't let Ariel leave her sight when he is outside Poseidon's reach. He stays in her greenhouse, helping her tend to her precious flowers. It is all she lets him do after breaking out. Ariel holds a worn watering can in gloved hands, a straw sun hat sitting on his head. He doesn't see the need for it when summer has hardly begun, but Erato made him. She, too, has a hat on.

"Erato?"

They walk down the thin side aisles made of oddly shaped stones. The fountain gurgles in the background. Ariel waters the upper rows, as he is tall enough to do so. They go on their way, taking a short break under the magnolia trees in the far corner. A porcelain tea set lays on a silver tray, Erato pouring them both a cup.

"I'm still waiting for that apology," she says. "What happened last night?"

"I told you already." Erato sets her cup down. "I

should've felt your presence. But I didn't. I want to know why."

"I..." He doesn't have an answer that doesn't incriminate Urania or himself.

"Did my sister help you?"

"Maybe she did. Urania told me I had to be home before midnight. I don't know why, but—"

"Oh, so she did that again? How many times have I told her not to mess with the auras of the divine? You could've died out there!" She drags a hand down her face. "I swear, her head is in the stars most days. Obsessed with her silly prophecies."

"Should I not have listened?" he asks.

With a huff, she prepares to take a sip, only to slip in a terrifying question. "So who was the man of the hour?"

Ariel nearly chokes on his tea. "...Man? I don't remember a man. I went out by myself. For a walk."

She peers over the edge of her cup at him. "You only get like this when it comes to him. Were you with that demon last night? Let me come clean, I don't think seeing him any more is a good idea. He might hurt you."

"Asmo? He would never." He rolls the idea around in his head, sure he is right. "He's different when he's around me, Erato. He wouldn't dare try anything."

Although she doesn't seem sold on the idea, they both have been through this circular argument one too many times. There is simply no use in it. "Well... whatever you say. For your sake, I hope you're right."

There isn't a sign of Asmodeus for a whole week, a thing he secretly laments. Ariel spends his time doing mundane tasks for the Muses, like pruning Erato's rose bushes. He has little to do other than wait. When will his shadow return to him? Will he be angry and cross? Or will he decide to quietly brood and let his emotion sit on his face like a warning sign?

He wants Asmodeus to be mad at him. He wants to watch his carefully put together mask crumble and for the demon inside to pull itself from that husk so he can see the real Asmodeus uncensored. After all their time apart, he wonders what that might look like.

He might have said he didn't want to hurt him, but what would he say to the opposite? He is so sure that Asmodeus would let him break him in half and rip him open with his bare hands and teeth. To wrench his guts from that shell of a body, to watch as his vision fogs over with blood; the idea is almost romantic to him.

Ariel will be the monster under his bed, lingering in the shadows until his time comes. He will hunt him with bloodied feet across the Cathedral grounds, the drum beat of fear the only noise in Asmodeus' head. When the time comes, how will it be? He will savor the moment as he sinks his fangs into him. He will tear his heart into a million little ribbons, just as he has waited to do since day one. Ariel has been cognizant of his own life from the moment he was given shape in that primordial sea foam. He wasn't born to be remembered or do anything worth admiration. His life's purpose is to relish in his own pleasure. He is pretty and simple. In the few short seconds after indulging himself, when he is full and sated, his life is at its peak.

"Ariel, are you even listening to me?" Calliope's stern voice brings him back to the present. She doesn't even bother looking at him, nose in her open book. Her nails drum against the wood of the table. "Ariel?"

"I'm listening."

"If you'd prefer we pause the lesson and take a break, we can do so." She spares a glance from the page she's on. "You don't look well. Did you get enough rest last night?"

He lets out a yawn as he covers his eyes. "I tried to."

They sit near the only source of natural light in her tower, an oval window. It's "good for the soul" as Calliope has told him, but all it does is give him a headache. Light streams in from behind the Muse, casting the rest of the room in shadow. Tall bookshelves line the walls, a narrow spiral staircase ascends to a lone room at the very top of her tower.

235

"Well, I implore you to try harder," she says. "Shall we continue? It's essential that you pay attention this time."

She prattles on about chastity this and penance that. Not that he minds, with how surprisingly smooth and soft her voice is. Calliope wields it with the grace of a painter. It is laughable that she really thinks he gives a damn about what she has to say. Just as she goes to speak once more, the horns sound off as if on cue.

"Ah, is it already that time?" She pinches the bridge of her nose with a sigh. "We didn't even cover half the material I had planned."

"Wow, what a shame." As soon as the words leave his mouth, she angrily scribbles in the margin of her book. Except the ink doesn't write into the page, instead transferring onto Ariel's skin. Countless insults scratch into it, but they are nothing he hasn't been called before. Calliope looks so smug with her head held high. She had better be careful, or her crown will slip one day.

Calliope leads him inside to the library. Now he has to deal with the second oldest, Clio. He hasn't seen her in centuries, cooped up in her library all these years. She has a wreath of olive leaves around her head, black hair pushed off her round face. She holds a heavy leather bound book at her side, a pair of rounded bifocals at the tip of her nose. Her golden robes are opaque, no glitter like Erato or Urania.

236

Calliope and Clio dislike making a big show of their appearances, more focused on their craft. What a boring way to live.

Clio mutters to herself, shuffling between the maze-like halls of golden shelves. Ariel holds a stack of books in his arms, assisting Clio in her rather mundane duties. "Everything has to be in its place," she says. "Without order, we would be no better than demons, living on pure whim."

He doesn't have an answer to this. He must say though, her brief lectures on the history of the gods are rather entertaining. Today's lesson is on Hera and her Garden. As if he didn't live through it all himself.

"Now, you must first understand, I'm not one to sugarcoat things." She talks at him in a similar way to Calliope, their voices both having a similar velvety quality. "So I would implore you to take my word as nothing but the truth. For without the virtue of honesty, where would we be?" She has a habit of asking him rhetorical questions. Ariel follows her as she speaks, straining to hear her. Clio doesn't bother to speak in his direction half the time. "...What do you think about that?"

"About what?"

She pauses to adjust her grip on her book. Many pages are dogeared or bookmarked with a strip of fabric. "The lesson."

"I wasn't listening."

"Sometimes I question Hera's decision to put my younger sister in charge of you. She always was soft when it came to the rudimentary. But, that's what I'm here for; to correct her mistakes. As I was saying, I must tell you the way things came to be, as is my calling as a Muse."

They pause below a recess among the bookshelves, in the very heart of the library. A tall painting of Hera sits among bright lights, glowering down at the pair from her throne. She holds a decapitated man's head in her hand.

"Do you know who that is?" Ariel doesn't get time to answer. "That's Zeus."

She lets it sink in for dramatic effect, but he doesn't understand the need for it. "She overthrew him, tired of the chaotic way he ran things. He had much to pay for, too much, in fact, that he ended up paying for it in blood. I know not where, or if, he's buried. But, it matters not in the grand scheme of things.

"Our wonderful Goddess of the Heavens crafted the Garden of Eden into her personal paradise, a place where the gods would live in peace under her reign. All gods live there." Clio side eyes him. "Well, except you." He'll remember that. "It's an honor to live among the rest of the pantheon, you see. It's where you belong. I don't understand why you would want to leave in the first place. Was it really so bad?"

"It was boring and stale like you," he says.

Clio wags a finger at him. "Now, don't go acting smart, otherwise you'll have to stay here even longer. None of us want that, now do we? I certainly don't."

"Why am I here anyway?"

Her smile is so condescending, as if she has waited years to say this to his face without consequence. "Because it's what our wonderful matriarch believes must be done. You've had it good for too long. It's time for you to be put in your place."

As Clio rounds the corner, she runs into Poseidon and nearly drops her stack of books. That is what she gets for trying to act like they are any better than him. He peeks over her shoulder at his captor, and his grin makes him want to puke.

Clio claps her hands together and sucks up. "It's such an honor to have you in my humble library. What's the occasion?"

"I came to retrieve my fiancé," Poseidon says.

Ariel takes a step back. "How many times do I have to tell you I'm not your fiancé, you delusional old man?" The hand that grabs his shoulder sends a chill down his spine.

The projector whirs to life. All light disappears as the stars show themselves and the rest of the room submerges into darkness. He expects Poseidon to be rough, to hurt him again, but he keeps his distance on the bed as they sit under the starlight. He stares at the ceiling in silence.

"I can't see it anymore," he says after a while. "Maybe my eyes are getting old."

Ariel dares to ask, "...See what?"

"Your little star. It twinkled so brightly before, but it's like someone snatched it out of the sky." Poseidon reaches as if he could grab these fake stars himself. "Where'd you put it?"

"I don't know what you're talking about."

He turns to caress Ariel's chest and his fingers are cold to the touch. "Oh, there it is. How on earth did you hide it from me?"

He slaps Poseidon's hand away. "Don't touch me. And I'd appreciate it if you'd stop rambling, you're creeping me out more than usual."

"I don't indulge in the imaginary. What I speak of is the metaphysical. That little pearl you have is something special. Out of all the treasures I've pillaged, I've never seen a thing so perfect." The so-called pearl shines in his eyes, a light that settles in Ariel's chest. "I need it."

May as well go along with it, no reason to anger him without reason. He stretches out on the bed, watching

Poseidon's transfixed face follow his every move. It is about time he return to his place beneath him. "Why would I give it to you? Maybe I'm saving it for a special occasion—or special someone."

He blubbers like a beached whale gasping for air. "No! It's mine! More importantly, you're mine! You have to do whatever I say."

Ariel stifles a laugh as he runs a hand through his hair. "You're like every other man, the moment I have something you want, you're like a dog begging me for food. As if I'd ever give anything to you."

Poseidon stands over him like he has so many times now. But Ariel's in control this time. "I'll make you then."

"If you think hurting me anymore will persuade me into handing it over, you're stupider than I thought." He yawns into his palm. The more he pokes at him, the more Poseidon loses his composure.

He tries to crawl over him, but Ariel shoves a playful foot into his chest. "It's not like I enjoy hurting you, it's simply what must be done. Hera wants me to kill your passion." Tired lines etch into his face and he clenches his fists against the sheets. "If I can do that, she'll let me back into the Garden. I'm tired and old, I don't have time to worry about whether my actions are good or not."

"Who cares what that old bat has to say?" he asks.

Poseidon laughs at that. "Trust me, I don't. I'm sure you can understand looking out for number one? It's all you do, as much as you claim to care for my nephews. I know what kind of person you are."

It is Ariel's turn to laugh, but his hurt ego gets the better of him. Still, he has half a mind to mask it as sarcasm. "What kind of person am I then? Hopefully a cute one."

He leans over him again, and this time he doesn't mind. It is almost fun taunting him without any sign of consequence. Not like that will stop him, though. "A filthy leech. You suck people dry to satisfy yourself. I've watched you flit between lovers for so long. If Ares had more sense, he'd have done something about it long ago." Poseidon shakes his head and brushes Ariel's foot away. "But love clouds his judgment. If it were me..."

A smirk draws itself onto his lips. "I see now. You're jealous of them."

His anger flares back up with a sudden change in the tides. His rough hand snakes along his thigh, a bit too tightly for his tastes, but it's mild compared to what he's been through. "You see nothing! I'm not jealous of him, what– what kind of stupid idea is that? Now stop distracting me and give me that pearl!"

"Is that why you hurt me so often?"

Poseidon's armor finally cracks as he freezes. "They don't

know what to do with a being such as yourself! My nephews are far too young and naive to know what you really are. You're one of the first, a primordial. You should be worshipped like the divine being you are."

He tilts his head and his eyes glow inside the large man's shadow. "Maybe you should convince me that you're the right man for the job."

The longer Ariel holds his gaze, the deeper he falls. For there exists depths even the God of the Sea knows nothing about. Ariel is the whale who will swallow Poseidon whole, but unlike Jonah, he won't survive to tell the tale. Fireworks go off in Poseidon's eyes, hardly even noticing the snare around his neck.

But the usual fragrance of sex carries something heavier tonight. Even Ariel can sense the finality in the desperate ways Poseidon tries to please him. It is a state he has grown to expect in the men he courts, a despair that tears them apart at the seams while he watches from the box seats. No matter what they do, nothing is ever enough. Ariel takes and takes until the only thing they have left to give is themselves, and by the gods do they give. Poseidon kneels before his body like it were a temple. The old man begs for his life as he worships him, but Ariel has no mercy in his heart. Every tongue that rises against him must fall.

After the pathetic display, a wonderful vision comes to

him in his dreams that night. Red light drowns out all other colors. Ariel lies on the ceiling of the Cathedral lobby, staring up at the floor. A man cowers at his feet who weeps pitiful tears. Once he raises his head, it is Poseidon's face that stares back.

Ariel trembles with rage and pounces on top of him, ripping into his neck with his teeth. He peels Poseidon's face off, and the bloody white of his skull shines in the dark. He expects for the stench of death to fill the air as he devours this poor man's body, but something sweeter tantalizes his senses, the fragrance of honey and fruit.

Pomegranate seeds spill out from his broken chest. and Ariel plunges his hands into the sticky mess. He takes fistfuls of honey into his mouth. Bones snap as he forces the rib cage open ever further to lap at the remnants, going as far as to lick his fingers off. Ariel caresses himself with a softness only he can give himself. Honey coats his skin with a perfume so thick it fogs his senses.

A single flame reduces Poseidon's corpse turns to ash. It lingers along the marble and builds into the silhouette of Ares. Ariel lays back, sticky fingertips running over and between his thighs, beckoning his lover closer.

"Look at me," he says. "At how plump and ripe I am. Perfect for picking."

He longs to be squeezed between Ares' hands like a grape,

to have the juices worked out of him until he is dry. Ariel's legs wind around his molten waist and his toes curl in anticipation for what is to come. His heart is so full and heavy with want, it might just burst at the seams. Ares picks his petals off one by one, even the pain giving him pleasure.

He stares up at the Cathedral floor as blood oozes through the cracks in the walls and doors. With each tremor that shakes through Ariel, an ocean of red engulfs them. After they crash together like blazing meteors, their separate silhouettes are hardly discernible. Is there anything sweeter than giving himself completely over to the one he loves?

Chapter Nineteen

The Third Chorus

Tragedy and Comedy enter the observatory. They crowd around the shell with glasses of wine. Tragedy frowns at the star map on the ceiling as they speak among themselves.

"Is something the matter, Melpomene?" Comedy asks. "Is the news today rather boring?"

Tragedy sips her wine. "The Fool falls for The Rose again. Even with a different face, you'd think he'd know better."

Comedy gives a gentle sigh and takes Tragedy's hands in hers. "I find it rather exciting, don't you? Love is so wonderful, isn't it?"

"It's predictable. Where's the death and destruction? The pain and suffering? Where's the tragedy?"

They view the past through their masks, but their faces

are empty and hollow. They have no attachment to the scenes they view. The story is but a play for their viewing pleasure, a thing they appraise with expert eyes. Something is off, but they refuse to openly say it, as it isn't their place as the audience. They have to watch til the end from the sidelines.

Chapter Twenty

Smoke

The taste of honey coats his mouth. Sweat drenches his skin and there is a warm mess inside his slacks. Dry blood sticks under his fingernails. He hardly remembers the content of the vision he had, other than the overwhelming ecstasy he felt. His heart pounds in his chest and his knees are weak when he stands. A cold breeze blows over his heart. After his run in with Asmodeus, he has turned into even more of a hermit, refusing to leave his hotel room altogether.

He paces his room. He has been trying to build the courage to act on his passion and see Ariel, but he isn't like Asmodeus. Ares prefers to think things through and every possible outcome only spells doom. But then, a knock catches his attention. Medusa stands at his door, her face hidden by the fringe on her hat. She seems to have one for every occasion. But even he can recognize her gaudy choice in fashion.

He props the door open. "What do you want?"

"Is that any way to greet a messenger?" she asks.

"I heard about what Stupid did and I sincerely apologize for his actions. I hope you still want to do business together."

"I repeat, what do you want, snake?" He goes to shut the door in her face, but she keeps it open with her hand.

She grins into his face. "I have an errand for you, a chance for you to see your little rose again."

"The Cathedral? You know I can't just walk in there, my Mother forbid it."

He lets her in after all. She takes a seat by the window. Medusa tilts her sunglasses down a smidge and slips an envelope from her clutch. It's royal blue, with a moon stamp sealing it in red wax. Medusa slides it over the coffee table. "It'll be explained once you get there."

He snatches it from the air and peels it open. "You've been cordially invited to The Blue Lounge. Located near–" the address has been drawn out as a street corner "–at midnight. We hope you enjoy your relaxing stay." He turns the paper over to see if there's anything else on the back. There isn't. "This is a joke, right?"

She files her nails, only half-listening to him. "You read it, didn't you? Go to the address. That's all you need to do."

"There isn't an address here, it's just a drawing…"

"You'll know it when you see it. It's hard to miss." She checks her watch. "You should get going, by the way. Don't want to miss your appointment."

"So you expect me to wander the city until it shows up?"

"It'll come to you," is all she says before leaving the room.

Ares showers and changes clothes. Tucking the invite into his jacket pocket, he marches out the front door. He wanders down the cold, dark streets and alleyways to find that stupid lounge. After half an hour, he gives up. He's been neglecting to feed himself and he is rather irritable, but Ares doesn't have an appetite for poorly made mortal food. He sits on the street corner under a dim street light and a deep blue light glows behind him. A slight warmth sneaks through his suit. Is this supposed to be the lounge? There's no indication. It has been so long, he can hardly remember if there's any other liminal spaces he should know of.

It is a typical coffee shop done up in shades of blue, with black tinting the windows. The Blue Lounge is written on the door in golden lettering underneath a poppy flower carved into the wood. He shoves it open, and a bell rings above his head. Ares has to slip his sunglasses off to see anything inside. The furniture is plush, with thick velvet curtains that cover the windows. Other guests slouch in their seats or lie face down on the tables, snoring into pillows set under their heads. Empty cups of tea sit in a high pile on a far counter. There are dark blue hookahs on a handful of tables.

A tall figure descends from a thin flight of stairs next to the door, one thin hand leading him down. His skin is blue, platinum hair thin and wispy, eyes golden. A blue sweater and fleece pajama pants hang off him, stars and moons cascading across the fabric. A little night cap leans to one side of his head.

"Do you have an invitation?" He speaks with a hoarse voice, as if Ares had been the one to wake him. He shoves a hand in his face.

"It's been ages since you've visited Eden, Hypnos."

"I hardly have time to visit the pantheon these days. Too much drama and fighting for me. I prefer to be where it's nice and quiet. Besides, dreams won't tend to themselves, will they?" He pulls the blue envelope out of his pocket and Hypnos silently takes it. The God of Sleep feels it, sniffing at the traces of cologne on it. The envelope bursts into blue flames, disintegrating before their eyes. "Welcome... take a seat... relax..."

Ares watches Hypnos walk out of sight. He was sure

there would be more to that interaction, but it seems that his presence here will be taken at face value. He takes a seat by the window. Another man sits on the other side with a hookah between them. He has a darker vibe than the other god with how he leans back in his seat. Black butterfly tattoos cover his folded arms. He stares at the ceiling, and his white hair falls over his face. His legs are folded, foot fidgeting in the air. His slacks look rather dusty for Ares' tastes.

His eyes don't move from their place on the ceiling, speaking with a voice of gravel. "It's been a while, Ares."

"Thanatos, I take it?" he asks. "Still up to your old tricks?"

It's almost nostalgic to see all these old faces from years prior. Although he was never close to any of Nyx's children, they were much more sociable than his Mother. "So what do you need me for? I'm sure you two are more than powerful enough to do whatever job this is."

"The gorgon requested our help." Hypnos shoves Ares' chair in for him.

"...and she gave me the job like I'm one of her lackeys?"

Hypnos stares at him, fingers tapping against the top of his chair. "You remember that dream you had, don't you?"

"Should I?"

"Who do you think made that possible?" Thanatos asks.

"So, again, what am I doing here?"

Hypnos offers him one of the black hookah hoses. "I think you should relax first. You've had quite a stressful life. We all need a little bit of relaxation, isn't that right?"

Hypnos lights the charcoal and taps Ares' shoulder to take a hit. The smoke tastes vaguely of blueberry. A few minutes of smoking, and the room spins. His vision blurs, somehow turning upside down as he dissociates out of his own body. Ares floats in the air, left to stare down at himself. His form has a wavery, smoky effect like he is underwater. When he tries to use the chair as an anchor, his hands go through empty air. The twins watch him flail with amusement in their eyes.

"This is a job better suited for Medusa, but you'll have to do." Thanatos reaches into his pocket and shoves over a pair of black shears into Ares' foggy hands, the handles theta symbols. They are the only thing he can properly hold on to. "You're going to cut those Muses' threads."

The shears are a considerable weight, Ares clutching them to his chest with both hands. "Why don't you just do this yourself?"

Thanatos shakes his head. "We choose not to directly involve ourselves in petty matters such as this. That's Eris' job."

"So, let me get this straight," he says, "I'm going to sneak in and murder them?"

"Is that a problem?" Hypnos asks.

Ares tightens his grip around the shears in an effort to strengthen his resolve. "If it means I get to see my Love again, I have no choice but to do this."

Hypnos tugs Ares down to the floor by his jacket. "You should get going before Hecate leaves without you." A vague light shines through the curtains that Hypnos ushers Ares outside towards. Hecate stands in the street, two lit torches at her sides. She has a thin black veil and layers of high skirts on, a pair of hunting boots poking out at the bottom. As he grows closer, he makes out the outline of her two other face as their eyes shine from underneath their covering. Moths flit about her. Two other arms poke out at odd angles; one carries a large worn key, the other caressing a live snake.

She speaks with three differently pitched voices, blending together at different intervals. "You'd be best to stand close to me, prince."

Inside the sphere of her light, Ares has a near physical form. A fog covers the rest of the city in a lifeless grey. All the color has been sucked away.

"What'll happen otherwise?"

"You'll lose yourself forever." Hecate moves on her way with Ares by her side. He can hardly tell where anything is on this plane.

They half walk, half float to the Cathedral along empty streets, the massive glittering jewel of the gods looking nearly abandoned in Limbo. She uses her key to unlock the great doors, passing through them as if they weren't there. They wander the halls at a brisk pace. Hecate is silent the entire time. They run into Urania, wandering the halls with her candle. Ares tries to step out of her way, but she passes through him with a shiver.

He nods to her. "Is she one of them?"

Hecate shakes her head. They continue into the library and up hidden stairs. The pair enter a small loft room. Clio is asleep in a bed in the corner. She has her own personal bookshelf over her window. An open book lies against her chest. She must have fallen asleep reading.

Ares stands over her bed with the shears in hand. As he opens them, Atropos appears over him, in all her shadowy glory. Her eyes are sightless, hands winding around his. She guides him to reach into Clio's chest, reeling out a string as thick as fishing wire. Its golden sheen is dull, glowing only near the end.

"It's about her time," Atropos says in a breathy voice.

"...Are you not going to ask why I'm doing this?"

She wrenches the heavy shears open, poising them

around the taut line. "I don't ask questions. People die all the time. Who am I to object?" With a quick snip, the string is cut. It falls apart into dust in Asmo's hand. "Another drop in the bucket."

The rise of Clio's chest slowly ceases and she dies peacefully in her sleep. With her final breath, a white butterfly leaves her lips. It flutters about the room in the torchlight before fading away.

Ares lingers in the room while Hecate turns to leave. "We don't have time to sit and ponder, prince. The night only lasts so long."

He stares at the shears in his hands. "But what did she even do?"

"Sticking her nose into business not her own." Hecate continues down the stairs with him.

"You mean with Ariel? How has he been, by the way? I haven't seen him in forever, can you tell me?"

Hecate side eyes him with all three pairs. "I know nothing of his condition. Right now, it would be best to focus on the task at hand."

"Ah... you're right." He has to steel himself for what's to come. Listening to orders is what he's good at. It's all he knows. Even though he may be the right hand to his sister's left, Hera calls all the shots. Maybe it's time he finally go off on his own after all.

They move onto Calliope, alone in her solitary tower. They walk under the awning single file. Ares climbs the spiral staircase to her secluded room, but she isn't there. Her writing desk is empty, and the chair has been knocked over as if in a hurry. From below, they hear Calliope's cry. "Urania, what in Hera's name are you doing!?"

The two Muses stand in front of the wide window. Urania forces Calliope against the glass, with a dagger to her elder sister's throat. "I'm doing what I should've done a long time ago, sister."

Ares catches a glimpse of her eyes as she turns, and amber cat eyes stare back. Deja vu washes over him. He knows these eyes, but he just can't place them. In Urania's distraction, Calliope manages to twist her arm enough to deliver a swift knee to the stomach. Urania only falters for a moment as she's bent over, but manages to catch her with a backhand swing of the knife. Blood sullies the gold silk of Calliope's robe, spattering onto the floor and wall. She yelps, but is determined to get out alive.

"What has gotten into you!?"

Urania covers her face and cries. "I'm sorry, I'm so sorry... I don't know what came over me!"

Calliope is hesitant to approach, but lets her guard down for the slightest moment to comfort her sister. "It's alright, you just need to tell me —" She's cut off as the dagger enters a gap in her ribs. Blood pours out over Urania's hands and robes as she removes the blade. Horrorstruck, tears fill Calliope's eyes. "...Why?"

Urania holds her close, corralling her over to the window. She leans in close to whisper something to Calliope before throwing her out the window. The glass shatters and the distant thud of her body hitting frozen earth is barely audible. Urania grins from ear to ear and cackles with an eerie laughter that fills the tower. Those cat eyes focus again on Ares. She presses a bloodstained finger to her lips, shushing him not to speak of this. Her candle sits on the table in front of the broken window. Urania takes it before heading for the door. There is only the one way out.

"Shouldn't we do something?" Ares asks.

"We can't. Besides, this situation isn't ours to step into. The Muses are both dead, our job here is done." She glances out the window at the moon, still high in the sky. "And with time to spare. Shall we get going, prince?"

"Could we visit someone, just for a short moment?"

"...Just a moment."

Ares leads this time, doing his best to stay in the circle of light. But his excitement gets the best of him. It has been so long since he last saw his Love, he has to look before they leave.

Hecate unlocks the door and they phase through it like every other one. Except something is wrong. Even though he hasn't stepped foot into this room, the scent of death sits in the air. Where is Ariel?

The clam shell in the middle sits open and that familiar silhouette glows in the dark. Except, on closer examination, it looks nothing like him. Blood red runs through previously pearlescent curls. The face that turns to him isn't Ariel, it is...

"Aphrodite?" Blood drips down her face and chest. Aphrodite holds a heart in her hands, chunks of which have been eaten away. A golden aura surrounds her. Her skin turns plump and soft the more she feeds. Below her lies Poseidon with his chest torn open. "My Love, what have you done?"

Aphrodite watches him with glowing eyes and his blood boils. How is his uncle dead? He was supposed to kill him! He grows dizzy and the room spins. Ares finds it difficult to focus. His form loses its shape as flames lick up his suit. He trembles with a rage he cannot push down any further, until his entire body bursts into an inferno. His mind goes blank.

He comes to in the Blue Lounge. A migraine pounds behind his eyes as the morning sun peeks over the horizon.

Hypnos sits across from him with a cup of coffee. "How'd it go?"

Ares refuses to speak of the horror he saw.

Chapter Twenty-one

The Black Cat

An unexpected face greets Aphrodite today. "Urania?" she asks. "What are *you* doing here?"

Urania stands over her bed, holding her nose at the stench in the air. "I came to wake you up, dummy. You really don't have to call me by that drab name any longer, Aph. It's about time I can let my hair down."

With a flourish of her hand and a poof of glitter, a pair of red cat eye glasses poof between her fingers. As she slides them on, her features shift and sharpen. She runs her hand through her hair and platinum blonde leaves her fingers. Her pupils turn to slits, eyes fade to gold. She smirks down at her with red lips, a beauty mark on her right side.

260

Aphrodite groans at the sight of the witch. "I should've known it was you, Eris. But where's Urania? Did you kill her?"

"Oh, she's around, probably having a wonderful dream somewhere. So don't worry about it." Eris presses a finger to her cheek, lips twisting to the side in deep thought. She bats her eyes at Aphrodite. "Although I can make that happen if you want."

This doesn't impress her. "You realize what'll happen to you, don't you?"

"You're worrying about me and yet you murdered Poseidon in cold blood?" Eris doubles over with laughter. "They'll kill you once they find out, you know! A one-way ticket to smiteville!"

Aphrodite rises at last, stretching sleep out of her limbs. It's as though she's been asleep for ages. "They have to catch me first. Besides, who'll be able to kill me?"

Eris shrugs. "You've got me there. Not many can stand toe-to-toe with the infamous Goddess of Love and live to tell the tale."

Now that she's gained back the weight she lost, the clothes she pulls into are snug. "So tell me, what made you come to this sad city?"

Eris steps around the shell, careful not to get too close to

261

the newly awoken goddess. "I go where the party is, and what bigger party could there be than with you? Besides, my Mother sent me to help you. She said, 'Eris, I need you to collect Aphrodite for me,' and *I said–*"

"Why does Nyx need my help?"

With a poof of glitter, a hand mirror appears in Eris' hand. She toys with her hair in the reflection. "Oh, she wants to get rid of Hera or whatever. I don't ask a lot of questions because then she talks forever and I don't have time for that, you get me?"

Aphrodite snorts out a laugh. "Kill Hera? When I'm all the way down here? How does she expect me to get back to Eden? Fly?"

She shifts the mirror away for but a moment. "I've got everything sorted out already. We just have to take a little trip down to Tartarus and it'll be smooth sailing from there. At least that's the plan."

Eris motions for her to stand. She flattens the mirror between her hands and it turns into a little fairy wand complete with a crystal star on the tip. She waves it around a few times for good measure before tapping it on the top of Aphrodite's head. Glitter rains onto her clothes.

"So what do you suggest we do now?" Aphrodite asks.

Eris paces, flicking the wand around as she speaks. "Well,

we can't just sit here and do nothing. Besides, my Mother's expecting you." She pauses to grimace at Poseidon's corpse. "But the only one who can take us to the station is that little prince of yours. I propose we pack up your things and wait for him."

"What a thrilling plan," Aphrodite says, deadpan. "How long will this take?"

A laugh sneaks out from Eris. "Oh, I don't actually know. Let's hope it's soon! In the meantime, we can catch up like old times!"

She blinks. "How thrilling. I suppose you'll want to have a stupid tea party like usual?"

Eris waves her wand and a cloud of glitter rains down upon them. A party hat materializes atop Aphrodite's head. "Oh, you remembered!" she croons, holding the wand to her chest. "I'll make sure to cook something up great for you two once you get to the Underworld, that's a promise."

Aphrodite tries for the door, but it's locked. "Eris.."

"You can't leave yet! This is an invite-only party and only your little boy toy is allowed in!" She adjusts her glasses and tucks a stray hair out of her mouth. "So just sit back down and let's have a little talk."

Eris sits at the edge of the bed and pats the space beside her, which Aphrodite has no choice but to take. She folds her arms over her chest and lays back, almost forgetting the corpse splayed out behind her.

"What should we do about him?" Aphrodite asks. "I don't really have the taste for ugly men at the moment."

"Well... we can always throw him out the window?" Eris asks, tapping her chin with her wand.

She sighs, unsure of how long she can handle Eris' annoying voice for. All she has to do is keep Asmodeus in her thoughts and drown out her rambling.

Chapter Twenty-two

Fire

Asmodeus lingers around the Cathedral, creeping at the very edge of the gate. He digs his teeth into his cigar, keeping one hand tucked in his pocket, the other clutching a bottle of vodka. The Cathedral has gone dark in the coming days. No light can pierce through those thick stained glass windows.

In his drunken stupor, he decides it would be a good idea to wander past the gate, zig-zagging along the lawn. He trips over his own feet–twice to be exact—as he crawls to the Cathedral's wall. Asmodeus stands, knees wobbling, yet he takes another swig of vodka that he barely tastes anymore.

"Fuckin' Ares... fuckin' Ariel... what do they think I am? A fuckin' joke?" He pounds on the glass with the bottle. "I'll show them."

He goes on like this until his hands turn numb. Asmodeus gropes on the ground behind him, and his fingers curl around a hefty rock. Putting all his frustration into his swing, he repeatedly smashes it against the glass. It splinters and shatters, leaving a dark hole tat leads into the Cathedral. He punches out more glass so he can pull himself into the lobby, but hits the floor   head first. The pain is the only thing to throb through the fog as he curses and clutches his forehead. A small dribble of blood comes away on his glove. Great, yet another thing to ruin one of his suits.

Does the universe hate him? Is this all Hera and The Fates' doing? It is not his fault he never received her blessing. Asmodeus hasn't done anything wrong in his entire life, he swears by it. He was a good child. He holds no ill will towards any of his previous victims, only regret, even though every one of them did deserve it. Is it his fault they sold their souls or that he had to crush them like cheap chalk in his hands?

But then, in the dark of the Cathedral lobby, the real question rears its ugly head; does Ariel really love him? What does it matter? Love is just another kind of ownership. You stake a claim, you offer your price, and that cute face is yours forever. Except in this case, Ares has him beat as far as a bid goes. Even so, it doesn't phase Asmodeus one bit. Every contract has loopholes to exploit.

He stumbles along at a leisurely pace, a self-satisfied grin slicing his face in half. He can picture them together now, spending the rest of their lives together until the eventual heat death of the universe. Then it will all start over again and again. Asmodeus makes it up to his room, but finds the door locked.

He fumbles with the handle, unable to comprehend why it isn't opening. What the fuck? "Ariel? It's Asmodeus."

No answer. Maybe that damned Muse has the key. Time for some more aimless wandering around this fucking maze. He spends close to an hour looking for her room, only to follow the sweet scent of flowers and summer air back outside to the greenhouse. He finds the glass doors open, revealing a dying garden on it last legs. Plants wither and flowers wilt in their pots. Erato sits near the back with dirt staining the ends of her black robes. She doesn't raise her head when he enters, too focused on holding Calliope's hand. His footsteps leave burn marks on the blessed ground.

"So where's the key? ... Hello? You alive?" He snaps his fingers to get her attention.

"It's in the fountain." There's no sense of colorful cheer in her voice. It's dead like her flowers. "I don't care what you do anymore. You can have him for all I care."

267

"What?"

"You heard me. I want you both to leave us." Erato looks back over her shoulder, eyes red from all the crying she's been doing. Asmodeus actually gives Calliope a good, blurry look. She lies there, unmoving.

"You realize she's dead, right?" he asks.

"Shut up! This is all your fault! If Aphrodite didn't come here, she wouldn't have attracted your attention. None of this would've happened." She lets out a mournful sob, covering her eyes with a hand. "I'm all alone now, thanks to you! They thought they could alter her ways, but it's clear she can't be changed. You can have her. She only brings trouble."

"This has to be a trick." He shifts closer to the fountain, keeping an eye on the twinkle in the water.

"Just take the key and go," Erato says. "I don't care where, just away from here."

Asmodeus places a hand in the water and reels back, with a contact burn on his skin. "Holy water? Really?" he hisses.

Erato is done speaking apparently. He rolls his sleeve back, gritting his teeth for the pain that is to come. He quickly dips his hand into the elbow deep water, taking a second to pluck the key out, skin burning white hot all the while. He collapses onto the stone floor, cradling his hand against his chest. The skin is raw and bleeding, barely able to make a fist. Any movement of his fingers and they scream at him to stop. Now he has even more trouble climbing back to Ariel's room, needing to use the wall to keep himself steady.

He unlocks the door and shoves it open with his good hand. "Ariel?"

Asmodeus slips into the room and collapses onto his stomach. The shell is wide open, with fresh cut roses littering the floor. But he doesn't expect Aphrodite to sit on the plush blankets in place of Ariel. She wears a white blouse, a purple ribbon around her neck. Her hair has been tied back into a braid. She too holds her hand, pressing a damp cloth to her thumb. The smell of blood swirls its way into Asmodeus' nose. He slowly gets back onto his feet.

"What're you–how're you–?"

"Don't ask questions you don't want the answer to," Aphrodite states. She removes the cloth and the fragrance only grows stronger, Asmodeus needing to cover his nose. His stomach growls. The impulse comes over him to sink his teeth into her neck and drink her blood until he is drunk off of it. But he can't possibly do that.

"I'm here to get you out," he says through his hand. She hardly notices Asmodeus' injury. "I'm fine, by the way. Just hurt my hand a bit. But again, just fine. What about you?"

She shows her thumb. There is a little gash in the center.

"I pricked myself on a thorn. It's nothing. But it's about time you showed up." Asmodeus' grin is hungry. He kneels before her, gazing up at her like she is some celestial body. But all he gets back is a thousand yard stare. She slides off the bed and heads into an unseen opening in the wall. "I'll be just a moment. I'm going to take a bath."

Asmodeus follows her in, shoes clicking against the tile. An oval tub is against the right wall of the bathroom, a sink with a full-length mirror on the opposite wall. Piles of linen towels hit the ceiling with various shampoos and soaps in the window sill. The circular window is crystal clear as it peers out into the endless sky. The bathroom has a sterile scent to it. She runs the bath and sits on the edge. Asmodeus casually plops down next to her with a smirk, smoking all the while.

"Why are you looking at me like that?" she asks.

He shrugs and exhales smoke.

She frowns. "Not going to talk?"

"There's nothing to say at this point."

She trails a hand through the warm water. Candles light themselves along the window sill. "What do you want?"

"That's an obvious question, isn't it? You, of course." He takes his cigar from his mouth. Asmodeus purposely moves into her line of sight once she looks away. Smoke trails from the corner of his mouth as he tugs at his suit jacket with a frown. Aphrodite shifts away again, but he leans back over.

"Giving me the cold shoulder all of a sudden?" He chuckles, cold and humorless. "Is this entire situation not your doing? Although there is some kind of debt I should repay you, no? After all, if it weren't for you, I'd be dead." He steps in front of her again, planting himself on the very corner of the bath. He spreads his legs, interlocking his fingers between his knees. His lips twist as he spits out his next words. "...*Thank you.*"

"I didn't stop Ares for your sake." She looks more annoyed at him being grateful than anything else.

"I implied nothing of the sort, now, did I? Don't go thinking I don't realize you're as self-serving as I am. I know you don't really love me." She looks at the floor, probably out of guilt. "Or am I wrong in that assumption? What other reason could you have to have intervened?"

Aphrodite looks him in the eye as she stretches a hand out. Asmodeus meets her halfway in order to hold it. "Love," she answers. "Now, I want to make a deal with you."

Another laugh of his rings out against the bathroom walls. "You really mean that? You really think I'd make a deal with you?"

"Why wouldn't you?" she asks. "You make deals with people all the time. Besides, I think you'll be interested in what I have to offer."

No matter how irked he is by her treatment of him, he perks up. "Is that so? What are the terms?"

"Well, I thought you'd enjoy being at an unfair advantage. I know how much of a masochist you are."

Smoky, thick desire rolls off of him at the implications. "Hm… you know me far too well. The terms, then?"

"If you can get me to where I need to be, I'll give you everything you've wanted from me," she says.

He hums like the cat that got the cream. Her answer leaves much to the imagination, but it isn't necessarily a bad thing. Will all his waiting finally end? "That's a very risky offer, you know. I'm sure you realize what the implications of a deal like this are, yes?"

Aphrodite flicks hair back off her face. Even after being trapped, she is as vain ever. "I'm well aware. I wouldn't be making it if I didn't already know what I was getting into."

"And to think you would give yourself up so easily? For a man like me?" The words seem negative, but there's nothing self-deprecating about his tone of voice.

"You're the one who wants me," Aphrodite quips. "Maybe I'm just being nice."

"Very nice indeed." A thoughtful look sets on his face. He rests his elbows against his thighs, leaning over to her side. "I take it you want me to worship you or something before we're done?"

"Rather presumptuous to assume I want you to be nice, isn't it?" she asks, monotone.

Asmodeus has to turn away and bite into his thumb. "You're really just a tease, aren't you?"

Like whiplash, her twinkly grin brightens her face. "I'm not as innocent as you think I am."

"Oh, I knew that from the moment I looked at you all those months ago." He takes a long drag from his cigar to prep himself, but he doesn't exhale the smoke. "Now then, shall we get started?"

"What do I do first?"

"Here." He gestures for her to come closer. "This is the easiest part, by the way."

Hesitation strikes at the most inconvenient time. Aphrodite's hands are as soft as he remembers. He closes his eyes as she is the one to initiate the kiss. The smoke turns a shade of purple as it leaves his lips.

"Is that it?" she asks.

He takes a deep breath and slips his eyes shut. Removing the glove from his right hand, he holds it out into the light. A curly script slowly writes itself above his thumb, Aphrodite's name shining as if it were fresh ink. He flexes his fingers, humming at the new addition. "Your turn."

She presses a hand to her neck, sucking in air between clenched teeth. Just as she did with him, he pays her pain no mind. "...What happened to me?"

"Just a little parting gift from me, think of it as a token of my affection." Aphrodite dives for the mirror, hands on either side of it. She cranes her neck from side to side, zeroing in on the purple kiss mark, whipping around to face him. "What did you do?"

She accuses him as if it wasn't something she signed up for. Here he thought she knew to read the fine print. "I seal my deals with a kiss, you see." He rubs at the fresh tattoo on the back of his hand. Aphrodite presses a hand to her lips. "Sad that you can't feel the real thing yet?"

The hand tightens into a fist. That rebellious look is back in her eyes. "If we ever get that far."

He takes a sharp breath. "You have little faith in me. Need I remind you who you're dealing with?"

She says, "a two-bit demon."

Asmodeus wags a finger at her. "And you're nothing but an absolute brat. But I still love you, don't I?"

He slips his jacket off and undoes his tie, but keeps a steady gaze on Aphrodite as he goes through the motions painfully slow. Button by button, he undoes his shirt, opening it enough for her to get a good look at his firm chest. Names write themselves onto his skin, only to be crossed out with a dash; dozens of them, all dull and fading. He cups his chin, making sure she can see his name on the back of his hand.

"See all these names? Proof I always keep up my end of the bargain—and I don't intend on going soft on you just because of our history. Business is business." Asmodeus stands in front of her, and leans to the side to get a better look at her own brand, eating up every inch of bare skin. Aphrodite stares back. He leans close to whisper, his hot breath brushing against her cheek. "There's no reason to act so coldly, you know."

"I have nothing left to say to you," she growls.

He takes a quick look around the high walled bathroom, then back to the window. Gears visibly grind in his head. "Now, how do you propose we get you out of here?" Aphrodite maintains her distance, a vacant glaze over her eyes. Asmodeus messes with the window, in a rather good mood after sealing their contract. If everything goes as planned, maybe she will pick him over Ares? "Tell me, are you afraid of heights at all?" he asks.

She delivers her answer with all the humor of a corpse. "Would I be where I am if I was?"

They must make an odd sight, walking through the streets half-dressed. Asmodeus doesn't really care how they look, focusing on getting as far away from the Cathedral as possible. A fire burns in his chest as he takes the lead, not from anger, but nerves. He has limited time to get home before one of Them comes to retrieve him. All Asmodeus can do is keep his eyes forward. Any one of the people passing by them could be one of his brothers in disguise, or in the absolute worst case, Hades himself. He almost wishes he would send his pompous brother Lucifer rather than have to deal with his Father's temper.

Aphrodite is silent beside him, not that he minds. Less distractions means less to think about. They trudge on through the streets. He watches lesser demons eye her, Asmodeus having to force forward a commanding air. Vultures, all of them. As if he would give them the satisfaction of even touching her. He follows the faint sound of music, a steady bass line pulsing in his ears. From across the street, The Black Mamba's sign blinks at him. He makes a move to cross the street, but Aphrodite puts up resistance.

"...What's the problem?"

"Do I really have to go in there again?"

His usual rough-looking colleagues loiter outside. He looks back over his shoulder. "We'll be fine, alright? These pond scum wouldn't dare try anything." He tosses a smirk in for extra measure. "Not when there's a prince in their midst."

She follows along while Asmodeus does his best to

intimidate with the state he is in.

"Look who just showed up!" a man yells.

"And here we thought you were above making visits to our little spot?" another woman quips. "Or is this for business?"

"Here we thought you were all about pleasure, eh?"

They all share a laugh at his expense. It takes immense effort not to pop off on these lowlifes, but he has to bear it with a grin.

"And who's your little friend, Asmo?" The woman leans in close to Aphrodite, cigarette holder between her fingers. "She's a looker."

"Don't touch the merchandise," he says.

She leans back with a frown.

"To save me time, tell me, where's the Lady of the House exactly?"

"Her usual place. You of all people should know that better than anyone." She folds her arms. "You are the only person she trusts, after all."

He has to laugh at that one. "She treats me like a squatter."

"And you're saying you're not?"

Asmodeus has had enough of entertaining these fools, pushing through to the front of the line. The same bouncer holds a clipboard in his clawed hands. "Name?"

He stares up at him. "You know me, man. It's Asmodeus."

"It doesn't ring a bell," he says as he unclips the red rope. "Cute friend, by the way. Try not to enjoy yourselves too much."

The club has blue lighting this time around. A slow, dreamy track sets a mellow mood for their visit. Asmodeus grabs them an open booth and orders them each a drink. He wraps an arm around Aphrodite's shoulders. She seems put off to say the least.

He has to yell over the music. "C'mon, loosen up a little bit!"

Aphrodite looks out to the crowd. "I really wish we didn't come here."

"We had to, baby. I need to speak with Medusa about something."

"Couldn't I have stood outside?" she asks.

He shakes his head. "I can't risk something happening to you. For fuck's sake, I just broke you out of jail practically. The least you could be is a little bit grateful."

She eases up under his touch. "There we go, just relax, have a drink."

He reaches into his pants pocket to retrieve a bottle of pills, screwing off the top. He took it before he left for the Cathedral. They look like the same black ones the other club goers are taking. He shakes out a few into his palm and downs them with a sip of his drink. After only a few moments, they kick in. His anxiety plummets, and his flame sits low and blue as he slouches.

"What even are those?"

"What, you've never seen designer drugs before?" His usual crisp tone warps. "You should try em, they really know how to take the pressure off, y'know?"

Aphrodite takes a tentative sip of her drink and eyes him with vague concern. "Should you really be taking those? Don't we have somewhere else to be?"

He waves a hand at her. "Ah, what do you even know? You've been stuck in that Cathedral for how long now?"

"What does that have to do with anything?" Asmodeus shoves a pill into her hand, closing her fingers around it with a pat. "A gift. Don't say I never did anything for you." She frowns and tries to put it back in the bottle, but Asmodeus grips her by the sleeve. "You'd really turn down the time of your life like this?" He gazes at her with twinkling eyes and a pout. "You only have to take it once. That's all I'm asking."

She stares down at the pill in her hand, decidedly downing it with a sip of her own drink. She keeps a hand

279

around the glass and stares into the black wood of the table. "...You doing okay?"

"I feel like I'm going to be sick," she mutters.

"That's how I felt at first, babe. You have to power through it." He nods matter-of-factly. He only tells half the truth, however. This pill, the answer to all his problems, will make sure they stay together this time. "If you're going to get sick, the bathroom's in the back."

She leans over the table, her forehead against the edge. Her hair hair glints in the light and Asmodeus has the urge to run his hands through it. It is so beautiful and silky, how could he not? But then she sits back up. Her playful nature winds down a bit, loose hairs sticking to her face. "It's really hot in here, isn't it?"

Aphrodite fans herself with a folded up napkin, as if it would do any good at quelling the pervasive heat.

"I'm used to it." He shifts closer to her. "I thought you liked it warm?"

"*Warm,* not stuffy. I feel like I'm melting." She sits in discomfort, although the glow in her cheeks is nothing but attractive. He tucks one of the stray locks of hair off it and his hand lingers along her jaw.

She leans in equally as close. "You're acting rather strange."

"You're just so pretty, I can't help myself." Asmodeus presses a hand to his chest. "My poor heart just aches every time I look at you."

An odd feeling radiates through his body. It is different than his usual high, a sickly sweet undertone in his throat. Love is all he can think of. All he wants is for her to pour her heart over him. He doesn't even care how overpowering it would be, preferring her love in its rawest form. "God, I love you," he whispers to her.

At least she gives a half-hearted smile. Even that makes him forget to breathe. "I already knew that, didn't I? But I can't help but feel there's something else you're not telling me. What is it?"

His gaze floats over to the dance floor, tugging Aphrodite along. Normally Asmodeus would get high out of his mind while he visits Medusa's club, but he has to keep a relatively level head to make sure she stays out of trouble. Aphrodite's well-being is his priority.

"I'm not sure what you mean," he says, trying to put her worries at ease. "Let's dance, shall we?" He muscles their way to the very middle, Aphrodite bumping into him every now and then. Asmodeus makes an effort to vibe with the mellow music, but she only watches his silly display. They are close enough that they can easily whisper into each other's ears. "What's the matter? Not having fun?"

"You didn't answer my question." She stands still.

"What question? I thought we were dancing."

"I want you to say it." Her features scrunch up as her anger rises.

Asmodeus acts as coolly as he can, whispering in her ear again. "If you want me to tell you how much I love you, I'll gladly do so."

"That's not what I mean, you're avoiding the question!" Her breath is like fire on his neck. He lets his fingers float along her waist. He isn't too sure he wants to cling to her when she is like this—wouldn't want to lose a finger or two.

"Add it to the list." Aphrodite doesn't look very satisfied with his answer, but it is not exactly a problem he wants to deal with. He can put it off for later. "You still wanna dance with me?"

"I don't feel like it. Besides, it's not like I know how." He stifles a laugh. "A goddess that doesn't know how to dance? Don't worry, I'll teach you."

He tries to get her to move along to the sensual beat, get her to loosen up for him. They dance in the dark among the mass of sweaty dancers, wholly absorbed in themselves. As time passes, Aphrodite finds the rhythm, even going as far as tugging her braid out. They grind on each other. The bass blares and it is as though Asmodeus' skin is vibrating apart. A vague red haze rings his senses, and the sound and lights blur together, like a neon mixed drink that he greedily gulps down. Aphrodite must be in the same boat.

"You need another drink, baby?" he asks. Asmodeus has to put his ear next to her mouth to even register she's speaking. Her hair swirls in soft, glittery hues that gather around her shoulders. She gives a curt shake of the head. "I'm okay... I'm good."

He glances back to their table. "We can go sit back down if you like?"

"We can do *whatever* you want." Already flirting a bit? She sure isn't one to waste her time once she's in the mood.

They return to the relative privacy of their booth. Aphrodite assaults her next drink with fervor. Her head lays on the soft back of the seat, seemingly staring at empty space. Asmodeus nurses his bourbon, glancing to her every now and then. Should he say something?

"You doing okay over there?" he asks.

"What do you care?"

"Because I just do."

"You don't have to lie. I know you only care about when you get to sink your teeth into me." She lays out on her side, letting out a sigh. "I already sold my soul to you, so what else could you possibly want out of me?"

"I want more than that," he mutters, swirling the remainder of his drink around. "Did that thought ever cross your pretty head?"

"Once or twice."

An extended pause falls in their laps. Asmodeus cough into his hand. "I need to wash my face."

She abruptly sits back up. What a lousy way to fake being tired. "Why don't I join you?"

He holds eye contact with her, challenging her with his stare. "Is there something you want to say?"

She tilts her head. "I think you talk too much. Have you ever tried not doing that?" Again with the overt implications. As badly as he wants to give her what she wants, it will have to wait. Just another thing to add to his growing laundry list for when he gets out of this disgusting body. He eases out of their booth and she stands beside him. "The thought has crossed my mind once or twice. Are you planning to do something about it?"

"Sure. *After* you wash your face."

He takes her to where the bathrooms are. More demons loiter in cliques in the hallway, their smoke clouds floating near the ceiling. Asmodeus lets her guess which door it is.

"It's on the left," he says.

"I knew that!" She shoves the door open.

The tiled floors are blood-red, everything else a shiny black. It is cramped, neither having much wiggle room, Aphrodite having to lean against the counter. He turns the water on, accidentally elbowing her as he washes off his face.

"Ah, sorry." He goes to splash himself with more water, but Aphrodite grabs hold of his wrist. His heart races. "Do you need something?"

The hungry eyes of an animal stare him down. "Perhaps."

"I'd love it if you'd let go. Trying to wash my hands and all." She says nothing. "I'm telling you to let go."

"Are you telling me what to do?" That's when Asmodeus knows he made a mistake. Her eyes glow that familiar rainbow hue. A wave of heat rises through his body as she runs a finger under his shirt sleeve; the only way she can get at any bare skin. Asmodeus has to hold onto the edge of the sink to remain standing. It is as though his brain scrambles the longer she touches him. A layer of pink slowly blots out all other color.

He manages to gasp out a breath. "Please! I'm sorry!"

She releases him. Asmodeus' knees give out and he has to use his bad hand to catch himself. Thank god he can barely feel pain. There is still a dull throbbing in his fingertips. Aphrodite demurely checks herself in the mirror, acting as if she didn't just try to completely bewitch him.

"I thought things were going smoothly?" he asks.

"I wanted to remind you who's in charge." She looms over him like the shadow of death itself. "Don't ever tell me what to do."

Asmodeus seethes and loses his cool. He yells, "pardon? I didn't realize there was a hierarchy here?"

She eyes him from her side. "I'm sorry, who just collapsed? It certainly wasn't me."

"I still own your soul, or did you forget that?" He sneers at her.

Aphrodite doesn't miss a beat. "Tell me, which one of us is truly being owned here? As far as I'm concerned, you're nothing but a guard dog. Besides, what do I need a soul for? It's just something to be used for leverage, like anything else." She sits on the counter, tugging Asmodeus close by the knot of his tie. "So, let me ask, who's in charge of who now?"

He actually swats her hand away. "Don't speak to me like I'm a fucking plaything. It's about time you show your true colors, Aph."

"And here I thought you liked it when I did this?" She presses a foot into Asmodeus' crotch, his dick betraying him for the last time. "I don't."

"You're lying again, Asmodeus," she says.

"You should really warn a man the next time you decide

to spontaneously flirt." He puts on a bitter smile. "I would've had a good line picked out."

"We're not flirting."

Asmodeus nods, slow and cautious. "Ah, so we are, then."

They stare into each other's faces, seemingly at an impasse. "Would you kindly remove your foot from my crotch?" he asks.

"Give me a good enough reason to." She presses it down a little bit harder.

Asmodeus brushes her foot to the side and steps between her legs. He forces her against the wall, hands under her armpits. "I don't need a reason to do anything. But, now that I know we're flirting, why don't we turn up the heat a little bit?"

She cocks her head. "I'm already sweating. How much cornier can you get?"

Despite her bratty attitude and compromised position, he can tell she is enjoying herself. Perhaps a little too much. He pushes in further, forcing her to spread her legs more. His hands float down over her thighs. "I suggest you to put this position to memory, by the way. You'll be in it quite often in the near future."

Even without truly touching her, he can sense the

tension. He takes a deep breath to smell the sweet blend in the muggy air; sweat, alcohol, and... honey. A knowing grin cuts his face in half, an a spark of black tints his eyes like a shark at the first signs of blood in the water. "See that? I know exactly how to get your blood running," he pauses to wet his lips, "among other things, that is."

The bathroom door eases open, Asmodeus unable to keep it closed from the spot he's in. "Hey! There's someone in here already!"

Medusa dips her sunglasses low, a neon yellow scarf wrapped around her head. A black bodysuit adorned with a daisy pattern shines in the light. "There you are, Asmo." Medusa cranes her head around the corner. "Who exactly are you dry humping today?"

"...Uh... No one."

"Really? Whose crotch are you grinding right now then?" She looks from him to Aphrodite, who makes no effort to hide. They don't answer her. "Well?"

"Well, I think it's about time I tell you–I broke her out–"

"You didn't."

"...I did." Medusa pulls him by the collar, away from Aphrodite and out into the hall. "I can't believe you! You realize what you've done, right? The weight of this?" She looks back to the goddess lingering in the doorway. "And why would you bring her here of all places!?"

"Well, I need your help," he says.

Her lips twist into a sneer. "I'm in utter shock. You really thought it was a good idea to bring her to my place of business? You know who's going to show up, right?" She shoves a hand into his chest. "You know he's probably on his way right now!"

He avoids her accusatory gaze, looking down at the way they came in. "As if he'd actually show up himself–"

"You kidnapped a goddess, Asmodeus! Right out of Hera's sanctum!"

"And what of it?" he asks. "You think your Father would send one of your stupid brothers over this?" Medusa throws a hand out to Aphrodite. "You remember who she is, right?"

"As if I could forget?"

"Then you must remember how everyone hates her guts. I don't have time for this, you know. Just get out here before you make things worse." She lets out a deep groan. "You couldn't have just met me at the apartment?"

"I–"

"Wasn't thinking, I know. Get out here."

The three make their way out of the bathroom, Medusa artfully slipping through swathes of people under the influence. Asmodeus and Aphrodite not so much. She props a nearby door open, waving the duo into a dark room. Comedy and Tragedy sit at the bar with more bottles of wine around them. A pile of tulip bouquets lean against the legs of their stools. They all have a little card with *"From Medusa"* written on them in red.

Medusa is rather serious as she greets them, giving them both a solemn hug. "I'm sorry for your losses."

"Ah, it's alright! There's no use in dwelling on the fact they died," Comedy says. "Isn't that right?"

Tragedy quietly cries into her glass of wine. "How can you say that? They're dead!"

Comedy shrugs. "Why don't we celebrate their lives rather than act like we're at a funeral? We should save the tears for then." She giggles at herself. "Remember when Clio scolded me for laughing too loud in the library?" Tragedy doesn't answer. "Anyway, it's not my problem that the story was ridiculous! I couldn't do anything else other than laugh!"

"She had fiction in her library?" Tragedy asks.

"I don't know, did she?" She takes a sip. "Anyway, where was I? I forgot, haha!"

"Do you ever stop talking?" Comedy lightly smacks her arm.

"I'm trying to remember them in a good light, okay! They were practically blood."

"I didn't really care for either of them, but you're right," she sighs.

"Ladies, we have guests." Medusa claps her hands, gesturing to Asmodeus and Aphrodite as if still they are a couple.

Tragedy swirls her drink before downing the rest in one go. "Who else did you drag in here against their will?"

"Don't say that, watch her turn us into her next statues!" Comedy snickers into her hand.

Tragedy's delivery is dry. "Please, put me out of my misery."

They sit on the other side of the bar. Medusa pours them each a glass of the same wine the Muses are having. Asmodeus pops another pill and almost falls out of his chair with how much he slouches. He takes shot after shot that Medusa serves him until all the colors blur together into a neon rainbow. He swears he can feel the universe unfold.

"You'd better be paying me to replace this alcohol." Medusa leans against the bar.

"Huh?" He leans close with a hand to his ear.

"I said, you're fucking out of it," she says.

"Pssh you're out of it!" He grumbles, going to take yet another shot. It's empty, though. "Hey uh... bartender what's up?"

"You've had more than enough."

"I'mfuckinfine!" Asmodeus leers at Aphrodite, alcohol strong on his breath. He makes an effort to enunciate as he spits out each word. "How bout you? you look pretty fine to me."

He goes to touch her and the pretty lady frowns. "Asmo, you're drunk."

"Yeah I'm high too what about it?" Asmodeus speaks to Medusa without turning to her. "Deuce I need your help."

"With what?" She pours Tragedy another drink. "Stowing your date away?"

"Yeah!" He fires a finger gun at her. Comedy cackles at him as he falls out of his seat. He gets back up as if he didn't just smack his head on marble flooring. "The fuck you laughin' at blondie?"

She ignores him, turning to Tragedy. "So, which of us will do the honors?"

"I suppose I have no choice, do I?"

With a smack to the shoulder, Comedy laughs. "Nope!"

With yet another dreary sigh, Tragedy shuffles out of her seat and down a set of stairs beside the bar. Asmodeus didn't even know they were there. A cold draft enters the hot room. He unbuttons half his shirt and tousles his hair. They follow after out of curiosity, but hopefully it won't kill this cat. Death would really put a damper on his high.

Tragedy's voice drifts from below. "You have someone to explain yourself to, little prince."

Asmodeus stumbles along the stairs beside Aphrodite, feet sliding step by step. He can barely register where his limbs are anymore. They reach the bottom, and piles of skeletal bodies make up the walls. He didn't know there was a catacomb under this shitty night club. You learn something new every day.

In the middle of the room, a dead tree sits with wilted branches. Coffins line the small hill of black dirt. A woman sits upon it, a long scythe grasped between her hands. She is bald, her upper half bare save for a large, bloodstained ruff collar. Layers upon layers of skirts fill out to a rather regal silhouette, colored black and purple. Ravens perch all over her.

Tragedy climbs the hill. "Merope, I have to contact the Underworld."

"Who wishes to speak?" Her voice is as fragmented as Hesperia's, but much lower pitched.

"Melpomene and," she looks back to Asmodeus, "guest?"

Merope nods, slow as a snail. "I'll just be a moment."

Merope's eyes close and smoke pours out from her eyes and mouth to fill the space. They stand in endless darkness.

"State your case, Muse. I have limited patience." A silky baritone implores her. A pair of white eyes glow through the gloom. "Who sent you to contact me?"

Tragedy bows her head. "I requests your assistance."

"Why would I want to help you, a Muse?" Fake flames flicker to life throughout the chamber, and the smoke morphs into the vague shape of a throne. A dim glow settles onto Hades' visage. He sits on his throne of black wood, leaning a hand against his bearded face. His long, messy hair frames his face that blends into the shadows. A five-pointed crown sits atop his head. His chest is bare, with robes of swirling smoke. He glowers at Merope. "You had better give me a good reason for intruding."

A sigh like a spring breeze comes from beside him. Persephone makes a grand entrance, sitting just out of sight in the shadows. She leans over his shoulder, keeping a gentle hand on his arm. "Aren't you acting a bit rash? Why not hear her out first?"

"I suppose I could." Hades waves a hand. "Speak."

"With all due respect, I assume it's something to do with one of your sons," Tragedy says.

A roaring fire lights from behind the throne. "Excuse me!?" He stands, squaring his shoulders. "Which one of them did it?"

"From the faint smell of alcohol I picked up," Tragedy crosses her arms, "I'm lead to believe it was your youngest."

"...*Asmodai*." He spits it out through gritted teeth. Persephone can only grin back at her husband. "Persephone? Is there something you know?"

She looks away and runs a hand through her curls. "I *may*... have let him go."

"*You what!?*" he yells.

Persephone holds a hand up to stop his rant before it begins. "We couldn't just keep him here for another millenia–"

"He's the baby!" His nails dig into the armrest. "He needs to be supervised! You know how he is!"

She folds her arms. "He needed to learn for himself how the world is."

Hades throws a hand out. "And we can clearly see how well that's gone after what happened with that red-haired whore!" He holds a hand to his forehead. "I wish you would've discussed this with me, Dear."

"You would've said no," Persephone says.

"...And we can both see why that would be my answer, yes?"

She runs a hand over the back of his throne. "Would you calm down so we can fix this?" She nods to Tragedy. "I doubt she wants to waste her time with our pointless arguing. I already let him go, all we can do now is try and find him."

"I suppose you're right," he says. He slumps forward with his hands clasped together. "Forgive me for my outburst."

Tragedy nods along. "You're only trying to parent them."

He sighs. "At least *someone* understands where I'm coming from."

Tragedy clears her throat rather awkwardly. "So, may we move on with this?"

"Let's."

The rest of the chamber is rough bedrock, sharp angles somehow managing to form beautiful architecture.

Hades surveys the open chamber. "So, where is he, then?"

"You mean your son?" Tragedy asks.

"Yes? Asmodeus? Where is that little fuck?" He spits out, balling his hands into fists. "Once I find that damn child I'm never letting him out of my sight again!"

She glances around. "Ah, about that..."

"Do you know where he is?"

Her cloak swings as she scans behind her. "I actually, uh, don't know where he went off to... he was just here a moment ago."

Hades' eyes twitch as he lets out a loud scream. *"You had better fucking find him, then! Or do I have to do everything myself?"*

Asmodeus cowers in the doorway, just out of sight. Fuck, fuck, fuck... he is so fucked. If he thought he was in deep water before, he is as good as dead now. He crawls up the stairs after he trips over his own feet, tugging Aphrodite with him. He may be sober with how fear pumps through his veins.

"What's going on?" Aphrodite asks. "Why is your Father so pissy?"

"We have to fucking go!"

"Where?"

"Anywhere but here!" Asmodeus drags her out of the private room. Medusa calls after him, but gets lost in the crowd. They have to get out of this choking heat. He shoves the double doors open and steps into the cold air.

Chapter Twenty-three

Butterfly

Once they are back out in the cold, Asmodeus acts rather strangely. He keeps his eyes low and hands shoved into his pockets. Gone is the aggressive desire and drunken stupor, checking every few moments to make sure Aphrodite is still by his side as they walk down the curb.

"We have to get as far away from here as possible," he says.

"What are you on about?"

Asmodeus stops dead in his tracks and rakes fingers through his messy hair. To her, he looks more like a rabid animal being ever so slowly pushed into a corner than a dignified prince. She can see it in his bloodshot eyes, desperation to do whatever he can to escape. He takes a deep, gasping breath as his possible outs grow smaller and smaller.

"Do you hear that?" His voice cracks as he presses his palms to his ears. He shrinks in on himself, kneeling on the wet pavement. Asmodeus quietly whimpers things to himself Aphrodite can hardly make out, in a tongue she can't understand. She stares down at the man she pledged her love to all those months ago. What exactly could make him quiver in his shoes like a small child?

"I don't hear anything," she says.

"It's the train–they're really coming–fuck, fuck–" He tugs her down to his level, the stench of alcohol wafting over her face. "They're going to come and everything's going to be ruined—"

She tugs out of his grip. "Who, Asmo?"

"I shouldn't have done this! I'm so stupid!" He grips the sides of his neck so tightly he breaks skin, and black blood oozes out. "You have to go back!"

"I thought we had a deal?"

"My Father will void it. He'd never allow something like this to happen!"

The wail of a train whistle cuts through the city streets, the sky darkening to a blood red the longer it goes. There is the sound of wheels on a track growing closer, only for it to fade out entirely once it's on top of them. Asmodeus' face drains of color and he ceases his breakdown. Back is his sarcasm and snark. "Took you long enough to notice I was gone, Father."

"I don't have time for your games, Asmodeus." Hades' voice slithers around them. "Get up. We're leaving."

Aphrodite glances over her shoulder to catch none other than the God of the Underworld standing behind her. Even though she is never had the pleasure of meeting him, other than at a royal christening or two, the name sends a minor shock through her. Hades in the flesh. But none of his generation frighten her. He has chosen to trade his robes for a shiny suit and tie.

He keeps her silent with a glare. "So, we meet again, Aphrodite."

Persephone stands nearby in a high-collared pink dress. Pleated ruffles swallow her, and the little crystals sewn into the fabric glint in the light. Cerberus growls and bares his teeth at Aphrodite. "I suggest you step away from my son."

"It's not her fault, Father!"

"You think I don't know what she's done? She's arguably the worst out of all the gods in Hera's heaven!"

Asmodeus' voice rises. To think he would dare speak

back to his own parents like this. "She hasn't done anything!"

"It matters not what promises she made. Did you forget what she did to you?" Hades leans down to his level. "She didn't do it—"

"But she did." He nods to himself, a hand gripping his son's shoulder. "She was the one to lead you astray, was she not? She charmed you and when the dust settled, where was she?"

Asmodeus mutters, "with Ares."

"She didn't care about you." Persephone kneels on his other side, taking Asmodeus' face in her hand, inspecting his right side. Angry tears bubble up from within. "Is that why you choose to hide your face like this?"

"No! I'll do anything! Just please don't make me go back, please!" He actually grovels before them.

"You know we have no other choice." She straightens and tightens her grip on Cerberus' leash.

"Would you prefer we leave you for Hera to find?" Hades shoots a look to Aphrodite. "I'm sure she's already contacted her, isn't that—"

"She doesn't know anything about that, Father," Asmodeus says. "She's the one who put Aph in that tower."

"Why do you insist on buying into her charade? She's pretending!" Persephone's beautiful face dampens with disappointment.

Asmodeus eases back onto his feet, trying to hide Aphrodite from their glares. But there is only so much of her this small man can cover. "You're so set in your old ways, you can't even realize she isn't what you think."

"What is she, then?" Hades scoffs.

He challenges his stare with one of his own. The little prince musters all his confidence to utter a single word. "Mine."

He slips off the glove from his left hand, Aphrodite's name shining in the light.

Hades expression darkens with such anger, she swears he might accidentally snap. *"You little shit!"*

Asmodeus backpedals. "Father, please..."

He rushes toward him with a finger in his face. *"You'll wish you were dead when I'm through with you!"*

"Just hear me out, will you!?" Asmodeus holds his hands out to keep him at bay. He glances to Aphrodite, and there is a fondness in his eyes, a manic gleam bordering on obsession. He keeps his gaze on her as he speaks. "If I go, she has to come with."

"As if I would agree to such a thing." Hades nods to the ground beside him. "If you aren't next to me in the next two seconds–"

Asmodeus drops to his knees, hands clasped together. "Please, please, please! I beg you to reconsider!"

"What are your intentions with her?" Persephone asks.

"...What?"

"We asked you a question, Asmodai." He tilts his head. "It seems you've already made a deal with her, so what will you do when the time comes for her side to be fulfilled?"

Asmodeus looks down to the side, avoiding their expectant faces. "Can't we talk about this later? There are other things more important—"

Aphrodite speaks up. She's watched this scene as a bystander for too long. "You plan on devouring my soul, don't you?"

"No!"

"No?" they ask in unison.

He only clams up even more. "...Shouldn't we be getting home?"

Hades presses his face into his hand, voice muffled. "Fine. We can discuss this on the ride home."

With that momentarily settled, Persephone snaps her fingers. The world inverts on them. Darkness surrounds her, a heavy heat on Aphrodite's shoulders. Their glowing eyes are the only thing she can see. Persephone's shoes click on marble floor as she pulls Asmodeus to his feet.

Hades tosses an insult over his shoulder. "Are you coming, harlot?"

Electric lights flicker to life from either side of the large tunnel. Aphrodite follows the trio out onto the platform. Columns descend from seemingly impossible angles. Indistinct chatter echoes around her, like she is in a crowd, but the room itself is empty. In the middle, their train sits, coughing smoke into the underground, the door to their compartment sitting open. Smoke billows out from open windows, as well as from the engine. The train's metal is warped into the vague shape of what it is trying to be. Aphrodite can make out a ghostly shadow standing in the threshold, checking its watch.

Hades drags Asmodeus to the train, their silhouettes reflecting in the floor. His hand grips the back of his son's neck like a puppy as he forces him into the first cabin. Persephone steps in with Cerberus afterwards. Aphrodite is the last to board. The parents sit directly across from their son. Asmodeus has his face in his hands, looking at Aphrodite with an expression unbecoming of him. His shoulders and posture are tight, lips a firm line. Again, what could Asmodeus possibly be fearful of? She takes a seat close to him, but he shrinks away.

The train slowly begins its descent, rolling away from the warm lights, and into darkness. For the first while, none of them speak, let alone look at each other. Something is about to change, for this is the end of the line. She doesn't know what will happen. The click of the wheels on the tracks is all Aphrodite has to focus on, watching pale lights briefly illuminate the inside of the carriage.

Persephone loosens her grip on Cerberus' leash, letting him curl up on the bench next to her. "Asmodeus," she says in a soft voice, "are you ready to answer us yet?"

"I guess I have no choice, do I?" The glow from outside ceases to exist. Black covers them. "I didn't want things to get this far... I never thought you'd have to see the real me again. I never wanted you to, but I suppose I can't get everything." He lets out a pained cry, the sound of his fist making contact with the wall ringing out. "Story of my fucking life."

He lets out a deep sigh, eyes flicking to stare into her face. His words drip, weak and limpid. The purple glow grows larger as he gets closer to Aphrodite to vomit out his feelings. "I just want you so badly, I guess I didn't think things through. I'm sorry. But–but maybe now that Ares isn't here, maybe you'll want me back this time? What do you think?"

"*Asmodeus.*" Persephone is as tired with this as he is.

"Mother, please! I know you think I'm stupid, but I can't

fucking help it, okay!?" His hands hover over Aphrodite's and tears drop onto her skin. "I tried everything, I did everything you wanted, but why did you abandon me?"

"I'm sorry?"

The glow intensifies, illuminating their faces in color. A maniacal grin plasters onto Asmodeus' face. She is close enough to kiss him. "I'm not going to let anyone get in the way this time, you hear me? I'll do anything to keep Ares from you…" He trails off, biting onto the bottom of his lip. "It'll all be worth it, won't it?"

Hades pulls him back to scold him. "You have to let her go, Asmodai."

Just as quickly, his emotions slingshot him back into a puddle of tears. "You're one to talk, Father!" A flash of light fills the inside of the cabin, as Hades' eyes brighten. "Did you not kidnap Mother? How is this any different!?"

"Do *not* bring your Mother into this!" He shoves his son against the seat. "This is between you and her!"

Asmodeus looks down at his hands, his scream drowning out the train. It's full of anguish. "Stop the train! Please! Stop it! I don't want her to see me!"

"I can't do that," Hades says. "We all have to face ourselves at some point."

They roll into cold light that Aphrodite has to shield her eyes from. Once she adjusts, the sight before her is pathetic. Hades stands in the middle of the compartment, and Asmodeus cowers in the very corner on the floor. Back is his lavender skin and ram horns. He weeps   tears of pitch as Hades keeps his eyes downcast, stiff as a statue.

"Asmo?" Aphrodite leans over to get a better view, but he turns further away.

"No! You'll think I'm disgusting!"

"Please, you can trust me." He lowers his hands just a smidge. His left eye is its regular purple, but the right is milky white, that half of his face marred by deep burn scars. He loudly whimpers.

Persephone kneels down beside him, pressing her son's crying face into her shoulder. "It's okay, it's alright," she whispers, keeping her eyes on Aphrodite. The emotion in the room fails to seep under her skin. She doesn't know why she should feel sorry for him.

Hades speaks with absolute contempt. "*You* did this to him."

Aphrodite isn't sure what else to do but apologize. "I'm sorry–"

"Don't bother. It won't fix anything at this point." He

turns to Aphrodite with a sniffle. To think an intimidating figure such as Hades would be brought to tears. "I only allowed you to come along because it's what he wants. I would rather see your pretty head on a pike for what you've done to him, but he's unable to get over his silly love affair."

Asmodeus nudges his Mother off to better lash out at him. "Don't say that! It meant more than just an affair!" He crawls over to Aphrodite, holding her hands. "Please, don't listen to him! It wasn't your fault, you didn't know Ares would be there–just–blame it on me!"

"You have to let go," she says.

"I'm not letting go of you this time, didn't you hear me before? I love you! I'm not going to let anyone or anything get in the way of us!" She can only stare into Asmodeus' good eye. His whole body shakes, and he collapses, tears overflowing. His lone eye remains locked on her face. "Why won't you let me have you?"

The train rolls into the station. They collectively stare down at Asmodeus. Cerberus stretches out his legs, awakening from his nap.

"You will *not* speak of this to anyone." Hades lifts Asmodeus as one would a crying child. "Against my better judgment, you'll stay with my son for the time being, until this all blows over. No one can know you're here. You know nothing. Do we have an understanding?"

The hell hound wanders beside Aphrodite.

"I don't have any other choice, do I?"

Hades humorlessly grins. "There's always death."

"...I see." She pulls herself to her feet as he brushes past her. Persephone takes Cerberus' leash in hand once more.

They step off the train and onto the new platform. The station is as ornate as the last. Just like before, it too, is empty. There is an eerie silence throughout. Aphrodite keeps her eyes forward. All she cares about right now is getting to wherever they plan on staying. Today has been a very long day. She is coming down from her minor high, and she isn't used to everyday aches and pains.

They trek through empty brick streets, and Aphrodite has to cover her mouth to keep from choking on the thick fumes. Lights dance from windows, making the silhouette of their shadows shapeless. Dozens of blocks pass by and her feet grow weary. The colors shift from red and black to shades of purple, the buildings on the street newer brick. It seems as though they are either brothels or bathhouses. The sky is the same malevolent purple she remembers.

Hades and Persephone stop at the metal gate to

Asmodeus' estate. "We're here."

Persephone pauses to look over her shoulder. "Coming?"

She picks up the pace, but sways with exhaustion. As they usher her through, the front door shuts behind her. Aphrodite climbs the stairs to the portrait. The colors are fading, a thin layer of grime obscuring the smaller details. "He still has this up?"

Persephone stops beside her, sighing at her ignorance. "You really still don't understand, do you?"

She gestures to the painting in question. "What I understand is that your son is obsessed with me."

Hades adjusts Asmodeus in his arms. He's stuck between a rock and a hard place, as he ascends the right flight of stairs. "Let me put my son to bed and we can discuss things."

Persephone lets Cerberus loose. Hades saunters down a dark hallway and out of sight. The wood floors creak under his footsteps, as he returns a few minutes later. He whistles low to his pet, running his fingers over Cerberus' head as he comes to his side. Aphrodite taps her foot impatiently, and Persephone snorts out a little laugh.

"What?" she snaps.

"Nothing."

"You have something to say?"

She rests a hand on Aphrodite's shoulder. "You might be older than both of us, but you act as if you're Asmodai's age. Have you not learned anything in all your years?"

"Of course I have! I've learned that trusting people only gets you hurt. It's something that you should've taught your son before he met me."

A grimace darkens Persephone's features. "Bite your tongue! He doesn't know what to make of his feelings, that's all. You on the other hand, you know exactly what you're doing."

"So what if I do? Is there any harm in looking out for myself?" Aphrodite wraps her arms around herself like a cocoon. She fake cries as an attempt to garner sympathy. "You people act like I'm a monster. I have feelings too, you know! Sure, I killed that ugly bastard Poseidon. But besides that, don't I deserve a happy ending like everyone else? Don't I deserve love too?"

Cerberus growls as Persephone levels an icy gaze onto her. "You don't know what love is, you witch."

She throws her hands in the air and stomps up the stairs. "You don't understand me! None of you do! I don't know why I waste my breath."

Aphrodite leaves the Goddess of Spring behind to find her room. It has been a while, but she is sure she can trace the steps. That familiar pink door comes into view and she collapses on her big bed. In hindsight, she almost appreciates Asmodeus for all the work he put into it. She stares into the vanity mirror and lightning lights up her reflection to reveal Tragedy and Comedy beside her.

Tragedy holds her mask over Aphrodite's eyes. "It's about time. One of your suitors is on his way and his soul burns like the sun. The little prince has been scorched before, but will you too melt like Icarus, lustful rose?"

"Who do you think you are to preach to me?" She swats the mask away. "I don't even know you people, how did you get in here?"

Comedy giggles. "We always give very good advice, you know. But people seldom follow it. It's a real shame you don't like listening, we're really trying to help you out here."

"I don't need your help! Just leave me alone!"

Aphrodite stands and screams her frustrations out. Another bolt of lightning strikes and the duo are gone. She throws herself onto the bed to shove her face into a pillow. What she thought would be a nice break is looking to be even worse than the Cathedral. At least Poseidon isn't here to grope her anymore.

Act III

The Underworld

Chapter Twenty-four

Fallen

Ares remains at the Blue Lounge after his discovery at the Cathedral. It is almost as if Hypnos is trying to keep him here. For what, he hasn't the slightest clue, but he can only drink so much tea before it grows old.

Thanatos is nowhere to be found, having disappeared at some odd hour of the night. Ares has finally been able to do what Hypnos has so subtly egged him towards, true relaxation. He's had much time to stew with his thoughts without Aphrodite or Asmodeus to worry about.

He sits at the same table for days, watching his surroundings until they blend into an abstract swirl of blue. The color that once enraged him, turns into a source of peace. He is Hypnos' only customer. All the others have left at this point. The light that illuminates his table casts the rest of the cafe in darkness.

It's in those shadows that he finds his solace. But those two, creatures of desire that willingly hide from the light, are no stranger to the dark. Ares, who once thought that the blazing sun of Eden was the only thing that mattered, blinded by his Mother's forceful will, realizes he is not meant to follow. Ares is no one's soldier, not anymore. So he trades his red suit for black, and throws away the rings along with everything that evokes the opulence of the Garden. With the fire that fuels his heart, he will carve his own path.

The bell rings as the front door opens, but Hypnos doesn't pay the new patron any mind, instead keeping his place near the door. A flash of blonde hair tells Ares exactly who he is dealing with. Eris slips into a seat at his table, still in the white robes from Eden.

Ares asks, "what do you need? I don't remember asking for help from a witch."

"You're one to talk, seeing as you're in love with one." She drapes an arm over the back of her chair and folds her legs. Her eyes twinkle in the light as she stares him down. "I come with news, ripe fruit for the picking."

With a flick of her wand, a golden apple materializes on

the table between them. "All you have to do is–"

"I'm not playing any of your games, Eris." Ares too, leans back in his chair, an unimpressed air about him. Her confidence falters at the calm energy he exudes. "I assume you know where they are?"

"How'd you know they were together?" Eris bends her wand with both hands.

"Where else would they be?"

"Fine, you win," she says. "You should be glad I don't have time to play with you, I have a party to throw." She wiggles her fingers in the air and closes them into a fist, sliding a black boarding pass across the table like she's dealing cards. "You have a train to catch, prince."

He leans over and inspects it. The boarding pass' gold lettering tells him it's only one way. "What is the meaning of this?" he asks. "Where exactly did he take her?"

Eris grins and raises her crystal wand. "Why don't you take a ride down to your relatives and see for yourself?"

With that, she taps her wand over her own head and she poofs into a cloud of glitter. Ares inspects the pass further, and the destination would surprise him if he didn't already have a hunch of where they were hiding. Of course, the Underworld. There is no other place that slime ball could take her without him following.

Chapter Twenty-five

Soft

Today marks the beginning of the end. It's as though the days previous were a lucid dream, one he is only just waking from. Asmodeus takes in his surroundings; the plush bed under him and the ashtray full of spent matches on the nightstand. He stays completely still, not even bothering to blink, and it rushes back to him in waves. He left Medusa's club and was forced onto a train back home by his well-meaning parents.

But most of all, the image of Aphrodite shines in all her splendor. Her face is devoid of anything he can put a name to. There's nothing in her eyes as she looks upon him. As it is, she is the valuable queen, and he is but a pawn. He almost doesn't care how she treats him, as long as he gets to bask in her presence. She could even eat him alive.

Hunger gnaws at his bleeding heart, and after waiting all this time, he knows the love of his life will reject him. But all he can do is wait for her to open up and give herself to him. Even if nothing changes, he will never let her out of his heart. Asmodeus is afraid of the only thing that may save him, learning to let go.

When he tries to sit, his neck and back ache with pain he's never felt before. He admonishes himself for being overly careless and ambitious. Medusa was right, he never would have gotten caught if he stayed low instead of painting a spotlight on his back. All Asmodeus wanted was a place to hide Aphrodite for a little while. But he found a way to fuck even that up. A hard knock resounds against his door, to which he asks, "what do you want?"

"Asmodai, I want to discuss last night with you. Will you let me in?"

The illusion of choice is obvious when the doorknob turns open before he can answer. Hades blocks the only way out, but it's not like Asmodeus has the energy to bolt. Everything about his Father seems frustrated and tightly wound.

"You realize the gravity of the situation you've gotten yourself into, correct? Everything you do reflects back to me, did you know that, Asmodai? That's why I had to keep you where you're safe. You've gotten me into a very precarious situation. I meant to return her where she belongs, but do you know what I noticed?"

"...What did you notice, Father?" This isn't looking very good.

He taps his chin and his eyes float over Asmodeus' room. "There's just something off about her. Have you noticed? Something... different. Why is that? Do you know, Asmodai?"

He tries not to crack under the pressure as his Father stares him down. Maybe something *has* been different about her, but it's nothing he would notice. "I don't know what you're implying. What exactly do you think we did?"

"Asmodai, you know I don't have time for bullshit. What happened to her?" he asks. "I know you know something. Stop hiding it from me."

Asmodeus wrings his hands and searches for the right words. "I might have noticed..."

"Get on with it, boy."

"She's sick, isn't she?" he asks.

"Please tell me you're not stupid? She's pregnant, Asmodai!"

Hades lowers his face into his hand and the weight on Asmodeus' shoulders grows with each passing second. He isn't sure what to think, he's never seen his Father like this before.

"You're joking, right? We haven't done that in... god who knows how long."

"Do you think Hera cares about that? Why do you think she's tried so hard to keep Aphrodite imprisoned? She doesn't want word of Ares and you fighting over her getting out!"

"But, can't you just–"

"No, I can't 'just deal with her.' Hera is one of my equals. She could easily strike me down as I could her." Hades pauses. "And what would you do without me? Who would be my heir?"

Asmodeus says, "Lucifer, of course."

His Father paces in front of his bed, clenching and unclenching his hand. "I hardly trust any of your brothers, you know this. Lucifer in charge?" Hades shudders at the thought.

Asmodeus has grown used to being lectured on a daily

basis, so he keeps his eyes on the floor. He doesn't understand why any of this is news. Hera and his Father have been at odds since before he can remember. "So what does Aphrodite have to do with this?"

Hades sits on the edge of the bed and all the anger drains from his face. A heavy sighs leaves him as he focuses on the ceiling. He can't look Asmodeus in the eye. "We told you before that she's bad news, didn't we? I think it's in your best interest to let her go."

"Stop trying to separate us!" Before he can continue, Asmodeus throws back his covers, and slips on a fresh dress shirt from the dresser. "You're wrong about her, Father, we love each other!"

"How are you so sure?"

"And this pregnancy bullshit?" he scoffs, avoiding the question, even he knows there's an inkling of truth. "As if that'll change anything, even if it's true!"

Hades hasn't in him to stop Asmodeus from leaving. He prowls down the halls—angrily buttoning his shirt up all the while—to the only place she could stand staying; her old room. He hasn't stepped foot in it since their falling out, afraid he would fall to pieces if he lingered for too long. He doesn't even know when it happened or what triggered it, but as the lonely days stretched on, the hunger grew.

Asmodeus was a man without water, without food, perpetually in a state of yearning. The thing in question was clear, but the waiting–oh, the waiting–pushed him closer to the edge. To have something, the very thing you have wanted your whole life, right at your fingertips, but still unable to call it your own? Truly maddening.

But, now he can fix all his mistakes. Her door is open a crack and as he reaches out a hand, the reminder of his unfortunate visage shines in the doorknob. He is sure he has disgusted her enough. The things that worked before don't seem to do the trick, his overt attitude only hurting his chances. Is that not what drew them together in the first place? Surprisingly, it opens, and the fragrance of flowers creeps out. Aphrodite appears as shocked as he is, clearly not expecting him to be standing outside her room first thing in the morning. She has a towel laid over an arm, curly hair let down.

"What are you doing?" she asks.

"I- uh-" He stumbles and stutters for a good few seconds. "...Good morning."

She blinks, and refuses to look directly at him. "Could you move? I'm trying to remember where the bath is."

He steps out of her path. Aphrodite glances down each side of the hall, decidedly wandering down the left. He follows at a distance. "I could help you find it—"

"I'll be fine, but thanks."

He goes on so he can stay beside her for just a little bit longer. "--This castle is bigger than it seems. You'll get lost without my help. I hardly think you remember where everything is."

She pauses to throw a glance over her shoulder. With a soft scowl, she asks, "you'll be needing a bath too, I assume?"

He chooses not to retort, instead pointing a finger down the hall. "It's the third door on the left."

Aphrodite quietly tuts at herself. "I could've figured that out myself."

"I'm sure you could've."

Asmodeus watches her slip into the room. He waits a few moments before going in himself, not wanting to come off as too eager, not after everything that happened yesterday. When he steps in, the focus of his affection has stripped. Clothes leave a trail to the gigantic bath. The brick walls and floor are old and worn. Aphrodite wades knee-deep in the water. Roses float around her and steam rises from the surface, Asmodeus unable to do much but stare. He is a moth to a flame.

"Plan on coming in any time soon? It's lonely in here." She shoots him a fiery look.

Asmodeus removes whatever clothes he just put on when her back is turned, and sinks into the hot water. He keeps to the wall, too afraid to creep into her bubble. However, Aphrodite shifts closer as she ties her hair up. It takes all his determination to keep his eyes at face level. Somehow, she still finds the energy to be a tease after everything that has happened.

"You'd best be careful, my patience can only go so far." Asmodeus only allows himself her face to focus on, choosing to zero in on her softly pursed lips.

"And here I thought you wanted to lose control." She blows a stray hair off her face. "All that big talk and yet here you are, hiding inside this empty house."

His voice drops to a whisper. "I just don't want to hurt you."

She laughs at him. "You can't hurt me even if you wanted to! No one can."

"What of my Uncle?" Asmodeus quickly averts his eyes so she can't burn them out with the daggers she points at him.

"Excuse me? What about that dead bastard?" Her voice

echoes through the bath.

All he can do at this point is ramble. "I don't think you realize how much I love you, I just don't want to hurt you like he did--"

"*I'm fine!*" Aphrodite screeches. "Sure, he treated me like a common whore, but he got his just desserts in the end. Poseidon is no more! He's gone! I beat him!" She strokes her own soft skin, and even through she seems to only be a plump and delicate woman, hidden strength coils within her muscles. It's no wonder everyone both fears and worships the primordials.

He goes on as if he didn't hear her. "—you're not as okay as you think, Aph. You've been acting strangely! You're not the same woman I fell in love with, something has to be wrong."

"...I said I'm fine, didn't I?" The anger dies down, leaving a single burning flame. She holds herself now as she turns away. "But even if I weren't, what's the use in acknowledging it? I'm supposed to be a powerful goddess, I don't have time to deal with pain. I've *dealt* with it by killing him, isn't that good enough?"

"...You can't ignore it forever," he says. "I'm sure after the ordeal you've been through, I can only imagine how you feel."

She snaps, "I'm not even close to being traumatized! You know nothing about what I've been through!"

Asmodeus grows closer even as she hurls insults at him, hugging her from the right side. He rests his face against her shoulder and stares up into her eyes, as he's done so many times before. "You're the only thing I want in this world. Nothing—not even this can come between us, I promise."

She doesn't know what to do, he can read it on her face like a billboard. Aphrodite, The Goddess of Love, the woman who indulges in intimacy on a daily basis, freezes.

A tiny voice squeaks out of her, "let go—"

"I'm not letting go." Tears get caught in his own eyes, watching her cry like he never has before. She winds her emotions into a taut line when she is around him, so he hasn't had the chance to see her vulnerable. "Never again." They cry together for a few minutes. Aphrodite pulls away toward the center of the pool and once the light hits her, his own sadness drains away. Her entire being, down to the way she holds herself, brings him back to an era long gone. Back to when he thought they were together. Even her voice carries a nostalgic softness.

"Asmodeus." At last, her smile, the one ray of light he has, warms his face, but her words stab at his heart. "I know you care, but that beautiful fantasy you have of me doesn't exist. She's gone. She's never coming back."

"Don't you think I know that? I only want you–it's all I've wanted!" he says.

"I'm all that's left." Even as her tears shine in the light, Aphrodite holds her head high. "You always knew that I'd hurt you, and I'm sorry for what I've done. I know you think I'm the love of your life, but you're wrong about me. I'm only going to hurt you again. Why can't you see that?"

He has nothing to say to that. She climbs out and dries off as if she hadn't just verbally struck him down. She slips on the shirt she has worn for the last twenty four hours and leaves. Once the door closes, the little prince cries his heart out.

After a few minutes of calming down, Asmodeus wanders the hallway back to Aphrodite's room. He knocks on her door but gets no answer. "Are you there?"

The door muffles her voice. "I don't want to talk anymore."

"I know, I'm sorry, but..." He isn't sure what to say anymore. Why is it that he's lost his quick wit? "Maybe... maybe we could move on from this? I can't fix this, I can't fix anything. I know that."

To his surprise, the door eases open enough for half of her face to fit through. "If you know that, then why do you bother trying?" She yawns into her hand, looking rather weary.

"Are you doing okay?"

Her nose crinkles as her expression darkens. "Why do you care? … For your information, I'm just tired. It's not like I'm sick or anything," she mutters. "Now, can you get out of my room?"

Aphrodite closes the door in his face. The creaking of the floorboards tell that she has gone back to bed. He waits. Her voice rings out. "Do you still need something?"

"…No."

"Then can you, I don't know, leave?" she asks.

With nothing left to do, Asmodeus decides to wander. There is no sign of his parents, who have seemingly disappeared from the manor. So he descends the stairs, taking a right into the open den area, and shoving the curtains closed. He settles on one of the couches, and with hands folded over his stomach, he means to keep an eye on the upper hallway. Just in case Aphrodite decides to leave her room, of course.

With a snap of his fingers, he lights the fireplace. The crackle of burning wood is the most pleasant background noise. Aphrodite is the source of his anxiety as well as the only thing that can soothe it. As time passes, the knot in his stomach unwinds. All they can do is take this a day at a time.

Chapter Twenty-six

Fear

The dark room greets her as Aphrodite jolts upright, holding the covers against her chest. The rain continues to pour outside her window as if she expects anything else. A heat lingers among the cold, radiating from the center of the room. A shadow stands out in the armchair.

"Asmodeus?" she calls. A loud snore is the only answer she gets. Aphrodite flicks on the lamp beside her to show that he is, indeed, asleep. His head leans to one side as he slumps in the chair. His shirt is half-buttoned and his shoes lie upside down on the carpet. Standing next to him, she stares on. She doesn't know when she would get a better chance to see his face at peace. If it weren't for the scars desecrating his features, his beauty could rival that of an angel. She asks again, "Asmodeus?"

He stirs from sleep, groggy and soft. "Ah, what are you doing up already?" A loud yawn sneaks up on him.

Aphrodite tightens her grip on the sheet she drapes around herself. "What are you doing in my room?"

He takes a long while to answer, rubbing at his good eye with his thumb. "I wanted to be here when you woke up."

"*Ah.*" The corners of her mouth quirk up.

"What?"

"How cute. Don't tell me you're getting soft on me."

Asmodeus makes a face and turns away to sulk. The armchair is too heavy to move. "I'm not cute."

She shifts back in front of him. "Sure you are."

His eyes focus elsewhere. "Did you do something new with your hair? It looks curlier today."

"Don't try to change the subject," she says. While he isn't looking, she takes the chance to slip into a silky nightgown, roses embroidered along the hem. Aphrodite tosses her hair back, and tugs a knot out with a finger.

Asmodeus leans forward with his elbows against the

armrests. The chair is much too big for him. "I'm sorry... for earlier. I admit I went a bit too far pestering you. I just don't want to lose you again."

She leans close to the vanity mirror, one hand on the counter, the other roughly brushing her hair out. "But what this is all leading to then? Do you not plan on going through with the contract?"

"I..." He crumbles. "I didn't want any of this to happen, not like this." He digs his claws into the armrests and squeezes his eyes shut. "I was bluffing, okay?"

"*Sure,*" she snorts out.

"You have to–you believe me, don't you? I just wanted to get you out of there!" he sputters. "I had to do whatever I could to do that! It was all a smokescreen! You think I ever plan on collecting your share?"

Aphrodite stares him down. She rubs at the tattoo on her neck with a scowl. "A deal's a deal, is it not?"

"I could talk to my Father? Have him annul the contract?" A lopsided grin paired with the hopeful twinkle in his eye shows just how deluded he is. What he hopes for is but a pipe-dream, an impossibility.

"You can't just do things and think everything will turn out alright, Asmo. You can't play games with people and expect them to love you back." She's had enough of this circular argument filled with empty promises. Even as hypocritical as she is, she has to convince herself she's right in the end. "What's going to stop you from killing me? Even this could be an act to get me to drop my guard."

"You really think I'm faking my love for you?" His tone is hollow. His seat and the side table knock back when he stands. "Don't you even try implying that!"

"Or what? You'll kill me?" Aphrodite looks back at him. "Do it then. Take my soul."

"No!" he whimpers.

With her own hand around her neck, her fingers glide along the middle of her chest and lightly press against her heart. "It'd be easy for you, I'm sure. Ripping my heart out without raising a finger... or would you prefer something more passionate?"

"Please... stop it.. I love you." Thick tears roll from the corner of his eye.

"Maybe if I keep talking you'll snap and eviscerate me." She can't stop the visceral words from flowing, like one can't stop the tides from changing. "How would that be? My body ripped apart, strewn across this room." She eyes the decor with a sad shake of her head and pouting lips. "The stains would never come out. Even if you replace the carpet or the wood itself, it'd still be there–for you." Asmodeus kneels on the floor, mumbling out apologies, claws tearing marks the finely embroidered carpet. His chest heaves as he cries. Aphrodite squats down a few feet away, cupping her face in her hands. "I imagine you'd keep my head as a memory, so you could always look at me and torment yourself."

"Why are you doing this to me?" His burning eye locks with hers.

The smile she gives him is sickly sweet. "You should know better than anyone that love is a cruel thing."

Asmodeus crawls to her, but she evades his attempt at grabbing her ankles. "I can fix this! I can talk to Ares, I can convince him to do something!"

She retreats to the bed, wrapping an arm around the post. The straps of her nightgown droop over her shoulders. "He'd burn you to a crisp before you ever opened your mouth."

"It'd be what I deserve," he says, "after everything I've put you through. If you were the last thing I saw, I'd go to the guillotine with a smile."

Her smile remains steadfast, but it doesn't reach her eyes. "You're completely obsessed, you know that?"

He grins back. "There isn't anyone who deserves it

more."

She digs in the wardrobe, pulling out something that she never wore; a pink robe as equally as thin as her gown.

"Where are you going?"

Aphrodite pulls the door open, only giving "out" as an answer.

"You can't leave the grounds, if my Father catches you–"

She pauses only for a moment to allow a laugh to bubble out of her. "I didn't say anything about leaving the castle, silly."

"Then where are you going?" Asmodeus nearly trips over his own feet in order to follow her. He has to rush to keep up with her long strides.

She marches down the hall. "Outside, of course!"

He rubs at the tears still shining on his face. "But it's pouring out?"

"Your point?" she asks. Asmodeus follows her down to the ballroom. There is a thin coat of dust over the chandelier and staircase banisters from disuse. Aphrodite hops down the path from the terrace, step by step. The greenhouse is at the end, but it is abandoned. She doesn't mind the rain in her hair as she stands at the door.

Asmodeus calls from the safety of the awning. "Get back

here!"

"I want to see if the door is still there," she says, trying for the handle. It refuses to budge.

His voice grows closer. He uses one of his suit jackets to shield her from the rain. "It's locked. There's nothing in there anymore. Can we go back inside where it's warm, please?"

"Where's the fun in that?" she scoffs.

"We've been through this, Aph. You're not getting sick like last time."

"What happened to the demon I fell in love with?" She pivots to face him, rain dripping down their faces. "Can't you at least try to have some fun?"

Asmodeus looks at her with sadness in his eyes. The bags are deeper, with frown lines between his brows. "That's the kind of thinking that got us here in the first place. Can we please go back inside now?" Aphrodite steps to his side to take the hand he offers. They stroll back into the ballroom like a pair of lovers taking a break from the afternoon weather. But the softness only lasts so long, Asmodeus squeezing her hand. "I'm not letting you go as easily as I did before. Even if this manor were to burn down, nothing can separate us."

"I appreciate the gesture, but–"

He holds a finger to her mouth to shush her. "I know it's not realistic, but can't we enjoy the time we have together? Pretend like nothing's wrong—for a little bit?"

Asmodeus leads her to stand underneath the chandelier. The dust has been wiped off, its hundreds of dangling crystals glinting in the light. Even the mural is brighter, its wonderful colors glowing like they were just laid down.

"When did you have the time to do that?" she asks. "We haven't been gone that long."

The static of a record player echoes from a far corner. A piano ballad plays, only for it to pause and restart. Asmodeus is unable to hide his annoyance, yet he pulls Aphrodite in with an arm around her waist.

"You're not seriously trying to get me to dance, are you? Is that what this is?"

He beams at her with a wide grin. "C'mon, let's have some fun while we still can."

He leads for a minute before they find their rhythm, even if it is only swaying back and forth on the ballroom floor. Aphrodite holds onto him like it is their first night together again. She doesn't even mind when the record plays for the third time or how her feet ache. The chandelier lights up Asmodeus' face, and she sees him in a way she has neglected for so long. There are things in her heart she refuses to look at, things that creak and moan, but for a single second, she finds the feeling that she's been yearning for, love.

For the first time in her life, regret fills her like liquid cement. She freezes in her tracks and their dance falters. Aphrodite breaks down into bittersweet, ugly tears. If only she could go back to a time when she had the world wrapped around her like an old blanket, when all she had to worry about was what she would get up to next to get a rise out of Ares.

But everything is slowly spiraling out of her control, and all she can do is watch as it falls through her fingers like water; down, down, down the drain it goes. Back to zero she goes, racing down into oblivion like a shooting star. There is no use in pretending, she has no one but herself to blame anymore.

"Are you alright?" he asks. "Did I do something? I'm sorry–cut it! Cut the record!"

The music comes to an abrupt stop.

"You don't need to worry about me, Asmo." She dabs at her eyes with the back of her hand, smiling through the tears. "I'll be fine."

"But you're not fine! See? I told you something was

wrong," he says, taking her hands in his. "Let's go back upstairs, you should be resting."

"I don't need any more sleep!" She pulls herself free and heads for the den. He remains at her side the whole way, continuing to pester her with well-meaning suggestions.

"Don't walk so quickly! You should sit down! I'll make you some tea!"

As much as she usually adores being fussed over, it is rather odd coming from Asmodeus of all people. Something has to be wrong for him to act like this. "What are you hiding from me?" she asks as she whirls around.

"Nothing!"

Aphrodite tries to make her way to the stairs, but Asmodeus nudges her to the couch. He even pulls it closer to the fireplace as she uncomfortably watches him struggle.

He pants, "you're not cold now, are you?"

"If I say no will you stop?" He dabs at sweat on his forehead, taking a seat beside her. "I'd love to, really, but I just can't in good conscience let you treat yourself like you did before."

"*Before?*" she asks.

"Did I say that?" Asmodeus forces a grin, one she only brings out when he's hiding something. "I meant, you know, like... before this all happened?"

Aphrodite straightens her posture to better tower over him. She watches him squirm under the spotlight of her stare. "I really don't. Why don't you tell me?"

"You'll kill me if I do." He preemptively gets off the couch so he has a head start. She rises along with him, her face darkening the longer he takes to answer. "So, uh... you're pregnant."

Asmodeus is about to make a run for it when he seems to realize she hasn't moved an inch. Her lower lip quivers with the threat of a crying fit, but Aphrodite's eyes remain hard and cold. "What do you mean 'you're pregnant?'" she asks. "That's not even possible. How the hell would you even know that?"

His fingers curl around empty air as he gropes for something to say. Leave it to a man to fail to have the right words at a time like this, but he eventually gives her what she wants. "My Father—he told me! I'm sure he wouldn't lie to me, he's had several sons, after all."

She wipes at her watering eyes as she asks, "so who's the father? Does he know that too?"

"...I'm sorry, I don't–?"

"What good are you if you can't even answer a simple

question!?" Aphrodite throws her hands out as if to knock into something, but there is nothing but an armchair nearby to smack. "Whose child am I carrying? Is it yours?"

A softness returns to her face as the thought enters her mind. She presses her palm to her stomach, her fingertips digging against the thin fabric over her skin. It could be his, or Ares', or even... his. Like whiplash, she slingshots back into the black at the mere possibility of it being Poseidon's child. If only she could get a definitive answer, then she would know if she should rip it from her womb herself. She would rather fling herself from a high window than give birth to such a thing.

"I don't know that, Aph. *We* don't know that... not yet." Asmodeus keeps a safe distance from her, but there's a tenderness in his voice she can't quite place.

She sneaks away into the foyer with a hand along the railing. He stalks after her, muttering curses under his breath. "Don't tell me you want to be a Father now?"

"What if I did?" He takes the cigar from his mouth and waves it towards her. "You think I'm just a cruel, heartless creature, don't you?"

"Am I wrong?"

"I have needs and wants outside of you, you know!"

Aphrodite ascends the first few steps while keeping her eyes on the portrait. She has him right where she wants him. "Whatever you say."

"What words are you trying to put in my mouth?"

"I'm not doing anything, Asmo. You want to have a baby with me, right?" she asks.

He bites down on his cigar once more, muttering, "maybe I do!"

A knock at the door rattles through the entire mansion, cutting their conversation to a close. Asmodeus ushers her back into the den, leaving her to rest on the couch. He edges closer and closer, letting the door swing open. A black cat waits to be let in, winding its way around his legs. He cranes his head back around to the den, but makes sure to lock the door.

"I can't believe you left me behind!" Eris' voice whines. "After I cleaned your clothes, too! Talk about being thankful."

She lays on the couch across from Aphrodite, propping her head up a hand, displaying a golden apple in the other. There's a mischievous glint in her eyes.

"And who the fuck are you?" Asmodeus asks.

"Did Aphrodite not tell you about me?" She spares him a glance as she adjusts her cats eye glasses. "How typical. I'm your friendly Goddess of Discord." Eris extends a hand toward Asmodeus, and a force drags him across the floor so she can better grip his chin. She appraises him with a critical eye. "What happened to you?" A grin escapes her solemn front, pressing a hand to her lips in mock shock. "If only your parents had let Hera bless you, you wouldn't look so... ugly." He growls, but she shoves his face away. "Now, Aphrodite, let's have a little chat."

"I have nothing to say to you."

"Are you sure about that? We still have much to discuss." Eris tosses her golden hair over her shoulder. "I thought I told you, my Mother wants to have a little meet and greet with you, or did you forget the moment you laid your hungry eyes on this little man?"

Aphrodite acts as snobbish as Eris. "If Nyx thinks I'm going all the way to Tartarus just to catch up, she can forget it. I'm staying right here."

"Did you knock your head when you fell from Eden, Dear? This disinterested act isn't helping you look any cuter." Eris lets out a dramatic sigh, placing the apple in the air. She steeples her fingers together while grinning from ear to ear. "It's finally time to get down to business. Now, I was hoping your actual partner would be here, but this small fry will do."

"We have no business with you," Asmodeus says. "I'm not that short, either!"

"I'm here for Aphrodite, not you." She takes a look at the decor with an unimpressed nod. "I didn't break you out of jail just for you to lounge around in some cobweb-infested house, you know! I think it's high time someone give you a wake up call."

"How do you intend to do that?" Aphrodite asks. "Why have you been following me around all this time, Eris?"

She purses her lips and gives a little shrug. "One could make the argument that I'm here on Her behalf, but it couldn't be farther from the truth." Her tone turns cold once she stands. "My only interest is to see everything go up in flames, you see. Just think of how pretty it'll all be! And *you'll–*" she fires a finger gun at Aphrodite "–be the catalyst for it all. Nyx has so many plans for you."

"Why should I believe anything you say?"

"Oh, you're going to believe me." She spins the apple with a finger as it dangles mid-air. "All you have to do is bite this apple, and everything will be shown to you. Easy, right?" Eris snickers. "You won't be needing those washed-up gods' help, when you have me at your disposal."

Eris takes a step away from the apple, and Asmodeus

eyes it with suspicion. "There has to be a catch, right? I've been in the business long enough to know nothing comes free."

"Think of this as a gift." Her voice lilts into condescension. "There isn't even a contract. I don't need anything in return from you." She waves them along. "Now... bite it. Both of you."

Asmodeus holds it in his hand and the fruit glows at his touch. He brings it close to his mouth, Eris looking as though she might burst with anticipation. "If we do this, will you leave?"

"It'll be like I wasn't even here," Eris says. He takes a single bite and collapses onto the couch like a marionette having its strings cut. Eris saves no time and whirls onto Aphrodite next, something manic about the excitement in her grin. "Your turn, Aphrodite."

She nudges Asmodeus' shoulder, but he doesn't budge. "Is he okay?"

Eris shrugs at her like it is the least of her worries. "He's completely fine, I never said there wouldn't be side effects. Now, why don't you join him? When you wake up I'll be gone."

She hands her the remainder of the fruit, watching her

348

every move. She takes a bite from the other side and her eyes grow heavy. The light swirls together at the edges of her vision into a blur of colors. The apple drops to the floor. Aphrodite descends into herself, numb to her surroundings.

Chapter Twenty-seven

Nightmare

When Asmodeus comes to, there's something off. Nothing particularly concerning, but the thought still nags at him. The weight on his heart has been lifted, which certainly isn't unwelcome. Aphrodite lies beside him, still out cold. He reaches out to rouse her, but the hand that extends isn't his. It is reminiscent of a time spent within a corpse.

"Aph?" Even his voice is different; smoother, silkier.

He touches his face; only perfect skin and stubble are under his hands. There is definitely something wrong. Yet, there should be nothing wrong about being beside her. He is exactly where he wants to be, is he not? Nonetheless, he carefully nudges her by the shoulder. He runs his hand down to rest on her thigh. Even in this old vessel, he can feel every inch of her. He can actually touch her and feel the heat on her skin. The implications are hazy, but he isn't sure if he cares. He pulls her into a tight embrace.

Breathing in the soft scent of her, like salt off the sea, he cries, "please, wake up."

Her eyes stare back into his face, glancing at the arms around her. "Asmo? What's going on?"

"I think I've been granted a new face. Isn't this strange?" He presses their foreheads together. Aphrodite's hands wipe at his tears. This only makes him cry harder. "It fucking worked! She wasn't lying!" He impulsively kisses her face, over and over and over. Asmodeus mumbles "I love you" into her skin.

For the first time in forever, he hears her laugh. "What is with you?"

"I've been waiting to do this for so long. Now I can touch you as much as I want." He is still hesitant and soft with her, not sure how far he can push the envelope yet. It has been so long since that night alone. Asmodeus is afraid to say he's grown rusty. But nothing can interrupt them this time. No curfew or even Ares himself could tear him from her. He settles with holding her pretty hand, gazing into her eyes. Yet deep down, he is conscious of the darker urges he has been ignoring; monsters in the abyss. What is it about Aphrodite that makes him so... soft? So very unlike himself. What is a son of Hades doing acting like a smitten teenager?

He has the opportunity to fix his mistakes. They are finally together. The Fates have given him a second chance. This is what he has wanted all this time, isn't it? He is waited, planned, and lied. Now the moment has come. But when he stops and thinks, he falters. What does he want? Is this it?

He has spent so much time building it up in his head, like a grand chateau, that it has been the only thing in view. Why does he even want her? Because he loves her, is what he tells himself. To spite the gods above that cursed him, to prove that he is good enough, and to prove that he is more than just the life that has been thrust upon him. If he could get a taste of the things they are able to experience, perhaps his life will turn around.

All of this nonsense falls to the wayside when he looks upon Aphrodite's face; a thing so sweet, he could spend the rest of his time putting her features to memory. Everything about her is soft and round. So the question is posed once more; what does he want? To be remembered. To mean something to someone. Because love is the only thing that can't die. Sex grows old, highs wear off, but that passionate flame is something that can last forever. A thing that he doesn't need to routinely chase after, for he has the key to it right in his arms; his Rose, molded to be perfect and beautiful. Does a creature like him even deserve such a divine being?

The two grow closer on the couch, hands entangled, faces close. "How'd you do this to me, Aph?"

"Do what?"

"For the first time, I feel alive." His mouth twists into a frown. "That doesn't make much sense, does it?"

"No, I understand completely." The way she nods gives the impression of knowing, but he is sure she is only saying it to put him at ease. Aphrodite rests her hand over Asmodeus' chest and his black heart swells. "It's such a small thing, that you don't even realize it at first. Like a little seed that just needed water."

And like water she falls over him, into his arms again for a brief kiss. They fall into perfect stillness, Aphrodite resting her head against his chest. With their bindings broken, there's nothing to fret over. Asmodeus triumphed over Ares in the end, just as he knew he would, or so he wishes to believe.

"What is that?" she asks.

His eyes fall to the coffee table, an oversized cake sitting on a silver platter before them. Dozens of candles cast a dull glow that's more ominous than warm. On the sugary frosting "Welcome Home" is written in gold cursive. He grumbles, setting Aphrodite back in her original seat. He straightens his jacket as he inspects the mysterious cake.

The smoke trails from the candles seem to swirl directly above into an amorphous silhouette, tinted gold. Eris manifests in the air, glitter raining down from her body. Her wide grin is rather off putting. Confetti falls from the ceiling. She blinks, her hair wavering like flowers in the breeze. They stare.

"Hello, welcome–"

Asmodeus' stomach drops. "Why are you still here?"

Her face and voice lower, darkening into something surprising for her glowing exterior. "Is that any way to greet me after everything I just did for you?"

Aphrodite is at his side. "He didn't mean it. We're just... surprised. You said you wouldn't be here when we woke up and, well, here you are."

"I lied," she says. Eris floats around them, a silver fork poofing into her hand. She holds it out for one of them to take.

"Now, are you going to eat your cake? I made it just for you."

"We're not hungry," Asmodeus says.

"Hm. Suit yourselves." The metal erodes and rusts in her grip, disintegrating. The cake melts away onto the floor, the tiers toppling over themselves. "To think that all my hard work, gone to waste." Eris pauses, tipping her head back to look down her nose at them. "I would've taken the cake if I were you. You just love making things difficult, don't you?"

"The fuck are you on about?"

"I've already said too much." She wags her finger with a sneaky laugh, full of things that only she is privy to. Eris eyes them like subjects in a petri dish. "If I told you, you just wouldn't understand." A sigh escapes her. "It's so sad it's come to this, but actions have consequences."

"Stop being so fucking vague, you old–" Asmodeus fails to get the rest out, his tongue unable to form anything coherent.

The Goddess of Discord laughs in his face. "What's the matter? Cat got your tongue, little boy?" With a snap of her fingers, a wave travels out. A visible vibration distorts the air until everything, except Asmodeus and her, are trapped in absolute stillness. Aphrodite sits like a statue, unblinking and cold. She shoves herself into Asmodeus' space, face reflecting in her golden eyes. Raking nimble fingers through her wavy hair, she drops the exuberance.

"I dare you to finish that sentence and see what happens," she says. "Let me remind you, I'm not here for you, I'm here for Aphrodite. We have grown up things to talk about." Eris floats over her, snapping her fingers in her face. "What's the matter, Aph? It's time to stop pretending. You know you can talk to me, right? Hello? What's the matter with you?"

Far off, near the stairs, Aphrodite's voice descends, monotone and dry. It lacks all feeling as if speaking alone drains her. "I heard you the first time." Asmodeus completely forgets Eris, tripping over himself to get a look at her. There she stands, atop the stairs below the portrait. Her back is to him, dark red hair swirling down her back, dress bright against the white around her; a splatter of blood across snow. She stares at the painting.

"Aph–"

"What are you doing in my dream, Asmo?" Aphrodite asks seemingly no one in particular. She looks back down the stairs to him and her expressionless face is so familiar, yet her eyes hold a raging fire in them. "Did you do something to me?"

"...I don't know what you're talking about?"

Her attention wavers, looking through him now that he doesn't have the answer she is looking for. She brushes past him as if he isn't there. "Eris, has something happened?"

"Well, you see—"

"Why am I over there?" She nods to her double, frozen on the couch. Her raw anger seeps out with each word, a malevolence weighing down on them, but her face gives away nothing. When Eris fails to answer, Aphrodite stares. She holds the other goddess' eye, circling around her, waiting for a sign of weakness like a lioness cornering its prey.

"Must be a fluke in the system," Eris says. "There isn't supposed to be two of you."

She keeps her eyes low, Aphrodite turning to face herself. At last she lashes out, picking her double up by the neck. Her fingers clamp down, staring into the empty face Asmodeus loves.

"What is this? Where are we?" Aphrodite asks.

"I can't answer that."

She tosses the body away like one would garbage. Asmodeus, of course, catches it in his arms. Aphrodite considers him, her mouth drooping as emotion inflates her features like a balloon; anger, rage, and most of all, hatred.

357

Her once beautiful green eyes overflow with red as she weeps blood. Aphrodite takes slow steps towards him, leaving shining footprints on the tile. The lights flicker and shift in color, bright red washes everything out. The illusion of a beautiful woman melts away, her true shape coming up to the surface like a bloated corpse.

Something feral and wild, a beast that only craves flesh and ruin. The perfume she wears stinks of death, and blood drips down the middle of her forehead. Her heart glows through her chest like a beacon, a lighthouse. The beat of it drums in his own ears as if it were his own. As that light grows closer, it bathes him in warmth, and Asmodeus is but a moth to a flame. He can't move, doesn't want to, as an ecstasy he has never experienced fills him, letting out a sigh like he is taking a dip into a hot bath.

"This is who I really am—or did you forget after all that time we spent together?" She kneels on the floor and blood oozes from her skin. Fabric tears as she rips into her dress, destroying her clothes, letting the scraps fall where they may. Her voice doesn't fit the situation, sounding almost like she is bored with this game. Aphrodite speaks slowly, taking pleasure in the anticipation she ushers. "You're mine. It's been too long since I've been able to let loose. You know what I'm going to do with you, don't you?"

"Please, please tell me." He breaks out into a nervous sweat; his throat and clothes all too tight. His body is on the verge of bursting from the building heat inside him. Asmodeus tightens his fingers and remembers the other Aphrodite in his arms, drawing him from his fever, yet the skin he touches is made of plaster and paint. "I, I can't do that anymore. Not now."

"What's the matter? Come play with me, let's lose ourselves." She rolls around on the floor, smearing blood in every direction, and openly groping herself. Her fiery eyes remain fixed on him. "Come closer, I know what you want, what you need." Running a finger over her lower lip, she squeezes her breast. "More importantly, I know what you fear."

The fireplace erupts behind her, overflowing and spitting out embers. The couches and table catch flame and smoke spills into the foyer. Asmodeus desperately searches for Eris, but she's nowhere to be found.

He whimpers, "no."

"What did you just say?"

"I... I can't. I don't love you anymore. Not like that." He holds the fake Aphrodite to his chest with wet eyes. "You love that fucking doll? Is that it?" Her voice pitches high as her patience wears thin, screaming at full volume. *"She's not real, Asmo! She's just a shell!"* She is on top of him in an instant, movements stuttering like a rusty doll, tearing his fantasy away from him with ease. *"I'm going to destroy everything you love, you fucking bastard! You're going to regret denying me! This will be the last mistake you ever make."*

Her ribs crack as they snap one by one, fingertips digging into her chest through her sternum. She rips open her chest, her heart transforming into a gaping maw with dozens of rows of teeth. Blood sprays every which way as it snaps and writhes about.

"I will speak this into existence." She forces the mannequin's head into her heart's mouth. Fear paralyzes him, gluing his feet to the floor. "You will lose everything dear to you, every scrap of happiness that you have will scatter with the wind."

She shoves the body into the seemingly bottomless pit of the mouth until she is gone from sight, eaten whole. Aphrodite stands before him, nude and painted with blood. There is no one else, just the two of them staring each other down. She cups his face, her skin cold as ice.

"You know the best part? The cherry on top?" she whispers into his ear. "I'm going to be the one to do it."

She bites down into his neck, and with a jerk, she rips his head off. Asmodeus hardly feels a thing as his vision spins around the room, as she tosses him to the floor. The image of Aphrodite standing over him with that same serene grin is the last thing in his eyes. Even after being slaughtered by his lover, a trace of fondness lingers. Asmodeus will remember this moment for the rest of his life.

Chapter Twenty-eight

Emptiness

Aphrodite wades through a lake of black pitch back to the waking world. It seems as though she lost hours, unable to remember what happened before she slept. She only recalls vague sensations of calm before anger overwhelms her. It was all over in an instant, passing before her eyes like a bird in flight. Asmodeus was there–is there–right beside her, the weight beside her proof enough.

Eris promised them things would return to normal, that their pervasive problems would be fixed, but where is she now? Gone are the traces of melted cake and loose confetti, a rotten apple core on the floor the only proof she ever visited.

She goes to stand, but a throbbing pain keeps her in her seat. She is forced to keep a hand over her abdomen as it radiates down through her hips. The thought that her guts may spill out enters her mind, but she can only wait for it to end.

Her vision is blurry, looking through wavering water at the figure that stands in front of her. Aphrodite can tell she is pretty—not as pretty as her, of course—but her face blends together. She has no recognizable features beyond a pair of white eyes and dark lips, clutching her black skirts in her hands. The woman is barefoot, but there's no sign of mud on her feet. How did she get in here? She hardly even considers Asmodeus' prone form. The ongoing storm roars from the windows, the manor creaking at its call.

"It's about time I found you, Aphrodite." She grins so sweetly at her. "You nearly drove my daughter mad trying to find you. But the moon never fails to rise, isn't that right?"

"How did you get in here?" she asks.

Her grin, full of pearly white teeth that glint in the light, spreads across her face. "Don't play coy, you know who I am. The one who brings days to their close?"

Aphrodite bristles at the realization. "I thought I told Eris I wasn't interested?"

"We've been watching you, the only ones who've ever

looked out for you. I'm here to show you the way if you ever need to flee this dreadful place. Would you really turn down this offer?" Nyx offers her a hand, but the longer Aphrodite looks, the more impossible it becomes to tell who she truly is. It could be an elaborate glamour for all she knows. "Shall we get going?"

"But where? I have to wait for Asmo to wake up," Aphrodite says.

"You wanted to see the greenhouse, didn't you?" She asks this as if it was her own fault she couldn't get in. "He told you it was empty," Nyx gets close to whisper a secret, dark hair falling over her shoulder, "he lied."

"I figured as much."

She lets out a little chuckle. "He didn't *want* you to be able to leave. He's afraid, like all men are of powerful women, that once you realize you don't need him, you'll leave again."

Aphrodite steals a glance down to Asmodeus, and her blood runs cold at the sight of him. As if she's going to let another man try and stifle her. Even if he loves her, it'll be his own fault if he forces her hand. She might've been able to stop Ares, but she won't be so merciful. "So you're saying it's unlocked, is that it?"

"Come with me and I'll show you," Nyx says. "But it's a

secret. You have to promise me you won't tell anyone about it." She gets lost in her eyes momentarily, held by that commanding gaze. Nyx holds out her hand once more. "Do you promise?"

"Of course! I'm not one to break promises," she lies, while sliding her fingers through Nyx's. She pulls Aphrodite outside, leaping from the terrace to the first stone step, making it a game to try and not dirty her feet. The rain pours down on her, but she doesn't seem to notice. Aphrodite follows her, as any normal person would, by walking along the path.

"Everyone's been keeping so many things from you, but I won't. It would really be a disservice."

"Why would I ever need to revisit the Garden?"

Nyx makes an odd face, amused, but there's something she can't name that's there. "You'll see in due time, just follow me."

That generates more questions than answers, ones Aphrodite doesn't care in ever asking. They descend on the greenhouse and Nyx stands at the door with a hand on the knob. The rust and other detritus peels off, making it look good as new, and she pulls it open like it was never locked. Stepping into the greenhouse, it is as she expected it to be, abandoned.

Nyx walks confidently, not even seeming to mind the low hanging leaves brushing against her face. Large roses line the walkway and their sweet scent flows around them. She thought the greenhouse was much smaller on the outside, but Aphrodite doesn't recall the door being this far back. Nyx says nothing, the two having no sort of conversation until they find the door made of a darkness that absorbs all light. Hundreds of red butterflies rest upon it, their wings idly twitching.

"Just remember, come visit before you enter Eden," Nyx says. "I hold the key to all your wishes."

The light fades to black and the temperature drops, leaving Aphrodite in the overwhelming gloom. She looks at the rest of the greenhouse behind her, the walls closing in until it is about the size of her room. Flowers wilt and rot away, leaving empty and cracked pots, their dead leaves littering the previously pristine floor. The cold air caresses her skin like the touch of a corpse. All that's left is the door, wide and imposing. She stares into that blackness, and it stares back.

Aphrodite grows restless as the days crawl by, they seem to

last forever. At least far longer than her time spent in Eden. Although, it is rather difficult to perceive time when the sky is but an empty black void. She has no idea whether it is day or night, as it all looks the same. Spending most of her time in the confines of her room, she may as well be back at the Cathedral.

Neither Persephone or Hades have intruded much on them, Aphrodite sneaking through the halls as silently as she can muster, things creaking and bumping in the darkened parts of the manor. A heavy coat of dust clings to everything.

She watches the fake sky through her bedroom window, wondering if Hera were to ever float down from her paradise and grace their house of sin. What would she say once she saw what Aphrodite's become? She can picture the disgust and outrage on her face, but she doesn't care one bit. Maybe this is what her life has been leading to; a bad ending of her own design. So what she does in the meantime shouldn't matter, right? She can do whatever she wants.

She sits at her vanity while Tragedy and Comedy stand behind her. Comedy has a hand on Aphrodite's shoulder and a mocking grin on her lips. "What are you thinking about?"

Aphrodite cups her face with her hand, toying with the jewelry box's lid. "Nothing at all."

"It's about him, isn't it?" Tragedy asks.

Aphrodite glances back at them. Comedy lies on the bed, leaning back on her elbows, and wiggling her bare feet against the carpet. "You don't have to lie, especially not to us," Comedy says. "You're naive to think we don't already know every thought that crosses that feeble mind of yours."

She ignores the insult. "Can't you just stay as voices in my head?"

Tragedy tilts her head. "Voices? We're as real as you are."

Aphrodite folds her arms and looks out the window for the fiftieth time today. "What sort of advice can you give other than cryptic statements?" she asks. "Nothing worthwhile, I imagine."

"You should listen to us." Comedy's face reflects hundreds of times in the droplets on the window. "We would hate if something were to happen to you."

"Is that a threat?"

"I'm just saying, we give very good advice," Tragedy's voice moves beside her ear, "that you should listen to."

"I don't listen to ghosts." Aphrodite shifts away.

"A ghost? We're the reason you're even alive. We're the reason why everything is the way it is."

"I'm sure you are." Aphrodite goes to leave, hand poised

on the knob. Tragedy's ghostly hand wraps around her wrist, keeping her in place.

"Do you realize you're expecting?"

She pulls her hand out of her cold grip as her features distort with anger. "Why does everyone think they know more about myself than I do!? First Asmodeus, now you two?"

"You are," Tragedy insists. Her expression is mournful, but she isn't sure if it's any different than her usual. "You should be thankful for such a blessing, some would kill for a child."

"Why would I be thankful for a thing I didn't even ask for!?" Aphrodite snaps. "If you want it, you can have it! I'm not about to be a mother!"

They laugh at her. "Like you said, we're only ghosts. All we can do is make sure you do the right thing."

"I'll do whatever I want!" She opens the door, only for a half-asleep Asmodeus to confront her. He seems to be on the grumpier side today, not giving her enough time to speak. "What are you yelling about now? Some of us are trying to sleep."

"It's nothing," she says. "If it's such a problem, why don't you ignore me?"

"The walls are thin," he says, dryly. "Besides, what if you need me at some odd hour?"

The way she crosses her arms and looks away with a huff makes his place apparent; some dark hole far below her where the light never reaches. And as he views her like the distant moon, the weight of her empty life on her shoulders lessens. Asmodeus fell in love with a force of nature, an uncontrollable wave that is bound to swallow him whole. Maybe he is stupid for believing in love so strongly, but she knows it is all he has in his sad life. She could never convince him otherwise.

Aphrodite only has it in her to reply with a weak "I won't."

"How are you so sure?" Asmodeus leans against the wall, obviously prepping for another argument, but she has nothing more to say, her face as tired and sad as his. She leaves her door open as she shuffles back into bed, lying on top of her covers. "Are you feeling alright?"

Aphrodite once wanted to feel it all, every high and every low there is to be had, until the fluctuating emotions drove her mad. She thought of romance as a gift to give freely, wrapped in pink paper. But once opened, it was everything and nothing all at once; violent yet gentle, melancholic yet cheerful. It was never enough to fill the void inside her. The burning flame that's lead Aphrodite all her life flickers, and she knows they're reaching the end. The hunger for love is gone. Maybe Poseidon did his job after all.

She stares at Asmodeus in the vanity's reflection as he enters the room and ignores his question. "You know," she says," all I've ever wanted is romance. I didn't want any of this to happen—you believe me, right?"

He sits on the other side of the bed, out of her line of sight. "I could've guessed that much. But you can't make people love you the way you want, Aph."

"Don't you think I know that?" she asks, rolling over to better see him. Aphrodite could stare at his back all day. Maybe she is wrong, maybe she isn't who she thought she was. "But is it so much to ask for?"

"Maybe for another man, but not for me," he says as he twists around to face her. Asmodeus kicks his shoes off and they meet in the middle, obscured by the veil of lace that surrounds the bed. He takes her hands in his. "I know I don't mean much to you, but I'll love you until the day I die," he breathes. "Will that be enough?"

He holds her so close as if he could squeeze his love into her. This is their funeral, their last goodbye, and yet even now this scene is just another climax to her. Aphrodite's walls crumble and tears squeeze out from the corners of her eyes.

"I want you to make love to me," she whimpers. "Make me forget everything he did." Asmodeus lays her down like they're newlyweds on their honeymoon, only without exuberance that would come with such a thing. He treats her like she is made of porcelain. While his hands fumble, the more his soot stains her. She rambles on, effectively pouring her heart over him. "I hate feeling so empty! I try and I try, but even after all this time, I don't feel anything for you."

Aphrodite trembles, grabbing at the thin nightgown she has worn for days and shoving it over her head, leaving her nude and most of all, vulnerable. This is the only way she knows how to bare her soul to men, by getting undressed and hoping they see her for what she really is; a bitter, lonely woman who longs for love.

"That's alright," Asmodeus mutters, as he kneels above her. Shadows fall over his face and she can't make out his expression, but she can tell he's putting on a tough front. "I'll still love you regardless. I don't even care if you hurt me at this point, it's not like I'm worth much in the grand scheme of things. I'm just a demon, after all."

"Don't talk about yourself like that!"

"What's it matter anymore? It's like I suspected all along, you don't care about me." His voice wavers and tears fall onto her bare skin. "No matter how much I try and love you, my name won't be the one to go down in the history books. When this is over, everyone will forget about me—even you."

Aphrodite pulls him down without any of the passion both are so used to. There is nothing but an aching sadness that lingers between them, an understanding that things will never be as they once were. The end of their love is upon them, but they choose to prolong its death for just a little bit longer, long enough for them to raise it up for one final farewell. She takes him in her arms and they comfort each other the only way they know how.

There is no heat on their skin as they make love, both cherishing the other. The scent of his cologne and cigar smoke, the roughness of his stubble against her face as they kiss, even down to the way he holds her hand; it all brings out a fondness in her she never thought possible. But none of it matters, for their love is going to fizzle out by the morning.

Chapter Twenty-nine

Loathing

Watching someone sleep has never been a pastime of his, but Asmodeus could watch Aphrodite for the rest of his life. He lies beside her the rest of the night, intertwining his hands over his stomach. All he has to do is play the part of the dashing prince and pray with fingers crossed that things go his way. But of course they will, love always beats out the odds, and if last night is any signifier, things are finally turning out his way. Aphrodite stirs and rolls towards him, and the moment he gazes on that face all his thoughts melt away, his heart and breath faltering.

"Did you sleep well?" he asks.

"Since when are you a morning person?" She stretches her arms above her head.

"Maybe I'm in a rare mood."

She gets out of bed and rubs sleep from her eyes. She is ethereal this early, the low light throwing dramatic shadows over her curves, as if their shared breakdown was but an episode. She takes her time in brushing her hair at the vanity, Asmodeus more than content lying in bed, getting to watch her like a fly on the wall.

Aphrodite catches him in the mirror. "Do you need something?"

He shakes his head. "Not a thing."

She resumes her brushing. "Whatever you say."

Asmodeus lets out a little sigh of content as he catches her rubbing the tattoo on her neck. "Something the matter?"

"What will happen once this is over?" she asks.

"You don't need to worry about that." Asmodeus swings his legs off the bed and steps behind her chair. "Everything will be taken care of, trust me."

"You have yet to tell me how," she snaps.

"I can't say for certain. Why don't we wait to discuss it

until my Father gets back?" He leans down to whisper in her ear. "In the meantime, we can do whatever you like."

"What does it matter what I like?" Even though her snapping is uncalled for, he doesn't mind anymore, like the weight on his heart has lifted. He isn't sure why, but he feels as though something is about to change very soon. Whether it's good or bad, Asmodeus is unable to tell. "Did you have something in mind?"

He pretends to check himself in the mirror, his usual cockiness returning to him with a smirk. "I'm not doing anything of the sort."

They stand on the terrace, rain dripping from the awning. He is thankful for this respite from the weather and Aphrodite hounding him for answers, but can't she allow him some relaxation? They can deal with this problem later. There is always the option to put unpleasant things off.

But what will he do about Ares? He is sure to show up eventually, but Asmodeus doesn't have that answer, choosing to deal with it once he gets there. He glances to Aphrodite, who is shoving her feet into a pair of loose boots. He found them in one of many closets. She has a grey raincoat on, hair tucked under the hood.

"Are you ready?" Asmodeus steps onto the path, umbrella tucked at his side, just in case a certain someone gets caught in the rain again. She rises with a yawn to his side, pulling her sleeves back over her hands. "Isn't it cold out?"

"I *told* you to bundle up," he says. "It's not my problem you decide to not listen."

"I'll be fine!"

They walk down unsteady ground and into the forest beyond. There is little life here other than the trees, moss and lichen clinging to their bark, the ground littered with their needles. The forest absorbs all sound here, even their footsteps–which should be crunching dead leaves–are eerily silent. They walk on.

"Where are we going?" she asks.

"Somewhere no one else can hear us." The deeper they go, the more the trees blot out any semblance of light. They eventually reach a small plot of willow trees, beyond it a lake of surprisingly clear water. A wooden rowboat sits on the bank. Aphrodite lingers farther back the closer they get. "What's wrong?"

She doesn't look at him, transfixed by the boat. "Nothing."

"Why don't you come over here then?" Asmodeus offers

a hand for her to take.

"I'm good where I am."

Aphrodite actually takes a step back. "I don't particularly like boats."

"I thought you loved water?"

"You know how it is," she says. "Interests change."

"Well... I kind of planned for us to take a little ride. So, if you don't want to, we can just go back?"

It seems that she has so much to say, but she bites her tongue and steps into the boat in the end. "It's okay, we can do it–but just for a little bit."

He pushes the boat out and gets in himself. They row down the edge, close enough for them to stop if she wants him to. "Is something still wrong?" he asks. Water drips off the oars as he rows, Aphrodite holding the umbrella in her lap. "You don't have to keep lying."

"I'm not."

He stops his rowing to rest a hand on her knee. "Then why have you been acting so strangely? I can hardly hold a conversation with you lately, and after last night... I don't know unless you tell me."

"Can't you just believe me for once?" She comes off rather harshly.

He isn't sure what avenue to pursue. He knows this line of questioning will most likely turn into an argument, but he has to know. "Not until you tell me the truth."

"I *am* telling the truth, Asmo! Why can't you just leave me alone!?" The boat rocks as she jolts forward in her seat.

"...You know what? No, I'm not going to leave you alone!" He didn't intend to let it all out, but now that he is doing it, Asmodeus can't stop from airing out all his grievances on this secluded lake. "And you know what else? This is all *your* fault! This is all happening because of you!"

Aphrodite tries to out yell him. "I didn't do anything, you delusional bastard!"

"You're the reason my face is ruined!"

"You think I asked for this?" She throws a hand out to their surroundings. "Everyone around me treats me like a wild animal and I have zero say. I hope you let Hera kill me so I don't have to listen to you anymore!"

"Maybe I will!" he huffs.

"I hope you do." Aphrodite crosses her arms like a pouting child. What happened to the woman he made love to? Why is she acting like this? "You're only confident with a mask, without it, you're just a scared little man!"

He sneers. "What would I be afraid of?"

"Being alone," she screams. "I'm the only one who's ever

listened to you!"

This is what lights his short fuse. She grins in all her smug beauty and he can't wait to give her a taste of her own medicine. But even now he can't bring himself to spew ugly words at her. He loves her too much to truly hurt her.

She hacks out a laugh. "How did you think this would turn out, Asmo? This isn't a fairy tale. This is real life. You knew what you were getting yourself into the first time you ever took my hand."

"But you said–"

"I say a lot of things." Aphrodite stares him down.

"Let me ask then, what exactly am I to you? I thought you loved me."

"Oh, I do. Of *course* I do! But don't act like you forgot what you were getting yourself into."

"I just thought, maybe I could help you," he says, his resolve crumpling like wet paper.

She leans over him, her hair falling out of her hood. Her eyes gleam even in shadow. "I've got news for you, I don't need your help. You thought you could change me, make me soft enough for you to stomach, is that right?"

His voice shakes with emotion. "That's not it."

"I'm going to say it for you so you can get the memo, alright?" Asmodeus hides his face in the collar of his jacket so she can't see him fall apart. "Look at me when I'm talking to you." He refuses. "Maybe if you just kept your stupid mouth shut, things would've been so much easier for us. But you just had to tell Ares off, didn't you?"

He gingerly touches his scarred face. If she would only listen to him. All he wants is someone who listens to him, to have someone by his side that won't realize how despicable and pathetic he is. But she always has to have the last word. Even though she makes him cry and question himself, he wants nothing more than for her to be herself. No one, neither Ares nor him, can convince her to change.

"I love you," he says. "You can yell at me all you want, but I'm still going to love you."

"Get me off this stupid boat."

Asmodeus rows back into the bank, helping her out despite everything, for even if she were to break his heart a million times, nothing would change. She doesn't look at him on their way back to the manor. Leaving the umbrella closed at his side, he lets the rain soak him. As they reach the terrace, the faint smell of tea—earl grey, to be specific—wafts through the air. A glass-topped table and three sets of metal-legged chairs are set on the concrete. His Mother's favorite tea set sits in the middle, the one she only brings out when company visits.

Who would have any reason to come to his estate? Well, other than...

"Ah, there you are," Ares' smooth voice floats from the open ballroom door and his red blinds him. Asmodeus' head spins as sudden whiplash slams into him. He tries to reach out for Aphrodite, but she is no longer by his side, instead rushing to meet Ares. The raincoat lies in a heap in the wet grass, his hand dumbly groping at the air.

"What the fuck," is all Asmodeus can mutter to himself. Ares and Aphrodite keep their chatter quiet, at least quiet enough so he can't make it out. Ares doesn't acknowledge his presence until his parents come out to join them. They are dressed in matching silver silk; a high collar dress with layers of hanging lace to accent Persephone's silhouette, making Hades seem under dressed in his blousy shirt and slacks. His Father's hair has been tied neatly back and he finally sees the resemblance between them. Asmodeus could very well be his spitting image.

"Asmodai, why are you standing in the rain like that?" Persephone asks, ushering him onto the terrace. "Why don't you join us? We haven't had company in ages!"

"I'm fine, Mother." He allows her to slide his seat in however, unable to say no to anyone anymore. She pours him a cup of tea and sits beside Hades. "Why is *he* here?"

"Who, your cousin? He came to visit, of course." Persephone drops a spoonful of sugar into her tea, the metal clinking as she stirs. Rainwater flows from the gutters and patters along the edge of the patio. The rain is the only thing Asmodeus has to distract him from Ares being here. "Why else could he be here?" She eyes his still full cup. "Will you drink it before it gets cold?"

"I don't want any tea, Mother," Asmodeus says.

"Listen to your Mother." Hades meets his gaze while taking a sip from his own cup, and they both seem nervous. Hera's side of the family doesn't just show up for some tea and chatting; they only intend to get something done. That thing, for Ares, is clearly taking Aphrodite away from him. "This isn't something you can argue your way out of."

"Father–"

The way Hades places the cup down and how he flexes his knuckles so subtly, warns Asmodeus that his Father is serious. "Whatever reason he's here for, we have to oblige him. We're family, after all. It's like I told your brothers, and I'm telling you now–"

"'Family never separates,'" he mockingly says. "In this case, I think an exception could be made."

Aphrodite and Ares stroll over to the table, Aphrodite sitting between Ares and Asmodeus. She laces her fingers together under her chin, fawning over Ares to the point that Asmodeus could puke. But he can't do anything, as his Father says, so he sits there, with his shoulders hunched, angrily sipping at his perfectly brewed tea. But even his Mother's tea can't soothe him at a time like this.

"How have you been holding up?" Ares asks. He knows it is directed to him, but Asmodeus still makes a show of eyeing the other three, hoping one of them answers over him. "I really would love to put this all behind us," he pauses to spit out his name, "Asmodeus."

"There's really no reason to be so formal," Asmodeus says, forcing out a grin to at least try and please his parents. "We're family after all, aren't we? And for your information, I've been holding up just fine, no thanks to you."

Aphrodite runs a finger along the rim of her cup with a bored glaze over her eyes. "He's lying, you know."

"I'm not lying!"

Ares lets no trace of the ruthless soldier seep through, his dexterous fingers perfectly poised around his tea cup and platter like he is only a prince accustomed to the finer things. But that is what makes Asmodeus resent him even more–

both of them, actually. Aphrodite and Ares act like they are so far above him in their kingdom in the clouds, that everyone else pales in comparison to each other. Ares shows no anger or hatred towards him, and Asmodeus can't help but wonder, why not? Is he not even worth being hated?

He watches them laugh over tea together and he is aware they feel nothing. He is nothing in their eyes, just a stepping stone for them to daintily leap over in the creek, a thing to momentarily consider and forget thereafter. It is this fact that drives him to prove himself and do things his family would call borderline suicidal. He can't–and won't–ever let Aphrodite go. He would rather die than do that.

Ares grins, and Asmodeus' blood pressure skyrockets, squeezing the spoon so tightly it crumples. "What's wrong, my dear cousin?"

Asmodeus shifts his seat halfway out and the table jostles from him moving. He can't do this, he can't possibly play pretend anymore. "Don't give me that bullshit. You came here to kill me, didn't you?"

The God of War holds out his cup for Persephone to refill. She sends daggers Asmodeus' way, but he's too deep to stop. "What are you talking about, Asmodeus? Kill you? I would never." He takes a long sip of tea. "Not if I don't have to, that is."

"Ares.." Persephone keeps her husband from shoving out his seat as Asmodeus did. "I thought you said you wanted to solve this passively? You didn't mention anything about killing my son!"

"Don't worry, my wonderful Aunt," Ares says. "As long as your son listens to this new deal I have in mind, everyone will come out of this happier than before – well, except for him."

Asmodeus stands with his hands clenched at his sides, leading Ares to do the same. "Well?"

"You look like a wet kitten," Ares notes with a grin. He slides a hand forward for him to shake. "I'm trying to look past a previous transgression of yours–not for my sake, for yours. You broke our previous deal, but let's pretend it never happened. I know you never intended on following through, but maybe this time you will."

"If I wanted to be insulted, I'd speak to my older brothers, so if you actually want to make this so-called deal, you know where to find me!" Asmodeus turns to stroll into the ballroom, but Ares lays a hand on his shoulder.

"You're not understanding me, are you? Forgive me for rambling." He bends at the waist so they're at eye level. "You're going to give Aphrodite back to me and I'll let you keep your life." Ares speaks to her over his shoulder. "My Dear, this involves you, as well."

Aphrodite has yet to move from her seat, hardly taking a sip of her tea. "Why must you make this so difficult?"

"I do it because I love you. One of us has to make the difficult decisions, so I may as well be the one to do it." His grip tightens around Asmodeus' shoulder, asking a question to them both. "Tell me, is there anything I need to know?"

"Oh, I'm only pregnant," Aphrodite says rather casually. "It's not like I'm dying or something. No big deal."

Ares goes silent, but Asmodeus can't escape his grip no matter how hard he tries. "What did she just say?"

His parents pretend to busy themselves by chatting about the weather. "Wow, we sure have been getting a lot of rain lately, huh?" Hades asks.

"I hope we could do without it for a day or two," Persephone says.

"If you'll excuse us for a minute, Uncle." Ares motions Aphrodite over with a wave of his hand, shutting the open door behind them. He stands before it with his hands on his hips. "Explain."

"What else is there to explain?" Aphrodite asks.

Asmodeus and her can't even look at each other, let alone

Ares. "I'm pregnant and that's all you need to know."

"I don't care about the what, I care about the how." He pauses. "Do you even know whose child it is?"

"That's irrelevant, don't you think?" Asmodeus shifts closer to her, only brushing their hands together. With how things have been, he is sure he would lose a hand if he did anything more. "She's having a baby and that's all that should matter. Who cares who the father is?"

"I do. There's only two possible people it could be," Ares states. "But seeing as how one of them is dead, that only leaves me. That child is mine."

Asmodeus blurts out, "yeah? Well, what if I want her to stay here? Doesn't what I want matter?"

Ares has a good laugh for a full thirty seconds, wiping a tear from the corner of his eye. "Why would I care about what you want? You're the reason I had to come down to this dirty mansion in the first place! Why do you think you're entitled to anything?"

While they yell, Aphrodite wanders down the staircase to the rest of the ballroom. "Aph, we're going home now. You won't have to stay in this mess any longer."

She tilts her head at Ares. "I'm not going anywhere."

"What do you—"

"And who do you think you are, telling me what to do?" Aphrodite yells. "I can't go back to Eden with you, I killed your Uncle. Don't you remember what Hera does to those who kill other gods?"

Ares goes to lean against the railing with a sigh. "I know perfectly well, I've seen every execution we've had. I'm sure my Mother can be persuaded just this once."

She nearly tears her own hair out with how she tears at her curls. "There you go, calling her your Mother still! She isn't a Mother, she's a monster in a crown!"

"She's all I have left! As if you could even understand what losing family feels like." Ares is oddly quiet for what should be an explosive argument, but she has pierced a weak spot in his armor. "All you have is yourself and that's all you need. But haven't you ever thought about what I want?" She doesn't answer. "Of course not. You never do. I want a family, someone to take care of outside of myself. I'm sick of fulfilling your every whim!" He dusts his hands off, adjusting his suit jacket. "I think you need some time to think your decision over, so I'll return to you in a week's time. I know you'll make the right choice, my Dear."

Ares brushes past Asmodeus, hardly paying him any attention as he steps back outside. Asmodeus descends the stairs to try and comfort Aphrodite. She stands in the middle of the room, back under the chandelier where they danced, clutching her hands to her chest.

"Are you alright?" he asks, going to put his hands along her shoulders.

"Don't touch me." He flinches back as if her voice smacked him. "I want to be alone right now, alright?"

Asmodeus tucks his hands in his pockets with a stiff nod. "I wish I could do something for you."

"There's nothing anyone can do for me now. I've dug myself into a hole I can't get out of." Aphrodite tugs at the thin fabric along her chest, saying nothing while she stares at the mural on the ceiling.

"Don't worry, I'll figure something out to take your mind off this." He smiles at her but she doesn't return the gesture. "I love you, and I want to see you happy again—even if it's only for this week we have together."

"You're so silly," she mumbles, placing a hand against the threshold to the den. "I'm sure whatever you think of will be wonderful."

Aphrodite disappears around the corner and grey drenches his world. Asmodeus drops onto the bottom stair, unable to take the weight of the world crumbling around him any longer. The glass patio door opens once more and his parents climb down to sit on either side of him.

"We couldn't help but overhear," Persephone says, smiling and holding Asmodeus' hand. "I'm sure it seems horrible now, but it'll be fine once it's over. You'll see."

"Can't we do anything for her?" he asks.

"You can't help someone who doesn't want it." Hades pushes off the stairs, using the banister for leverage, and dusting his suit off. "I'm afraid this is happening whether you like it or not. The only thing we can do is watch from the sidelines. It isn't your Mother and I's place to stick our noses into other people's business. Besides, Aphrodite has been headed down this road for years."

"I beg to differ! Can't anyone change their Fate?" Asmodeus stares down into his hands, clenching them so tightly that his claws dig into his palms. "If she won't do it, I will."

"How do you intend to alter another person's Fate?" Persephone asks.

Asmodeus gets up and whirls around on them, a finger in the air as he stumbles over ideas. "I'll... I'll throw a party! The greatest party that anyone's ever been to! I know she'll most likely leave, but surely that will persuade her otherwise?"

His parents share a look, but refuse to say the obvious. Hades asks, "I suppose we have no choice but to help you throw this little party?"

"My mansion looks fine! I don't know what you're..." Persephone rubs at the dust along the wall. "I'll hire some of your Father's underlings to help give this house a good scrubbing." She presses a hand to her chest. "I'll be in charge of decorating, naturally."

"I'm sure Asmodai will love the gaudy colors you pick out," Hades says, dryly.

Without looking away from Asmodeus, she says, "I'm going to pretend I didn't hear that, Dear. Now, let's get started, shall we?"

Persephone lifts her skirts and turns the same corner as Aphrodite without another word, leaving Father and son by themselves. Hades stares at Asmodeus with such longing and worry, but his son can't see it, for his head is stuck in clouds he will never see with his own eyes. The fact of the matter is that Asmodeus will never leave this place alive.

Over the next few hours, well into the evening, Persephone employs every manner of lowly demon to clean Asmodeus' manor while she weaves decorations out of pure light. Hades directs them himself, a cane of black wood resting between gloved hands, rapping it on the floor whenever one of them makes a mistake. Asmodeus leans against the foyer's stairs railing, he isn't allowed to help. His parents check in to make sure everything is to his standards; does he prefer black or purple? Velvet or silk? Eventually he gives up and lets them do whatever they want.

All this time, Aphrodite has locked herself in her room, only leaving when no one else is around to see, creeping silently as a cat through his manor. Asmodeus has to see her tonight, however, as he has the dress his Mother made specifically for her. He hasn't seen it himself, but he knows it has to be beautiful.

With a hand raised to knock, Asmodeus hardly expects Aphrodite to saunter towards him from the bath. The pink silk robe she has on is barely tied shut, leaving most of her bare chest out. Asmodeus' mouth hangs open. She makes no effort to cover up whatsoever.

"What do you have for me? A little present?" Aphrodite takes the hanger he holds, pushing past him into her room. Asmodeus peeks inside from the safety of the hallway. She unzips the garment bag to peek inside, and he can faintly make out the shimmer of red velvet. "When do I need to be ready?"

"Well, the party doesn't start for a few more hours, so we still have some time to kill," he says. "Why? Did you have anything in mind?"

"I only want to know when to be fashionably late. The party can't start without me, isn't that right?" Her robe slips over her shoulders a bit, but he can only stare at her back. She aims a wicked grin at him as she proceeds to brush her hair out. "But we can do something if you like–after I get ready." Aphrodite pauses. "You can come in and sit, you know?"

He enters and closes the door behind him, carefully settling in the armchair. There are thoughts that come to life as he looks upon Aphrodite, like so many little strings of lights being plugged in. Paranoia gnaws at every part of him until it consumes his being, as he only has so much time before Ares returns.

Her answer will be obvious to all in attendance. No matter how much she says she can't return to Eden, Asmodeus can't shake the feeling she will leave again. But that can't possibly be true. He loves her. But the fact is that she doesn't love him like he wants her to. Asmodeus will never be able to match up to that perfect romance she envisions in her head; an unattainable dream.

What will he have to do to keep her? Persuasion won't work on the charmer of men herself. No one can tell Aphrodite what to do—so what options does he have left? His heart aches as the truth dawns on him, like the stabbing of a blade in his side. As much as he would love to pull the knife out to relieve himself of this pain, to forget this strange thought, it is the last thing he should do. He loves Aphrodite more than he loves himself. So, it is with a heavy heart that he must do the unthinkable; kill The Goddess of Love.

Now don't misunderstand, he would do anything for her, give her any piece of him she wants! Nothing is too much if it means professing his love. But there comes a time when a line must be crossed in order to keep the things you love and hold dear. During the last night of the masquerade, he will lay her down on the same bed they made love on, and strangle every last bit of softness out of her.

How can he imagine doing such a thing? Love makes even cowards do the previously unthinkable. Asmodeus broods with these intrusive thoughts as he watches Aphrodite doll herself up. She catches him watching, and grins before going back to her makeup. Perhaps he won't need to go to such extreme measures, maybe this next week will go as planned?

The clocks strike nine and fill the manor with a mournful

noise, one Asmodeus only notices now, as if all living all this time with no purpose made him numb to his surroundings. "I should probably get going," he says. "Wouldn't want to keep my parents waiting any longer."

"Of course," she agrees, dabbing powder onto her round face. "You know where I'll be if you need me."

Asmodeus departs rather awkwardly, fumbling with the door knob as he closes it, and scurrying back downstairs. A thousand demons fill the ground floor of the manor, some lounging against the walls or near the door, but all have solid-colored suits on; golds and reds, blues and greens, every color of the rainbow shining under the chandeliers. Except for black, for it is too severe a color for the mood Asmodeus wants to keep for the next week. Black is the color of the void inside him, a thing he would rather forget altogether... until Ares returns.

The furniture in the den and dining room have been all shoved against the walls to make room for the sea of guests. Although Asmodeus knows none of them by name, it is as though they are his best friends coming to bid him farewell. Farewell to where, he isn't sure, but perhaps it is to this phase of his life? Yes, of course!

Everything will go his way and Aphrodite will stay with

him, as it should be. He strolls into his room, making an effort to not come off as too eager or nervous, for princes like him have reputations. But all Asmodeus wishes to do is skip along like his heartbeat and soar above the petty familial drama that plagues his life.

He changes into a suit that's never worn of glittering purple. It is mostly so he can remain in her field of vision no matter how crowded the manor becomes. The sequins fade from purple, to pink, then to red at his knees. Slicking his hair back with extra gel, he stares at the cracked mirror in his room with a bright smile, but the longer he holds his own gaze and truly inspects his appearance, it deflates along with his ego. Is he fooling himself, thinking that this will work out in his favor? What if things go wrong at the last minute?

Asmodeus turns away from the mirror to spy his Mother creaking his door open. Pastel pink chiffon cascades down into a hoop skirt, with birds and flowers embroidered in white thread. A white ruffled collar is around her neck, her thick curls braided into a bun.

"Are you doing alright, Asmodai?" Indistinct chatter flows up from below. "It's almost time for the party to start."

"I'm doing fine, Mother. I 'm just a bit antsy." She sits along the side of his bed and beckons him to sit beside her.

Persephone holds him close, taking his hand in hers. He isn't sure why she is acting so strangely. "Is something wrong? Where's Father?"

"Nothing," she says. "I can't help but regret not being closer to you when you were young. It's something I'll always regret. But I want you to know how proud we are. *So proud.* No matter how this ends, we'll always be here for you."

"What are you trying to say?" He looks up at her like he is a child again and she encompasses his whole world. When his older brothers would ostracize him, she was always there. Asmodeus has nothing but love for his dear Mother.

She sighs. "I worry about you, I do nothing but worry these days. Let me ask you; what will you do if this doesn't work out? If she leaves you?"

He lets out a whimper as he squeezes Persephone's hand. "...I don't know. I don't like thinking about it, it scares me too much." Asmodeus pauses before shaking his head. "It's not that I can't let go, I hold on so tightly because I'm afraid I'll never find anything like her again. I don't want to be alone."

She kisses his forehead. "You won't be. You'll always have us to fall back on." His Mother tugs his jacket tighter on him. "Now, you have a party to start."

They share hopeful grins before returning to the foyer, where the festivities have officially begun. All the electric lights have been shut off in favor of dozens of candelabras and torches set throughout the manor. Aphrodite descends the stairs in her off-the-shoulder red velvet dress like royalty, hair swooping over one shoulder. Asmodeus stands on the foyer landing, a glass of red wine in hand as he takes hers. He doesn't look to the crowd, having only eyes for her, staring transfixed like the fool he is. It is like there is nobody else here, this night only made for them.

They descend into the belly of the beast. The pair are the focal point of the party, the eye of a churning storm that's sure to sweep them away. But they pay no mind to how the guests prance through the rooms. As they sway through them, each is furnished to match its respective color; the den is gold, the dining room blue, and the upstairs halls draped in violet.

But the black ballroom is one place where none dare to tread for too long, they pass through it without lingering, keeping their eyes on anyone close to them for the time being. None wish to think of the blackness of death, the eventual end of this week-long party, instead focusing on each other's rosy cheeks and the music that drowns all else out.

Drapes of black velvet cover the tall windows to the terrace, glittering in the candlelight like the void of space. The mural above them seems almost menacing, twisting the features of Aphrodite and Asmodeus' painted faces into ghouls. The clocks strike the hour and the party pauses for an extended beat. The music cuts, the laughter ceases, and Asmodeus and Aphrodite stare at each other for the short few seconds until they ease back into their joyful celebration.

The front door opens and Hades enters with his pitch black suit, a single tulip tucked in his jacket's buttonhole. Hades looks down at the carpeted floor, avoiding the cluster of dancers altogether. Instead, Persephone and he stand on the stair's first landing, directly beneath Aphrodite's portrait. They watch Asmodeus pass by, arm in arm.

Two other figures, Comedy and Tragedy, also stand at the top of the stairs in their beautiful gowns. Neither party speaks, as there is nothing to say at this point. To speak of the bad ending would be like cursing the one scrap of happiness Asmodeus has left. The least they can do is give him this.

Aphrodite grows weary after six days of partying and drinking, deciding to take a brief nap in the quiet of her room. Asmodeus waits at the foot of the stairs, watching her back disappear like he has so many times before and he knows what he must do. He glances to the clock's hand quickly reaching midnight, and the thought of Ares returning sinks its teeth into his every thought. His fingers twitch and his palms sweat... can he possibly go through with it? He follows her rather clumsily, staring at the pink door until his eyes lose their focus. With stiff legs, he slips into Aphrodite's room like a thief in the night.

She lies prone in bed, her dress shimmering in the low light as she breathes. Asmodeus kneels beside her and takes it all in one final time. Her messy curls, the light smearing of her lipstick; all these imperfections are what make her more beautiful to him. It is a shame he won't be able to see it anymore.

He runs his open hand along her bare collar, even now hating how he stains her. She smiles and mumbles in her sleep. Asmodeus' face goes blank as he pushes down every emotion he has and places his hands around her neck. He repeats one thought to himself like a mantra, *I love you.*

But before he can squeeze, his Father's voice calls out to him. "Asmodai!"

He has no choice but to roll off the bed and scramble through the door as Aphrodite stirs underneath him. His slicked hair falls out of place over his forehead, no matter how he tries to smooth it back down. Once he makes it out to the foyer, his Father stands at the open door, the storm raging outside. The guests have been parted to either half. A solid figure cloaked in black, a red mask obscuring his face, stands at the foot of the stairs with a pair of rapiers on either hip. He doesn't speak. But even with the mask on, that red eye glares at Asmodeus.

Chapter Thirty

The End of Love

Hades poses a question to Ares, "so, that's how it has to be then?"

"I'm glad you finally see my side of things. It took you long enough," Ares says.

Asmodeus' confused voice rings out. "Father, what's going on?"

Aphrodite reaches the lobby in a daze, a siren blaring in her head. Hades doesn't look at her as he beckons Asmodeus down, but he doesn't budge. Hades crosses the carpet to stand at the bottom of the stairs.

"We've come to an understanding."

"So I have to let her go, is that it?" Asmodeus asks.

"Don't be difficult now, Ares has come to retrieve her," Hades says. "You knew this would happen."

He blurts out anything he can think of to keep the conversation going. "But what about the contract?"

"Consider it cancelled." He approaches his son with a smile, laying a hand on his shoulder. "Now, if you'd just step aside, we can end this mess."

He pulls out of his Father's grip, leaving him gripping thin air. "No."

"You're *going* to let her go."

Asmodeus covers Aphrodite with his body as if he of all people could stop Ares from doing what he came to do. "No I'm not."

Ares calls from below, "I told you he wouldn't agree! This is why we have to do things my way."

Why do they speak of her like she isn't here? She has more than a say in what happens to her, does she not?

"I'm not going," she says.

They stare at her in shock. Hades bristles at the

interruption, hand tight around the banister. "You're going wherever we tell you, you indignant little–"

"Don't talk to her like that!" Asmodeus snaps.

"Who are *you* to talk back?" Hades steps toe to toe with him. "I always knew you were mouthy, but this is pushing the envelope, Asmodai. Hand her over."

"So you're just going to take my baby away from me? I don't think so."

"For the last time, that's *my* child!" Ares' voice rings out. He locks eyes with Aphrodite, his stare as cold as ice. It is the same she has seen on his face before the beginning of every battle, knowing Ares intends to fight for her until there is only one man left standing.

Asmodeus leans over the railing. "It's my child now!"

Hades has little to say to this, throwing a look to Ares. Flames lick up Ares' spine, forming a fiery crown around his head. They grow from orange to blue as his anger rises. Despite the way he shakes, Ares manages to keep his voice steady. "Do you realize the situation you've just put yourself into? What you've forced me to do now?"

Asmodeus shifts his weight to his back foot and tucks his thumbs into his pockets. "I don't see what you mean, big guy?"

"So you don't even know how much you've just fucked up?"

Asmodeus scoffs, "it's nothing I won't be able to handle."

"You realize that's my baby, don't you?"

"I got to her first." He stabs his thumb into his chest. "She's all mine. Our little deal has been off for some time, hasn't it? So why can't you understand that she wants to stay with me and not you?"

Hades sits on the stair with his head in his hands. Ares climbs the landing with careful steps, tossing one of the sheathed swords at Asmodeus.

"If it weren't for you, she'd be happy." He slowly draws his blade, it glints in the torchlight. "But you had to have your way, you had to ruin everything, and what do you have to show for it?"

"I'm staying right here, Ares!" She moves between them with her hands out. If she can only stop this before it goes too far.

He almost looks surprised at her. "What did you say?"

"Do you call being contained happiness?" Aphrodite asks. "You really expect me to be content in your Mother's stupid Garden?"

"You can stop now. You don't have to pretend anymore,

my Dear, that you enjoy being here. I know how badly you want to come home." Shadows darken Ares' face as he drags the edge of his sword against the gaudy wallpaper. "Everything will be over soon."

She has to duck her head as Ares takes a swing at Asmodeus. He can only block with the sheath, desperately trying to get his sword out to retaliate. Asmodeus tackles him into the wall. Paintings and vases fall and shatter. The little prince ducks down the stairs, shoving past the crowd. Ares leaps over the banister to follow him into the ballroom. The clashing of blades fills the old estate. Persephone is the one to usher the guests out of the estate.

Hades, however, sits on the stairs, bawling his eyes out. He can do little to stop them at this point. They know he is about to lose a son. Aphrodite rushes down after them with Persephone, crying their names out. She can't do anything but watch in horror as the blade slices through Asmodeus' suit, growing ever nearer to his skin. He puts up a valiant fight, but he isn't a trained soldier like Ares is. He doesn't have the stamina to keep up with him or his hard-hitting blows. Two pairs of hands hold hers. Comedy and Tragedy stand at her sides, watching the duel like it is the climax of a play.

Tragedy says, "it's time for you to go to her."

"No, I have to stay here! What if they need me?"

Comedy shakes her head. "The only way you can fix this is to follow Nyx. She has all the answers you need."

The door to the patio sits ajar. None of them notice Nyx standing out in the rain, beckoning Aphrodite to her. As her feet patter past them into the backyard, Asmodeus makes a break for her. Ares' heavy footsteps make up the rear. As she reaches the edge of the forest, she takes a single look back. Cuts cover Asmodeus' face and torso, all swings and jabs he manages to barely avoid. Thank the Fates he is still alive. But he drops his guard. He stares at her a moment too long.

"Asmo–" Silver pierces Asmodeus' side, blood pouring out and staining his suit. He clutches at the wound as he lurches over to cough more into his hand. Even as he stumbles, he continues down the hill to her. "Please, stop! You're going to die!"

"I'm not letting go of you!" He sounds out of breath and weak.

Ares watches after them. He makes no further move, for he landed the only blow he needed to. Lightning illuminates their faces in the dark. Aphrodite has no choice but to turn and flee, a little cardinal flitting between the trees. She runs and runs, even as her feet turn sore and sharp branches nick her face, for it is the only thing she can do. Somehow, she knows Asmodeus is still following her down. Deeper and deeper they go down the rabbit hole.

Chapter Thirty-one

Parting Ways

Asmodeus stumbles through the dark, bleeding out all the while. It spurts all over the hand he keeps over the glaring gash. He has little time left, his limbs growing heavier and heavier with each step he takes. But he has to make it to her, to tell her how he really feels. If he can just do that, none of this will mean a thing. The trees turn pitch black against a white sky and blood-red leaves cover the ground. He can hardly hear the rain anymore. Further down, Aphrodite collapses before a cave entrance, dug into the bedrock itself.

"I finally caught up with you!" he can barely speak as he gasps for air.

Asmodeus collapses in front of her, not even having the energy to crawl anymore. She pulls him into her lap, the cold rain soothing his pain. He can hardly raise his head. She's on the edge of his vision, a blur of red hair and pale skin, but everything hurts too much to move, so he can stares at the sky. His voice comes out raspy and weak. "Hey, Aph... I know you probably don't want to hear it right now, but it's funny–" a throaty cough interrupts him, blood on his tongue "–every time. Even right up to the end, I can't tell you how much you mean to me. I don't know anymore. Can you tell me what to do? I'm lost here. It stings all over. Hurts like a bitch. When is this going to end? Aph? Are you there?"

The sky obscures and the colors melt into each other. He can barely register the tears rolling down his skin anymore. A rose scent flows through the breeze. His heartbeat slows, his eyes are so heavy. He isn't ready to fall asleep yet, he still hasn't told her anything; how much he truly loves her, how much he appreciates her. If only he could get the words out before it is too late.

"I've only been able to find the words to say it all right now. How I feel. It's funny, right? I always come through when it's too late. We're going to end up somewhere amazing. Just us. You and me. Together like we used to be. Doesn't that sound great?" What he thought was rain is actually

Aphrodite's tears plummeting onto his face. "Right, Aph? ... Please?"

For the only time in his life, Asmodeus' heart bloats with an overwhelming fervor, much like the intent that brought him to lie here. It is all that he feels, the only thing he can feel, but there is none of the grit and fire.. Aphrodite's face passes over his blurry eyes in quick succession like a final slide show. He trips over his numbing tongue, a flood of words constricting his throat. This isn't happening. This can't be happening.

"I love you." The little prince makes his feelings known, with no one but Aphrodite to hear it. But even so, the hand that plucks at his heartstrings refuses to let up. This ocean of warmth and yearning for one single person fills the entirety of his frail body. For at every end, there is love.

Chapter Thirty-two

Blood

Fat snowflakes drift down around them. He lies in her arms like a limp doll, trying to shield him from the cold. Aphrodite half expects him to pop back up like nothing happened. Surely, it is all a joke, right? But as the minutes pass and his skin turns cold, she has no choice but to move on. When today ends, will she be able to go on without him? Can she even bear to return to Ares? Not after going this far, there is no turning back for her. She has only one way left to go, one path to travel.

Nyx stands just beyond the light in the cave's mouth. Her face is more put together in the dark. "It's finally time.

Welcome to my humble home; Tartarus."

"Just do whatever you have to already, will you?"

"What will you do with that one?" She uncurls a finger at Asmodeus' body. "Surely you don't mean to bring him in here?"

"I'm not leaving him out here by himself!" No matter how much she cries, the tears keep coming. She refuses to leave him behind, as it is the only thing she will ever be able to do for him. No matter how much he held out for her, or professed his love, she held him at a distance. She has to right her wrongs somehow.

Impatience crosses over Nyx's face like a cloud over the moon. "Have it your way then."

Holding him in her arms, she carries him into the dark cave. Wandering through the tunnel is like stepping on the night sky itself, dozens of little stars twinkle around her like gemstones. A single candle lights the way for her to follow. Blue mist pours past her and raven wings cast a long shadow on the walls as Nyx assumes her true face. She weaves a tapestry with expert precision while more litter the floor, extending farther into the cave to places she can't see. On the fabric, a single figure with red hair dominates the scenes she has spun. She focuses so intently on her weaving, she hardly notices Aphrodite.

"So you're just going to ignore me? After all the things I've done to get here?" Her voice lilts to and fro with unhinged frustration. Her entire appearance is messy, gone is the soft visage she prefers to radiate, anger and regret the only things left. "You're not even going to acknowledge me?"

Nyx raises a hand at her, and a throaty voice creaks out, "I'll be with you in a moment, child. To think a primordial such as myself would be this impatient."

The Goddess of Night turns away from her loom to face her. She is middle-aged, her face reminding Aphrodite of a crescent moon with how her long black hair falls to the floor. Her black wings twitch and the blue mist surrounds her head in the shape of a halo.

"I thought you'd never make it, you're just in time." As she speaks, white passes over her eyes like the moon coming out from the clouds at long last. "It's time for us to have a little talk, Aphrodite – just between us girls. Do you have any idea what I'm referring to?"

"You want me to kill Hera, I assume?" she asks.

She smiles, but it isn't pleasant in the least. "You remember. Now, if you'll just–"

"Before we do any of this, I want you to fix him!" She

glances between Asmodeus' body and Nyx. "You have to fix him! You can do that, can't you?"

Nyx leans back in her seat with not even a scowl on her face. "What are you talking about? Fix him? What, are you upset that you broke one of your little toys? You think someone's life is a game you can play over and over until you've had your fill?" She shakes her head like she were a doctor pronouncing her patient dead. "Let me make something clear here, for once, you don't get to make the terms. All you get to do is shut up and listen."

She shuts her eyes to keep calm. "What are your terms, then?"

As Nyx rises, her long sheer dress drags along the ground, standing even taller than Aphrodite. "You already know what must be done. That woman has grown far too arrogant for my tastes. Her entire generation is sickening to watch. So I'm going to give you a gift to make sure you succeed. But," she raises a thin finger, "you must give me your most prized possession in return."

Two crystal bottles float into her hands from the dark; one is empty, the other holds a red liquid. "I... I don't have much—other than my beauty." Aphrodite's eyes grow wide as she realizes the possible consequences and she nearly cries.

"So, what then? Are you going to make me ugly? Oh, I can't imagine living like that! Who will love me then?"

"Calm down, it'll only be a for a little while." Nyx poises to pop the star-shaped cork out of the empty bottle. "Is that what you'll be trading? This is your last chance to change your mind."

Once she nods, Nyx opens the bottle and a cyclone swirls out and surrounds Aphrodite. As it steals her looks, she turns gaunt and sickly. Asmodeus' body falls from her arms. The crystal fills with a glowing pink liquid, which she takes a swig from. While she wilts, the other primordial blooms, Nyx turning plump and firm, growing younger as the seconds pass. Aphrodite hides her face in her hands while the red bottle floats to her. She gulps it down without a second thought, willing to do anything if it means she gets her beauty back, for she is meaningless without it. Do people enjoy gazing at a night sky without its stars? Then what good is she?

Aphrodite clutches at her stomach and throat as they both burn, it is as though her insides are on fire. She coughs and hacks, the world tinting red at the corners. Anger courses through her veins, but Aphrodite can't find the energy to do more than cry. She falls to her knees before Asmodeus and runs her hands all over him, as if her new found power could somehow resurrect him.

"Please bring him back to life for me!" she begs.

Nyx watches with her hands folded over her chest. "I can't do that, but I'm sure you can if you put your mind to it," she says. "But it won't be the way you want, not with the magic you harbor."

"What the hell do you mean?" Aphrodite tears open his shirt and gapes at his bare chest. What does she do? She isn't a healer, she's never used her powers for more than bewitching men, but she must be stronger than she thinks. "I don't know what to do... you have to help me!"

"You're the Goddess of Love & Creation here, aren't you?" Nyx asks. "Why don't you simply will him to life?"

She presses her hands to his chest, focusing all her thoughts on the point where their bare skin meets, thoughts that have long since died and fell from the sky like shooting stars. With deftness, she plucks them from the sky to drop into her mental cauldron. The call of birds and the heat of Eden come back to her, surging through her fingertips with an energy as gentle as the current of a small river, something much unlike her. Aphrodite only knows how to destroy everything she touches. That glow leaves lasting marks the further she presses against his heart, ten little red pinpoints.

Nyx waves her along. "You have to speak it into existence

for the spell to finalize. What wish would you like granted?"

For so long, she has never wished for anything, only wanted and taken. To think such a simple thing as a wish could have tremendous power. Aphrodite throws herself onto Asmodeus, crying into his chest. "All I want is for him to stay with me, to live forever. I'll give everything I have left if it means I can see him again!" She continuously wipes at her tears, but nothing can stop them from flowing. Her makeup runs and smears the more she does so. "I'll keep you safe this time, I promise! We can live together like you wanted–please, just come back to me. I'll fix all my mistakes, just don't leave me like this!"

The marks on his chest dim until they disappear inside him altogether, his heart glowing a bright red. Its beating drums in her ear, but Asmodeus himself makes no movement, skin still cold. But the spot above his heart is warm to the touch, Aphrodite staring down into that red. It is the only part of him that is alive.

"What do I do now, what is this?" she asks.

Nyx peers over like a teacher surveying a student's work. "Oh, it's only his soul. Your incessant crying must have woken it." She lets out a heavy sigh. "Well, do what you must."

That red light blinks with each beat, holding Aphrodite's

gaze in a trance. Her eyes are flat as she shoves her hand deep inside Asmodeus' chest to pull his heart free. She even goes as far to caress it as if he could somehow feel it. Love does indeed make cowards do the previously unthinkable. For that is all Aphrodite is, a coward who only makes deals on her terms. And now there is no one left to object to what she must do; devour his soul. The only way she can keep it safe is to keep a piece of him forever with her. Aphrodite swallows his heart as it burns like the afternoon sun, warmth spreading through her.

She runs a hand over her the bump of stomach and thinks, albeit fleetingly, of the child–no, children–inside her. Aphrodite hopes their previous night together was successful, but if not, this act should solidify her chances. To have his child... what a pleasant thought at a time like this. She will raise them and be the Mother she never had nor wanted. Maybe she can pull herself together from the dredges of this mess, and build a new life?

But the glint of a knife enters her vision. Nyx shoves a heavy hilt into her hands.

"What is this?"

"With this dagger," Nyx says, "you shall pierce the Heavens and burn that accursed Garden down once and for all. Today is the day Hera is brought to her knees."

She throws a dark cloak at Aphrodite and ushers her out of the cave. "If you want to see your precious children one day, don't return unless it's with her head on a plate. Do you hear me?"

She climbs back to Asmodeus' estate. The rain and snow has come to a halt, not even a breeze breaking the tranquil silence. But this calm isn't something to be wondered at, for she is the eye of the storm coming to uproot Hera's Garden. Dozens of owls perch in the trees to watch her. She is sure Nyx will keep an eye on her before she ever steps foot into Eden, but the only problem is how she will get past Ares. He is too intelligent to not know what she is up to.

Among the blood-spattered grass, he waits for her on the terrace steps. Ares stares as she stops near the greenhouse. He is up before she can make another move. No matter how close she gets to freedom, he thwarts her plan by hooking an arm around her waist.

"Where do you think you're going?" he asks.

She doesn't try to get out of his grip, knowing she's been had. "I have to do this."

"Do what? Destroy your life more than you already

have?" He pulls her around to face him. She never would've expected him of all people to be sorrowful at Asmodeus' death, but here he is, forcing back tears. "I'm not letting you do this to yourself! You're coming home with me, do you understand? It's over. I'm not fighting with you anymore!"

"You're the one who doesn't understand." She keeps her face low so the hood can block her face. "I have no other choice but to fight back. Hera has to die."

Ares runs his hand over her cheek like he has so many times before, but horror crosses his face, and he gasps at the feel of her skin. He throws her hood off. She expects him to be disgusted at her haggard appearance, but he holds onto her even tighter. "You made a deal with Nyx? You know she's nothing but a dirty liar, right?" He looks past her into the forest. "Why would you do such a thing?"

"This is the only way I can win. I'm not strong enough to be her on my own." Aphrodite smiles, a kaleidoscope of colors mixing in her eyes.

"I'm not listening to this! For all I know, she tricked you and you're going to get yourself killed! We're going home, do you hear me?" He drags her into the greenhouse, locking the door behind him. "Now show me how you did it."

"I don't know what you mean? Do what?"

"There's no point in playing games, Aph. We both know that *I* know that you were going back and forth. Why else would you try and sneak your way in here?" She takes him by the hand through the mess of hanging plants to the door in the back. Once she grabs the handle, the red butterflies flutter away. Bright light leaks through the crack that blinds her momentarily.

"It was a door this entire time?" He squints into the overwhelming light, more butterflies daintily floating through the open door. It grows in size, until it's large enough for both of them to fit through at once.

"What did you think it was?" she asks.

Taking a step through the threshold, the door closes on them. Ares turns to grab the knob, but he wraps his fingers around empty air. Noises creep into existence; a gurgling stream, the call of a songbird, the rustle of a gentle breeze against her cheek. Vast fields of green stretch as far as her eyes can see, tall grasses that sway in the wind. The sky is a beautiful blue. Even in the sunlight, stars twinkle, barely visible behind rolling clouds of fluff. It is almost nostalgic to see her previous home again.

A dense forest of oak greets them. Even in the summer sun, it's rather foreboding. They have to maneuver over thick roots, an effort just to keep their footing on the uneven ground. All the animals that flit by are a bright white, feathers floating down with the fallen leaves.

Eventually, an obstacle is met, the forest cutting off in favor of a finely manicured lawn. White cows graze along the remainders of uncut grass, peacocks meandering alongside them. They pay them no mind other than a confused look before returning to their business. A paved path cuts through the dense green, leading to a high gate of glittering gold. She stops a few feet away.

Ares places a hand on the gate, easing it open just enough for them to get through. Aphrodite wanders ahead, gazing at the Garden, the giggle of the Hesperides intertwining with the calls of birds. She passes her hand through the leaves of a giant willow as they pass by. The nymphs relax against their trunks or high up in the branches.

His hand probes inches away from her face as they walk side by side. "Are you alright?"

She flinches at his touch. "I'll be fine. This is only temporary."

"Are you sure?"

"I'm sure." Their conversation falls flat afterwards, Ares subtly correcting her path with a hand on her side. Hera's temple enters her field of view. They must be at the middle of the Garden. Vines crawl along the otherwise pristine marble, an empty throne sitting just past the entrance. More peacocks flock around the premises. Golden apple trees sit beyond it, reaching taller than the rest. Filled baskets sit in the sun.

Ares swerves straight past the temple without looking back, brushing loose branches out of the way as they step off the path, descending into the more unkempt parts. Bugs buzz in the air, growing thicker with trapped heat. He takes her hand, the slope rocky and steep.

"Where are we going?"

"Somewhere special," is all he says.

A lazy stream announces itself as they push through vegetation, a cliff edge greeting them. Off in the distance, even denser forests present themselves, the sun an ever present halo in the sky. A room is etched into the rock itself, seemingly by hand. A four-poster bed sits by its lonesome in the back corner. Carefully placed candles dot the walls, rugs covering the floor. Ares allows her to survey the room, busy lighting the candles.

"Is there some reason you brought me here?"

He lays back on the bed, stretching out upon the mass of blankets and sheets. "What a silly question. Why else would

425

I?" He pats the spot beside him. "I'm going to talk you out of this."

He undoes his shirt and tosses it to the side. Under the soft light, Ares keeps his eyes on her.

"I can't," she says. "I don't have any time to waste."

Despite her words, she stands beside the bed, hands clutching the thin garments she's worn all day. Ares crawls over to her to cup her face. His warmth is a thing she's missed dearly. "What will you do otherwise? It's not as if you've anywhere to go. We already saw what happened when you're left to your own devices." His fingers trail along her cheek. "I think it's in your best interest to stay here. I'll make sure to keep you safe." A small laugh escapes him. "Tell me, did you really make a deal with that demon?"

"What makes you say that?" Ares shakes his head. "The mark on your neck. You didn't really think of selling your soul to him, did you?"

"I had no other options." Aphrodite rubs a hand along her neck, the tattoo fading as the time passes. "It was the only way out."

Ares comes over her like a gentle summer breeze, thick arms wrapping around her shoulders. He presses kiss after kiss against her neck, moving her way up to his cheek. "Then there's nothing left to stop me, is there?" His voice is heavy with desire. But there's a tinge of sadness. "I'm not about to let you ruin yourself over some silly grudge."

Her emotions bubble over; crippling guilt and anxiety. She tries to hide the tears in her eyes. "No, don't! I'm ugly–"

Ares cuts her off. "What? You think I care about what you look like? Is that what's stopping you?" He nuzzles against her, crooning into her skin. "I only care that you're happy, my Love. I want to see you – and our children – propser." When she still cries, Ares turns an even softer shade. "I love you. We'll always be together. Even if we're separated, whether it be distance or even death, I'll always be with you," he rests a hand over her heart, "forever in your heart. That's a promise."

The fire within her builds and builds into an inferno, but unable to let it spill over, she grows antsy and chews on the inside of her lip. It is clear she so desperately wishes to strike the match and let it all burn, but Ares is the only thing keeping her from doing so.

"I love you too," she mutters. "But I'm not letting you get in my way, Dear." He sits in brooding silence. His face is blank, the rising anger that she thought would be there is nonexistent. She lays a hand on his shoulder. "Are you okay?"

The fire comes with such force it gives her whiplash. "Do I look okay to you? I don't think you possibly can understand how I feel—how I've felt—for the past few *centuries*. You can't understand! No one can! I've lost everything, I have nothing left!"

His voice rises like a hurricane's wave, building until he can't hold it back any longer. Ares; the Destroyer of Men, one of Eden's Great Generals, the God of War himself, he breaks down. Tears of lava melt their way down his face, his sobs wracking his body as an ocean of tears spills forth. Aphrodite can do little but watch and wait. She has no pretty words to give, no platitudes to say that could put him at ease. The armor has been thrown to the side, the masquerade has been lifted, and without his mask, who is Ares but a broken man trying to swim against the current?

"I miss you!" he cries. "I would give everything I have left; my blood, my sweat, my tears, my body—" A whimper breaks his voice, leaving naught but ashes left. "I just need you to stay." She reaches a hand out, but Ares reels back, staring at it. "You must think I'm foolish for feeling this way, don't you?"

"You can't help it more than a flower can't help but bloom." She places a hand on his knee, sitting beside him on the bed. She has no choice but to lie now. "I'll stay with you. I won't go through with it."

"...Are you sure?"

"I don't want to hurt you anymore than I have. I've killed your own kin and that's something I can't take back. I'm not going to take your mother from you."

"Of course you would say something like that at a time like this." He doesn't bother dabbing at his eyes, letting the trails of tears sit, glimmering on his skin like jewels. His words have a sugary coating of nostalgia. "You so often convinced me of things when we were younger, just little stupid things–you nearly made me believe I was adopted, just with the conviction you held. I knew you were wrong, but no matter how wrong you'd be, I was always there by your side." He looks down into his lap. "My Mother tried to tell me – even warn me about you – that you were bad news, that you would lead me astray. But you're the only thing I ever truly believed in." The sun dips low for the evening, casting orange and purple shadows onto the cave walls. Crickets chirp incessantly; the perfect background noise for a cool night huddled together. "You showed me what it was like to feel free."

He holds her without looking into her eyes, without trying to kiss her, without any semblance of selfish possession. She basks in the innocence of it all, fulfilling the need to just be held. The tightness leaves his body, uncurling out of a shell he has stayed far too long inside of.

"Can I just say something before this is over?" she asks.

He holds her that much tighter. "Of course, my Love."

As she speaks, Aphrodite finds herself stumbling over tear-stained words. "Whatever way this story ends, I want you to know, that I have nothing but love for you. I always have." She takes a long look into Ares' face, for it's the last time she'll be able to. "I can't help but ask—no, beg—for forgiveness... for everything I've done. I know it won't bring back your Uncle, but I don't know what else to do."

He wipes at her tears with a finger, the smile he gives tasting bittersweet. "You did what you had to, but none of that matters anymore. There's no fight left to be had – it's over. All we can do is move on."

She even finds it in her to grin back, even as she pries opens the coffin full of unspoken feelings that lies within her heart. "They say people meet for a reason, did you know that? It's so silly... even now you're teaching me things about myself I never knew." Aphrodite cries harder, yet her smile is steadfast. "But I'm so happy right now, ecstatic really!" She pauses, so she can genuinely put thought into her final words.

"Because–well, because I got to know you. You've changed me in ways I never would've expected. So.. thank you."

She presses her lips to Ares' forehead. A rainbow blooms in her eyes, and she has no choice but to charm him to sleep. She doesn't even have to use pheromones to do the trick. "I love you. Everything's going to be okay from now on, I promise."

She looks out to the starlit sky, the warm hues waning as blues take their place. In the back of her mind, she knows she can't put it off much longer. A sense of clarity comes over her in the intimate light with Ares. If they want her to be a wicked witch that manipulates others, why not exceed their expectations? Why stop there? She will turn into their worst nightmare.

Chapter Thirty-three

The Witch

Under the cover of night, Aphrodite descends upon Hera's temple. As she passes through the Garden, she envies its endless grace and perfection. Things that she gave up for this opportunity. The weight of the dagger in her cloak keeps her mind steady. She knows what must be done. Sneaking in as silently as a mouse, she finds her bed chambers empty. How curious.

The last thing she expects is for Hera to know about her own assassination. She thinks she is invulnerable. So why would she be afraid? The moonlight falls onto her throne and lo and behold, the woman has been waiting in the dark this entire time.

"What do you want, crone?" Hera can hardly see her in the shadows. With how decrepit Aphrodite looks, she must think nothing of her. "What possible reason do you have to be in my temple at this hour?"

"I come bearing gifts." She does her best to make her voice raspy and thin. A fake golden apple materializes in her hand as she stretches it into the light. "I shall reward this apple to the fairest in Eden. But seeing as how neither Athena or Aphrodite are here to take the crown, it looks like you win by default, My Goddess."

"It's not like it was a competition anyway!" Hera haughtily laughs. She holds a hand out for her prize. "Hurry up and hand it over! I don't have much time to waste."

Aphrodite hobbles over, keeping the apple just out of reach. "Ah, what ever is the matter? Has someone struck fear into your heart?"

"I heard from the grapevine that Aphrodite is planning on trying my patience tonight. I let her live once, but I will not be so merciful this time." She taps her scepter against the floor, grabbing at the apple. "Will you give me it already?"

"Forgive me, you'll have to come over here to get it. Stairs are such a burden on my poor old hips. Surely you can understand?"

There she goes, rushing down from her throne to give Aphrodite a piece of her mind. But it's exactly where she wants her to be. "Are you calling me old!? Who are you to—" She rams the dagger into Hera's gut, tearing the hood from her face. Fear shakes through Hera's face. Her cry of pain is the sweetest music. "*Aphrodite!?*"

"It's me! I did it! I tricked you, you old bitch! *I win this time, you lose!*"

Hera hardly falters so she stabs her again. And again. And again. And again. Until she turns her pretty robes into a bloody mess. But she knows it won't be enough to end her. She throws her cloak off. Hera cowers before her. Red overtakes her view until it's the only thing she can see anymore. Endless wrath and anger fill her veins. Blood oozes from her eyes and nose until it covers her. Aphrodite tosses the knife away, wanting to feel the life leave Hera's body with her bare hands.

She screams but Aphrodite blocks it out. "I'm going to keep the promise I made so long ago. Prepare to meet your end, so-called Goddess of the High Heavens. 'This is the least you deserve. This is my mercy laid upon you.' Is that not what you told me? Or did you pray that you could keep me contained?"

"Please, let me live! I beg you!" She grovels at her feet. "I'll take back everything I've done to you! I'll give you whatever you want!"

Aphrodite shoves her over with a foot. She circles her like a bird of prey. "You've already taken everything I have! I've given up my entire life just so I can have the pleasure of killing you. I don't want what you have to offer. Nothing can bring back one of the men I loved."

"Please don't–"

"Enough talk! I'm tired of listening to you! All you do is spew lies! I'm going to shut your mouth for good!" Aphrodite's silhouette morphs and shifts. Bones snap out of place as she grows. A wondrous red light shines from her eyes. It illuminates Hera with a brightness rivaling the sun. Her skin singes and her retinas burn out.

"What are you!? You're a monster!" She tears one of Hera's arms off with a flick of her finger. Blood sprays over the temple floor.

"The more you speak, the more limbs I pluck off one by one. I'm the beginning of life itself. I'm the witch you cower from in your beds at night. I was destined to outlive you, so don't act surprised that I've come to collect. It's time for your chapter to come to a close."

"No!" She blindly gropes on the floor, trying to reach her throne. Aphrodite opens her mouth full of razor-sharp teeth. Her cheeks split, her jaw unhinges like a snake. The light intensifies until crimson blots everything out. Hera can't even utter a final scream before Aphrodite wipes her from existence. Like a thief in the night, she disappears from the temple.

She stalks Eden with bloodied feet. Anything that reminds her of Hera, she destroys. At least she is with her departed husband now. They can both rot for all she cares. She has never been so alive before. With this power that courses through her veins, she can do anything. She can change the fabric of time and space if she put her mind to it. As an unleashed primordial, the world is her oyster. She drifts through the dark without thought, stumbling through the door back to the Underworld. Aphrodite is barely conscious of her own surroundings anymore. The only thought that consumes her is taking what she has been promised.

She returns to Nyx's cave, the other primordial sitting with a mirror. Aphrodite tracks blood on the floor.

"So, you're finally back?" She can hardly tear herself from her own reflection. "I assumed you succeeded?"

"I did what you wanted," she yells. "Now give me back what's mine!"

"Ah, ah, ah—I'll be needing that knife back." Nyx holds out a hand. "You know, it's so wonderful having beauty like yours. It's been so long since I've been young. Do you think I could hold onto it for a few more minutes?"

She shoves the blood-stained dagger into her hand. It's still wet. As Nyx takes it, the blade nicks Aphrodite's finger. A droplet of blood, hardly noticeable against the layers that paint her, oozes out. An intense throbbing pulses from her fingertip that crawls up her arm, making her eyes grow heavy. "What did you do to me!?" Aphrodite thrashes out at Nyx, but she's seeing double. She wavers from side to side. "I'll kill you too!"

"How does it feel to be the one being used?"

"Give me my beauty back! I did what you wanted!" She tries to swing at her, but stumbles into the cave wall.

"I imagine it feels horrible," Nyx tuts. "I bet you want to rip my head off, don't you?"

Aphrodite stares down at her wrinkled hands. It is like her feet are cemented to the floor. She can hardly move with how lethargic she has become. "Am I dying? Is this what death feels like?"

"Hardly." Aphrodite falls to the floor. Nyx kneels over her, a hand on her stomach. "You're just going to take a little nap. Where Hera failed, I'll succeed. You're too much of a threat to keep you alive, but too valuable to kill. So, I thought, why not settle?"

She tries to wrench Nyx's hand from her, but she hasn't the strength. "What are you going to do to my babies?"

"I'll see to it that they're taken care of. It's unfortunate you won't be there to watch them grow up. I'll keep a close eye on them—just for you." She pets her head. "It's alright, you can sleep soundly now. Your job is done."

It is like she is being sucked in by a whirlpool. Her vision fades to black and Aphrodite falls ever further down the drain.

Chapter Thirty-four

Love

She makes contact with soft sheets. Feathers burst out from the pillows. When she opens her eyes, a white room greets her. Even her dress is as white as freshly fallen snow. She's all alone. There is an eerie silence. Plush curtains cover fake windows. Hundreds of vases filled to the brim with black roses litter the floor, piling up to the edge of her bed.

"Ares? Erato?" she calls into the emptiness. She clutches at her stomach. "..Asmo?"

No one answers. The audience watches on. It's too late to call for help. The lustful rose, who thought herself so sure and confident, breaks down into tears. There is no one left. She has thrown away everything she holds dear for self gain, having no one else to blame but herself now. Aphrodite wades past the roses into the next room.

It is an exact copy of the other, but the floor is empty. A projector sits beside the doorway, turning on the moment she enters. Rows of empty seats are set up and she takes one in front. House lights illuminate the screen that unrolls. Her old self stares back on the wall. Highlights of her time with Ares and Asmodeus play, and she's the main character in her own movie.

The memories fly by so fast until it reaches Asmodeus' death. His cry rings out, and his body lingers on screen for an eternity. She isn't sure what to feel, frozen in place as she is, so she cries. She balls up in the seat and cries her eyes out. The screen fades to black and just like that, her movie is over. Their movie is over. Except there is no audience to file out, for she is the only spectator. The spotlight shines and blinds her.

This is the end.

Except there are no credits that roll, no curtains that fall to hide her graceless, tear-stained face. There are no bows for the leading lady to take. The Audience stares on and Aphrodite stares back.

Made in the USA
Monee, IL
14 February 2020